"[A] sparkling, deeply satisfying tale."
—Karen White, *New York Times* bestselling author

"Wax offers her trademark form of fiction, the beach read with substance." —*Booklist*

"Wax really knows how to make a cast of characters come alive . . . [She] infuses each chapter with enough drama, laughter, family angst, and friendship to keep readers greedily turning pages until the end." —*RT Book Reviews*

"This season's perfect beach read!" —Single Titles

"A tribute to the transformative power of female friendship, and reading Wendy Wax is like discovering a witty, wise, and wonderful new friend." —Claire Cook, *New York Times* bestselling author of *Must Love Dogs*

"Quite a clever, fun little novel . . . If you're a sucker for plucky women who rise to the occasion, this is for you." —*USA Today*

"Just the right amount of suspense and drama for a beach read." —*Publishers Weekly*

"Beautifully written and constructed by an author who evidently knows what she is doing . . . One fantastic read." —Book Binge

"A lovely story that recognizes the power of the female spirit, while being fun, emotional, and a little romantic." —Fresh Fiction

"Funny, heartbreaking, romantic, and so much more . . . just delightful!" —The Best Reviews

Books by Wendy Wax

A WEEK AT THE LAKE
WHILE WE WERE WATCHING DOWNTON ABBEY
MAGNOLIA WEDNESDAYS
THE ACCIDENTAL BESTSELLER
SINGLE IN SUBURBIA
HOSTILE MAKEOVER
LEAVE IT TO CLEAVAGE
7 DAYS AND 7 NIGHTS

Ten Beach Road Titles by Wendy Wax

TEN BEACH ROAD
OCEAN BEACH
CHRISTMAS AT THE BEACH (NOVELLA)
THE HOUSE ON MERMAID POINT
SUNSHINE BEACH

SUNSHINE BEACH

WENDY WAX

BERKLEY BOOKS, NEW YORK

BERKLEY

An imprint of Penguin Random House LLC
375 Hudson Street, New York, New York 10014

This book is an original publication of Penguin Random House LLC.

Library of Congress Cataloging-in-Publication Data

Names: Wax, Wendy, author.
Title: Sunshine Beach / Wendy Wax.
Description: Berkley trade paperback edition. |
New York : Berkley Books, 2016.
Identifiers: LCCN 2015043729 | ISBN 9780425274484
Classification: LCC PS3623.A893 S86 2016 | DDC 813/.6—dc23
LC record available at http://lccn.loc.gov/2015043729

PUBLISHING HISTORY
Berkley trade paperback edition / June 2016

PRINTED IN THE UNITED STATES OF AMERICA

10 9 8 7 6 5 4 3 2

Cover art: Seaside patio © Imagin.gr Photography / Shutterstock;
Mediterranean style terrace © Andrei Nekrassov / Shutterstock;
Outdoor lamp © La Forza Deztino / Shutterstock.
Cover design by Danielle Mazella di Bosco.
Interior text design by Kristin del Rosario.

This is a work of fiction. Names, characters, places, and incidents either are the product of the author's imagination or are used fictitiously, and any resemblance to actual persons, living or dead, business establishments, events, or locales is entirely coincidental. The publisher does not have any control over and does not assume any responsibility for author or third-party websites or their content.

*For my parents, Elaine and Ken Wax,
who gave me a beach for my birthday and a childhood spent
cartwheeling across sugar-white sand and floating in the warm
salt water of the Gulf of Mexico. I miss you both.*

*And for "Aunt" Sonya and "Uncle" Irwin,
longtime family friends who owned and ran the Rellim
(Miller spelled backward!) where I spent so many magical
summer days. The hotel of my youth has been gone for many
years, but my memories of it remain.*

*Although my Sunshine Hotel, and the characters who own, run,
and visit it are fictional, I hope they'll give you at least an idea
of how lovingly I remember the real hotel that inspired it.*

ACKNOWLEDGMENTS

As always, thanks go to my longtime critique partners, Karen White and Susan Crandall, talented authors and BFFs with whom I'm grateful to be sharing this crazy journey.

Thanks, too, to my agent, Stephanie Rostan, who is also very talented at what she does and can always be counted on to tell it like it is.

In every book there are an amazing number of small details that can have great impact. Rebecca Ritchie has once again helped me envision what a space can be and answered countless questions. Tito Vargas shared information on construction and its cost. Thomas Lange, Chief of Police (Ret.), St. Pete Beach, Florida, offered insights into policing a small beach community and how a case might be dealt with "then" and now.

I've taken liberties and exaggerated where necessary. This is, after all, a work of fiction and "making things up" is a critical part of every novelist's job description.

Prologue

She climbed onto the diving board and waited until she had
an audience. Waited for the fathers to look up from their
newspapers. The mothers to stop fingering the smooth ivory
mah-jongg tiles.

The winter residents were gone, the cottages closed up. But
the beach club was open. Children spent entire days running
from the pool, across the white sand beach, into the Gulf of
Mexico and back again—stopping just long enough to build
a sand castle or etch a hopscotch board—while their mothers
sat at card tables arranged in the shade and gossiped. She had
no idea what their fathers did during the sweltering weekdays,
but on the weekends they came to lie on the chaises, or stand
in the water talking business while they threw pennies into
the pool for their children to dive after.

She checked to make sure her audience did not include her
grandparents or her parents, who would be somewhere on the

property making sure everything ran "like clockwork." Or her bossy big sister. Or the lifeguard who'd "closed" the pool so that he could spend his break k-i-s-s-i-n-g her sister behind a palm tree.

When she had everyone's attention she took three short running steps, bounced once on the end of the diving board, and dove headfirst into the deep end of the swimming pool just like her daddy had taught her. She did not come up. Nor did she emit so much as a single bubble.

The scorching summer sun cast shimmery beams all around her as she hung motionless beneath the surface. It was perfectly quiet here; the *rat-a-tat* of the jackhammers digging up the cottage patios silenced. She was queen of the water kingdom and all the subjects that dwelt in its depths.

Above her she could just make out figures standing near the edge of the pool, a group of dark shapes leaning over, peering down. She imagined them holding their breath as carefully as she was holding hers. Trying to decide whether someone should jump in after her.

When no one did she began to swim toward the shallow end, slicing through the water with a long gliding breaststroke, her long blond mermaid hair streaming behind her. Silent and smooth, she used the same stroke with which she flew through the night sky in her dreams, soaring high above the ground free and unbound, pulling hard with her arms and legs to make sure she didn't fall. Or get low enough for anyone—or anything—to touch her.

It wasn't a huge pool, not Olympic sized or anything, and she knew every inch of it. According to her Nana, she'd learned to swim in it before she could walk. Had been swimming its length underwater since she was three. She was five now and could do ten full underwater summersaults without coming up to breathe.

Almost out of air, she reached for the wall, ready to surface to gasps of relief and admiration. But when she stood and wiped the water from her eyes there were no oohs or aahs. Just her know-it-all sister, who'd obviously told her audience that there was nothing to worry about and who was giving her the evil eye for being in the pool when she wasn't supposed to be.

Regally, she stepped out of the pool keeping her eyes straight ahead and her head up so that the diamonds in her tiara would sparkle in the sunlight. Without so much as a nod, she accepted the towel from her sister, then draped it across her shoulders like a cape. She did not deign to speak nor even stop to accept the ice cream sandwich her Pop Pop offered her as she swept down the path to the family cottage. Everyone knew that a queen should never be ignored. And the people the queen loved most should not be allowed to die or disappear.

Chapter One

Madeline Singer was fairly certain that the number of former suburban housewives who went on to have relationships with rock stars was too small to be statistically measurable. Which might be why she felt like Cinderella that May evening as William Hightower handed her out of his boat and onto the dock at the Lorelei Restaurant and Cabana Bar. If, that was, Cinderella had to color her hair, suck in her stomach, and wore a size too large to make *America's Next Top Model*.

Perched on the edge of U.S. 1, the multitiered Islamorada landmark served good, basic food, poured potent drinks, and drew a mostly laid-back crowd for its nightly sunset celebrations. Tables surrounded a thatched hut of a stage and spilled out onto a half-moon of beach where you could eat with your bare feet buried in the sand and your eyes pinned to a truly spectacular sunset that played out over the Florida Bay.

Remnants of sunlight glinted off the black hair lightly threaded with gray that brushed William's shoulders and cast his sharply angled face into shadow. "Should be interesting to see what kind of reaction we get to the new song," he said as he retrieved his guitar case from the boat and slipped an arm around her shoulders.

"Everybody on Mermaid Point loved it," she reminded him. "You got a standing ovation."

"Yeah, well, let's not forget Mermaid Point is surrounded by water. The residents are a captive audience."

Maddie laughed but did not concede the point. She may not be a musician, but she knew a great song when she heard one. Will had written "Free Fall" in September not long after she and the rest of the *Do Over* crew had finished turning William Hightower's private island into what was supposed to have been a high-end bed-and-breakfast but which he'd turned into a sober living facility. It was the first song he'd written after more than a decade unable to make music at all. The first he'd ever written without the benefit of drugs or alcohol.

"And not that I don't appreciate it," he added. "But I don't think you're completely objective."

"True," she said. "But I was a William Hightower fan way before I ever met you." That had been back when he was building a name as a southern rocker, and Wasted Indian had been climbing to the top of the charts. "So let's not go questioning my musical taste."

His dark eyes creased with amusement. The spider's web of lines at their corners attested to all he'd been through. He dropped a kiss on the top of her head, then headed for the stage.

Maddie leaned against a vacant post not far from the bar that afforded an unobstructed view over the already packed tables that fanned out from the stage. A waitress handed her a glass of Pinot Noir, which she accepted gladly. She sipped it as Will and the musicians he'd cobbled together set up. Her eyes scanned the stage, the crowd, and the sun that hung in midair poised for its swan dive into the bay. She had only one more day with Will before she'd drive up to Bella Flora, the house that she, Nicole Grant, and Avery Lawford had nursed back to life and which had now become home. There they'd have to figure out what, if anything, they could do about the show they'd created, lost control of, and then quit so publicly.

Conversation ceased as William stepped up to the microphone. All eyes, including hers, fastened on the man who had once hung in poster form on her bedroom wall. William Hightower might be sixty-two, but he'd come out of rehab a little over a year ago for what he'd vowed would be the last time, looking hot as hell.

With a salt breeze and a pinkening sky for background, Will laid out his losses with a pain-roughened voice. He'd lost his younger brother and the woman who'd borne his son to drugs and excess. The pain had only mounted as he disappeared into every vial and bottle he could find in an attempt to hide from the hurt. Tonight he hid nothing, singing with his eyes closed, his fingers lithe on his guitar strings, his body taut with emotion. The crowd's response was equally visceral. When he finished, Maddie's were not the only cheeks wet with tears. She'd expected that. What she hadn't anticipated was the naked hunger that shone in the eyes of his female fans.

He sent her a smile over the heads of the women who mobbed him after the set, and she managed to smile back even as she struggled to tamp down her jealousy and uncertainty.

She'd learned over the last months to stop apologizing for her body or even trying to hide it from him, though the stomach sucking was a reflex with a mind of its own. He insisted he wasn't comparing her to anyone; that she, a fifty-one-year-old mother of two and grandmother of one, turned him on just the way she was.

But if Will's mind didn't stray to all the women who'd come before her or to the tsunami of female adoration that was currently washing over him, Maddie's did. A lifetime spent as a suburban housewife prepared a woman for a lot of things. A relationship with a man like William Hightower wasn't one of them.

...

"You were fabulous," she said on the boat ride back to Mermaid Point. "Could you feel how the audience reacted to 'Free Fall'? God, they loved it. They were hanging on every word."

"Yeah." Steering with his right hand, he pulled her onto his lap with his left. "I didn't expect to get the same high, you know, performing straight. But it's a definite rush. Kind of like a shot of adrenaline to the heart."

His body was hard and warm against hers. She could practically feel that adrenaline coursing through him. When they reached the house, Will emptied his pockets onto the bedroom dresser and began to shuck his clothes.

"I'm way too wired to go to bed," he said pulling on swim trunks. "Want to come for a swim?"

She'd become used to taking off her clothes in front of him, had been unable to argue his unfailingly positive physical reaction to her, but his reception tonight had proved that while she might have tamped down her insecurities, she hadn't shed them completely.

"I think I'll stay here and start getting my things together." Unable to meet his eyes, she glanced at the items he'd pulled from his pockets. There were two cocktail napkins with names and phone numbers, one of them written in bright red lipstick. A crumbled photo of . . . "Is that a naked woman?" She moved toward the dresser for a closer look. "I didn't know anyone owned a Polaroid camera anymore."

"Hmmm?" Will asked as he reached for a towel.

"This." She held the photo up by one corner. "This naked photo."

He turned to look at the photo Maddie held between her fingertips. He snorted. "Given who I think shoved that in my pocket, I doubt it's remotely recent."

"Someone shoved a naked photo of herself in your pocket," she repeated dully.

"Um-hm."

"And this is . . . ?" She scooped up a wisp of red lace, dropping it when she realized what it was. "A thong." She could hear the note of disbelief in her voice.

"Seems to be." Will shrugged and smiled. "You sure you don't want to come for a swim? It's past resident curfew. We'd have the pool and the hot tub to ourselves." He shot her a wink.

"I'm looking at a thong that a complete stranger placed in your pocket." A thong that she doubted would make it over one of her thighs. "And all you're thinking about is going for a swim. With me."

"Absolutely." He leaned down and brushed his lips across hers. "What else should I be thinking about?" He asked this as if every female at the Lorelei that night hadn't spent the evening mentally undressing him and would gladly swim naked to Mermaid Point, like some Sexual SEAL Team Six, if invited.

Maddie hadn't dated in close to thirty years and she'd never dated a rock star, but she was pretty certain that freaking out over groupies or calling attention to all the women William could have sex with instead of her was not a good idea. She shrugged as casually as she could. "I don't know. I've never been in this situation before." She looked at but did not touch the thong.

"It's nothing," he said tucking the towel under one arm. He hadn't bothered to put on a shirt and she couldn't help watching the play of muscle as he shrugged again. "It just goes with the territory. You walk up on a stage and . . . seriously, Maddie, there's no accounting for what some people will do or assume."

"Right."

His eyes held hers, but he didn't argue the point. "I'm just going to do a few laps. I'll be back in a bit."

Maddie knew him well enough to know that a few laps could be anywhere from fifty to infinity. Swimming had been his go-to stress reliever during and after rehab, and he typically swam twice a day out of habit, she thought, as much as necessity. She stood out on the balcony and watched him slip into the pool; it and the ocean beyond glimmered in the moonlight. Only a few years ago she'd dreamt of empty nesting only to have that nest filled with an aging mother-in-law, an unexpectedly pregnant daughter, and an unemployed husband who'd lost everything, including his job, to Malcolm Dyer's Ponzi scheme. Two desperate years of hanging on and staying afloat had followed. Now here she stood on the bedroom balcony of William Hightower's private island, an outcome she'd never imagined in her wildest dreams.

Inside she began to empty her drawers, carefully avoiding the items that still littered Will's dresser. Then she got undressed, slid into bed, and lay listening to the rhythmic splash of his flutter kick. Somewhere in the middle of lap thirty-five she finally fell asleep.

Chapter Two

Avery Lawford pushed a stray curl off her forehead. Eyes half closed she stumbled toward the kitchen relying on her nose to lead her toward the all-important coffeepot.

"Here you go." A mug of coffee, warm and wondrous, was placed in her hands.

She breathed in its dark, delicious aroma, then took a first sip. Her eyes opened another notch as she moaned with pleasure. "You are a fine human being."

"And a careful one," Chase Hardin said as she took another sip. "I know how to read warning labels." His finger skimmed across the T-shirt she'd slept in. A gift from Kyra Singer, who knew her well, and that read, *I Drink Coffee for Your Protection*.

She could feel his eyes on her as she took another sip. She sighed with pleasure as the liquid caffeine began to rouse and warm her.

"Okay, guys, I think it's safe to go about your business now," Chase said.

A utensil clattered against a hard surface. The refrigerator door opened. After an especially heavenly sip she opened her eyes all the way and took in the kitchen. Which looked as if a hurricane had swept through it. Chase's father Jeff sat at the kitchen table, his walker beside him, the morning paper folded to the sports page. Chase's son Josh was in the process of wolfing down a bowl of cereal while his brother Jason helped himself to eggs from a pan on the stove.

Muzzy with sleep Avery blinked away a vision of Deirdre Morgan, the mother who'd abandoned her for decades and then reappeared without warning, standing at that very stove demonstrating her newly acquired culinary skills.

"I'm going to drop the guys at school, then take Dad to his doctor's appointment. If he's got the energy I'll take him to the job site with me." Chase now ran what had once been their fathers' construction business. Avery had been working with him since she'd come back from Mermaid Point. Where the mother she'd only just forgiven for abandoning her had crumpled at her feet and died of a brain aneurysm. Avery looked down into the swirl of creamed coffee, blinking away tears as she tried to dislodge the image. Her hand shook as she raised the cup to her lips.

"If the day ever comes that I'd rather sit at home like an old fart than visit one of our construction sites, I'll let you know," Jeff snapped.

Chase nodded to his father but made no comment. Pulling a crumpled bakery bag from the back of a cabinet, he carried it to the table. "I managed to save you exactly one glazed donut," he said as he placed the bag in front of Avery. "Next time you're going to have to hide them better."

She extracted the donut from the bag and pinched off a bite knowing as she began to chew the sugary confection that if Deirdre were there, she'd be lobbying for Avery to trade the donut for a fat-free yogurt.

"Have you guys got your lunches packed?" Chase asked. He was running full throttle while she was still trying to get up to speed.

Mouths full, both boys grunted in the affirmative.

"Is there anything I'm supposed to sign, deliver, or do that I don't already know about?" Chase, who had a lot of years as a single father under his belt, prodded.

They shook their heads.

"Are you sure?"

There were two identical eye rolls. The chewing didn't stop.

"What do you have going on today?" Chase asked Avery.

"Hmmm?" She downed the last of her coffee, managed another bite of the donut, and blinked up at him. "I'm going to finish those sketches for the O'Reilly addition. And I had some ideas for the spec home on Davis Island." She enjoyed being a part of the company their fathers had built. Being busy helped, but it hadn't eliminated the aching sense of loss she still felt for the mother she'd lived so much of her life without. Nor did it erase her worry over whether *Do Over* could be salvaged. And if they did salvage the show? What would it be without Deirdre, who'd put her personal stamp on every property they'd touched?

"Do you have time to help me pick up the boys' Explorer from the repair shop later?"

"Um, sure." She took another sip of coffee, willing the caffeine into her bloodstream, and her thoughts back to the present. "I'm wide open today. Tomorrow I'm going to Bella Flora—Maddie and Nikki should be there in time for dinner. I thought I'd stay there at least through the weekend. We've got to figure out our next moves." She swallowed. Deirdre's absence would be even more palpable when they were all under one roof again. Especially Bella Flora's.

"Are you okay?" Chase asked quietly as he took her empty cup and carried it to the coffeepot to refill it.

"Yes," she said automatically. "Thanks. I . . ." Her voice trailed off as she accepted the coffee, cupping the warm mug between both hands.

She was once again blinking back tears as the boys put their empty bowls in the sink. Chase took his father's plate, added it to the stack, and reached to open the dishwasher.

Avery waved him away. "Go ahead. You'll be late. I can load the dishwasher."

"Thanks," he said, pecking her on the cheek. "I'll text you when the Explorer is ready."

At her nod he shooed the boys out the door, then hovered at his father's side as Jeff maneuvered the walker through the kitchen. A few minutes later the garage door rumbled shut.

She was sorry to see them go. Sorrier still when the quiet that she would have once treasured, descended. Alone was not good. Alone in the silence was even worse.

"Get over yourself," she muttered as she stood and carried her coffee cup to the sink. As she loaded the dishwasher and tidied the kitchen she began a mental to-do list. She continued that list as she showered, stuffing her mind with concrete tasks to be completed. After dressing quickly, she fled the house. Her memories of the mother so recently regained, then lost, came with her.

. . .

Nicole Grant knew it was pointless to be pissed off at *The Millionaire Matchmaker.* She also knew she should not be watching it. And yet here she was doing exactly that. Again.

Stifling a curse, she raised the television remote and snapped off the program, incensed that the woman had so successfully commercialized and sensationalized what Nicole had once considered a delicate and highly personal service.

Grumbling, she retrieved a handful of nuts from the bowl on the coffee table and popped them in her mouth. As the founder of Heart Inc., Nicole had found spouses with specific pedigrees, personalities, and even genetic traits for a long and notable list of clients to whom discretion was key and a million dollars didn't even qualify as pocket change. And she had done it without exposing them to public humiliation, using the f-bomb as an adjective, or scolding/coaching them on their pickup lines and appearance in front of a television audience.

The Millionaire Matchmaker didn't even belong on the same planet as Nicole's Heart Inc. once had.

Once. She downed another handful of nuts.

Once, Nikki had been famous for the wealth and status of her clientele, the charm with which she handled them, the plush offices that she'd maintained on both coasts, the famous and wealthy elbows she'd quietly rubbed. She'd been considered *the* A-list matchmaker and dating guru, had written a bestselling book of advice, had been *the* expert in her field— quoted in national publications and on network programs.

That had been before she, and a troubling number of her clients, had lost everything in Malcolm Dyer's three-hundred-million-dollar Ponzi scheme. Before the world discovered that Malcolm Dyer was not just her financial advisor but also her younger brother. Whom she'd practically raised and foolishly loved and trusted.

Not even helping the FBI put him in jail had cleansed her of the taint of that relationship.

"You really need to stop binge watching that show." Joe Giraldi handed her a glass of Chianti and raised his own in salute.

"I know." She'd been knocked down often in her life but never had this much trouble getting back up. Somehow her willpower and resolve, which had seen her through the loss of her business, her savings, and her reputation, had now deserted her. "I just can't seem to help myself," she admitted as he sat down beside her. "I don't suppose you have any family connections that might like to put out a hit on her?"

A dark eyebrow quirked upward in amusement. "Well, my Nonna Sofia has been willing to fling a curse now and then. But a hit? How many seasons of *The Sopranos* did you watch while I was out of town?" As a special agent in the FBI's financial crimes unit, Joe traveled often. It was his hunt for her brother that had brought him into her life.

She sighed. For someone who'd worked her way out of poverty to the top of her field, she now spent an embarrassing amount of time on Joe's couch with a television remote in her hand.

She took a sip of the wine. In her experience alcohol could smooth out the occasional bump, but it was pretty much never the answer. Still she hoped it would calm the bubble of anxiety that now seemed to perpetually simmer inside her.

"Dinner's ready. It's gorgeous outside. Are you up for eating on the patio?"

"I'd go a lot farther than the patio for your manicotti," she said as her stomach, which was clearly unsatisfied with the junk she'd been filling it with, rumbled with hunger.

She followed him out the open slider to the table that overlooked the pool, Biscayne Bay, and a slice of South Beach now twinkling in the distance. She smiled her thanks as he pulled out a chair for her, then watched him sit across from her. When he'd first started dogging her on the beach at Bella Flora during his hunt for her brother, she'd had no idea that his stern good looks hid a warm and generous heart. Joe Giraldi was full of surprises, most of them good.

She took another sip of her wine hoping it would calm her.

"Are you sure you're feeling okay?" he asked.

"Absolutely."

Although he read faces for a living, Joe didn't call her on the lie. And he was far too much a gentleman to bring up her appalling lack of direction since *Do Over* had come to such a horrible end.

She still ran daily and continued to hunt down and eradicate the gray hairs that tried to infiltrate her auburn hair, but she could no longer afford the physical "tweaks" that had once seemed so important. Most of her vintage designer wardrobe had been sold. The only remaining luxury from her previous life was the classic Jag, the first expensive thing she'd bought for herself. They'd have to pry the keys out of her cold, dead fingers.

The breeze was soft and warm. The blue sky had begun to pale. She drew in a deep breath of salt-tinged air and instructed herself to pay attention and enjoy the moment. Tomorrow she'd make the four-and-a-half-hour drive to Bella Flora midway up the west coast of Florida. There she, Maddie, Avery, and Kyra would deal with their new reality.

"How long do you think you'll stay in Pass-a-Grille?" Joe asked, seemingly reading the turn her thoughts had taken.

"I don't know. I guess until we figure out what, if anything, we're going to do about *Do Over.*" They'd all been licking their wounds to varying degrees since September. It was now the beginning of May, time to either move forward together or separate to follow their own paths. Maddie and Avery had become close friends, the first real friends Nikki had ever had. Would that friendship survive if they let go of the show? And what exactly would she do for a living if that happened?

"You know you don't have to do anything until you're ready," Joe said quietly, once again seeming to tap into her thoughts. "You can just stay here and 'be.'"

"Be what?" she asked.

"Be with me. Relax. I don't know. Clearly, watching and starring on reality TV hasn't made you happy. I don't imagine you'd be any happier eating bonbons and watching soap operas?"

"You mean as opposed to living one?" she asked.

White teeth flashed. "Seriously, Nikki. You've got money from your portion of the sale of Bella Flora if you insist on continuing to pay your own way. Or you can let me take care of things while you write your story and set the record straight before your brother has a chance to put his version out there. Maybe that would help you move on. So that we can get married."

She turned her attention to the Caesar salad he'd prepared. Malcolm had petitioned for the right to accept a hefty advance for his story, money he claimed would go to the investors he'd bilked. A move possibly meant to impress a parole board, though she doubted that money would ever make it to his victims.

She chewed carefully, aware of Joe's eyes on her. He was right about her being stuck. But the idea of sitting back and letting Joe or anyone else take care of her, well, it would never work. And as for marriage, she loved him too much to deprive him of what he deserved—a far less jaded woman whose eggs had not yet expired and who could give him the children he wanted.

She looked up into Joe's intelligent brown eyes and read the sincerity in them. She'd hit the relationship jackpot and could not in all conscience cash in her chips.

She set her fork down. "I've been married twice. And I sucked at it."

"It's not a skill you develop," he said. "I'm pretty sure it's a matter of choosing the right person."

"Said the man who's never been married," she said wryly.

"True. But I know what marriage can be." Joe said this with the quiet assurance of someone whose parents and grandparents had been together for over half a century each. "I know who and what I want."

Somehow he'd decided she was that person. A fact that both amazed and frightened her. FBI agents were trained not to take no for an answer.

"Ready for the main course?" he asked.

"Yes, but I can . . ."

"No, I've got it."

She took another long sip of Chianti as he disappeared into the house. This was their last night together for a while. This was not the time to hash out their differences or debate their feelings. This was a night to be enjoyed.

When he returned she ate every bite of the meal he'd prepared, and turned the conversation with a deft and intentionally lighter hand. When they'd finished and he drew her up from the table and pulled her into his arms, she gave herself to him without reservation. Deirdre Morgan had been full of life one minute and dead the next. Nicole was determined to make the most of this moment. To create new memories that would never be forgotten when their relationship came to its inevitable end.

She only hoped she'd have the strength to let him go when the time came.

Chapter Three

"Listen, Nigel, if you take the day off, I promise that the next time Daniel comes to see Dustin we'll give you an exclusive." Kyra Singer offered the lie with a straight face and crossed fingers as she wheeled the jogging stroller down Bella Flora's bricked drive.

"Nice try, luv," the lanky paparazzo replied from his position in the middle of Beach Road, exactly three feet from Bella Flora's property line. "But I didn't just fall off that turnip truck now, did I?" The Brit wore board shorts, flip-flops, and a Hawaiian-print shirt. Multiple cameras hung around his scrawny neck. The rest of his pack was missing, presumably off hunting more impressive celebrity game. Nigel Bracken was nothing if not single-minded, that single thought being to capture shots of Dustin with his movie star father, Daniel Deranian.

Since Dustin's birth two and a half years ago, Kyra had dressed the two of them in an array of disguises to avoid detection. Daniel, who had access to professional hair and makeup people, had passed himself off as an old man, a convincingly attractive woman, and a UPS deliveryman in order to visit his son.

Nigel lifted a camera and aimed it at them, and she knew he was framing them against Bella Flora's wedding cake façade; making the most of the pale pink walls, banks of windows framed in white icing trim, and the bell towers that topped a multi-angled barrel-tile roof and jutted up into the powder blue sky.

She nodded and prepared to go, but the photographer turned his lens and aimed it directly at Dustin. When he began to zoom in for a close-up Kyra bent over, intentionally blocking Nigel's shot, then took her time slathering sunscreen on Dustin's sturdy arms and legs even though he'd inherited his famous father's golden skin, which never burned, along with his brown heavily lashed eyes and silky dark curls.

Nigel continued shooting. Which meant the photographer was now taking pictures of her ass.

"Okay, little man." She handed Dustin his favorite ball and whispered, "Hold on."

Jaw tight, Kyra pushed the jogging stroller down the driveway. As they left the drive, Nigel backed toward the beach, blocking the road so that she'd have to get close enough to give him his money shot of Dustin.

Not today, she thought, her hands tightening on the stroller. At the last moment, she broke right and headed toward the bay.

"Dustin go to beach!"

"We will, sweetie.," she promised, leaning over as she pushed the stroller onto the sidewalk that ran along Boca Ciega Bay. *Just as soon as I lose the photographer.*

Ignoring Nigel's yelp of surprise, she began a slow jog, which took them past First and Second avenues. Careful to appear unhurried, she subtly increased her pace with each block. She had no doubt she could outrun him; the man was wearing flip-flops after all, while she had on her running shoes and was pushing what was for all intents and purposes an all-terrain vehicle. Plus she'd seen him with a cigarette dangling from his lips plenty of times. Nothing about the man's physique led her to believe he'd ever set foot in a gym. But she didn't want to simply outrun him; she wanted to lose him altogether.

At Fifth Avenue she doubled her speed, though she was careful not to hunch forward or look too intent. Kyra kept her eyes straight ahead as the concrete balustrade whipped by, and ignored Nigel Bracken's shout when he apparently noticed the gap between them growing. The sound of his flip-flops flapping against the sidewalk brought a smile to her lips.

"Hey!" Nigel's shout carried on the breeze, but she pretended not to hear him, accelerating once again as she widened the gap between them.

She continued north past the small park that sat between Ninth and Tenth. At Eleventh she snuck a peek over her shoulder and saw Nigel bent over with hands braced on his thighs, wearing only one flip-flop and breathing heavily. His cameras dangled down around his ankles.

Gotcha! She smiled with pleasure as she cut across the street and out of sight. At the end of the short block, she crossed Gulf Way, jogged north a few blocks, then took a crossover onto the beach.

"Ha!" Feeling ridiculously victorious—were there medals for eluding paparazzi?—she pushed the stroller down to the hard-packed sand at the water's edge.

"Beetch!" Dustin yelled jubilantly as she turned the stroller north and headed toward the castle-like Don CeSar Hotel.

"Beach!" she shouted back as she settled into a comfortable walk that would allow them both to enjoy the sights and sounds.

Brightly colored kites swooped and fluttered in the sky. A parasailer hung suspended high above the water, towed by the speedboat to which it was tethered. Jetskiers and windsurfers skimmed across the slightly choppy surface while landlubbers set their own pace, some running or walking with intent while others meandered from shell to shell. Small children ran in and out of the shallow water with shrieks of delight.

With each step the huge pink hotel grew larger. When they reached it with no sign of Nigel, she stopped and extracted Dustin from the stroller. They settled happily at the water's edge where they built their own version of the Don with thick hard-packed walls decorated with coquina shells, mud-dribbled turrets, and a moat that filled with water with each new wave that came ashore.

A text dinged in and she lifted her phone, hunching over it so that she could read the screen. *lifdink let. Ticks lightner.* Kyra snorted at her mother's attempted communication, which as always left a lot to be desired. Madeline Singer's thumbs and her iPhone were not exactly simpatico. She debated whether to call or to query the message, but decided if there was anything urgent her mother would have called.

"Catch ball!" Finished with the castle, Dustin retrieved his beach ball and hurled it without aiming. It landed in the surf and he was after it before Kyra could stop him.

"Hold on, you!" She sprinted after him hooking an arm around his waist and lifting him onto her hip before wading in after the ball. "If we're going to play catch we have to get farther from the water. How about up there?" She pointed toward a stand of dunes near which a catamaran nestled on its pontoons, its lines clanging slightly against its mast.

"Boag!"

"Yes." Together they pushed the stroller back the way they'd come, then maneuvered it up into the softer sand.

Positioning herself in front of the sea-oat-topped dunes not far from the catamaran, she tossed the ball carefully to Dustin. "Good catch!" she said as he caught and clasped it to his chest. Before she could prepare herself, he threw it back. It whizzed past her knees, rolled between the dunes, and disappeared.

"Ball!" Dustin ran past her in pursuit of his ball.

Kyra went after him. She found him crouching near what appeared to be a low wall of sand against which the ball had come to rest. A wall that ran the width of a property she'd never even known was there.

She scooped up Dustin and his ball taking in the No Trespassing!!! sign that rose out of a patch of grass and sandspurs. But it was what lay beyond the low wall that had her frozen in her spot trying to understand what she was seeing.

She'd walked and run this stretch of beach hundreds of times, had noted the homes both new and huge and old and funky as well as the condos that perched above it. But she'd always assumed this stretch of sand and scrub was somehow attached to one of the buildings on either side of it.

Despite the sign and its exclamation points, she settled Dustin on her hip and moved closer, drawn by something she didn't really understand. A low-slung building with glimmers of grime and salt-caked plate glass overlooked an equally bereft concrete pool filled with trash. Drifts of sand clumped with debris covered everything, reminding her oddly of pictures she'd seen of Pompeii. She stepped through the low-walled opening, her sneakers crunching on sand and gravel and broken glass, half expecting to see plaster casts of bodies overcome by the Florida equivalent of molten lava. This place felt that way—abandoned unexpectedly and in a hurry. A jungle of palms and sea grape trees had sprung up around the edges of the property, wrapping around each other, squeezing out air and sun. Roots and tropical vegetation poked up through the concrete deck, climbed the building's concrete walls, and hung from its tarp-covered roof.

Not sure why, she walked to the building and pressed her face against the murky glass. The long side of the building was an open space that contained tattered groupings of furniture. An ancient Ping-Pong table sat in front of one glassed area. Card tables lined another. The back wall was punctuated by doors labeled with signs she couldn't make out. The L at the eastern end of the building appeared to be a dining room, its tables and chairs still in place. Faded artwork hung crooked on the walls. Shredded ceiling-to-floor curtains hung in corners.

Dustin wrapped his arms tighter around her neck, unusually silent. He did not ask to be put down, but he didn't ask to leave, either.

"I'm just going to take a peek at what's down this sidewalk," she said to both of them as she followed a narrow concrete walkway that curved and branched to an assortment of square, concrete buildings, all roughly the same size. Tarps had been stretched over the flat roofs. Signs affixed to each door carried names, all of them beach related: Starfish Suite, Coquina Cove, Horseshoe Haven, the Happy Crab.

A hotel, then. Small and intimate and definitely of another time. She'd never noticed it from the road, either, hidden as it was by the overgrowth that surrounded it, but given its proximity to the Don CeSar she'd know where to look for it.

Slowly she retraced her steps to the beach pausing near the No Trespassing!!! sign for a last look.

The property was in horrible shape, but it hadn't been condemned or torn down. This was prime beachfront. Perfect for a lavish new home. Or even a small condo building. This property was worth millions of dollars and yet it sat like the land time had forgotten. The question of course was whom did it belong to and why had they left it here to rot?

Chapter Four

The day had already begun to fade but the sun had not yet set when Maddie pulled her trusty minivan into Bella Flora's driveway behind Avery's bright blue Mini Cooper and Nikki's green Jag.

Bella Flora's plaster walls glowed a dusky pink. Her white trim had begun to shadow. Her barrel roof looked burnt red against the lightening sky. She was elegant and beautiful, yet warmly comforting. The sight of her sent Maddie flashing back to the day she'd arrived and met Nicole and Avery for the first time, all three of them aghast at the sorry state of their shared remaining asset. Out of desperation they'd brought her back to life not once but twice. Bella Flora had done the same for them, sending them all down a path that none of them had envisioned. That she belonged to Kyra and Dustin now and had turned into "home" was beyond amazing.

"Geema!"

Maddie had barely extracted herself from the driver's seat when Dustin launched himself out of Bella Flora's large wooden front door, down the steps of the windowed arcade, and through the front garden toward Maddie.

He hurled himself into her arms and began to cover her face and neck with noisy kisses. She kissed him back just as noisily, both of them laughing as Kyra came to join them.

"Mommy tolded me I could stay up 'til you gots here," he said happily.

"I see that," Maddie said, cuddling his sturdy warm body close as she leaned over to kiss Kyra on the cheek. "Have you had your bedtime story yet?"

"He's got it all picked out." Kyra pulled Maddie's suitcase and hanging bag out of the backseat. "Nikki just got here a few minutes ago. I thought we'd have munchies and drinks over sunset once Dustin's tucked in."

Maddie carried her grandson into the high-ceilinged entry and felt Bella Flora enfold her. The first time she'd stepped into this foyer it had looked and smelled more locker room than grande dame. A trapped bird had winged by them in a mad escape. If there'd been the slightest alternative, she, Avery, and Nikki would have turned and fled, too.

She peered into the formal living room and study to the left and right of the foyer. A formal guest bath lay across from the elegant staircase that led to the second story. The central hall led past the formal dining room and Casbah Lounge with its Moroccan-tiled décor and on to the eat-in kitchen and salon. Nikki and Avery stood in front of the salon's floor-to-ceiling windows that overlooked the loggia, the pool, and the pass, where the Gulf and bay came together.

"The pool house is clean and available if anybody's interested," Kyra said after hugs and greetings had been exchanged. "Or we can double up upstairs."

Avery hesitated and Maddie knew that although she'd spent time at Bella Flora since they'd lost Deirdre, had even helped Kyra move into the master bedroom suite, which Deirdre had claimed upon her then-unwelcome arrival, it was hard to be in the house without thinking of the woman whose interior design had so transformed her.

"Why don't you bunk with me?" Maddie said. "I have the extra bed and bathroom. It'll be like a slumber party."

"Thanks." Avery's smile was a bit wobbly. "That would be great."

"I'm not going to complain about having a bedroom and bath to myself," Nikki said. "We've been forced to share a single bathroom far more times than is healthy for any friendship."

They shuddered in unison at the memory of five women and Dustin sharing the tiny prefabbed houseboat bathroom on Mermaid Point. They'd shared at Bella Flora out of personal necessity, but the grim accommodations on the last two renovations had been only one of the network's attempts to "keep things interesting."

"Amen to that," Avery agreed.

"As soon as I put my things upstairs, I'll get the drinks organized," Nikki said.

"I'll get the snacks." Kyra dropped a kiss on Dustin's head, which was already burrowed into Maddie's shoulder. "Happy dreams, little man."

By the time they'd gathered out on the pool deck Maddie wasn't the only one yawning. They sat in the cushioned wrought-iron chairs Deirdre had selected, a far cry from the Goodwill castoffs they'd begun with, and watched the sun slip toward the horizon. A few people fished on the jetty, and a lone windsurfer cut across the water beyond it. It was quiet with only the rustle of the palms and the thrum of insects.

A bottle of red wine and an assortment of their favorite appetizers sat on the wrought-iron dining table. "I bought the caviar in Deirdre's honor," Kyra said watching Nicole load up a cracker.

"The woman did know her gourmet foods," Nikki said.

It had taken time to warm to Deirdre Morgan, who had deserted her husband and their then-thirteen-year-old daughter, Avery, to become a Hollywood designer to the stars, and who had reappeared after Avery's father's death. She'd proven that people and their actions weren't always as they seemed, and Maddie had done what she could to help Deirdre reconnect with her daughter. Deirdre's sudden death had left an unexpectedly large hole.

Avery eyed the bowl of Cheez Doodles before plucking one out and holding it between two fingers. "These don't taste quite as perfect now that I can't taunt Deirdre with them," she said quietly.

"Oh, I'm sure she's up there tutting over your food and clothing choices," Nicole said reaching for her wineglass. "But it does feel strange to be here without her."

"The first night I slept in the master bedroom, I put on my fanciest pajamas," Kyra admitted as she snagged a Bagel Bite.

"What, the ones with the T-shirt that has only one hole?" Nikki asked.

Avery popped the Cheez Doodle into her mouth as they laughed. But Maddie saw her eyes glisten.

"To Deirdre." Maddie raised her wineglass to Avery.

"To Deirdre," they echoed, raising their glasses in return.

For a time they drank and ate and watched the sun continue its descent toward the Gulf. Bella Flora's thick walls hunched protectively around them.

"I'm pretty sure I'm too tired to come up with a good thing tonight," Avery said. Coming up with one good thing to toast at sunset was a ritual Maddie had instituted during that first desperate renovation of Bella Flora when coming up with even one semi-positive thing had been a challenge.

"Me, neither." Maddie yawned again. She was glad to be back, yet already missed Mermaid Point. She was someone there with Will that she wasn't anywhere else, even here with Kyra and Dustin and the women who'd unexpectedly become her closest friends.

"Seriously, Maddie? You're sleeping with a man formerly known as William the Wild and you have nothing to offer?" Avery teased.

"I have a child present," Maddie said with a nod toward Kyra even as her cheeks heated.

"Yes, the child doesn't want to hear about her mother having carnal knowledge of a former rock icon," Kyra said.

There was laughter, but a picture of Will onstage bathed in the warm glow of a spotlight formed in Maddie's mind. He looked so natural there, more comfortable in his skin than she'd seen him anywhere except out on the water poling his skiff over some backcountry flat. "I'm not planning to kiss and tell," Maddie assured her daughter. "Speaking of that, I didn't see any sign of pests."

Kyra shrugged. "Nigel and a few of his colleagues show up now and again. I managed to lose him this afternoon, and there was no sign of him when Dustin and I got back from the beach."

"Good. Maybe there are some real celebrities in town," Avery said. "It would be nice to have some privacy while we figure out our next move."

Nikki groaned. "I'm going to need more wine if we're going to talk about that now."

"We can save it for tomorrow, but I don't think it's going to be a long conversation," Avery said. "I'm grateful we were able to take time to regroup. But our options haven't changed too much since last fall."

"Definitely drinking now." Nikki topped off her glass and did the same for the others.

"I've left several messages for Lisa Hogan's replacement," Kyra said alluding to their former nemesis at Lifetime. "To see if they'd be willing to change the focus of the series. And, um, overlook the fact that it wasn't just Lisa we told where to, um, shove their pitiful and spiteful budget."

Maddie winced. "We may have burned a few more bridges than we meant to." It had been a wild night. A brief moment of heady freedom followed by cataclysmic disaster.

"We should be able to pitch other networks now that we have a track record of sorts. HGTV would probably be the best fit," Nikki said.

This time it was Avery who groaned. She'd been pushed out of her original HGTV series *Hammer & Nail* after the network turned her into the Vanna White of the DIY set and her ex-husband, Trent, into the star of the show. Then Lifetime had taken the renovation show they'd envisioned and made it over into a mean-spirited reality TV show. "No, thanks," Avery said. "I'd love to find a way to produce something of our own. Even if we started with a pilot that would demonstrate our vision for the show to potential backers."

"Me, too," said Kyra, who'd also been pushed out and devalued over the last two renovations while forced to watch as Dustin was used to draw viewers and unwanted media attention.

"If we did something of our own it would have to be local since we can't afford to travel," Avery said. "And we'd need an interesting property owned by someone with an actual renovation budget."

"If we go it on our own, we'd have to fund production, too," Kyra said. "I mean, I can shoot and edit pretty economically, but we'd need at least another production person and we'd need more in the way of editing than I can do with my own equipment."

They'd all gotten a lump sum when Bella Flora had sold. But given their debts and their lack of real income, that money was dwindling, not growing.

"And we wouldn't even have the insulting pittance the network gave us," Nikki added. There was another silence.

"We can all live here," Kyra said. "We wouldn't have a mortgage or rent payment or anything, but we still need to pay for utilities and food and, I don't know, I love Bella Flora and I still can't believe Daniel bought her for Dustin and me, but she's not exactly cheap to run or maintain."

"Elegant grande dames never are," Maddie said looking around her. "We owe it to her and ourselves to figure this out."

"I thought we weren't going to actually talk about this until tomorrow," Nikki said over the top of her now-empty wineglass. "Do I need to grab another bottle?"

"No," Avery said. "We're done. But I'm glad we've laid out the basic options so that our subconsciouses can mull them overnight."

"I don't think my subconscious is in mulling mode," Nikki said. "I think it's ready to start shrieking. All of these options have a certain nightmare quality to them."

"I still think we have a great opportunity ahead," Maddie said. "We just need to choose a path. I'm sure we can figure it out together." She said this with all the certainty she could muster. But there was far more wishful thinking wrapped up in her pronouncement than she wanted to examine. The last time they'd had this conversation she'd insisted that the future looked so bright it would require sunglasses. But at the moment she'd settle for a flashlight and a really good road map.

Chapter Five

If Nikki's subconscious had spent the night mulling, it hadn't reached any significant conclusions. She woke early, still unsettled from the stray thoughts and worries that had floated through her dreams, her stomach in a knot. Not yet ready for coffee and unable to face food, she pulled on her running clothes, laced up her sneakers, and let herself out of the house. On the sidewalk that paralleled the beach, she stretched against the low cement wall in the early morning hush that matched the muted sky.

She jogged slowly, feeling her body loosen, nodding to the occasional passerby. At the Paradise Grille, already opening for breakfast, she took the steps down to the beach and headed north toward the Don CeSar.

As she ran, she scanned from the Gulf, across the beach, and up past the dunes and crossovers to the buildings at the beach's edge. She passed other runners and a few early sun worshippers who were already spreading their blankets and setting up chairs. There were meanderers, too, and shell gatherers who moved from spot to spot with the concentration of art lovers at a museum. There were nods and smiles. No one, least of all Nikki, felt compelled to speak, but the atmosphere was friendly, hospitable. As if they all knew how lucky they were to be here at this particular moment.

She'd discovered Joe Giraldi running behind her on this very beach when he'd decided she was the FBI's best chance of getting to Malcolm. She could picture Joe's broad shoulders, the way they triangled down to slim hips and what could definitely be considered washboard abs. His interior was even more attractive. He was so many things the men she'd dated and even married were not. If only he were willing to leave things as they were, she knew the ever-present knot in her stomach would loosen.

Nikki arrived back at Bella Flora with a pleasant ache in her calves and feeling far more relaxed than when she'd left. She found Maddie in the kitchen staring into the refrigerator and scribbling on a yellow pad. The kitchen was a warm and welcoming space with its Spanish tile floor, reclaimed wood countertops, and soft green glass-fronted cabinets. Sunshine poured in the floor-to-ceiling windows and dappled the wood kitchen table. The coffeemaker gurgled sending the scent of dark roast mingling with something cheesy. "Mmmm, smells good. What's in the oven?"

"Egg soufflés I had in the freezer," Maddie replied. "I thought we should have something special for our 'business' brunch."

"Sounds good to me," Nikki said pulling a coffee mug from the cabinet.

"I think there's enough fruit and coffee cake to round out breakfast, but I'm going to have to make a grocery run. It looks like Kyra and Dustin have been living on cereal, Goldfish crackers, and peanut butter and jelly sandwiches. I'll pass the list around so everyone can add any special requests."

"Great," Nikki said. "What can I do to help?"

"Could you set the table? And then maybe pour orange juice into this pitcher and cut the rest of the pineapple into the bowl of mixed fruit?" Maddie placed the juice and pineapple on the counter. "The soufflés should be out in twenty minutes." She moved with an easy competence, the only one of them with bona fide homemaking credentials.

Thumps and murmurs from above indicated the others were up. Footsteps sounded on the back stairs. Maddie poured a cup of coffee, added cream and sugar, and put it into Avery's hands as she entered. Nikki's mother had been too busy working multiple jobs trying to keep a roof over their heads to spend any real time creating a homey atmosphere beneath that roof, but Nikki had come to appreciate the warmth and comfort of a real home that Maddie had created in each of the places they'd found themselves.

"Bless you," Avery said lowering her face to the mug and inhaling the scent. "I don't suppose you have . . . ?"

Maddie placed a small chunk of coffee cake into Avery's other hand.

"You are magnificent." Avery's eyes opened another notch. She sniffed appreciatively. "Are those egg soufflés?"

"They are."

Avery smiled with pleasure. Her eyes opened fully. "I'm going to nominate you for sainthood. What do you think of Madeline Singer, Patron Saint of Mornings?"

Maddie laughed. "I'm not sure my soufflés merit that degree of religious zeal. They are the never-fail version, nowhere near as fancy as their name implies. But thanks for the vote."

"Hey, they're poufy and filled with cheese," Avery said after another long pull on her coffee. "Is there a patron saint of stomachs?"

"If there were, I'm pretty sure you'd already know about it.

I don't understand how you can eat all the crap you do without gaining weight," Nikki said.

• • •

Everyone was present and accounted for by the time the soufflés came out of the oven all golden brown and impressively puffed up.

"I love egg soufflés," Avery said.

"That's just because they're as close to a Cheez Doodle as anyone's willing to give you this early in the morning," Nikki pointed out.

"True," Avery agreed. "Maybe next time we should try crumbling Cheez Doddles on the top."

Everyone dug into breakfast with gusto. Avery gave them a few minutes before calling the meeting to order. "So," she asked after a last forkful of soufflé. "Do we want to discuss each possibility and go over the pros and cons? Or should we take a vote and see if we already have a consensus?"

"Why don't we take a vote and see where we are," Maddie said.

"Okay, all in favor of pursuing a conversation with Lifetime's new production head say aye."

Nikki raised her hand. "Aye."

"All in favor of approaching other networks?" Avery said.

Again, Nikki responded with an "aye." Maddie joined her.

Seeing his grandmother's response, Dustin raised his hand and chimed in with a loud "Hay!"

"All in favor of finding a project and producing *Do Over* ourselves as originally envisioned?" Avery's hand went up the moment she'd finished speaking. Kyra's joined hers.

"Does the vote have to be unanimous?" Maddie asked.

"Good question," Avery said. "That would be nice, but I'm not sure how we're going to get there."

They considered each other. The decision was large. The risks even larger no matter which choice they made.

"Listen," Nikki said. "I'm tired of working for other people and being abused in the process. I've had more than enough humiliation to last me pretty much forever."

There were nods and murmurs of agreement.

"But renovating and producing on our own, not to mention purchasing airtime? That's a lot to take on. And to find investors we'll need real numbers and time for fund-raising. We could spend a year figuring it out and trying to secure the money." Nikki shook her head. "And that could be a year without income."

There was a silence as they all absorbed this.

"I'd like to find a way to do our own thing," Maddie said finally. "But I think Nikki's right. We need to pursue all of our options so that we can make an informed decision."

"Agreed," Avery said. "But we need to find a renovation project to even come up with a budget. And the only way I'd agree to go back to Lifetime or any other network is if the renovation, and not humiliating us, is the focus of the program. Which means *we* choose the project so there are no unpleasant surprises."

There were murmurs of agreement.

"Since we need to stay local I can ask Chase and his dad to keep an eye out in the Tampa market." She paused for a sip of coffee. "And whatever we choose needs to be architecturally interesting with some sort of . . . history."

Nikki pushed her plate away, her appetite disappearing as she contemplated the number of hurdles they were going to need to jump.

"I saw something unusual yesterday that might be worth taking a look at," Kyra said wiping egg and coffee cake crumbs from Dustin's hands and face. "It's just up the beach. I stumbled on it by accident."

"Really?" Avery asked. "Is it a bungalow? Or one of the smaller Mediterranean-style houses?"

"Not exactly." Kyra shifted uneasily in her seat. "It's a small hotel not too far from the Don CeSar."

"We've never done a hotel before," Maddie said. "Is there a For Sale sign? Or a real estate company listed?"

"No. It doesn't seem to be for sale." A strange look crossed Kyra's face. "And it's just sort of sitting there . . . abandoned."

"That's odd," Maddie said, her eyes on Kyra's face.

"Yeah and that's not all," Kyra said. "I Googled it early this morning. And I got a lot of hits."

"Oh?" Nikki brightened. "Did somebody famous own it? Or sleep there? An interesting history would definitely help pull an audience."

"It has a history, all right," Kyra said. "Only it's not a happy one." She paused. "A man died there under mysterious circumstances in the early fifties. The main suspect disappeared the same day and was never found."

Chapter Six

If you wanted to know anything that had happened on Pass-a-Grille since the first homestead was established in the tiny fishing village back in the 1880s, the man to ask was John Franklin, who had grown up in its two and a half square miles, sold a good share of its real estate, and striven to preserve its history for most of his eighty-plus years.

Avery, Maddie, Kyra, and Dustin arrived unannounced at the small bungalow that housed Franklin Realty and found John's wife, Renée, at the reception desk giving a potted plant a stern talking-to. As head of the Pass-a-Grille Garden Club, and the person who'd orchestrated the restoration of Bella Flora's original gardens, Renée could coax and/or command desired results out of most anything with a trunk, stalk, or petal. Avery thought she was pretty good at coaxing desired results out of people, too.

"Hello. How great to see you." Renée moved toward them, her smile warm and welcoming, her suntanned arms already reaching out for Dustin. Recognizing a grandmother when he saw one, Dustin leaned toward those arms and happily accepted the hug and kiss she gave him. "I heard you were gathering at Bella Flora," she said running a hand through layers of short gray hair. "Come on in. John's in the conference room. I've got coffee and cupcakes."

Dustin's smile grew. "Cut cakes! Choc cut, Neh Nay?"

"Absolutely," she replied leading them into the room with its mahogany table and chairs set in front of a large plate glass window. It was here that they'd signed the papers selling Bella Flora to a then-unknown buyer.

"Well, hello." John Franklin stood.

They came one by one to hug him. His shoulders were stooped and his cane stood at the ready. But his basset hound eyes were sharp and the ruff of white hair encircling his bald head gave him a rakish look. His weathered face was wreathed in smiles. "I heard you were all back. It's wonderful to see you."

He motioned them to seats and Renée hustled out briefly, returning with a tray of drinks and cupcakes. Dustin's was placed on a large paper napkin in front of him. He wasted no time in lifting it in both hands and aiming it toward his mouth.

"Now then, to what do we owe this pleasure?" the Realtor asked jovially. "You've already got the best property on Pass-a-Grille." He had believed that even when Bella Flora smelled like a men's locker room and had varmints living in its vacant rooms. As it turned out, Avery thought, he'd been right.

"We were hoping you could tell us something about the Sunshine Hotel," Kyra said.

"Ahh." He busied himself creaming and sugaring his coffee, but his eyes had lost some of their sparkle.

Renée took the seat next to him. The husband and wife exchanged glances.

"What is it you'd like to know?" he asked.

"I happened on it by accident the other day when I was out on the beach with Dustin," Kyra said. "We've been here on and off for almost three years and I never even knew it existed."

He nodded in acknowledgment, but said nothing. Renée shifted in her seat.

"It seemed strange that it would just be sitting there rotting away. But there was no For Sale sign or anything," Kyra said. "Do you know who owns it?"

John looked down into his coffee cup, but still made no move to pick it up. "Yes."

"I looked it up online," Kyra said. "It opened in 1942 and was owned by a man named Ezra Handleman."

The Realtor nodded but made no comment.

"Most of the articles were about a man, one of the Handlemans, who died there in the early fifties. His wife disappeared the same night. Police named her as the main suspect but they never found her."

"Yes." The Realtor exchanged another glance with his wife. Both Franklins remained uncharacteristically quiet.

"But I couldn't find any mention of the hotel or the Handleman family after the hotel closed in the eighties," Kyra added.

The Realtor nodded.

"Can you tell us anything about the current owner or the property?" Avery asked.

Renée reached over and busied herself straightening Dustin's crumb-covered and increasingly tattered napkin. Her husband watched her for a long moment.

"All I can tell you is that the owners have no interest in selling," John said.

"Well, that's not a problem," Avery replied. "We're not in any position to buy it."

"What is your interest in the property, then?" Renée looked up from the tattered napkin, her expression wary.

"We're looking for a project to renovate," Avery said. "Our relationship with the network is—under review." Though there had been some press at the time, the network had not yet gone public with their mass resignation, no doubt saving it for the finale of season two, which would air that summer. "We want to do a less exploitive version of *Do Over*."

"They were very heavy-handed with Dustin and with poor Max Golden," Renée said quietly referring to the owner of the home they'd renovated on South Beach.

Dustin, who had been single-mindedly consuming his cupcake, looked up at this. "Gax! Neh Nay!" He reached out a chocolate-covered hand and patted Renée's arm. Her features softened as he clambered onto her lap.

"We need a project, one we choose and control ourselves," Avery said. "And we need it to be as close to home as possible."

"I understand," the Realtor said. "Normally I'd love to see one of our historically interesting properties getting attention." John stirred his coffee carefully. "But in this case . . ."

"Couldn't you just ask the owner for permission to show it to us?" Avery interrupted, hoping to forestall the "no" that was clearly coming. "So we could determine whether it would even be a viable project?"

"The property is so interesting," Kyra added. "And it was so, I don't know, so sad to see it sitting deserted that way. Wouldn't the owners like to see it brought back to life?"

Kyra reached for the crumbled remains of Dustin's cupcake, rolling them up in the tattered napkin. John exchanged another glance with his wife, who had gone quite still.

"Maybe John knows of another Pass-a-Grille property that we could consider." Maddie sent Kyra and Avery a warning glance, which Avery ignored. All they were asking for was a look around.

"It's just down the street," Avery said. "Couldn't you maybe reach out to the owners and ask if . . . ?"

John looked more uncomfortable than Avery had ever seen him. Renée laced her hands across Dustin's stomach, seemingly oblivious to the cupcake crumbs and icing that smeared his shirt. She drew a deep breath. "The hotel belongs to my sister and me." Renée's voice was carefully neutral; her face was not. "John can show it to you if you really want to see it, but it's not a potential renovation candidate."

Maddie put a cautionary hand on Avery's arm, but Avery couldn't have stopped the question that sprang to her lips even if she'd wanted to. "Why not? Why wouldn't you and your sister want it renovated?"

Renée's chin came up, but her lips quivered as she lifted Dustin gently off her lap and handed him to Kyra. She folded her hands on the table. "Because our father died there the night my sister's mother disappeared. Presumably after she killed him." Renée's eyes were bleak. "And because all I've ever wanted is for it to be torn down."

· · ·

Nigel Bracken was the first thing Maddie noticed the next morning. He stood in his favorite spot under a palm tree just beyond the no-man's-land of scrub and sandspurs that separated Bella Flora from the path that led to the jetty and the beach. He wore neon orange swim trunks and what seemed to be his favorite, or possibly only, Hawaiian-print shirt. A fishing cap perched on his head, and he wore what looked like a brand-new pair of flip-flops on his feet. Two of his "pack" stood beside him, yawning over cups of coffee.

"Where are you ladies headed?" he asked when they emerged after breakfast.

"We're headed out for a walk," Nicole replied.

"Will Daniel or William be joining you?" the photographer with the bad teeth and the potato-shaped face named Bill asked hopefully.

"Afraid not." Kyra pushed the stroller down the sandy path toward the beach. Maddie, Avery, and Nicole formed a loose circle around her.

"How far are you going? What time do you think you'll be back?" the third photographer called out.

"Seriously?" Avery, who was bringing up the rear, turned to ask. "You want us to help you figure out whether to follow us or not?"

This, of course, would be like telling the fox when the henhouse would be most vulnerable, Maddie thought. And then opening the henhouse door.

Nigel shrugged. "Never hurts to ask, luv."

Maddie turned to stand beside Avery. Nikki turned, too, so that they stood shoulder to shoulder facing their common enemy.

"You're right," Avery said. "What's the point of you following us around all morning hoping for a clean shot you might never get?"

Kyra turned the jogging stroller around. "I agree. Why don't we just have a little photo op right now so you don't have to work up a sweat or anything?"

The three paparazzi conferred. "I wouldn't mind having some breakfast," Nigel said.

"It's not like they're doing anything we haven't shot a hundred times before," Bill said. "They haven't even had a good argument since Deirdre died."

Avery fisted her hands on her hips. Her lips tightened. "Sorry to be so disappointing."

"Yeah," Kyra said repositioning the stroller. "Take the photo or don't. Jeez."

The three conferred again. One of their stomachs rumbled loudly, which ultimately decided the matter.

Avery, Nikki, Maddie, and Kyra slid their arms around each other's waists. Without prompting Dustin took off his Mickey Mouse sunglasses, leaned forward in the stroller, and spread his arms wide.

"Gentlemen." Maddie nodded when the photo frenzy ended. The women turned their backs on the photographers and took the path to the beach.

"That was a good move," Nikki said as they walked down

to the hard-packed sand and headed north. "Maybe if we throw them the occasional photo op and keep things boring enough they'll give up and go away altogether."

"You mean cancel the orgy I had lined up?" Maddie asked drily.

"Yeah. You do that and I'll postpone that nude morning run I was considering," Nikki said.

There was laughter.

"I think we have the basis for a workable strategy here," Kyra said. "We just need to keep it up until some real celebrities show up."

"I'd settle for a couple of reality TV stars doing something stupid," Avery said.

"*We* are reality TV stars," Nikki pointed out.

"Not by choice. And not anymore," Avery replied. "And if the Singer women could detach from their celebrity attachments, we could probably run around naked without attracting the slightest attention."

"Speak for yourself," Nikki said.

The mood lightened further. In truth it was difficult to be negative with sugar-white sand sifting beneath your feet and a perfect blue sky overhead.

"Dustin will always be Daniel Deranian's son," Kyra said. "Whether I ever see Daniel again or not." She kept her voice even, but no one there thought this was likely.

Maddie understood far better now than she had when Kyra had first come home pregnant by a movie star, just how difficult it could be to resist someone that charismatic. William had been flying way under the radar when they'd first arrived to renovate Mermaid Point. Would that change now that he'd begun making music again? Maddie turned her face up to the sun trying to lose the thought in the sound of the waves washing onto the sand and the light breeze that caressed her bare shoulders. A picture of Renée Franklin's bleak gaze replaced it.

The Don CeSar Hotel's pink castle-like structure grew larger as they neared.

"So how far from the Don is the Sunshine Hotel?" Nikki asked. "I've run this beach a thousand times and never seen anything near it that looked in need of a major rehab."

"I know," Kyra said. "It's really hidden." She pointed toward the distant glint of sun on metal. "It's just up there."

"Near those dunes?" Avery asked.

"Between them. And if Nigel and his friends show up let's just keep walking," Kyra said. "It's not the kind of place you want to lead scavengers to."

"No, it doesn't sound like it. But that's exactly what we'd be doing if we somehow got permission to work on the property," Maddie reminded them. "This is Renée we're talking about. Their father died under suspicious circumstances more than sixty years ago, but it doesn't sound like she or her sister are anywhere near over it." Maddie looked out over the Gulf, but all she saw was Renée Franklin's troubled face. "Surely we don't want to exploit her the way the network's been exploiting us."

"No, of course not," Avery said. "I've asked Chase and Jeff to keep an eye open for potential projects, and I'm planning to check out the beach communities within driving distance of Bella Flora, but I don't know that we're going to have much of a choice," Avery said. "And who knows, maybe if we renovated the hotel, Renée and her sister could reach some sort of agreement. Maybe then they could sell it and be done with it."

"God, I just keep thinking what it must have felt like living so close to the place where such a horrible thing happened," Nikki said. "Renée's always seemed so upbeat and positive. I would have never guessed she had such a tragedy in her past."

"No," Maddie said. "A lot of wounds aren't at all visible." Weren't they all a walking testimonial to that?

"Well, all we're going to do today is take a look," Avery said. "There's no harm in that."

They were within hailing distance of the Don CeSar when Kyra angled the stroller toward the dunes she'd pointed out earlier. The catamaran's hardware clanged against the metal mast with a hollow ring, and the sea oats that surrounded the dunes swayed gently as they made their way through the softer sand.

Kyra extracted Dustin from the stroller, handed him into Maddie's arms, then retrieved her video camera from her backpack. Hefting it onto her shoulder, she led Maddie, Avery, and Nikki between the dunes. They stopped in front of the low concrete wall for several long moments trying to absorb what lay before them.

Maddie shivered slightly. Instinctively they moved closer together as they followed Kyra through the opening in the low concrete wall.

Chapter Seven

Maddie took in the drifts of sand and refuse that covered the gouged concrete pool deck and piled high against the corners of the L-shaped building. The scarred trash-filled pool gaped at them openmouthed. Brown-skirted palm trees, bulging bushes, and flowering vines had woven themselves into a thick green wall that blotted out the neighboring properties. The encroaching vegetation clung to the building and had taken root in the cracked concrete. The ends of a tarp that covered most of the building's flat roof snapped against its restraints like a sail against the wind. The sky was still blue and the sun still shone, but its angle cast long shadows across the abandoned property. It felt as if they'd stepped from one world into another.

"I can't decide if this is just sad or creepy," Avery said, though Maddie could see her eyeing the low-slung building, as if applying a mental tape measure.

"I don't think you have to choose," Nikki said. "It's both." Her voice had dropped to a whisper. "I thought Bella Flora looked bad when we first saw her, but she had great bones. Renée was right. This looks like a teardown to me."

There was the crunch of feet on gritty concrete and they looked up to see John Franklin approaching from the rear of the property. The Realtor leaned heavily on his cane, placing it carefully before each step.

"I wish you all could have seen the property in its heyday," he said when he'd reached them. "I lifeguarded here on weekends in the winter when it was filled with snowbirds and over the summer break for the local beach club members. My platform was right there." He pointed to a spot midway between the deep and shallow ends. "I used to give water skiing lessons out in the Gulf on weekends."

Maddie followed his gaze out over the low wall to the beach and the body of water beyond.

"The kids would run on and off the beach all day." An almost shy smile twisted Franklin's lips. "The teenagers used to hang out over there under that stand of palms." He nodded toward the clump of cabbage palms on the edge of the low wall, but his eyes were far away. "I kissed Renée there for the very first time."

Maddie's heart twisted at the affection in his voice. Once she'd believed she and Steve were in it for the long haul.

He led them past the listing covered patio that ran the length of the building to the double glass entrance doors. There he pulled a large ring of keys from his pocket and fit one into the lock. After a bit of jiggling he managed to push open the door.

What once must have been a bright sunlit space was dark and dank, smelling of ancient wet towels and bathing suits trapped in an airless space for far too long. Nikki gagged. A hand flew to her throat. She wasn't the only one swallowing hard in an effort to hold on to breakfast. Trying to breathe through her mouth, Maddie took in the long rectangular space. Cobwebs hung from the ceiling and clung to pretty much every available surface and fixture while dust bunnies (a far-too-delicate term given their size) covered the baseboards and climbed the corners.

"The terrazzo's not too bad," Avery said eyeing the gouged and filthy mottled floor.

"I'm assuming from your tone that's a good thing?" Nikki said.

"Well, it can be repaired and refinished. And it is original." Avery did a 360 taking in the decor.

Ancient rattan sofas and chairs with shredded vinyl cushions were arranged around brightly colored coffee tables. Mushroom-shaped table lamps and multiarmed floor lamps wore coats of dust. A Ping-Pong table sagged in front of the beachside plate glass. Old wooden card tables and chairs overlooked the covered porch and pool.

"It's like a midcentury time capsule," Avery said. "Deirdre would have a field day with this place." She swallowed and turned away.

"Those doors lead back to the locker rooms and sauna and massage rooms," John said pointing to the two openings in the back wall. "You can access them from outside, too, so you didn't have to go through the lobby."

A front desk took up the L near the entrance. Behind it a built-in wooden cubby still held keys on dangling plastic holders. A large sun-shaped clock with faded multicolored rays hung on the equally faded turquoise wall, its large black hands stuck at 12:05. A soda fountain straight out of *Happy Days* occupied the opposite corner complete with chrome stools with ripped vinyl seats, a mirrored back wall, and a vintage Coca-Cola sign. The Realtor ran a hand over the gold-flecked Formica countertop, then slid open the round-edged commercial cooler behind the fountain. "This was always stocked with ice cream sandwiches. It was kind of a help yourself on the honor system.

"The kitchen's through there." He opened the door to a small but utilitarian kitchen. "The dining room is this way."

A space too short to be called a hallway opened to the glass-walled dining room, which sat maybe sixty. Here the tables were white Formica and the low-backed chairs were wicker with vinyl cushions that had once been bright lime and yellow. The lone interior wall and the corners between the sections of glass were papered in what looked like a lattice pattern, no doubt intended to give the room a gazebo-like feel. That paper now hung in strips; the plasterboard behind it was blotched with almost as many water stains as the sagging roof.

John inhaled slowly, and from the beatific smile on his long face it was clear the scent in his nostrils was pure nostalgia and not present-day reality. His eyes were clouded with memory.

Doubling back, he led them through the changing rooms, which were lined with wooden lockers and cubbies as well as the saunas and massage room. Dustin climbed up on an antique scale, his weight barely tilting the bar that held the weights. Maddie, Avery, and Nikki abandoned subtlety to pinch their noses shut. Kyra, who couldn't spare the free hand from her zoom lens, appeared to be holding her breath.

They left the building more quickly than they'd entered, dragging in lungfuls of fresh salt air as the Realtor locked the doors behind them. Without fanfare he led them back along the concrete walkway. Maddie held tight to Dustin's hand, careful not to let him get too close to the jungle-height grasses and bushes, afraid of what might be living in or slithering through them.

The cottages were built of cinder block and looked far more utilitarian than whimsical despite the once-bright colors they'd been painted and the signs carved with beachy monikers. The units were locked, the windows boarded up. Roofs were swathed in a patchwork of tarps. Tropical vegetation had grown around, between, and up cottage walls.

Maddie turned, trying to get her bearings. "Is that Pass-a-Grille Way behind that wall of trees?"

"Yes," John said. "And that's Thirty-first Avenue beyond

all that overgrowth." He pointed to their right. "That's where guests parked their cars. There's a public beach access at the end of it."

He turned, taking the pathway that bisected the cottages and explaining the mix of one- and two-bedroom units, how they'd been situated and landscaped to provide maximum privacy in a space that was decidedly minimal. At the Happy Crab, which didn't look at all happy, he inserted a key into the lock and jiggled it. As he put his shoulder to the door, they heard the sound of small things scurrying inside.

"I hope to hell they're running and hiding and not getting ready to jump us," Nikki muttered. "I don't do rodents."

"I'm with you on that one," Maddie said as the Realtor finally managed to unstick the swollen wood door. Settling Dustin on her hip, she squinched her eyes partly shut so as not to see any small rodent bodies or scurrying cockroaches and followed Nikki and Avery inside.

The cottage smelled as bad, or possibly worse, than the main building, having less room for the smells to dissipate. It had its own small living room with one large window, a small eat-in kitchenette, and a profusely tiled bathroom. The front door had a jalousie window inset. Living room and bedroom windows were fitted with air conditioners and short blackout curtains. The floors appeared to be the same sand-colored terrazzo as the main building; it was hard to be sure given the layers of sand and grit that covered them. The furnishings hadn't fared any better and were coated in layers of dirt, dust, and grime. Signs of water damage were everywhere.

Kyra shot video of all of it and them. Dustin sneezed and clung to her neck. For the first time Maddie could remember, he did not ask to be put down.

Outside, Franklin locked the door behind them. "Excuse me for just a moment," he said moving toward the northern end of the walkway, which appeared to end at a huge hibiscus bush.

"What do you think?" Maddie asked as they huddled outside the Not-So-Happy Crab.

"It's interesting," Avery said. "I mean, all the buildings were pretty utilitarian in the first place and they're in horrible shape, but it's a prime example of mid-twentieth-century architecture. And anything midcentury modern is really hot right now."

"You're kidding, right?" Nikki whispered even though the Realtor couldn't possibly overhear them. "This place would be perfect for a remake of *Psycho*. But only *after* they fumigated."

"The fact that it's seriously in need of attention could work in our favor," Avery said. "They've only just managed to keep it from falling down."

"Renée wants it to fall down," Kyra pointed out.

"But she might change her mind if it were renovated and made attractive to a buyer," Avery said, her enthusiasm apparent. "This is an incredibly valuable piece of property that no one is making a penny from." She shot a glance at John, who'd come to a stop at the end of the walkway. "Plus it's barely a mile from Bella Flora."

"I don't know," Nikki said. "We'd need to put together a renovation and production budget before we could even consider soliciting sponsorships or funding of any kind. And I don't have any confidence that Renée would give her permission even if we could find the money. Or be able to talk her sister into it."

"And I'm not sure she should," Maddie said, setting Dustin on his feet. "She can't even bring herself to set foot on the property. I doubt she'll open herself up to the kind of attention that could surround a renovation here."

"Dawn!" Dustin pointed toward the Realtor and began to toddle toward him. They followed him to where John stood staring at a two-bedroom unit set apart from the others. Largely obscured by the overgrown hibiscus, its faded blue paint was chipped and peeling. Unlike the other units, it had no sign. Its door was padlocked and hurricane shutters had been pulled down over its windows. The other units had looked deserted; Maddie thought this one looked downright desolate.

"This is where Renée and her family lived after the war while her father was helping to run the hotel." John's voice was quiet, almost drowned out by the rustle of nearby palms. "She was the one who found him." They stood in silence for a time before John seemed to rouse himself.

"Would you like to see the hotel brought back, John?" Avery asked.

His shrug was anything but casual. "I don't know," he said finally. "In almost any other case I'd rather see something restored and enjoyed than torn down. But this isn't your usual situation. Renée has always wanted to make it disappear, though I doubt even that would ease the hurt and loss. Annelise was only five when it happened and she's never gotten over it." He lowered his voice so that Dustin wouldn't overhear him "Annelise is convinced that her mother didn't do it, that an intruder killed their father and abducted her mother, even though there's never been any evidence to support that."

He sighed and turned his back on the cottage. "But then what child wants to believe their mother could kill their father and then run away and leave them behind?" He ran a hand over his face. "We've had offers to sell the property 'as is,' but Annelise has refused them all. Their grandparents' will left the property to them equally and stipulates that they have to agree."

"But why leave it to rot?" Maddie wondered aloud. "What does that accomplish?"

"At first I think Annelise just wanted to preserve the time before her life fell apart," John said. "Then I think she convinced herself that there might be clues to what happened that night that would clear her mother's name and explain what really happened." He shook his head sadly. "She's become quite addicted to *Forensic Files* and *Cold Case* and the like and has been trying to get the case reopened for a decade. But then, she's never been a big fan of reality. She's always been somewhat . . . fragile."

Kyra stopped shooting. Slinging the video camera over one shoulder, she bent to pick up Dustin, who'd been eyeing a brightly colored butterfly.

"I think the Sunshine Hotel could be a great project for the new *Do Over*," Avery said. "Would you ask Renée and her sister to at least let us present a plan and a budget for their consideration?"

John leaned even more heavily on his cane for a moment, his face stark. Then he slowly straightened. "I'll ask," he said. "But I wouldn't get your hopes up. I really can't promise anything."

Chapter Eight

Avery spent the next two days alternately pacing Bella Flora, walking the beach, and trying not to jump each time a phone rang. She'd stayed on because she was incapable of going even as far as Tampa with things in such a state of flux. And because although being in the house that Deirdre had so vividly left her mark on was painful, being there with Maddie, Nikki, Kyra, and Dustin, who had been a part of her reconnection with her mother, somehow helped ease that pain.

Chase and Jeff had agreed to look in the Tampa area for possible renovations and Avery had driven the west coast beach communities as far north as Tarpon Springs and as far south as Fort Myers, but so far nothing had even come close architecturally or historically to the Sunshine Hotel.

She was sitting outside staring morosely over the pass when Maddie appeared. "Come on, I need a lift to the grocery store. Plus I could use some company and an extra set of hands."

At the store, Maddie flitted from aisle to aisle checking things off her shopping list while Avery glumly pushed the grocery cart, rousing only when something caught her eye.

"Seriously?" Maddie asked when she returned from the meat counter.

"What?" Avery looked up from her failed attempt to hide the pile of Twinkies and Ding Dongs behind the milk and cereal. "They were buy one, get one."

"That's what you said about the mac and cheese and Hamburger Helper," Maddie replied. "As a mother I can't stand by and let you choose nothing but junk food."

"It's not junk. There are meat and cheese in these products," Avery countered. "And there's a reason kale isn't considered a 'comfort' food." Defiantly she reached for a box of chocolate chunk double fudge brownie mix. "I just can't stand being at such loose ends. Sitting around waiting for someone else to make something happen is driving me crazy."

"I understand," Maddie said. "But I don't think overloading on sugar and carbs is the answer." Like a lion tamer who knows better than to turn her back on the big cats, she maintained eye contact as she gently pried the brownie mix out of Avery's hands. "Kyra's following up with the networks and Nikki's trying to come up with a list of potential funding sources. You could go ahead and work on a plan and a budget for the renovation. Maybe it'll turn into a *Field of Dreams* scenario. You know, 'if you plan it, the go-ahead will come'?"

"Or it could be more like washing your car and causing rain," Avery said, pushing the cart around the end of the aisle. "I'm so afraid of jinxing things."

In the chip aisle Avery swept a bag of Cheez Doodles from the shelf without slowing the cart. When Maddie only raised an eyebrow, Avery grabbed a second bag. She could do without the Twinkies and Ding Dongs if necessary, but a life without Cheez Doodles simply wasn't worth living. "What do you think the chances are we'll get a chance to present a plan to Renée and her sister?"

"I don't know," Maddie said. "Given what John told us, I

can't blame Renée for wanting the hotel to disappear. Plus there's the whole paparazzi problem. This renovation would get lots of attention whether we meant it to or not."

In the produce section Maddie picked through the fruits and vegetables, checking the bananas for bruises in the same way Avery was now examining the roadblocks that stood in their way. Without a doable renovation project there could be no *Do Over*.

"We've got to find a way to convince Renée and Annelise to at least look at what we can do."

"I think you should go ahead and put a presentation together," Maddie said again as they unloaded the cart at the checkout and then watched the items get scanned and bagged. "Realistically, it's our best shot."

In reality it was most likely their only shot. And if Avery had learned anything during the demise of her marriage, her ex-husband's hijacking of their original HGTV show, and the loss of her father's life's savings to Malcolm Dyer, it was that all of a woman's eggs were not safe in one basket.

"I was thinking it might be time to start looking for someone to handle the interior design," Maddie added as they pushed the bulging cart through the parking lot.

"No, not yet," she said too quickly. "I mean there's no reason to replace her now when we don't even have a project."

"We all know that no one can really replace Deirdre." Maddie's voice was gentle. She laid a soothing hand on Avery's arm. "But it only makes sense to start the search. I bet there are lots of designers who'd like to be involved who'd be completely different from Deirdre."

Avery blinked back tears—*tears*—as they loaded the groceries. Not trusting her voice, she remained silent as she slid into the driver's seat and fired up the Mini Cooper.

"Kyra's been tweaking the *Do Over* Facebook and Twitter pages," Maddie continued. "Maybe she can post what we're looking for. Finding someone different shouldn't be a problem given how completely unique Deirdre was."

Avery nodded but made no comment as she backed out of the parking spot, her eyes locked in the rearview mirror.

. . .

Traffic on Gulf Boulevard was heavy as they made their way back toward Bella Flora. They were sitting at a light when Maddie heard a text ding in on her phone. She looked down at the screen expecting it to be some forgotten grocery item from Kyra or Nikki, but it was from Will. She felt her lips twisting into a smile as she read, *Mornin', Maddie-fan. Out on the flats. A couple of your fish friends asked me to say hi.*

"I'm guessing from that shit-eating grin it must be Will," Avery observed.

The grin grew bigger as Maddie typed back. *If fiz knot lafing, tell fiz bi hack.*

She hit "send," then groaned when she realized what she'd sent. *Damn. Mint hi pack . . . back!*

"Good grief!" She tried again. *Tumps are two prick.* "God, I hate autocorrect," she said.

Avery snorted. "You know you can shut that off, right? In the meantime, wouldn't it be easier to call him back?"

"He's out on the boat," Maddie began. "I hate to disturb his fishing. I don't want to . . ."

Avery took Maddie's phone from her hands, scrolled down Maddie's contacts with one thumb while keeping her eyes mostly on the road. She'd hit Will's speed dial and handed back her phone before Maddie had finished protesting and well before she could have composed a legible response.

"Hi, Will." Maddie grimaced at the tremor in her voice. It had been only a week since she'd left Mermaid Point, but even the sound of Will's voice made her feel like a teenager crushing on a too-cute guy.

"Hi, Mad," he said, and she could picture him out on the water, the bright morning sun reflecting off his mirrored sunglasses, hiding the dark eyes that were undoubtedly scanning the shadows beneath the surface.

"I hope I'm not scaring away any important fish." She turned to look out the passenger window hunching into herself in an attempt at privacy, something that was pretty much unachievable within the confines of the Mini Cooper.

"Naw, I've mostly just been sitting out here thinking," he said.

"Ahh," she said. "Doing a little therapeutic fishing, are you?"

"I am." There was a smile in Will's voice, but there was something else there, too. "I heard from a guy at Aquarian, my old record label. They want to come down next week to talk."

"About what?" she asked, barely seeing the Gulf Boulevard hotels whizzing by.

"Recording 'Free Fall.'" He said this as if trying the words on for size.

"Oh." Her stomach went into a free fall of its own as she thought about what that might mean. "Are you going to do it?"

"I don't know," he replied. "But they're throwing all kinds of stuff at me." There was a wry chuckle. "I forgot what it was like when they want you."

"What kind of things?" She hoped the list of incentives didn't include women.

"Well, when I said I didn't want to travel they told me we could record in Miami. Then when I said I didn't want to work with studio musicians they told me I could bring anybody I wanted to record with me."

"Oh," she said, looking up to see the Don CeSar Hotel looming ahead.

"When I told them I really wasn't sure I wanted to do anything with the song, they offered me an obscene amount of money."

The Don's thick pink walls and white-trimmed windows whooshed by. A few blocks later they passed the massive hedge that she now knew hid the Sunshine Hotel.

"How obscene?" Maddie finally asked. After all, there were levels of monetary obscenity. Will had been a big name for a lot of years. He might have pissed away most of what he'd earned, but a fortune to her might not be enough to entice Will to walk across a street.

"Obscene enough to take care of the money I owe the bank. And to run the sober living facility for a year. I could subsidize a good number of residents who can't afford the stay."

"That would be pretty hard to say no to."

"Yeah."

Avery cut over to Gulf Way. The beach flitted past.

"When do you have to decide?" Maddie asked carefully. She did not want to picture what sort of temptation might be thrown in his path if he put himself back in the public eye. Or think about how that temptation might color how he saw her.

"I told them I'd let them know by tomorrow." He sighed and she heard him settle in the boat. "But I'm interested in knowing what you think."

Maddie fixed her eyes on the beach just beyond the row of parked cars and the low concrete wall that edged it, but she was picturing Will in the flats boat out off some small island.

She was ashamed of how much she hated the whole idea. How small she felt for wanting to keep things exactly as they were. How desperately she wished she could keep him all to herself.

"Well," she said, determined to kick her own wants and needs to the curb. She'd vowed to always tell him the truth even when it was hard. "As a longtime fan, I . . ." She paused to weigh her words, her insecurity at war with how much she knew the song meant to him and what it could do for the facility. "The song is fabulous." She swallowed and pushed forward. "And I think it would be a damn shame to keep it to yourself."

• • •

Nicole's legs had turned to rubber. Her chest heaved and the orange juice she drank for breakfast sloshed in her stomach as she jogged along the stretch of hard-packed sand. Her breathing turned ragged and it took everything she had to resist cutting her pace.

Footsteps sounded behind her. Her phone vibrated in her back pocket. Glad of the distraction, she pulled it out, thumbed the screen open, and raised it to her ear.

"We've got to stop meeting like this." The footsteps drew up beside her and she heard Joe's voice in stereo. There was a low rumble of laughter as he matched his pace to hers.

"What are you doing here?" she asked, trying not to wheeze. It had been only a week since she'd left Miami. Though she didn't plan to say so, she'd already begun to miss him.

"I had a meeting in Tampa. I don't have to be back in Miami until tomorrow." Joe spoke easily, not the least out of breath. His T-shirt was tucked into the waistband of his running shorts, which left his broad shoulders and bare chest open to view. He moved with athletic grace, his all-seeing eyes hidden behind government-issue sunglasses. She could see her chest heaving in their reflection.

"Great." That was the best she could do without having to gasp for breath.

"Are you okay?" he asked, automatically checking his stride.

"Sure." She drew in a deep breath and tossed her head back.

"Nikki, seriously, are you okay?"

"Yeah, just a little out of breath," she admitted as she brought her breathing under control.

"I have been known to occasionally have that effect on women." His lips quirked upward.

This was true. She could see the looks women shot him as they passed, the way they studied his body while pretending not to. "Is that right?" she drawled as they jogged by the dunes that bracketed the Sunshine Hotel.

He slowed to a walk just before they reached the Don CeSar, forcing her to slow with him. Her heart stopped pounding but her legs felt as if they might fold beneath her at any moment.

"Why don't we stop and sit and have a cold drink?" he suggested, already angling up the beach.

She was so grateful she could have kissed him. She did give him a peck on the cheek, but said only, "Okay." As if she were simply accommodating him. By the time they'd settled at a table near the Don's outside pool bar with a view over the beach, her breathing had evened out. They ordered sparkling water and she filled him in on the Sunshine Hotel and their lack of progress so far in finding a project. She didn't ask about his business trip or exactly what he was doing in Tampa, having learned that he would share what he could when he could.

A pelican caught her eye and she watched it soar high above the Gulf, its wings extended as it no doubt scanned beneath the surface for something worth diving for.

"I saw Malcolm." He said this quietly as if attempting not to startle her, but just hearing her brother's name sent the orange juice gurgling like a geyser in the pit of her stomach. As the special agent who'd brought Malcolm Dyer in and put him in prison, Joe had been sent to interview Malcolm a number of times. There was still a lot of money missing and unaccounted for.

Nikki did not ask how Malcolm looked or what he might have said. She could barely bring herself to think her brother's name, let alone utter it.

"He's asking to see you," Joe said. "He's promised to cooperate more fully if you come see him."

"But he's a liar." It had taken her far too long to understand this about the brother she'd practically raised.

"He is," Joe agreed even as he reached for her hand. "But if we can recover more of what he stole . . ."

She understood what he didn't say. A little emotional turmoil on her part was nothing compared to the possibility of returning more of the millions he'd stolen. She thought of all the lives Malcolm had ruined. All that he'd taken not just from wealthy clients but also from charities and average people who'd made the mistake of trusting him. People like Avery's father, Maddie and her family, and Nikki herself. Bile rose in her throat.

"I hate asking you to even consider this," Joe said. "Personally I don't even want you on the same planet with him. But professionally . . ." His lips tightened as his words trailed off.

"I know." If Malcolm had asked to see anyone else, Joe would be moving heaven and earth to make it happen. And not worrying about the inconvenience or emotional upset.

"You don't have to do it," he said.

Her hand wrapped around the icy glass of water as she stared out over the beach. Nikki would rather starve than have to look at her brother's too-handsome face, which had become so ugly to her. But this was not only about her.

"I'll be right back." She got up, walked quickly to the pool bathroom, then locked the door behind her. She felt better once she threw up. Afterward she splashed cold water on her face and rinsed out her mouth.

Back at the table she squared her shoulders and looked Joe directly in the eye. Quickly, before she could change her mind she said, "If you want to go ahead and set up the visit, I'll do it."

Chapter Nine

It was a beautiful spring evening at Bella Flora with a soft breeze off the water and a sky just beginning its metamorphosis from day to night. Nigel and his bunch had already taken their photos, determined that neither Daniel nor Will were there, and decamped in search of more interesting game. Dustin splashed happily in the pool never far from the Hardin boys, whom he idolized. Jeff Hardin had been ensconced in a chair from which he could "supervise" Chase and Joe at the grill. Kyra had begun setting the wrought-iron table on the loggia.

In the kitchen, Avery loaded a plate with appetizers whose common denominator was that they were composed of cheese products, then poured Cheez Doodles into a bowl.

"I think I hear Deirdre turning in her grave," Nikki said over the whir of the blender that held a first batch of piña coladas.

"Well, I'm not going to get all caviar and toast points at this late date." Avery swallowed back the emotion that crowded its way into her throat every time her mother was mentioned. Dread knotted her stomach at the thought of the interviews Kyra had scheduled for the next morning. "And I still don't see why we're interviewing potential replacements when we don't have a project or money to complete one, let alone pay a designer." She placed the plate and bowl on a tray. "Besides, midcentury modern is popular enough that there are lots of reproduction pieces and finishes available. I can handle the interior design."

Maddie stopped tossing the salad she was preparing. "You're going to have your hands full serving as contractor. And you know Deirdre would be the first one to insist we had someone on board to handle the design." She set down the tongs and reached for the bottle of dressing. "Nikki said she'd sit in on the interviews with us and Kyra will be there shooting video. We don't have to choose anyone tomorrow. Who knows, maybe Deirdre's spirit will make her preference known."

Avery made no comment as she carried the tray outside. She didn't need chain rattling or ghostly moans to know what Deirdre would have thought. Sometimes, like tonight when she'd ripped open the bag of Cheez Doodles, she could almost see Deirdre rolling her eyes and hear her uttering some droll observation.

Jeff, Chase, and Joe welcomed the appetizers without eye rolls or complaint. She'd barely popped a Cheez Doodle into her mouth before all three boys were clambering out of the pool to snag a snack. Leaving the tray on the table Kyra was setting, Avery headed back inside to sample the piña coladas and make sure they were fit for consumption.

Her mood had improved by the time they gathered around the table. Sun kissed, windblown, and barefoot, they were, she thought, poster children for beachfront living. When their plates had been filled, Maddie clanged a knife on her glass. "I'd like to thank Chase and Joe for providing the steaks and for so manfully grilling them."

There was applause and enthusiastic utensil clanging.

"And to Jeff for supervising them," Avery added.

"Hear, hear!" They raised their glasses in toast, then settled in to enjoy the meal.

Fueled by two and a half piña coladas, an unlimited supply of Cheez Doodles, and surrounded by the people who'd become her family, Avery felt her lips tug upward. She'd taken Chase and Jeff to see the Sunshine Hotel that afternoon and their reactions had confirmed her own.

"It's nice to see you smiling like that," Chase whispered, leaning closer. "I've been worried about you."

"It's been a good day," she said truthfully. One of the best since Deirdre had died. "Now if we can just get permission to renovate and put the money together . . ."

"Those aren't small things," he said.

"I know. But we don't have any real alternatives. And none of us are ready to give up on *Do Over.*"

When the main course had been decimated, Chase signaled to Josh and Jason. "Guys?"

The teens got up without protest and began to clear the table. Maddie took coffee orders and promised Key lime pie for dessert. Nikki went inside to retrieve what remained of the piña coladas, though Avery noticed that Nikki had barely touched hers.

The sun turned a golden red, then began its fiery descent as they lingered over dessert. It was a sight she didn't think she'd ever grow tired of. After practically licking their pie plates clean, the boys took Dustin inside to watch a movie and the adults settled in over second cups of coffee.

Chase slid his chair closer to hers and she felt Bella Flora wrap her arms around all of them. Glancing across the table, she saw Joe slip his arm around Nikki's shoulders. Nikki's eyes were pinned over Avery's head; worry lines creased her forehead. Her normal take-no-prisoners attitude was absent.

"I understand you have a project in your sights but that there's a problem getting permission?" Joe said to Avery when her eyes settled on him.

"Yes. I'm consoling myself that although we don't have a go-ahead, we don't have a definite 'no' yet, either."

"It's a great property," Chase said. "I think a combination of midcentury restoration outfitted with upscale modern amenities could make it interesting to a boutique hotel chain."

"What would it cost to renovate?" Joe asked.

"I need to finish a plan to come up with real numbers," Avery said. "But I'm thinking somewhere in the neighborhood of two hundred to three hundred dollars per square foot, which would put us in the neighborhood of two million plus another five hundred thousand on a new pool and grounds and landscaping."

Nikki's expression turned bleaker. "I don't see how we're going to afford that neighborhood."

"We might be able to bring it in for less," Chase said with a certainty Avery could have kissed him for. "Dad and I would like to participate, and I'm sure a good number of our subs would work with us at a discount if we can be flexible and work around their other commitments. I heard from Enrico Dante yesterday." He mentioned the roofer, part of a large Italian family of artisans who'd spread out through Florida and lent a hand on all three *Do Over* projects. "And I ran into Robby on a job in Tampa." Robby was the young plumber who'd worked on Bella Flora. "He asked about you all."

"It probably took him all this time to get over working with Avery in the first place," Nikki said, rousing.

"I don't think Avery was the one who threatened bodily harm when he had to turn off the water," Joe said. "It was a good thing I had hostage negotiation training."

"There was no air-conditioning and there were five of us sharing one bathroom," Nikki retorted. "Plus Kyra was pregnant. No jury with even one woman on it would have ever convicted us."

There was laughter. "You're right about that," Maddie said.

"Speaking of negotiation, what do you think it would take to get a go-ahead on the renovation?" Chase asked.

"Renée Franklin and her younger sister have to agree. Renée wants the place torn down and the land sold; her sister doesn't want it touched. She seems to think there might be clues there that would help explain what really happened the night their father died," Avery said.

It was the word "clues" that had her straightening and focusing on Joe Giraldi, but it was Maddie who asked the question now foremost in her mind. "The murder took place almost sixty years ago and the place has been closed up since the early eighties. Is it possible that anything could still exist that might help answer Annelise's questions?"

All of their eyes were now on Joe. Avery felt another stirring.

"Forensics aren't really my area," Joe said. "But it would depend."

"On what?" Avery asked.

"On what kind of evidence or leads they had back when the crime was committed. And whether any of it was properly preserved."

Nikki downed the last of a glass of water and turned to Joe. "Is that something you could find out?"

"I do know a few people in the Tampa office," he said. "And I suppose I could check in with the local authorities."

The stirring Avery had been feeling began to blossom into full-fledged hope. "I'm going to check in with John. Maybe Joe and his contacts will be enough to help us get our foot in the door."

• • •

Nikki walked Joe to the foyer the next morning. He pulled her tight against him and brought his lips down on hers. She lingered, reluctant to see him go.

"Get a room!" Avery came out of the kitchen and made

a point of walking around them. "Oh, wait, you already have one." The smile she gave them was forced. She'd made it clear that she was not at all in favor of replacing Deirdre yet and had done her best to talk them out of the interviews scheduled to begin in an hour.

"I wish I could stay," Joe murmured against Nikki's lips as Avery disappeared into the foyer bathroom.

"Me, too." She who had always believed in stiff upper lips and brisk good-byes looped her arms around his neck and pressed against him. *What in the world had happened to her?* Gathering herself, she dropped her arms.

"I thought I'd stop off at the Pinellas County Sheriff's Office before I head to the airport. They've absorbed what used to be the St. Pete Beach Police Department."

She took a step back for good measure. "Do you really think there's anything you can do?"

"It can't hurt to ask a few questions." He placed a finger under her chin and tilted her face upward. "And when you start talking to potential investors, don't forget to talk to me."

"No, absolutely not," she protested. "I hope we can make this happen, but it's not exactly a sure thing."

"What is?" he asked. "I'm not a pauper, Nikki, and I can't think of anything I'd like to invest in more than you."

His eyes slid over her in a warm caress. It took everything she had not to step back into his arms.

"I need some time here to help get things under way," she said in what she hoped was a calm, businesslike tone. "After that I'll go see Malcolm." Even the thought of it turned her stomach and sent heat flooding up her cheeks.

"Sorry to interrupt." Avery came out of the powder room and headed for the front door. "I'm just going to grab the paper." She pulled the heavy wooden door open, then gasped and went still.

There were shouts and scuffling sounds. Nikki and Joe moved to Avery's side. Which was when they saw the long line of people that snaked down the steps, out through the garden, and along the edge of the driveway into the street. A large number of those people resembled Deirdre Morgan. Nikki blinked. But when she opened her eyes, the Deirdres, who came in a variety of shapes, sizes, and ethnicities, were still there.

The first Deirdre in line was tall and muscular with short blond hair that fell in soft waves and curled over one eye just as Deirdre's had. The woman removed her designer sunglasses to reveal blue eyes the exact shade of Avery's and Deirdre's. Her blond brows were perfectly arched and feathered. Except for her build, she might have been Deirdre. In fact, she wore a white linen pantsuit with a V-necked black silk blouse and strappy black-and-white wedge sandals very similar to ones that Deirdre had owned.

It wasn't yet nine A.M., but she had a hint of five-o'clock shadow. "I hope you'll accept my condolences for your loss," she said to Avery. "I wept for days when I heard about Deirdre. As I'm sure you can see, she was a huge inspiration."

"Thank you." Avery's voice wobbled. "But why are you here and why are you . . . dressed like that?"

"I'm here for my interview." The oversized Deirdre's voice was deep, her Adam's apple large. "I spent the entire night in my car and I have been standing on these steps since before sunrise. And frankly," she said, her voice dropping an octave closer to its true timbre, "this girdle is crippling me." The Deirdre reached down and made a none-too-subtle adjustment.

"I know we all appreciate you coming," Nikki said. "But we're looking for an interior designer, not a Deirdre impersonator."

"What's happening?" Maddie and Kyra came up behind them. As a group they stepped out onto the front gallery.

"Durda!" Dustin's face lit with a smile at the sight of the Amazonian-sized Deirdre.

There were more shouts. Digital flashes went off. Nikki

imagined Nigel and his pack of paparazzi must be pissing themselves with happiness at this unexpected bonanza.

"The post did say we were interviewing interior designers, right?" Maddie asked.

"Of course." Kyra's eyes widened as she took in the crowd. Dustin began throwing kisses.

There were more shouts, more flashes, as the Deirdres jockeyed for position.

"Well, I cannot speak for the others," the first Deirdre replied, adeptly blocking the shorter, rounder Deirdre behind her. "But I'm both. And I went to considerable effort to be at the head of this line."

Joe was grinning now. "Now I really wish I could stay," he whispered in Nikki's ear.

"I am the founder and president of the Tampa Bay Area Deirdre Morgan Fan Club," the Deirdre continued. "Which I formed long before everyone else started jumping on the Deirdre bandwagon. She is the new Barbra. The new Divine Miss M. I'm already working on a tribute number for Inside Out, the premiere drag club in Ybor City, where *I* am the headliner."

Still grinning, Joe brushed his lips across Nicole's cheek. "I'll be expecting an update later. You okay to handle this?"

Nikki nodded numbly, then watched him weave his way through the throng. A petite Asian Deirdre, presumably unaware that Joe carried a gun, reached out and pinched his butt as he passed. One applicant held out a cell phone and shot a selfie with Joe.

Nikki inched back toward the door, taking Avery, Maddie, and Kyra with her, but the too-tall Deirdre followed, causing the line to surge closer.

Nikki teetered briefly, torn between laughter and horror. Avery's face had gone white; her body was rigid. The presence of so many "Deirdres" had to be macabre and upsetting. Still, Deirdre supplanting Barbra Streisand and Bette Midler in the hearts of gay men? Well, that was quite a legacy, wasn't it?

"Listen, honey," the first Deirdre said quite reasonably. "I know no one could or should replace your mother. But I am a huge *Do Over* fan. And I suspect we are all here in hopes of making a contribution to the series." The red lips tilted up into a sincere smile. "I mean, don't we all deserve second chances?" She tugged at the waistband of her undergarment, then reached into her matching white straw satchel to retrieve a résumé and an extremely glossy business card. "I am not exaggerating when I tell you that I have yet to meet a space I cannot improve upon. I also do a stellar Ethel Merman. You simply must conduct the interviews as advertised. I believe that even without the incomparable Deirdre, this show simply must go on."

Chapter Ten

As Avery had expected, interviewing replacements for Deirdre sucked. The fact that almost half of the interviewees were dressed like and impersonating Deirdre sucked even more. At first each Deirdre impersonator had been like a punch to Avery's gut. It took four or five before the shock began to wear off.

Clouds scudded across the sky throughout the day, finally blotting out the sun late in the afternoon. Rain began to tap against Bella Flora's windows and splatter against her tile roof just as the final applicant departed. Within minutes it was a deluge that curtained them off from the outside world.

"I'm glad it's raining," Avery said. She felt like a sponge that had been soaked in a sea of strangers, forced to absorb their stories and their credentials, then wrung out by their obsession with a mother she had barely come to terms with. "I'm not even sure I have the strength to get up off this couch, let alone leave the house."

"Me, neither." Kyra yawned. "But I might be able to make it as far as the Casbah Lounge."

They dragged themselves into the bar with its leaded

windows, Moorish arches and tiles, and red leather banquettes. Avery rummaged behind the bar finally coming up with a bottle of rum and an unopened liter of Diet Coke. Maddie returned with a bowl of Cheez Doodles and a plate of Bagel Bites.

Nikki mixed the drinks. Raised her own. "Well, that went better than I expected once we got the system streamlined."

They'd situated themselves in the formal living room, Maddie checking in each applicant, Avery reluctantly conducting the interviews with input from everyone including Dustin, who'd been especially fascinated with the "Durdras."

"I know it was hard," Maddie said. "But I kept thinking how much she would have enjoyed all that worship."

"It's true," Nikki agreed. "A few of them had her mannerisms down and a good number of them were actually talented."

Avery picked up a Cheez Doodle, put it down. "I don't care. I will slit my own wrists before I'll work closely with someone dressed up like my mother." She swallowed. "Besides, how creative can someone who's imitating someone else be?"

Dustin, who'd fallen asleep midway through the interviews and been laid down for a nap, wandered in rubbing his eyes. He climbed onto his grandmother's lap and burrowed his face into her neck. A thumb stole into his mouth.

"So who are our top three?" Nikki lifted her drink to her lips, grimaced slightly, and shoved it away.

Maddie handed Nikki the résumés on which she'd asked, make that forced, Avery to scribble notes, all of which had been negative. Between each interview they'd filled out a score sheet that included design experience, reaction to the designer's portfolio, as well as a compatibility score. Which was, of course, completely ironic given that they had not chosen each other and that Deirdre never would have made the cut if Avery had had the veto power she assumed she did now.

"Number one, shockingly, is Amazonian Deirdre," Nikki said. "And not just because he/she offered us free tickets to the drag club. His work was impressive and his portfolio included two midcentury installations."

Avery's stomach lurched at the real possibility that they might not get the Sunshine Hotel. Especially since they had no plan B.

"And I think he wants the job badly enough to work for the same amount we are. Which is basically nothing. Plus he's used to working on a shoestring, which is, unfortunately, still a budget we can only aspire to," Nikki continued.

"I liked him. And he is already in show business, so he wouldn't be thrown by the cameras," Kyra said.

They all looked to Avery, but she was busy examining the Cheez Doodle in her hand as if it might contain heretofore unexamined secrets of the universe. Or at least a means of ending this conversation.

"Second is Alice Lawrence," Nikki continued. "She was the tall, no-nonsense silver-haired woman who's done several hotels and a family compound. Bertrand Mirdeau was third."

"Wasn't he the elegant French gentleman?" Maddie asked.

"Yes, he had lovely manners," Nikki said. "He reminded me of a count I once had as a client. He kissed my hand."

"Well, there's an important talent," Avery said. "By all means let's hire him. Not that we have the money to hire anyone."

"Do we want to hold more interviews?" Kyra slid closer to Maddie and eased Dustin onto her own lap. "Because I've got about sixty more applicants. In fact the *Do Over* Facebook page kind of blew up after I posted that we were looking for a new designer. I just hope they all tune in for the Mermaid Point episodes."

"You know it's possible we have a larger audience than Lisa Hogan ever let on. Most of her energy went into keeping us on the defensive and off balance; the last thing she'd ever do would be to tell us we were part of a hit show," Nikki said.

"True," Avery said.

They sipped their drinks and nibbled on snacks as the rain continued to fall and thunder rumbled in the distance.

Nikki reached for a bottled water. "A big enough audience could make raising money easier. I thought I might go see Bitsy Baynard in Palm Beach. She's the only person from my former life who stays in touch. She might be willing to invest."

"I'm prepared to put in most of what I have left from the sale of Bella Flora, but there's not a ton," Avery said.

"Me, too," said Maddie. "I just need to keep back enough for Andrew's tuition and expenses."

Kyra's lips tightened. "I thought Dad was supposed to be responsible for that."

Maddie dropped her eyes but said nothing. She rarely mentioned Steve Singer. In Avery's experience no news was good news when it came to ex-husbands.

"I can contribute and Joe offered, too, though I'd really rather not risk his money." Nikki took a long pull of the water. "I was thinking that if we can't raise the two million plus, we might go after some form of crowdfunding."

Avery ran a hand through her hair, but it did nothing to clear her head. "I'm not prepared to choose any of the people who came here today. I will not work with anyone who gets off on dressing up like Deirdre. I don't even want to work with anyone who knew her. If we're looking for a fresh start, then let's have one."

No one looked at all happy with that, but no one argued, either. Avery didn't make the mistake of thinking that meant they wouldn't. "The only thing that really matters right now is nailing down the project." She reached for a Cheez Doodle, gathering her resolve. "I'm going to call Renée right now. We have to talk to her and her sister. And this time, I promise you I'm not going to take no for an answer."

...

It took three days to hear back from the Franklins. Days in which Maddie watched Avery hunch over a drafting table, crumbling and tossing rendering after rendering, and muttering to herself.

On the fourth day Maddie, Avery, and Nikki drove to the small neighborhood tucked behind a small inlet across from the Don CeSar Hotel, where Renée's sister Annelise Handleman lived. The homes ranged from untouched to newly renovated and were arranged in the shape of a nautilus with the outer edge of homes facing the water. Annelise's home was a well-tended forties-era ranch that commanded views of the Pinellas Bayway, Tierra Verde, and the stretch of Boca Ciega Bay that ultimately fed into the pass behind Bella Flora.

Renée greeted them at the door and ushered them inside. "This was our grandparents' house," she explained as she led them through a small formal living room that overlooked the water. "Annelise and I lived with them after our father died." They reached a dining area off a small updated kitchen. John and Renée's younger sister were already seated at the table.

John rose to greet them. Annelise remained seated but smiled up at them as they took their seats. "It's very nice to meet you," she said in a breathy childish voice that occupied a completely separate universe from her older sister's decisive tones. "Please have a seat."

As they settled around the table, Maddie knew she wasn't the only one marveling at how little the sisters resembled one another. Older by eight or nine years, Renée was tall and robust while Annelise appeared small and fragile. Renée's salt-and-pepper hair was thick, short, and decidedly low maintenance, her tanned face devoid of makeup. Annelise's hair was a thinning grayish blond cut in what had once been called a pageboy. Her features were soft and delicate, the whole more pleasing than any one part. Her bow lips were coated with a light coral lipstick and she wore a soft green twinset. But it was her eyes, a pale and unfocused blue, that caught Maddie up short. At Renée's request a small hummingbird of a woman named Mrs. Arnold served them coffee and pastries. At Renée's nod she excused herself and disappeared down a nearby hall as Renée took the vacant seat beside her sister.

"Now, then," John said after they'd murmured their thanks for the refreshments. "I believe you have something to show Renée and Annelise?"

"Yes." Avery stood and began to pass out the folders in which she had placed copies of her sketches and a brief write-up. She unrolled a large piece of paper with sketches and laid it in front of Renée and Annelise and then cleared her throat nervously. Maddie's throat was equally dry as she offered up silent prayers for a go-ahead from both sisters.

Renée leaned forward to study the drawing. Annelise simply sat and waited, her pale blue gaze pinned to Avery's face.

"Okay, then." Avery cleared her throat once more.

Renée gestured toward the drawing. "Take a look, Annelise. Please." Her voice was casual, but Maddie could feel the effort that had gone into keeping her emotions under control.

A few long heartbeats later, Annelise's attention turned to the rendering, and Avery began to speak. She covered the material quickly and clearly, ticking off the most important parts of her plan to bring the property into the twenty-first century while maintaining its mid-twentieth-century architecture, décor, and vibe. She'd brought sketches of the reception area, the dining room, and one of the two-bedroom cottages. She didn't bring up the budget, how much they hoped Renée and Annelise might contribute, or where on earth they were going to get the rest of the money because they'd agreed that none of that mattered until they had permission to renovate. Barely ten minutes later, she concluded with a "we will do everything humanly possible to bring it back to its former glory" and took her seat.

Annelise looked up from the drawing, her expression troubled. "But our house is going to be turned into a guest cottage. There'll be nothing left for the crime scene people to investigate." The words, uttered so clearly in the childish voice, sent shivers up Maddie's spine. "I know how cold cases work. I want . . ."

"Yes, we know what you want," Renée interrupted. "And I've told you that an FBI agent will be looking into the evidence and having the property reexamined before anything is touched." She turned to Nikki. "Isn't that right?"

Annelise turned her eyes on Nikki, who shifted uncomfortably in her chair. Maddie, who could almost see Nikki's internal debate over how much to say, did the same. Getting a go-ahead on the Sunshine Hotel was their only hope for keeping *Do Over* alive.

"Yes," Nikki said finally. "Special Agent Joe Giraldi is, a, um, close personal friend of mine. Of all of us, really. And he's promised to try to get any existing evidence reexamined and have the scene gone over again before work commences."

Annelise placed a finger on the rendering. Slowly she traced the main building with it.

"I think we should do it, Annelise," Renée said. "The place is falling down."

Annelise's finger moved to the long rectangle that represented the pool. She traced its lines almost lovingly. Renée sighed, her eyes closing briefly in obvious frustration.

"It's a good compromise, Annelise," John said. "We know how much the place means to you but we can't continue as we have. The structures are way beyond patching. It's this, or tearing it the rest of the way down."

Annelise's head snapped up. "That's what you both want, isn't it? To get rid of the hotel. So that everybody can forget." Annelise's voice had lost its breathiness. Her blue eyes had sharpened.

There were quick footsteps from the hall.

"Of course we want it torn down," Renée said, her fists clenching on the table. "It's crazy to leave it moldering." She paused, drew a deep breath. "But that doesn't mean any of us are ever likely to forget what happened there. Believe me, I've tried."

Mrs. Arnold arrived and hovered near the kitchen. John Franklin placed a hand on his wife's clenched hands. Renée, who had always seemed so calm and unflappable, continued to jangle with emotion.

Every family had its dance, Maddie thought as they waited for Annelise's answer. She knew firsthand how difficult it could be to change the steps. Barely breathing, she braced for disappointment while continuing to offer up prayers for a reprieve. Across the table Nikki, Kyra, and Avery did the same. Just when Maddie thought she might pass out from lack of oxygen, Annelise huffed and pushed the drawings away from her.

"I'm not agreeing to anything until I meet this FBI agent. I want to see his credentials and hear what he's prepared to do."

"Annelise," Renée said. "This is ridiculous. We're lucky they even want to . . ."

"I don't care," Annelise interrupted, her voice mulish. "That's what I want. And if I'm not satisfied, then the answer is no." She fixed her pale eyes on Nikki.

None of them moved. Maddie had to remind herself to breathe.

"All right," Nikki finally said with a brightness she couldn't possibly feel. "I'll check Joe's schedule to see when he might be able to come."

"Thank you," Annelise said prettily as if she hadn't just held all of their feet to the fire. Her smile was that of a delighted child, all malice swept clean.

Without prompting, they stood and prepared to leave before Annelise could demand anything else. As they said their good-byes and practically raced out the door, Maddie couldn't help wondering why the seemingly weakest dancer in the family appeared to be leading.

Chapter Eleven

The drive across the center of the state of Florida was flat and not, in Nikki's humble opinion, particularly scenic. Unless you were into palmetto and scrub and the occasional farm animal. She and Maddie were on their way to Miami via Palm Beach where they were having lunch with former client Bitsy Baynard so that Nikki could present her with the "opportunity" to be a part of the "new and improved" version of *Do Over*.

Bitsy was a celebrated hostess, so Nikki had confidence the lunch would be both pleasant and delicious. How Bitsy might feel about becoming a sponsor was less certain. Beside her, Maddie peered out the window as if there was something to see.

"Being at Will's recording session should be really cool," Nikki said.

"Yeah. It should be great." Maddie's hands clasped and unclasped in her lap as she turned to Nikki. "It's something I used to fantasize about when I was a teenager. You know, back when you could fool yourself into thinking that a rock star might somehow fall madly in love with an awkward teenage girl." Her voice was tremulous.

"Well, you're not an awkward teenager anymore, Maddie."

"No," she said. "I'm an awkward middle-aged woman who doesn't understand what a rock icon could possibly see in me."

"Oh no, you don't," Nikki said. "You are one of the smartest, most caring, warmest women I've ever known. And William Hightower is crazy about you."

"Right." Maddie did not sound convinced. "It's just that I'm wearing Not Your Daughter's Jeans in an effort to hold things in and three-quarter sleeves to hide my upper arms. My shoes are from Payless."

"You look great, Maddie. And I don't think Will gives a shit what you're wearing. If I'm understanding the situation correctly, the man has seen you naked on more than one occasion. He's also seen the *you* that's inside. And he's made it clear you are what he wants." Nikki almost laughed at how much easier it was to say this to others. How impossible it was to believe it about yourself.

"But that was before," Maddie said.

"Before what?"

"Before he was back in the world. Before he had, I don't know, unlimited choices. 'Free Fall' is going to be a hit; I know it is. And then women are going to be coming out of the woodwork and throwing themselves in front of him." She looked down at her hands, then back at Nikki.

"Maddie, even at rock bottom, Will could have had pretty much any woman who crossed his path." And probably had.

"Gee thanks," Maddie said drily. "I feel so much better now." She sighed. "It's just that when we met he'd been mostly out of circulation. Once he has a hit record there'll be women *littering* his path." She closed her eyes and drew a deep breath. "I feel so small and petty. I want him to be successful. I want the song to be huge, to remind everyone how incredibly talented he is. But at the same time I'd give anything to keep things just the way they are."

"I know." Nikki wished that she didn't, but she understood

completely. Change was never easy. But there was no point wishing for things to be different from what they were. "William Hightower is damn lucky to have you. And don't you forget it."

They both fell silent. Nikki found herself wondering if Joe would still feel lucky to have *her* once she explained that Annelise Handleman expected to "interview" Joe to see if he had enough experience to suit her. She held tight to the steering wheel as she imagined just how well that conversation would go down.

An hour later they were at the entrance to Bitsy Baynard's Palm Beach estate watching the curved wrought-iron gate open inward. Nikki drove the Jag onto the bricked drive and up a tree-lined allée. The landscaping fell away and the massive stuccoed Mediterranean villa appeared.

"Wow," Maddie said, taking in the courtyard with its tiered fountain; the jutting towers, wrought-iron balconies, and enormous arched windows. "It looks like Bella Flora on steroids."

"That's exactly what Kyra said when she ended up here for lunch," Nikki said as they walked up the rounded concrete steps to a long columned arcade.

They waited in the foyer with its glassy marine blue tile floor and sweeping double staircase. A chandelier hung from the domed ceiling high above their heads. Its dropped crystals sparkled in the sunlight. "I'm grateful Bella Flora's chandelier wasn't this big," Maddie whispered. "I'd still be cleaning it."

Bitsy Baynard greeted them with outstretched arms and a smile that brightened her long face. She kissed Nicole firmly on both cheeks and shook Maddie's hand as the introductions were made. "It's so nice to meet you," she said. "Since it's just the three of us, I thought we'd be casual." She led them through a central hallway twice as wide as Bella Flora's with broad archways that opened to large rooms on either side. Outside they took seats around a wrought-iron table that overlooked a large infinity pool and the lush, if manicured, tropical paradise that surrounded it. Snatches of blue sky and water teased just beyond.

"Your home is beautiful," Maddie said.

"Thank you. I understand Bella Flora is pretty gorgeous, too," Bitsy said.

A bottle of sauvignon blanc arrived at the table and was poured by a uniformed attendant. For a few moments Nikki allowed herself to miss the moneyed and glamorous life that had once been hers. Salads arrived along with freshly baked breads. Bitsy had been born into serious money, and inherited more, but she had an equally easy manner with guests and the people who served her. Once they might have chatted about common acquaintances and parties they'd both attended, but Nikki had become persona non grata when it became known that the person who had defrauded so many of the local elite was her brother. Grateful for Nikki's hand in arranging the marriage that had seemingly turned into a true love match, Bitsy was one of the few who had not tarred Nikki with Malcolm's brush.

The day was beautiful; the wine was crisp and dry. The salad, which was filled with chunks of crab and lobster, was delicious. Nikki was debating how best to bring up *Do Over* when Bitsy said, "I've really been enjoying your show. I binge watched season one. I had no idea you were so handy."

Maddie choked slightly on her wine.

"What's so funny?"

"None of us but Avery started out at all handy."

"Yes, that's half the fun," Bitsy admitted. "But I've loved watching the friendship form between you."

"Adversity and being forced to live in such close quarters will do that to people," Nikki said.

"I don't know." Bitsy took a sip of wine. "Some people in those situations just get nastier. Speaking of which, I think what the network has put you through is appalling." She set her glass down. "Is that all scripted ahead of time?"

Nikki snorted. "Good God, no. They just keep dropping these bombs on us, trying their best to humiliate us."

Bitsy shook her head in sympathy.

"We agreed to a televised renovation program. But that's not even close to what we got," Maddie said.

Nikki could have kissed her for setting things up so perfectly. "We've had a falling-out with the network."

"Oh?" Bitsy finished her salad and set her fork on the plate.

"Yes. We're looking at producing the next season ourselves," Nikki said, careful to keep her tone casual.

"My daughter Kyra is a filmmaker and can handle the shooting and editing," Maddie said.

"Oh, yes, I remember meeting her," Bitsy said as the plates were removed and the last of the wine poured. "Wasn't she involved with . . ."

"Daniel Deranian," Maddie said but did not elucidate.

"And Avery, our other partner, is a trained architect and licensed contractor who grew up on her father's construction sites. She did a show on HGTV called *Hammer & Nail*," Nikki stepped in to explain. "She's got a project already locked up. It's a really cool midcentury hotel right on the beach near Bella Flora. A mysterious death and disappearance took place there in the fifties."

Maddie shot her a look of surprise at the words "locked up," but mercifully kept silent.

"Interesting." Bitsy leaned closer. Sort of like a fish who'd just spotted the bait.

"Yes, all we need now is a couple of sponsors." Nikki jerked the bait slightly, then let it dangle. "I don't know if you've seen any of the press coverage but the upcoming season was shot in Islamorada."

"No, we've barely been in town but Bert loves fishing

down there. He's entered a few of the Redbone tournaments."
Bitsy motioned the server to bring dessert. "What kind of
property did you work on?"

"We were supposed to turn William Hightower's private
island Mermaid Point into a B and B," Nikki said.

"William Hightower." Bitsy said his name with reverence.
"I have always thought that man was hot." Her smile lit her
face. "Is he that hot in person?"

"He is," Nikki replied, careful not to look Maddie in the
eye. They were here to get Bitsy jazzed about the show and
eager to invest. The fish had just nibbled. The time had come
to set that hook. If that required offering up a slice of Maddie's personal life, so be it. Maddie's relationship with Will
had hit the tabloids and would be inescapable and undeniable
once season two hit the air in June anyway. "In fact, when
we leave here, I'm dropping Maddie off at a Miami studio
where he's recording a new song." She paused to let this sink
in. "They're dating."

Bitsy looked at Maddie appraisingly; that appraisal ended
in a very large smile. "Shut up!" She practically squealed.
"You are not!"

"I know it sounds completely crazy," Maddie said. "But I
actually am."

Sounding more like a high schooler than a society matron,
Bitsy peppered Maddie with questions, many of them
personal.

"I'm sorry!" Bitsy apologized as Maddie's cheeks turned
a bright red. "But you're living pretty much every woman's
fantasy."

"I know. I'm still trying to figure out how this happened,"
Maddie said.

The questions continued, but they were asked with such
honest enthusiasm and lack of malice that Maddie stopped
blushing and began answering.

Soon Bitsy was telling them that she'd known Bertrand

was "the one" the moment Nikki introduced them. "It took him a little longer to accept the inevitable."

"I stuttered the first time I met Will." Maddie laughed.

"She did," Nikki said. "I was there."

"And he was rude as hell because he didn't want us there," Maddie added.

"Also true," Nikki said. "If he could have tossed us off his island he would have."

"But he didn't." Bitsy cocked her head inquisitively. "And he clearly got friendlier. What happened?"

"I wasn't joking when I said I don't know." Maddie's smile was pure Mona Lisa. "But it's pretty great." All signs of Maddie's earlier worry had disappeared.

"Oh, God, how do I get an early look at the episodes?" Bitsy asked.

"Oh, I don't think . . ." Maddie began.

"I'm pretty sure I could get ahold of the entire season for a serious sponsor," Nikki interrupted.

Bitsy laughed as she happily swallowed the bait, the hook, the line, and the sinker. "Well, obviously I'll have to see numbers, but throw in a chance to meet William Hightower and I'm in."

Maddie opened her mouth to say something, most likely that she couldn't possibly use Will that way or some other such nonsense. Nikki shot her a warning look. After all, if Nikki was going to have to tell an FBI agent that he needed to prove he could be helpful to a possibly deranged woman, Maddie could ask Will to say hello to Bitsy Baynard.

"Done!" Nikki said, extending her hand.

Chapter Twelve

"Just text and let me know where to pick you up on Sunday," Nikki said to Maddie late that afternoon as she pulled the Jag up to the curb in front of SunSpot Studios. "On second thought, maybe you should just give me a call."

Maddie didn't respond to the jab about her texting. She was too busy searching for her backbone, the one that would allow her to open the door, get out of the car, then walk through the front door of the recording studio.

"Maddie?"

"Hmmm?" Her eyes were trained on the small sign above the entry of the perfectly ordinary-looking office building.

"You're not getting ready to walk the plank. You're here to watch Will record. And to enjoy yourself."

"Absolutely." Maddie grasped the door handle and eased out of the Jag. She stood on the sidewalk for a few moments holding her carryall in a death grip. *You're here to support Will. To be with Will.* "Thanks for the ride."

She watched Nikki drive away before crossing the sidewalk. Pushing through the front door, she entered a lobby done in cool grays and blacks with pops of turquoise and lots of glass and chrome. The glossy black reception desk was occupied by a stunning redhead in her early twenties. On the wall behind the desk, bold black letters spelled out *SunSpot Studios*.

The redhead looked her up and down. "Can I help you?" she asked in a tone that was neither warm nor welcoming and not at all helpful.

"Um, yes. I'm here for a recording session." Maddie squared her shoulders, lifted her chin.

"Oh?" A beautifully shaped eyebrow sketched upward. The girl had flawless skin, delicate features, and even white teeth. Her green eyes turned appraising and Maddie could feel her taking in the "mom" jeans and the less-than-firm flesh she'd gone to such lengths to camouflage. It took everything she had to resist the overwhelming urge to suck in her stomach. "I'm a . . . guest of William Hightower."

The eyes lit with surprise. That surprise was tinged with doubt. "Your name?"

"Madeline Singer."

The redhead pulled out a clipboard. Her eyes skimmed down it. Stopped. Widened. She looked Maddie up and down once more. "Let me buzz the studio." She held the receiver to her ear, not meeting Maddie's eyes. "Yes, I have a Madeline Singer here for . . . Oh. Yes. Okay." She turned to Maddie with a puzzled expression. "Aaron will be right . . ." Before she could finish, a thirtysomething young man with intentionally messy brown hair, a boyish face, and a salesman's smile was striding toward her. "There you are, Maddie! I can call you Maddie, can't I?" He grasped her hand in his and looked her directly in the eye. "I'm Aaron Mann. Aquarian Records. Will's setting up to lay down the guitar tracks. Let me take you back to the control room."

"Thank you."

"I hope Sabrina offered you something to drink?"

The redhead's face fell.

"Yes, of course," Maddie said. "But, I'm fine, thanks."

"Well you just speak up if you need anything," Aaron said. "Anything at all. We have instructions from Will to take good care of you."

Sabrina's beautiful mouth gaped slightly. Maddie couldn't resist aiming a smile and a wink her way.

Aaron talked the whole way down a narrow hall and around a corner emitting a barrage of words that flowed right over her until they reached the control room, which was furnished with a leather sectional, chrome and glass tables, and lighting so low that stomach sucking seemed unnecessary. Plexiglas-framed album covers decorated the walls. A control board that looked like it could pilot a jumbo jetliner stretched beneath a thick glass partition that overlooked a studio. The engineer who sat behind it was wiry with gnarled hands, tattooed arms, and a graying ponytail. He nodded briefly when Aaron introduced them. "Nice to meet you. I'm Wiley," he said in the raspy voice of a lifetime smoker before turning back to the microphone that hung in front of him. "Can you give me that again, Will?"

Maddie stepped closer to the glass, where she could see Will sitting on a stool in a darkened corner, his face illuminated by a single spotlight, a microphone in front of him. With a nod of his head he began to pick out the melody. His eyes were closed, his expression more peaceful than she'd ever seen it except in sleep. His fingers moved as if of their own accord. Each note that played from the speakers and reverberated in the control room sounded almost ethereal. She held her breath as she watched and listened. Even Aaron had fallen silent. It was like watching a bird take flight. Or a child reaching for its mother. Or praying in church.

When the last note sounded, no one moved. She thought

she heard the engineer sigh as Will adjusted his headphones and reached for a bottle of water. "I'd like to try that again," he said after he'd taken a swig.

The engineer snorted, then flipped a switch to answer. "Hell, no," he said, not even bothering to look at let alone ask Aaron. "I am not screwing around with perfection." He switched off the microphone and shot Maddie an oddly sweet smile. "Will and me worked together a good bit back in the day. I almost forgot what a perfectionist he is. Even stoned out of his mind he'd never quit trying to make it better." His gnarled hands moved bars and adjusted levers. "Why don't you go on in there and keep him from arguing while I get set up for the next tracks?"

The last of her discomfort faded when she entered the studio and Will's face lit up.

"Well there you are, Maddie-fan. I was thinking maybe you'd changed your mind." He set his guitar in its stand and walked to her, taking her in his arms and deftly turning her back to the control room as he brought his lips down on hers. The kiss was long and thorough, so thorough that Maddie's initial self-consciousness disappeared and she began to forget not only who she was, but where they were.

An exaggerated throat clearing sounded in the studio. "Sorry to interrupt you all," Wiley's voice rang out. "But the guys have gone all polite and whatnot. They're waiting to come in and cut the next tracks."

"Oh!" Maddie's head shot up. Her knees, which had begun to resemble Jell-O, stiffened.

"Don't waste one single second being embarrassed, Maddie," Will said as he let her out of the embrace but kept one arm around her waist. "I can promise you that was tame compared to the things that these guys have seen."

"No doubt," she said as the studio door opened and his bandmates Kyle, Dean, and Robert walked in grinning and pretending to cover their eyes. Despite their effusive greetings and Will's assurances, Maddie could feel her cheeks heating. They'd picked up their instruments and were teasing Will unmercifully as the studio door shut behind her. But as she took her seat back in the control room, she still couldn't help wondering whether Will missed having "the wild" tacked onto his name.

· · ·

Although she was more than a little ashamed of her wussiness, Nicole put off the conversation about Annelise Handleman and her expectations until Sunday morning. It was the middle of May, warm but not yet hot. They'd spent most of Saturday out on the boat and most of Saturday night in bed.

She woke slowly and reluctantly to sun streaming in through the sliding glass doors and the lovely scent of coffee brewing. She stretched and yawned and pulled the sheet up to her chin. It smelled of Joe and of their lovemaking, the memory of which twisted her lips up into a smile. She felt a hazy contentment steal over her, a sensation that was unfamiliar and unsettling.

Her smile fled. She did not do contentment. She had not pulled herself out of poverty by being hazy. Nor had she reinvented herself by relying on others. When she'd loved too much, her own brother had taken advantage of that weakness. At the thought of Malcolm her stomach twisted. The situation with Annelise wasn't the only one she'd been sidestepping.

"Are you awake?" Joe stood in the bedroom doorway in an old pair of running shorts, his bare chest tanned and lightly chiseled. A dusting of dark hair arrowed downward.

"Um-hmmm." The sight of his naked torso banished Malcolm from her thoughts and reminded her of her own nakedness. She sat up, pulling the sheet with her, though given what had transpired between them the night before and the night before that, it was undoubtedly a bit late for modesty.

"Are you ready for breakfast?"

She stretched again. "God, you're going to spoil me. Food, wine, sex. You're a hard man to resist."

"You've figured out my game plan." His smile was easy, his body and face relaxed. But his eyes were sharp as he came and sat on the side of the bed. "Now, why don't you tell me what it is you're worried about?"

She pulled the sheet tighter under her chin. "You're not planning to get out the rubber hose and the bare light bulb, are you?"

"Not unless I need to." His tone remained easy as he gently tucked a stray lock of hair behind her ear, then traced the curve of her jaw with one finger.

She shivered slightly at his touch. "Is this some sort of advanced technique devised by the FBI?"

"No, I just like touching you. But if it helps loosen your, um, lips, I might need to research the possibilities further." His eyes dropped to the outline of her breasts beneath the sheet, which were practically begging for his touch. She crossed her arms over them, the traitors.

Gently, he placed his hands on either side of her, then leaned in to kiss her. Her eyes fluttered shut as his fingers trailed down her neck and skimmed across the sheet.

"I can't believe you think you can seduce it out of me." Her voice came out in an embarrassing croak.

"I'm not sure who's seducing whom," he said, smiling down at her. "You can tell me what's bothering you before or after, but I don't think there's any question that we're going to make love." He lowered his head again and pressed a kiss to the curve of her shoulder. To the hollow of her throat.

His fingers reached for the sheet, but she held on to it. If they made love now, she'd never say what she needed to. Or maybe she'd say too much. "I promised Renée's sister you'd come talk with her so she could be sure she was comfortable with you." She closed her eyes but had no idea whether it was a feeble attempt to hide from his reaction. Or her own.

"She wants to interview me?" It wasn't irritation but amusement she heard in his voice. "Do I need to bring a résumé? References?" She opened her eyes to find him grinning. "Maybe she'd like to talk to my direct superior?" His hand settled on the sheet over her thigh. "I have no problem reassuring her that I'll do whatever I can to help."

She looked away, unable to meet his eyes, and she could feel him studying her. When she forced her gaze up to his, the last vestiges of his smile were gone.

"I don't understand why it's so hard for you to ask me for anything when I've offered you everything," he said quietly.

She pulled the sheet tighter, sat up straighter. "I hate asking. Especially when I can't offer anything in return." She hesitated briefly, then forced herself to continue. "I can't go talk to Malcolm. I want to help you and, and, everybody. But I . . . I know I told you I'd do it, but I can't. Even thinking about it makes me sick to my stomach."

She waited, miserable. Afraid he'd get up and storm off, afraid he wouldn't. He'd gone very still but she couldn't read his face anywhere near as easily as he could read hers. "You're mad, aren't you?"

"I am," he said. Though he didn't raise his voice, it had turned decidedly cool. "But not because you can't talk to Malcolm. I'm angry that you don't seem able to take me at my word. That after all this time together you don't really know me and don't seem to want to. To me a real relationship is not a quid pro quo. My speaking to Annelise and asking the locals to take another look isn't dependent on you talking to Malcolm. It isn't dependent on anything."

"But . . . I can't let you do that when I . . ."

"You're not *letting me*. I insist." He searched her face for something, but she could tell by the way his eyes shuttered that he hadn't found it. When he spoke again, his voice had gone a few degrees cooler and was as sharp-edged as a knife. "I've always assumed I'd ultimately convince you that we belong together for good. But I don't know." He removed his hand from her thigh. "It looks like I've grossly overestimated my abilities of persuasion. And just how much you actually care about me." Each word sliced through her, but it was the way he was looking at her that hurt the most. As if he were finally seeing her—the real her—for the first time. Just as she'd always feared he would.

"It's not . . . I . . ." Now when she needed them most, the right words eluded her. Her head fairly echoed with the old "It's not you, it's me," which was completely true. But she couldn't toss clichés at him now. Not when she could feel everything hanging in the balance, could feel him shutting down. Shutting her out. Looking at her as he had when they'd first met and she was nothing more to him than a potential link to the man he'd set out to apprehend.

"I . . . I didn't mean . . . I . . ." Her voice trailed off. She had nothing new to offer and certainly not the one thing he really wanted to hear. "I'm sorry." That was it, the best she had.

"So am I." He got up, his movements as tight and rigid as his voice. "But this is on me. You've been clear from the beginning. You've told me repeatedly that you have serious trust issues, that you won't get married again, that you don't see yourself in a family or as a parent. And I've refused to listen because I didn't want to believe you. Because I've always assumed if I just tried hard enough I could change your mind, scale all the walls you've thrown up to protect yourself. Like you were some obstacle course in a training exercise that I had to master." He shook his head, and the disappointment that peeked out from behind the iron curtain he'd drawn down on his emotions broke her heart. "I'm done living in denial. It's not really fair to either of us. What do you say we just call it a day and spare ourselves another world of hurt?"

Even then she might have salvaged things or at least delayed the inevitable. But she didn't have the words. Or the confidence that she'd ever be able to give him what he really wanted. No matter how much she wanted to or how hard either of them tried.

She nodded mutely, holding on to the tears that were welling in her eyes, swallowing back the emotion that clogged her throat. She simply sat there, her fingers clutching the sheet until he'd turned and left the room pulling the door closed behind him.

Chapter Thirteen

"You want me to do what?" Kyra quickly checked Nikki's face, but although her expression had been both guarded and strained since she'd gotten back from Miami, she didn't appear to be joking. "I'm pretty sure we're not with the network anymore. We quit. On camera." Kyra didn't look at Avery's face as she said this. It was during their heated show-down with Lisa Hogan that Deirdre had died. "I don't think they're going to just hand over a copy of season two. I can't even get the new program head to return my calls."

She'd put Dustin to bed and then joined the others out around the pool to watch the sunset. They'd fallen silent when she arrived, but she'd assumed it was because they were dishing about the details of her mother's "unbelievably fabulous" weekend with Will. Unlike Nikki, who'd been inexplicably tense and preoccupied, her mother had been grinning like a goon since they'd gotten back from Miami. Kyra definitely didn't want to picture her mother in bed with William Hightower or anyone else—there were some places a daughter's mind should not be forced to go—but it wasn't as if she was a child or anything.

"No one's suggesting you march in through the front door and demand a copy," Nikki said, pouring a strawberry margarita into a chilled glass and passing it to her. "But I've had to ask Joe to 'apply' for the privilege of trying to get the Handleman case reopened." She said this with an odd hitch in her voice. "And Maddie, to whom we will be eternally grateful, has gotten Will to agree to some kind of meet and greet with Bitsy Baynard. We're all stepping out of our comfort zones to do this renovation and shoot our own season of *Do Over*."

Kyra's hand tightened around the glass. "But I don't have an 'in' at the network anymore. There's no one there who has any reason to help us." She took a big gulp of the icy red concoction.

The three of them looked at each other, then at her. "No?" Nikki asked drolly. "No one at all?"

"No. Oh!" Kyra said as realization dawned. "Oh, no. Definitely not." She shook her head for emphasis. "I am not calling Troy Matthews." An image of the cameraman's smug face rose in her mind. She could see the dogged determination with which he'd shot image after image of Dustin to satisfy the network, could hear his snide comments about her relationship with Daniel Deranian in her head. The man was completely infuriating. "Especially not to ask a favor." She shook her head again in case they'd missed it the first time, then gulped down some of the margarita, barely tasting it as it went down. "He's not a friend of ours. He works for the enemy."

"Maybe," her mother said. "But he did help you keep Tonja Kay from getting her hands on Dustin and he did refuse to shoot Deirdre's collapse."

"Maddie's right," Avery agreed. "And it was his footage that got Lisa Hogan fired."

"He's always had a thing for you, Kyra," Nikki added. Avery and her mother nodded.

"Don't be silly. He never . . ."

All three of them looked at her. As if she were the one who was delusional.

"The fact that he's shown his interest with all the maturity of a middle schooler doesn't mean he's not interested," Nikki said. "Neither does the fact that you haven't wanted to see it." She picked up the pitcher and refilled Kyra's glass.

"And it's not like you'd be asking him for anything that could hurt him," Avery said.

Kyra lifted her margarita, gulped down half of it.

"We just want to make the episodes available to Bitsy a little early," Nikki added. "The season will be airing soon and it's not like she's going to share the videos with anyone."

They might have been wrestlers the way they were double- and triple-teaming her. Kyra took another gulp of her margarita, which was when she realized that she seemed to be the only one drinking.

"Maybe we should let Kyra process this for a little bit while we each share our 'one good thing,'" her mother said soothingly. "I'll start with the fact that we now have clear steps to take that could make this project a reality."

"My good thing is Bitsy Baynard," Nikki said. "Once Avery gets the numbers finalized and Bitsy meets Will, I feel pretty confident that she'll write a substantial check."

"This renovation and season three are for Deirdre," Avery said. "I'm dedicating them to her right here and now." Avery put her hand out. Maddie put hers on top of it. Nikki's went on top of theirs.

Kyra lifted her glass and took another gulp. There was absolutely no point in trying to stay sober when she'd never stood a chance of resisting their combined will.

"Are you in?" Avery asked.

"I'm in," Kyra said, grateful for the cushioning buzz from the margaritas. She laid her hand palm down on top of theirs.

"And my good thing is that at least when I call Troy and grovel, I won't have to see the cocky expression on his face."

. . .

It was almost ten P.M. when Avery slipped out of Bella Flora and backed the Mini Cooper down the driveway. The escape was unplanned. One minute she was sitting in the salon after everyone else had headed to bed, the next she was practically sprinting out the front door and heading to Tampa—and Chase—like a swallow making its way to Capistrano.

The porch lights were off and the house was mostly dark when she arrived. She let herself in the front door and found Jeff Hardin in the kitchen, where he was in the process of decimating a large piece of chocolate cake.

"Sweet tooth keeping you up?" she asked, startling him.

"Have to be proactive in this house," he said, recovering quickly and giving her a wink of the bright blue eyes he'd passed down to his son and grandsons. "I think Josh and Jason may be training for the professional eating circuit and Chase is no slouch, either. Got to be quick and relatively devious." He studied her face for a long moment. "I'm willing to share if you want to sit down and join me." He slid the plate closer to the place beside him. "Grab a fork and some milk if you want it."

Settling at the table, she took a generous forkful. "Mmmmm." She let the buttercream icing melt on her tongue. "From Alessi's?"

"Yep." He took a bite himself and then a sip of milk, his eyes closing briefly in contentment. He'd been her father's closest friend and longtime business partner, a second father in all the ways that counted. He kept silent as she took another bite. When she set down her fork and pushed the plate back toward him, he asked, "So, how's the project going?"

She sighed, the bitter taste of frustration replacing that

of chocolate and sugar. "It's not. At least not yet. Joe's coming in to talk to Annelise and Renée, but there's such a chasm between those two I don't know if they'll ever be able to agree. And even if we can lock the renovation up there's no guarantee we can put the money together."

He nodded but didn't interrupt.

"I'm just . . . I'm afraid I'm not going to be able to pull this off. That we'll lose *Do Over* and have nothing to show for the last three years. That everything will have been wasted." She snorted inelegantly. "And I never thought I'd say this, but it's just not the same without Deirdre."

Jeff took the last sip of his milk and wiped his mouth with a napkin. "I know how it is when things don't turn out like you expect," he said. "I never thought Margaret would go first." At the mention of Chase's mother Avery felt the old squeeze of envy she'd had for the Hardins' tight family unit after her own mother had run off. "Or that the same thing could happen to Chase. I never imagined being in the business without your dad." It was Jeff's turn to sigh. "But I've learned that change is the only constant. And that *nothing* that's come before is wasted." He gave her a lopsided smile and reached for her hand. "Come here." He enveloped her in a hug and she felt none of his frailty but only his strength. When he'd let go he said, "You've got us, Avery, whether you want us or not. And you've got Maddie and Nikki and Kyra—you're in this together. And I believe you can help Renée and her sister and maybe find a way to honor their parents by bringing that hotel back to its former glory." His smile was sad but certain. "I have every confidence in you. You do honor to your parents, too. You carry all the best parts of them."

He sat patting her hand while she cried. When she managed to sniff to a stop he rose, using both hands on the table to do so. "I'm going to bed. I think you should do the same."

She sat absorbing all that Jeff had said as she watched him navigate his walker down the hall to the suite she and Chase had built for him. Then she stood and walked to Chase's room. Removing her clothes she slid naked into bed beside him. "Mmmm," he murmured sleepily as he folded his body around hers and wrapped her in his arms. His breath was warm on her neck. "Who says dreams don't come true?"

. . .

Though she didn't plan to ever admit it, Kyra spent most of the next day working up the nerve to call Troy Matthews. Late in the afternoon, unable to take the pointed looks a moment longer, she strapped Dustin into the jogging stroller, stopped on the beach path just long enough for him to blow kisses to the waiting photographers, whose number had begun to dwindle, then turned and pushed the stroller onto the beach. When she hit the hard-packed sand, she broke into a slow jog and tried to give herself up to the salt breeze and the sunshine as gulls wheeled and cawed in a pale blue sky dotted with cotton ball clouds. It took a good half mile before her breathing evened out, another before her thoughts began to clear.

As she ran past the dunes that bracketed the Sunshine Hotel, she reminded herself that the call to Troy was not about her. If getting the Mermaid Point episodes to Bitsy Baynard could help jump-start the funding, then she would do whatever it took. A little groveling might make her ill, but it wouldn't kill her. At a quiet stretch of beach just past the Don, she stopped and lifted Dustin out of the stroller. He shed his tiny flip-flops and curled his toes in the warm sand smiling happily.

"Katsle!" he said. "Wanna katsle!"

Together they pulled the sand toys out of their mesh bag. As he toddled toward the damp sand and began to shovel mounds of it into the turret-shaped pail, she sat down, pulled out her phone, and dialed before she could chicken out. Best-case scenario, she'd get Troy's voice mail and be able to ask for what she wanted without actually having to speak to him. Four rings in, she was mentally composing a brief but friendly message. Then Troy answered.

"Well, talk about a blast from the past," he said. "I wondered how long it would take you to get in touch."

"I beg your pardon?"

"Well, I guess that's a start."

"A what?"

"A start. On the thank-you you owe me for getting rid of Lisa Hogan. You really want to close that loop before you ask me to help smooth things over and put a good word in for you with the new program head."

She scrambled to her feet, unable to take his smugness sitting down. So much for Troy Matthews having a "thing" for her. "I'm pretty sure we sent you a thank-you note," she bit out before remembering she did in fact need his help. "But we are, of course, really grateful that Lisa Hogan is gone. And I've already left a message for the new program head."

"You've left three. But who's counting?"

She drew a breath and began to pace the area around where Dustin sat. He was digging happily, his expression intent. Far better to focus on her son than the man on the other end of the line.

"What's he like?" she asked, clamping down on her temper.

"He's smart and he knows what he's doing," Troy said. "He's a lot less combative than Lisa. But you don't get too far at a network by being overly warm and fuzzy."

There was no arguing with that. Which was one more reason why they were better off taking control of their own destiny.

"What do you need?" he asked.

"Who says I need anything?" she asked. "Maybe I just wanted to say hi." Or maybe she'd rather just slit her wrists and call it a day.

"Let's not pretend we don't know each other," Troy said. "It's me you're talking to, Kyra. The person who's been shooting you, warts and all."

Kyra gritted her teeth and drew in what she hoped would be a calming breath. He did know her, and she was going to have to stay as close to the truth as possible if she had any hope of getting what she wanted. "I'd like a copy of the Mermaid Point episodes," she said.

Silence.

"Just to see how they turned out," she added carefully.

Still no response.

"And for Avery. She's having a hard time. I think it would help her be prepared if she could see how things were, um, handled." She told herself to stop talking, but she was afraid if she did he'd hang up. For all she knew maybe he had. "Listen, all we want is to see the programs. I won't share them with anyone." *Except Bitsy.*

"Why do I feel like you're not telling me everything?"

She wanted to say that that's what came from skulking in bushes and portraying people in the worst possible light, but she was so glad he was still on the line she said only, "I have no idea."

Dustin toddled over and reached toward the phone with a sandy hand. "Who is at?" he asked.

"It's Troy."

"Broy!"

He broke into a smile and a little cartoon light bulb lit up in Kyra's head. "Someone wants to talk with you," she said. Then she crouched down and held the phone up to Dustin's ear.

"Hello, Broy!" Dustin said, clutching her hand. "I'm bidding a katsle!"

She couldn't hear what Troy said, but her son smiled all the way through it. Then he said, "Bye-bye, Broy!" and toddled back to dig some more.

The line was quiet when she got the phone to her ear. "Are you still there?"

"Yeah," Troy said. "I gotta go. But . . ." He hesitated and this time she managed to keep silent. He hesitated for so long that once again she feared he'd hung up.

She was about to abandon hope, when he finally said, "I'll see what I can do." She'd just begun to breathe again when he added, "In exchange for a favor to be named at a later date."

Chapter Fourteen

Joe arrived for the meeting with Annelise and the Franklins looking every inch the seasoned FBI agent that he was. He greeted Maddie and Avery warmly, but only nodded to Nikki as he entered Annelise's home, his manner cool and professional. Just as it had been when he'd first been tracking Malcolm and had seen her only as a potential accomplice.

He was far friendlier to the Franklins and to Renée's sister, whose pale blue eyes were pinned to his handsome face as if he were the savior she'd been praying for. He took the proffered seat at the dining room table while Mrs. Arnold flitted from Annelise's side to the kitchen and back again serving them cold drinks and offering food that no one wanted. At a nod from John Franklin, she retreated.

"Thank you for coming to talk with us," Renée said.

"My pleasure," Joe replied, his attention focused on the two women. With no fanfare, he opened a folio he'd brought with him and slid a piece of paper to both Franklins and Annelise Handleman. "This is a brief bio to give you an idea of my background and experience. I'm currently a special agent in the financial crimes area. It was while hunting down Malcolm Dyer that I first met Nicole, Madeline, and Avery." He did not allude to his relationship with Nikki, nor did he give the slightest hint that he had brought her close to tears with his lovemaking and asked her to marry him. His amusement at his need to present his credentials might never have happened.

Renée, clearly aware that Joe had no need or reason to sell himself, flushed slightly in embarrassment. Annelise read each word and jotted several notes, presumably preparing to conduct an in-depth interview.

"Since it's apparent that Agent Giraldi is extremely experienced and is doing us a very large favor, I suggest we listen to what he has to say before asking any questions," John Franklin said at a look from his wife.

A flash of anger lit Annelise's features, sharpening them briefly. So far Nikki hadn't noticed much middle ground. Annelise Handleman careened between "all in" and "not there."

"Thank you," Joe said. "I've spoken with the Pinellas County Sheriff's Office, who were responsible for policing the beach back in 1952 and who are once again in charge due to the closing of the St. Pete Beach Police Department. They have a relatively new cold case unit; an Officer James Jackson who grew up around here is part of it."

"You know the Jacksons," John said to Renée. "They live on Vina del Mar. I believe J. J. used to deliver the afternoon paper when there still was one. His older brother is also with the sheriff's office."

"Officer Jackson has already pulled the case files and is willing to take another look."

Renée gasped in surprise.

"But I thought *you* were going to reopen and reinvestigate the case," Annelise said.

Joe smiled easily at her. "Despite the way it looks on television, Ms. Handleman, special agents and other law enforcement officers aren't allowed to just take off to conduct unauthorized investigations. I do have a boss to answer to. But I can and will check in with Officer Jackson and lend a hand if anything falls into my area of expertise." He didn't look at Nikki.

Emotions flickered across Annelise's face so quickly it was hard to separate them.

"Thank God I made sure the cottage is still there," Annelise said. Her voice and body vibrated with energy. "Maybe they'll find new trace evidence that couldn't be detected then! Or run fingerprints through the Automated Fingerprint Identification System. That didn't even exist until the late sixties." The woman was practically levitating above her seat. "I've watched every episode there is of *Forensic Files* and *Cold Case*. They use new technology on old evidence to solve crimes all the time."

Joe's gentle smile pierced Nikki's heart. "I'm sure you know from watching those shows that the likelihood of anything surviving in the heat and humidity all these years is pretty low," he said.

Disappointment etched Annelise's pale face. Renée's face revealed less, but she, too, was hanging on Joe's every word. A reminder that it was her life and her father's death that they were discussing.

"The truth is that although the crime scene shows are incredibly popular and the new technologies are very exciting, the majority of cold cases are solved through old-fashioned detective work," Joe continued. "Someone committed to looking at the case with new eyes. It's possible Officer Jackson will unearth new evidence or an eyewitness. Or someone who knows something but wasn't willing to step forward then."

"I was an eyewitness," Annelise said. "Only no one believed me when I said I saw someone in our cottage that night.

Because I was only five they thought that I dreamed it or made it up."

"You did like to make up stories," Renée said. "The wilder the better."

John took Renée's hand.

"I didn't make the man up." Annelise's voice had taken on that childish note. The faraway look in her eyes made them even eerier.

"Can you tell me what happened?" Joe asked Annelise softly.

"I woke up, I didn't know why. I was thirsty and I had to go to the bathroom. Or maybe I heard something. I got up to go to my parents' room, and while I was walking through the living room I saw someone standing in the shadows in the corner. Only when I told my mommy and daddy that somebody was there they told me that I was dreaming."

"No one got up to look around?" Joe asked.

She shook her head. "No, and they wouldn't let me stay in their bed, either."

"And did the shadow person talk to you when you went back to your room?"

Annelise shook her head. "He wasn't there anymore. And then I thought maybe I did 'magine it."

"You said 'he.' Do you remember what the person looked like?"

Nikki knew she wasn't the only one holding her breath as Joe coaxed answers from Annelise, whose voice had turned increasingly childish.

"No. But I could tell it was a man. He was wearing black clothes, heavy ones."

Avery and Maddie's eyes were pinned to Annelise. Joe was jotting notes on a yellow pad. "He didn't speak to you?"

Annelise shook her head.

"Will you try something for me, Annelise?" Joe asked.

Annelise nodded solemnly.

"Close your eyes and think really hard. Try to see the man in the shadows."

Annelise closed her eyes. The rest of them watched her, barely breathing.

"Can you notice anything else about him? Was he tall? What about the shape of his face? Did he have a beard or was he clean shaven?"

Her eyes closed tighter as if she were straining to see. "He . . . there was something really scary about him because he stood so still. Like a statue." Her voice came quick and frightened. "He was standing next to the bookcase and his head was—" Her eyes flew open in surprise. "He was even taller and bigger than my daddy. I didn't know I knew that. Nobody ever asked me about the man. They all thought he was just in my 'magination." Once again Annelise pronounced the word as a five-year-old might. She spoke only to Joe as if the rest of them weren't there.

"I'll make sure Officer Jackson knows to ask you about the man. A sketch artist might be a good idea—to see what else you may have noticed without realizing it," Joe said. "Did you hear anything after you went back to your room?"

"No," Annelise said. "It was summer and the air-conditioning unit was on and those window units were really loud. Kind of like a freight train, Daddy said. But when I got up in the morning my daddy was dead. And my mommy was gone."

Renée slipped an arm around Annelise's shoulders. Her face was as white as her sister's.

"If I would have shouted or made noise, maybe the man would have left. And nothing would have happened." Annelise's voice was little more than a whisper.

"Or things might have gone south sooner," Joe said.

"You believe her?" Renée asked, her face still drained of color. "You think she actually saw someone?"

"I don't know. But the fact that she was a child doesn't

mean she didn't." Joe made more notes, then set down his pen. "Did the detective who investigated ask you about the man?"

"His name was Detective Anderson," John said. "He interviewed everyone. All the guests and the employees."

Annelise's eyes shimmered with tears. "He was mean. I hated him."

It was Renée who continued. "He ultimately concluded that Annelise's mother must have caused our father's death and run off since there was no sign of anyone else's presence."

"My mother never would have done that!" Annelise protested.

Renée glanced at her sister, who had lost the battle with her tears and was now crying silently. "There were people who were suspicious of Ilse and her motives for marrying my father from the beginning. Because she had such a thick German accent. And her English wasn't good. And also because my family and most of the guests and beach club members were Jewish. My stepmother wasn't."

John Franklin placed a hand over his wife's. "A lot of hotels and beach clubs were restricted back then. Renée's grandfather couldn't even buy that property in his own name. He had to buy it through someone else."

Nikki listened to the Realtor's matter-of-fact recitation. She would have liked to reach for Joe's hand but he was there in a professional capacity. And she seemed to have forfeited that right.

Joe made a few more notes before closing the folio. "I'm going to email notes of our conversation to Officer Jackson." He turned to Avery. "And if you can leave the Handlemans' cottage for last, I'm sure Officer Jackson will want to bring in a forensics team to have a look around."

Avery's eyes widened at how smoothly Joe had inserted the assumption that the hotel would be renovated. Nikki saw Maddie and the Franklins register what Joe had done a moment later.

"But you said there wasn't much chance there'd be anything helpful there." Annelise's tears had dried. All of her attention was now focused on the new investigation, not on arguing against the renovation, which had been presented as a fait accompli.

"I did," Joe said to Annelise. "And it might not yield anything. But I'm sure Jackson will want to run down every possibility." He looked directly at Nikki for the first time. "You never know when something is going to turn out to be different than what you'd expected."

He stood then, picked up the folio, and handed business cards to everyone but Nikki. "I've got to run, but I promise you'll be in good hands. And I'll be available by phone or email."

With that he nodded his good-byes, shook hands with John Franklin, and left. As Avery pulled out her notes, Nikki told herself she hadn't yet lost Joe completely. That someone didn't tell you they loved you and wanted to marry you one day and then simply write you off the next. That Joe might be hurt and angry, but that hadn't stopped him from batting a huge home run for her team.

• • •

After Joe had gone, Avery stood on wobbly legs, unsure of her approach. She'd come intending to simply explain the project, present the tentative budget, and hope for the best. Her backup plan had included getting down on her knees and begging. Now she waffled. Annelise hadn't protested Joe's assumption that the renovation was a "go." Did that make it safe to assume the project was on? She studied Renée's sister, who was busy making notes on her pad, head bent, tongue clenched between her teeth in concentration, her small hand wrapped tightly around her pencil. Nothing about Annelise seemed safe or certain. And then there was that old adage about how "assume" made an ass out of "u" and me.

Avery cleared her throat wishing that Deirdre was here

with her smooth certainty, her ability to steamroll with enough grace and charm to keep you from feeling completely flattened.

"So." She cleared her throat again. "I just want to say that I'm very glad that Joe's convinced the authorities to take another look at what happened to your father and, um, your mother."

Annelise's head jerked up at the last words, her unblinking eyes boring into Avery's. Beneath the pale eeriness lay the darkness of old hurts, the child who'd lost both of her parents without warning or explanation. Avery knew what abandonment felt like, knew what it was to yearn for answers that didn't come. Annelise didn't care about renderings or construction schedules or even how much the renovation might cost. Avery set aside the papers she'd brought and spoke directly to Renée's younger sister. "My mother was missing for a lot of my life, too. I was lucky enough to get her back recently. At least for a little while." Tears pooled in her eyes. "It was my father who gave me my love of building things. He's gone, too." She swallowed hard. "I want to restore the Sunshine Hotel. I want to bring it back so that you can find some of the good memories that happened there and so guests can make new ones." Her voice broke but she pushed on. "And I want to do it in our parents' honor. In their names. Yours. And Renée's. And mine."

Maddie reached out and took her hand and gave it a squeeze. Avery squeezed back. Her voice was thick with emotion as she continued. "If you let me do this, I promise we will take great care with every inch of your property. I promise we'll treat it like our own."

Then she stood still and waited, not even swiping at the tears that fell, until Annelise Handleman finally nodded and said, "Yes."

Chapter Fifteen

Annelise's agreement to allow the renovation demanded a celebration. The minute they reached Bella Flora, Maddie headed for the refrigerator and pulled out the bottle of prosecco she'd been saving. Kyra whooped at the news and grabbed her video camera while Maddie opened the bottle and filled champagne flutes.

Nikki accepted a glass and followed the others out to the loggia, but despite the excitement and her own relief that they finally had a project, she couldn't seem to let go of her distress at the distance that now existed between her and Joe. A distance she knew the others had noticed but had mercifully not yet brought up. A distance she was nowhere near ready to discuss.

"Well done!" Maddie raised her glass to Avery. The rest of them followed suit. "What you said was so beautiful and so moving."

"And effective," Nikki added, trying to let go of her worry.

"Thank you," Avery said. "I'm really excited that we've

got the go-ahead. But I'm afraid it was only dumb luck that I happened to say what Annelise Handleman wanted to hear."

"No," Maddie replied as they settled around the wrought-iron table. "It was your honesty that spoke to her. And I think it's important that we continue to remember that what we're doing is more than just a renovation."

More sparkling wine was poured and the celebration kicked into higher gear, but Nikki was still turning over Joe Giraldi's deft handling of Annelise Handleman and his dismissal of her when her cell phone rang. Imagining she had somehow telepathically induced him to call her, Nikki got up and moved to a quieter spot. Then she answered, expecting to hear his voice. Telling her that sitting next to her and pretending not to love her had been torture. That nothing she said or did could ever make him give up on her.

The voice that sounded in her ear did not belong to Joe Giraldi. It belonged to Bitsy Baynard and it was shrill with excitement. "The video arrived this afternoon. I've already watched two of the Mermaid Point episodes!" Bitsy exclaimed, barely waiting for Nikki to finish saying hello. "And you won't believe who called me!" Once again she didn't wait for Nikki to respond, which was fortunate because Nikki was still trying to pull her brain cells back into some sort of working order. "William Hightower called me! I just got off the phone with Wild Will!" Bitsy shrieked, her voice reminding Nikki of the old black-and-white newsreels of the Beatles' first U.S. tour. "There's going to be a concert! And he personally invited me to come with Maddie," wailed the woman who could have bought as many concert arenas and the people who performed in them as she fancied. "I am going to have a frickin' backstage pass!"

• • •

The sky was porcelain blue, the sun a bright yellow a handful of days later. It was a balmy seventy-eight degrees with a light breeze off the Gulf that stirred the sea oats and rifled the palms that surrounded the Sunshine Hotel. It was the sort of day that brought people to Florida and kept them from leaving. One any chamber of commerce would proudly call its own.

Like a fairy-tale character suddenly released from a witch's curse, the entire property had come alive and now hummed with activity as a steady stream of tradesmen came and went bringing their ladders, their meters, their swagger, and their energy. Avery stood on the concrete pool deck between the main building and the pool, not far from where John Franklin's lifeguard stand had once stood, like a captain at the helm of a ship. Chase and Jeff Hardin stood with her. Josh and Jason had taken Dustin down to the beach to toss a football leaving Kyra free to document the day. Maddie had set up a makeshift "lemonade stand" in the shade beneath the porch overhang while Nikki served as an additional greeter and escort.

Plywood was pried loose. Doors and sliders and any windows that could be budged had been propped open to the morning breeze and sunshine. Birds chirped in the trees, insects lighted on flowers and branches. The rustle in the underbrush no longer seemed ominous while the distant sound of boat motors came from the bay and Gulf sides. Avery imagined the buildings were breathing, drawing in great gulps of fresh air. For the briefest moment she could see Deirdre dressed in fluttery white linen impervious to the decades-old dirt and grime, every hair unaccountably in place. Her chest constricted painfully, but the tightness eased as the excitement she hadn't allowed herself to feel before permission was granted seeped into her bloodstream.

Enrico Dante, the roofer, was among the first to arrive. Small and wizened with a cue ball of a head hidden beneath a battered Rays baseball cap, he hugged each of the women effusively. A descendant of a roofer brought from Italy by Addison Mizner to help complete the transformation of Palm Beach, he had been the first Dante with whom she'd worked.

Avery scrambled up the ladder behind him to stand on the roof of the main building, which was in horrible shape even to her untrained eye.

"It will, of course, need to be replaced," he said after releasing the ragged tarp that covered the worst sections of the roof. "And we will make sure it is at a correct slope to avoid this pooling of water. I will look also at the cottages, but I think we will have to assume that the roofs there are in a similar condition."

A rainbow-colored parasail caught her eye, and she moved to the western edge of the roof to take in the view of sugar-white sand that stretched in both directions and the endless body of sparkling water that stretched westward.

"The beach it is beautiful from here," Enrico said. "You can see very far."

Avery nodded. Along the edge of the building, palm trees twisted toward the sky, their trunks swaying and palm skirts rustling slightly in the breeze.

"It's the perfect spot to watch the sunset, no?"

"Oh, yes," she breathed.

"And it could be also good for the sunrise," he said, turning and leading her to the opposite end of the roof with its eastern view over the cottages and the scrim of trees and bush that bordered Pass-a-Grille Way.

She went up on tiptoe. "A few more feet up and we'd be able to see right over those condos to Boca Ciega Bay. They're only two story."

"Yes. This is what I am thinking," Enrico said. "We must add a rooftop deck so that we can have magnificent views in both directions."

Avery felt a shiver of excitement. Raising the roof and

adding a deck would not only provide a magnificent place from which to enjoy the scenery, it would increase the square footage of the communal areas and greatly enhance the property. Raising the ceilings while they were at it would do a lot for the interior space. But each of these things would also add to the expense.

The worry about money was constant, a burden that grew heavier with each decision. She had chafed at the network for keeping the budget artificially low and putting them under needless pressure in order to keep things "interesting," but at least they hadn't been required to raise every penny. "Can you figure it both ways, Enrico? With and without raised ceilings and with and without the decks?"

"Of course. But we must have the decks." Enrico kissed his fingers and opened them in a classic Italian gesture. "This main one, I promise you it will be magnificent."

"Yes, I know it will," Avery said. "But I need to look at the cost very carefully. Our budget is . . ." She couldn't quite come up with a word that fit. "Tight" was too generous. "Almost nonexistent" too frightening.

"Do not worry," Enrico said. "I will work on this and give you my most 'beautiful' price. And we will also become sponsors. Like my cousin Mario did on the South Beach house. He has been lording this over me for too long to ignore."

"That's fabulous. Thank you!" A flush of gratitude warmed her. "I don't know where *Do Over* would be without the Dante family." But the truth was, to make these changes to the roof and raise the ceiling, the price would have to be not just "beautiful," but downright gorgeous. "I want to make sure you know, though, that although we're going to do everything in our power to shoot and air the series, we have no guarantee that what we shoot here will ever be televised."

"Pfft!" Enrico said dismissively. "I have no doubt that you will make this happen and show that network who they are dealing with."

God, she hoped so. Avery smiled and hugged the little man. "You're the best," she said.

"Yes, I tell Mario this all the time. Perhaps I will have to ask you to put it in writing."

Enrico began to take measurements.

"Raising the ceilings and adding the decks are both great ideas," Chase said with genuine enthusiasm when she explained what she had in mind. Though Hardin Morgan Construction had built a reputation on its new construction, Chase had a soft spot for historically interesting structures that matched her own.

"I like it, too," Jeff agreed.

"I'm just going to cross my fingers and hope like hell we're not going to have to replace all the support beams," Avery said. This was the real challenge when budgeting construction. Sometimes you just didn't know until you opened things up what surprises lay inside.

Chase wrapped an arm around her waist. "No point in borrowing trouble. We'll deal with bad news when and if it happens."

"Right." She banished budget worries for the moment and allowed herself to enjoy the warm glow of anticipation. It was a glorious day to be alive and an even better day to begin a new project.

"I hope you don't mind, but I asked John Freemont to come out today. He's the floor guy I told you about. An absolute genius with terrazzo."

Avery nodded.

"And one of Enrico's nephews is coming to look at the plaster work. Oh, and the company we get our hot tubs and Jacuzzis from said they'd take a look at the sauna." Chase abruptly stopped talking. "You haven't told me to mind my own business yet," he said. "Are you feeling all right?"

Avery laughed, shocked at how all right she was. "I kind of appreciate it."

"Hold that thought." He called out to Kyra, who'd been moving around, her video camera on her shoulder, documenting everything. "We need to record this for posterity."

Avery laughed again as he took her shoulders and turned her to face the camera. "Go ahead, say it again."

"Okay, here goes," she said, looking straight into the camera lens. "Chase Hardin has invited some of his subs to come give quotes and has offered to help on this project. And I am hereby admitting that I might actually let him."

Chase kissed her on the cheek and mugged for the camera.

"Good Lord," his father teased. "I think I see his head expanding as we speak. Keep this up, Avery, and the boy won't be able to fit it through a door."

Kyra moved off to follow Robby, who was on his way to inspect the cottages' plumbing. Jeff took a seat near Maddie's lemonade stand.

Chase cocked his head and studied her. "Are you as comfortable with the idea of collaborating as you seem?"

Avery studied him back, thinking of all the arguments they'd had, how disdainful he'd once been. How important it had seemed not to appear uncertain or needy. "Well, since the project's mine and there's no network cameraman attempting to make me look inept, I'm willing to listen. But that doesn't mean I'm going to do or agree with everything you suggest." There was only one general contractor on a job, and she was it. She could hire and fire. Cajole or reject. Anyone who didn't think she was capable just because she had blond hair, Kewpie-doll features, and a big bust could go screw himself.

"Fair enough," he said. "I'm going to go walk through the electrical with Reed Hampton." He offered his father a hand up, and the two turned down the path toward the cottages.

There was not a building or patch of the property that didn't need something, but even now Avery could see the end result in her mind's eye, could imagine people lounging around the pool, meandering to and from the beach through the opening in the low concrete wall, snagging an ice cream sandwich from the cooler, or bellying up to the soda fountain for a milkshake or a sundae. Being handed a vintage key at the front desk.

"Thirsty?" Maddie's voice pulled her back to the present. Avery drank down the proffered lemonade in a few greedy gulps and savored the moment, that moment before anything began, in which everything was possible and the need to compromise had not yet reared its head. She held out her glass for a refill as Nikki stepped out of the main building. Her hair askew, her face streaked with dirt, she looked far less put together than she had when they'd arrived.

She dropped into a chair, blew a limp bang off her forehead, and accepted a glass of lemonade. "Bless you," Nikki said. She closed her eyes and drank thirstily. "And I don't think there's enough air in the world to get rid of the smell in there."

They sat and sipped their drinks treasuring the shade, and the moment of quiet in the midst of the hurricane of activity that whirled around them.

"I could have hugged Joe when he told Annelise that the case was going to be reopened." Avery took a long sip of lemonade as her thoughts turned to the family cottage, which still sat locked and shuttered.

Nikki nodded and smiled at the mention of Joe. But her smile didn't come anywhere close to reaching her eyes. "And we have Will to thank for helping to bring Bitsy on board," Nikki said. "I'm pretty sure it was his call inviting her to the concert that sealed the deal."

"You're going to have a blast at that concert," Avery said to Maddie. "Being there with Will and a part of everything."

"Absolutely," Maddie said, but something flickered in her eyes. She'd sounded more excited about the lemonade.

"You did know about the concert, right?" Nikki said.

"Sure." Maddie looked down at the pitcher in her hand. "Well, I knew there'd probably be one. I just didn't think it would happen quite so soon."

An uncomfortable silence fell. Avery wasn't exactly a relationship expert but it was clear something was up with both Maddie and Nikki. Was she going to bring it up? Hold their feet to the fire to get to the bottom of it? Avery thought not. She'd stood and deposited her empty cup in the garbage, when she noticed a stranger walking toward her. He was tall and slim and wore a billowy pale blue shirt with white summer pants that confirmed he was not a tradesman. As he neared she noted the spiky blond hair and oversized tortoiseshell glasses. He removed the glasses, came to a stop in front of her, and put out his hand. "Avery Lawford?"

She nodded.

"Ray Flamingo." His grip was firm, but his hand was soft. His features were more beautiful than handsome. The blue eyes were slightly mischievous, his smile disarming. "I heard you might be looking for design help."

"Oh?" Avery asked.

"The design community is all agog," he continued. "And I missed out back when Ms. Morgan turned Bella Flora into a designer show house."

There was something in the way he said Deirdre's name that had her studying him more closely. "Have we met?" she asked.

"No, but I feel as if I know all three of you. I'm a very big fan of *Do Over*." The designer shook each of their hands enthusiastically, then retrieved a business card from the breast pocket of the linen shirt with the kind of flourish a magician might pull a rabbit from a hat and presented it to her.

Nikki excused herself. Maddie's eyes moved from Ray's face to Avery's, then back again. "I, um, I think I hear Kyra calling me," she said, though Avery hadn't heard any such thing. With one last look at the two of them she hurried down the path toward the cottages.

"We have budget issues," Avery said, looking at the thick white card with the bright pink outline of a flamingo and then at the designer's designer boat shoes and woven belt that encircled his trim waist. "Whoever we hire, assuming we do, is going to have to be creative. There won't be money to throw around."

"Not a problem. I enjoy a challenge. And I absolutely adore midcentury modern. This place is right in my sweet spot." He slipped his sunglasses into the V of his shirt. "Why don't you show me around and I'll give you my thoughts. If you like my ideas, I'll send you photographs of a few of my installations along with references. If you decide you don't want to work together, no harm no foul. But I really don't think that's going to happen."

"You're going to get dirty," she said, eyeing the pale blue linen shirt and white pants. "The property has been closed up and rotting for decades."

"All the more reason to get on with things, then," he replied, taking her elbow and walking to the main building. Inside he neither gagged nor pinched his nose. He walked through the space with a contemplative expression, stopping now and then to sigh with what seemed to be happiness or to examine a piece of furniture or blow dust off of a frame or knickknack. He went into paroxysms of ecstasy over the front desk and the soda fountain. In the dining room, he turned slowly with his hands clasped to his chest as he drank it all in.

He climbed onto the roof without difficulty or complaint. At his first sight of the view he said, "Good God, I hope you're planning to build a penthouse up here and charge people a fortune to stay in it."

"Hmmmm," Avery said. "Tempting. But we were just

discussing the idea of altering the roof line so that we could create a more expansive deck with 360-degree views."

"I love it," Ray said, doing a slow turn to take it all in. "I think we go for understated elegance—all clean lines and top-end outdoor finishes with nooks and seating areas. And of course we'd have to have a serious bar."

"Absolutely." Avery moved back to the western edge. "I was thinking that the bar could cantilever out over the pool and Gulf sides."

He smiled exuberantly.

Even the cottages didn't diminish his enthusiasm. "I love the idea of raising the ceilings," he said as they walked through a one-bedroom. "It'll really open things up." Outside a two-bedroom he tilted his head at an oddly familiar angle, then snapped a number of pictures. We should create new façades out of ten-inch-wide HardiePlank." He named a pressed concrete product impervious to bugs, water, humidity, and hurricane-force winds. "It'll have a clean sleek look but we can get it with a slight wood grain." He tilted his head the other way. "I'm seeing a burnished steel trim around the doors and windows and maybe squared hardware and light fixtures."

She found herself nodding in agreement with each and every suggestion that he made.

"It will be like designing a movie set intended to suck guests right back into the fifties, but with the best and sturdiest modern materials. With so few units the cottages are going to have to justify a high room rate."

When they finished, he looked as crisp and clean as he had when they'd begun. The only other person she'd ever known to whom dirt and grime refused to adhere was her mother.

"So," she said when they'd completed the tour. "Any questions?"

"You mean other than when can I start?"

She laughed. It was hard to resist someone who seemed to be as in love with the property as she was.

"I'll send you the references and photos," he said. "And I'm going to go ahead and pull samples of some of the finishes and materials I mentioned." He put the sunglasses back on. "As far as I'm concerned, we have a deal. Because I'm not one to take no for an answer. Never have. Never will."

By three that afternoon temperatures had climbed into the mid eighties and all but one of the subcontractors had departed. Maddie had folded up her lemonade stand, and everyone but Avery and Chase had gone back to Bella Flora. "We might as well start closing up the cottages," Chase said, rubbing the back of his neck and stifling a yawn. "Robby should be done inspecting the plumbing in the main building soon."

"I kind of hate to see them closed up now that they've finally had a chance to breathe," Avery said, pulling her sweat-soaked T-shirt away from her body. "I can't wait to make them habitable again."

"Yeah, it's a great property." He nuzzled the top of her head. "I'm glad it's going to get a second chance." He took off his baseball cap and ran a hand through his sweat-dampened hair. "Do you have the key?"

"Yep, it's . . ." Avery was patting her pockets when they heard a shout. They eyed each other at the sound of Robby's voice and started moving. The plumber waved excitedly as they approached the main building.

"What's up?" Chase asked when they'd joined him on the porch.

"I gotta show you something." He led them inside and through several doors to the women's locker room. "I had to take apart one of the lockers to get at a plumbing stack and I found something kind of odd."

Avery's heart sped up as they drew closer and she saw the

newly exposed section of wall. The thing Robby was pointing to wasn't something that needed to be repaired. It was, however, something that didn't really seem to belong hidden away in a women's locker room. It was a safe, one that would have looked far more at home in the bowels of a bank vault.

Chapter Sixteen

They spent the following week airing out the buildings and attempting to scrub away as much of the dirt and grime as possible. Ray scraped paint samples off the walls and cut swatches of wallpaper and fabric, shredded though they were, to send to the companies that had existed when the hotel was built for potential matching and comparables.

Determined not to lead the remaining paparazzi to the hotel, they staggered their departures each morning and took turns returning to Bella Flora at different times during the day. It was dirty and exhausting work that left them limp; some might say catatonic. Hiding their exhaustion when they straggled back in the late afternoons required almost as much energy as the manual labor they were performing.

With Renée and John still out of town following the Memorial Day weekend, they'd decided to keep the discovery of the safe to themselves until the Franklins returned. Despite the drawing of straws and a vigorous round of rock/paper/scissors, no one was willing to inform Annelise of its existence for fear she'd insist everything come to a halt until it had been removed and/or opened.

Kyra returned to Bella Flora from a supposed "beach run" with Dustin late that Friday afternoon to find what remained of their pack of paparazzi waiting on the beach path. She bit back a smile of satisfaction that the pack had now shrunk to a duo consisting of Nigel Bracken and his potato-faced cohort Bill.

"You're going to have to stir things up a bit, luv," Nigel said as she slowed to a walk. "Or I'm going to have to move on. I've put my trust in you and you've let me down. I've got alimony and child support to pay."

She blinked at the thought of Nigel Bracken as a father. "I'm pretty sure that's not our responsibility," she replied.

"Bloody hell it's not!" the photographer retorted, his companion nodding in agreement. "Ours is a symbiotic relationship. You give us photo ops of something worth photographing and we bring you an audience." He yawned theatrically. "Plus I'm nearly dying from the boredom."

"Symbiotic is a serious stretch," Kyra replied grimly. "More like parasitic. We don't *want* an audience that's looking for titillation."

"All audiences are looking for titillation," Bill said, taking a swipe at his very large, very sunburnt nose. "You and your mother are both dating celebrities and we haven't had so much as a glimpse of either of them."

"I am not *dating* Daniel," Kyra said. "And I definitely don't control his travel schedule." Her grip tightened on the jogging stroller's handlebar as she prepared to push around them.

The photographers snorted their disbelief. "Well, then maybe you'd like to flash a little something," Nigel suggested. "You know, give us a bit of *Girls Gone Wild*?" He raised his camera into position as if that might actually happen.

"That would do it," the other pap agreed amenably. "Just a little skin to keep the editor happy."

"Gosh, why didn't I think of that?" she asked, putting the

heel of one palm to her forehead as if she'd just realized she could have had a V8. "I'll tell you what," she said. "Why don't you wait right here while I take Dustin inside, you know, so he won't have to see his mother stripping in public. Then I'll take off all my clothes and come back out here so that you can take nude pictures of me. Will that work for you?"

Nigel's mouth opened then closed.

"That would be great!" Bill exclaimed.

"Wait right here," she said sweetly as she angled the stroller so that Dustin's sleeping face was not photographable. "I'll be back!" she called as she pushed past them. She kept the "just as soon as hell freezes over" to herself.

. . .

"There are worse things than having paparazzi wanting to take your photo," Nikki observed when Kyra carried the still-drowsy Dustin inside and tucked him into the corner of the sofa.

"Oh, what's that?"

"Having them leave because there's nothing worth shooting."

Kyra stared at her, nonplussed.

"I'm not saying you have to flash your boobs or anything. But as much as they are pond scum, Nigel has a point. I know Avery wants this to be a straight renovation show, but I'm not sure we'll be able to raise all the money we'll need or find a way to get it aired if no one even remembers who we are."

"Well, I'm pretty sure Nigel and his friend Bill are still waiting. If you think it will help, you can go on out and show them a little skin. Be sure and tell them I sent you." She knew she needed to calm down, but the fact that she was the one who had to control herself just made her angrier. "I'm so sick of them. They are barnacles on the dock of life as far as I'm concerned. Someone needs to scrape them off. I am not going to be turned into a Kardashian."

Kyra settled on the sofa with her laptop. As she checked the *Do Over* Facebook and Twitter pages, it was impossible to ignore the fact that the number of followers on both had leapt each time they'd had brushes with celebrity or disaster. Even her "designer wanted" post had picked up another five hundred Facebook fans. The shots of the "Deirdres" waiting in line for interviews had attracted even more.

Beside her, Dustin had curled into a tight ball, his breathing even, his thumb firmly planted in his mouth. She brushed a hand over his dark curls, studied his almost delicate features. He was so small and defenseless. So in need of her protection. And how would he fare when he got older and had to navigate on his own without her running interference, blocking unwanted camera lenses? Would he be comfortable with who he was and the circumstances of his birth? Or would he hold it against her?

Movement outside caught her eye. Still lost in thought, she watched the pool being cleaned. The pool guy wore a large straw hat that tied under his chin and a pair of dark glasses. His nose was covered in a thick stripe of zinc oxide. His T-shirt and swim trunks hung loose on his body as he vacuumed the bottom of the pool in long unhurried strokes, checked the filter, and added chemicals. He moved out of sight, presumably to inspect the pump.

A knock sounded on the kitchen door. She heard it open. Heard Nikki speaking to someone.

"The pool guy is here." Nikki stood in the entrance to the salon.

"Um-hmmm," she said, not bothering to look up.

"He needs to talk with you," Nikki said. "Now."

Kyra looked up in irritation, which fled when she saw the pool guy standing beside Nikki. He had removed the straw hat and dark glasses to reveal the dark curly hair, even darker heavily lashed eyes, and golden skin he'd bequeathed to her son. "Daniel." Her heartbeat sped up at the sight of him, a response she told herself was simply the result of being taken by surprise.

His eyes rested on her face before moving to Dustin's tightly curled body. "I thought I'd just pop in and see how you both were doing." He moved toward them with animal grace, his smile devastatingly eager and boyish.

He bent over and pressed a kiss to Dustin's tousled curls, then kissed her just as gently, the brush of his lips across hers reminding her of the first time he'd made love to her in his trailer on the set of her first—and last— major motion picture. When he'd kissed her as if she were something precious, as if all he'd cared about was making her happy. As if he couldn't believe his good fortune. She had been so unbelievably naïve.

"Nice getup," she said, nodding to the T-shirt with *Perfect Pools* lettered across it, the baggy board shorts. The stripe of zinc oxide still coated his nose and, she suspected, now dotted her cheek.

"Thanks. I have an hour before I have to return the truck."

"I hope you checked the filter while you were out there. I think there's something wrong with it."

His brown eyes lit with amusement. They were eyes designed to get a woman into a bedroom and keep her there.

"And there are two paps waiting outside in hopes that you'll make an appearance. Or for me to come out and flash them an interesting body part or two."

"I'd rather you keep those body parts here," he murmured.

"That's my plan," she said, reminding herself that she should not be showing those body parts to Daniel, either. "We've managed to bore the rest of them away. I think the last two are pretty close to giving up."

"Yes, well, unfortunately paparazzi have to make a living, too," Daniel said matter-of-factly.

"So Nigel told me. Apparently our dullness is wreaking havoc with his child support payments."

"It is a dicey thing," he replied. "We need each other to exist."

"Please," she said. "I beg you. Do not use the word 'symbiotic.'"

He smiled. "Done. I'm ejecting it from my vocabulary." Gently he lifted the still-sleeping Dustin into his lap, moved closer to Kyra, then settled him gently within the crook of one arm. A reminder that he was an experienced parent. That he had other children. And a wife. With whom he lived.

"The trick is not to make them go away, but to control the kind of coverage you get. And especially to get it *when* you want it," he continued as he slipped his other arm around her shoulders and pulled her against him, not giving her a chance to protest. As if she could have when she could feel that thing that bound them tingling and tightening. It was easy to be strong when Daniel Deranian was just a name in the headlines or a snippet in a movie trailer. In person he was more like catnip. Her own personal brand of kryptonite.

No. She might not be Superman but that didn't mean she was going to roll over, either. She was not going to be his "bit" on the side. She'd told him this and she'd meant it. More importantly, she'd promised herself. She scooted away from him.

"Kyra, you can't deny that we have pretty powerful chemistry together."

"I didn't do all that well in chemistry. But I remember that sometimes when the wrong things get mixed together they explode."

He smiled at this and inched closer, careful not to wake Dustin. "You know I care about you. And our son. It doesn't have to be complicated."

"We're not a package deal," she insisted. "I know you love Dustin and I appreciate everything you've done for both of us. Having Bella Flora is, well, it's huge. But it is complicated. You have a family and you're married to Tonja." If anything should have woken her up and ripped her out from under his spell, it was the mention of his vindictive movie star wife. Whom he'd repeatedly chosen over her.

She straightened and looked him in the eye. "I refuse to be someone you sleep with now and then."

"I'd like to sleep with you a lot more often than that." His tone was teasing, his eyes admiring. "I care about you, Kyra. I love being with you in every possible way. That's the best I can do."

Somehow, while she was all tangled up in the word "love" and the look in his eyes, he'd gotten close enough to nibble on her earlobe. His warm breath on her neck made her skin prickle with pleasure. Of its own volition her body began to strain toward his. Her eyes fluttered shut as she searched for the strength to resist him even as her head turned so that her lips could reach his. It was possible that the word "irresistible" had been created to define him.

"I am not going to sleep with you," she said hoarsely. "I'm not."

"I know." The kiss was devastatingly sweet and deceptively earnest.

Once again she felt herself surrendering. "No!" She pulled back, squared her shoulders. But the truth was if her protest hadn't woken Dustin, Daniel could very well have kissed his way to "yes."

"Dundell!" Dustin said happily, not questioning his father's arrival any more than he would question his departure.

"Dustbin!" Daniel replied equally happily, using the name Dustin had applied to himself when he'd first begun to talk. With a mischievous wink he slid his arm around Kyra's shoulders and pulled her tight against him.

And so she sat with Daniel's arm around her, their son sprawled across both their laps, smiling at their shenanigans. To all appearances they might have been a happy family roughhousing on the family couch. But though they were in fact bound together they were none of those things. And if she were going to protect her son, she'd better not let herself forget it.

. . .

Nikki came out of the kitchen to the sound of Dustin's giggles. Pausing to peek into the salon, her eyes were drawn to the sofa where Daniel, Dustin, and Kyra were knotted together in what appeared to be some sort of tickle fest. They were so tightly intertwined that it was impossible to tell where one body began and another ended. Despite the occasional mock growl or protest, their laughter was joyous. Though she knew the truth, to all appearances they might have been any happy young family delighting in each other's company.

The image sliced through her. This was exactly what Joe Giraldi wanted, what he deserved.

She turned away from the merriment. She hadn't had so much as a text from Joe since his presentation to Annelise. She'd agonized over whether to call and apologize. Whether to tell him how much she loved him. Whether to beg for another chance. Only nothing had changed. Including her inability to marry him and saddle him with a wife who did not have the courage to do whatever it took to start a family at this late date.

She moved slowly, her limbs heavy as if wrapped in a wool blanket she couldn't shrug off. It took eons to reach the back stairs, another millennia to drag herself up them. At the bathroom sink she splashed cold water on her face, then stared into the mirror at her ashen skin, the dull mossiness of her eyes. As if all the color had been leached from her. And not just on the outside.

Get a grip. She hated people who got all melodramatic and needy when things went wrong. She loved Joe and she loved being with him. But she didn't *need* him. And she sure as hell wasn't going to get all weak and weepy because he'd finally taken her at her word and moved on.

Bereft and alone, she walked slowly to her bedroom, where she closed the blinds to blot out the bright yellow sunshine and the soft blue sky. Then she pulled back the bedcovers and slid between the sheets, closing her eyes against the insistent prick of tears. *Could I be any more pathetic?* Her answer came as the first tears escaped and began to fall, dampening her cheeks, then building to an uncontrollable deluge. That answer was a resounding, soul-shattering, *Yes!*

Chapter Seventeen

Like the rest of her, Bella Flora's doorbell was not easily ignored. It chimed loudly, echoing through the foyer, up the front stairs, and down the central hallway. You might choose not to answer, but it was virtually impossible to pretend you hadn't heard it.

Maddie stood at the sink, her hands in soapy dishwater. Swiping at a stray hair with her shoulder, she waited for Nikki to get it.

The doorbell rang again. Which meant Nikki was probably once again doing her imitation of Sleeping Beauty. Something she'd been doing daily since they'd started the cleanup of the Sunshine Hotel, though Maddie was pretty sure her exhaustion, and accompanying sleep-a-thon, had more to do with Joe Giraldi's absence than the heavy lifting and cleaning they'd been doing.

Grabbing a dishtowel, she headed to the foyer, where she used a still-soapy hand to pull open the door. At the sight of her ex-husband she froze, her hands clutching the damp towel, a soap bubble on her right cheek. However disheveled she might be, Steve looked worse.

Steve Singer was still tall and thin but his shoulders were more stooped than she remembered. The face she'd once found so handsome had turned pasty. His hair was more salt than pepper and was in dire need of cutting. The gray eyes that stared back were wary and underlined by dark circles.

"Hi, Maddie."

"What are you doing here?" She leaned to the side in an attempt to see around him. "Is Andrew with you?" Their son was a student at Georgia State, where he'd been forced to transfer from Vanderbilt after their savings and pretty much everything else had been lost to Malcolm Dyer's Ponzi scheme.

"Nope. It's just me." He looked at her expectantly. "Is Kyra here?"

She looked back. "Is she expecting you?"

"Not exactly." He shifted uneasily from one foot to another. "But as I understand it the house does belong to her and my grandson. And I do have an open invitation."

Maddie may have made a face. Or it could have just been an attempt to keep the soap bubble from slipping toward her mouth. She hadn't seen him since Christmas when they'd spent an excruciatingly long three days being polite to each other, an ordeal she'd assumed she wouldn't have to repeat until the following Thanksgiving, which also happened to be Dustin's birthday.

"Are you planning to let me in?"

She wished she could say "no" and simply close the door in his face. Reluctantly, she took a step back to allow him to enter. With the dishtowel wadded in her hands she turned toward the stairs. "Kyra! You have—"

"Shhhh!" Kyra appeared at the top of the stairs. "I just got Dustin into bed and . . ." Her voice trailed off. "Dad! What are you doing here?" She came down quickly. Unlike Maddie, she hugged her father and accepted his kiss on the cheek.

"Do I need a reason to visit?" he asked, smiling too brightly.

"No, of course not," Kyra said. "I just didn't realize you had vacation time. I thought you'd be at work."

"I've taken a little time off," he said, his smile slipping a notch. "To regroup."

Steve had been either lying on a couch unable to get up or "regrouping" since their life had fallen apart and Maddie had been forced to step up and take over. It was not the loss of their things that had ended their quarter-of-a-century marriage, but Steve's loss of himself and his inability to forgive her for finding the strength to do what he could not.

"How long are you planning to stay?" Maddie asked.

"I don't really know," he said, attempting a casual shrug. Turning to Kyra, he asked, "Is there a bed available?"

"Yes, of course," Kyra replied quickly. "The pool house is empty."

They stood looking awkwardly at each other.

"Do you need help with your suitcase?" Kyra asked. "I was planning to edit a little video and have an early night, but I can . . ."

"No, I'm fine. I'll get my things out of the car and take them around back."

Since Steve had reminded her that she was not the hostess and her divorce papers confirmed that she was not responsible for feeding or caring for him, Maddie turned and walked back toward the kitchen.

"There's probably some snacks and cold drinks in the pool house, Dad," Kyra said. "Dustin will be so excited to see you. Are you sure you don't mind if we catch up in the morning?"

"No problem," he replied in a tone that had always indicated there was, in fact, a problem. "Just tell me what time breakfast is served and I'll be there all bright-eyed and bushy tailed."

It took every ounce of willpower Maddie possessed not to turn and tell Steve exactly when he might find breakfast and where he could then shove it. She smiled tightly to herself when

Kyra stopped climbing the stairs to say, "Oh, we don't have a formal breakfast, Dad. Everyone just kind of helps themselves. We're going to head over to the job site around nine tomorrow morning. Dustin and I will come wake you at eight."

• • •

"I think it's safe to unclench now," Nikki said the next morning when she and Maddie climbed into the Jag for the short drive to the hotel.

"Said the woman who's quite tightly clenched herself and has been giving Sleeping Beauty a run for her money." She eyed Nikki as she dropped the convertible top and then backed out of the driveway. "I've been thinking about looking for a poison apple. Or maybe calling the prince to tell him he needs to come kiss his girlfriend awake."

"Don't even think about it," Nikki said, turning north onto Pass-a-Grille Way. "I don't need a prince. I just need a little less manual labor and a lot more sleep."

"Right." Maddie turned her gaze out the window, where slices of blue water shimmered through the keyholes in the concrete balustrade that edged the bay as they passed. The breeze was warm and more than slightly humid. By afternoon the temperature would be close to ninety.

"Hey, at least I don't have an ex-husband moving in," Nikki said, deflecting as always. In Maddie's experience, getting the woman to talk about herself, let alone her actual feelings, could require the wile of Machiavelli and the brute strength of Hercules.

"I can handle Steve's presence for Dustin's and Kyra's sakes. I mean it's not like he's going to be here long."

"I don't know," Nikki said, her tone dubious. "I'm not sure Steve's planning to leave anytime soon."

"Why do you say that?" Maddie turned to watch the play of sunlight on Nikki's auburn hair. She could see her own reflection in the oversized sunglasses.

"I guess you didn't see the pile of luggage that came out of the trunk of his car this morning."

"No." Maddie had actually gone to ridiculous lengths not to pay attention to Steve's movements. Though she had noticed that the car he'd arrived in had rust spots and a dented rear door. "I don't think he believed Kyra last night when she told him that we all help ourselves to breakfast."

"I was glad you didn't cave when he started hinting about how much he loves your egg soufflé," Nikki said. "But I was a little worried about the way he was eyeing Dustin's Eggo waffles."

Maddie smiled grimly. "Kyra handled him pretty well. Especially when she took him up on his offer of help."

Nikki snorted. "Yeah, I don't think he was expecting to be put in charge of Dustin."

"Well, he could hardly say no when Dustin was so excited to be spending the day with his Geedad." Maddie's eyes clouded briefly when she thought of how different things might have been if only Steve had not been so quick to give up when things got tough. "The time together should be good for both of them. And it'll give Kyra time to edit that footage." She fell silent, her thoughts turning to William, who had bottomed out on a large scale and in the public eye. But where Steve had surrendered, William had conquered the daily struggle to keep himself clean and beat his dependency on drugs and alcohol. William had worked on his sobriety every day. He'd managed to rebuild his life even before he'd met Maddie. Now, it seemed, he was rebuilding his career.

"It looks like we're the last ones here," Nikki said as she turned onto Thirty-first and pulled the Jag in behind Avery's Mini Cooper, which was parked behind John Franklin's Cadillac.

They got out of the car, slathered on sunscreen, and pulled a small cooler out of the trunk. "Ready?" Maddie asked.

"As I'll ever be," Nikki replied, settling a baseball cap on her head and pulling her ponytail out through the back. "But I'm going to suggest we string up some hammocks out on the beach. You know, for the guests."

"Right," Maddie said drily. With the ponytail, the big sunglasses, and the bright halter top and shorts, Nikki might have been a mature Malibu Barbie. "Don't let Avery catch you snoozing on the job."

"God forbid," Nikki agreed. "That woman is a force of nature. Kind of like a miniature hurricane. She's half my size but I suspect she could blow me right over."

"Well, she is under a lot of pressure to produce."

"I know," Nikki said. "We all are."

Maddie pulled a straw hat down on her head, adjusted the brim. "Are you at all worried that we won't be able to pull it off on our own?"

"Hell, yeah," Nikki said. "But I don't see any way around it. Last time I checked, none of us had a whole lot of other viable options."

"Avery can make a living as an architect or building with Chase. I think Kyra could make it in film with enough help with Dustin. And Joe has asked you to marry him. Repeatedly." Maddie looked pointedly at Nikki. "Some people have options they're afraid to pursue."

"Not all of us are as fearless as you've turned out to be, Madeline Singer," Nikki said. "I just couldn't say yes to him, Maddie. I wanted to. Really I did." Her voice was practically a whisper. "So the 'Joe option' is no longer on the table." She sniffed suspiciously but she ended on a shrug. "Come on. Let's get to work before . . ."

There was a rattle and rev of a motor. A large panel truck turned onto the road and edged into a space around the corner. *A-1 Locksmith* was written across both sides.

Maddie and Nikki looked at each other, then hurried onto the path that led through the overgrowth and onto the concrete walkway that connected the cottages to the main building and pool. "I know it's crazy, but I've been trying not to think about that safe all week," Maddie said. "I mean it's such an odd place for it. It wasn't put there for the guests. And Renée had no idea it even existed." Maddie felt a stirring of excitement. "Do you think it's full of jewelry? Or something really exotic?"

"Personally, I'm hoping it's money. Right around two-point-five-million dollars would be good. That way we could stop worrying about the reno budget and just get on with it already." She smiled. "But I wouldn't mind if there was exotic jewelry in there, too."

Chapter Eighteen

Avery was standing in the women's locker room with John and Renée Franklin when Nikki and Maddie arrived with the locksmith in tow.

"Is Annelise coming?" Maddie asked.

"No." Renée's tone was almost apologetic. "I haven't told her yet. I thought it would be best to simply share what we find after we know what it is. Just in case it's something upsetting." John placed a bracing arm around his wife's shoulders. "I can't believe this safe was here all the time and I didn't know it," Renée continued. "My grandparents never mentioned it and there was nothing about it in their will."

They stood aside while John conferred with the locksmith, then watched eagerly as cutting tools were prepared.

"We're trying to preserve the lockers," Avery said. "Can you work inside that locker or should we remove them?"

"I think we're good," the locksmith replied. "Do you want the whole box to come out or do you just want to be able to access what's inside?"

"Renée?" John asked.

"I'm not sure." Renée's eyes were alight with nervous excitement. "Why don't we just open it and see if there's anything inside first?"

They stood in a small semicircle watching intently, their excitement palpable. The whir of a power tool meeting metal made conversation impossible. Even though Avery knew better, it was almost impossible not to fantasize about the contents. The safe could be completely empty or hold nothing more exotic than a child's baby teeth or some other sentimental object. But until proved otherwise, it could contain a fortune in jewels. "Am I the only one visualizing a treasure map?" she asked when the cutting stopped.

"I wish you were," Renée said. "But knowing my grandparents it's more likely to be a copy of Nana's matzo ball soup recipe. Or a lifetime collection of Sunshine Hotel and Beach Club postcards."

It wasn't long before the safe was open and an iron box pulled from inside it. The locksmith set it on the counter as directed and then departed, clearly not suffering from the curiosity the rest of them were experiencing. Stepping away so as not to crowd Renée and John, Avery, Maddie, and Nikki formed their own little expectant huddle.

"Well, here goes." Renée reached for the box's lid. "I hope we're not about to discover that those matzo balls were made from a mix." Her hands shook slightly as she raised the hinged lid.

The rest of them held their collective breath as Renée peered inside. Gingerly she withdrew a battered manila envelope, then shook it tentatively. The only sound was the rustle of paper. "Okay, jewels and gold are out. But a treasure map or a matzo ball recipe are still possible." Renée's voice and smile wavered. John stepped closer in an unmistakable show of support as Renée reached back into the safe, felt around, and pulled out a small cracked leather photo album. Lowering herself onto a wooden bench, Renée first opened the envelope and removed its contents. She began to leaf through a sheaf of yellowed documents.

"It's . . ." Renée looked down again. "My father's discharge papers are here. And this must be his and Ilse's marriage license." She held up two dog-eared black-and-white photos. "And this is Ilse and her mother." She held up a photo of two women of the same height and size with soft blond hair and identical smiles. "And this is Ilse in her wedding dress." Renée's smile was nostalgic. "It was made from a parachute that my father got hold of. Annelise used to love to hear the story. She has the framed picture of Ilse and my father the day they got married." She opened the photo album next and began to leaf through it. This time when she looked up, shock etched her face.

"What is it?" John asked.

"These photos are . . . They must be the rest of Ilse's family." Renée swallowed and flipped through another few pages. She looked up again, clearly stricken. "But these . . ." Her voice trailed off and the smile turned to a grimace. "I've never seen these before. I . . . I just never really thought . . . I mean I knew my stepmother wasn't Jewish. But my father used to tell us the story about how they met when he was working at American headquarters in Frankfurt after the war. How shy she was. How she never even looked at the soldiers like a lot of the other German girls did. And how she only ever spoke to him because she fell and hurt her knee and he insisted on taking her to the Red Cross hospital to get stitched up." She hesitated and something flickered in the back of her eyes. "I never expected . . . I didn't think . . ." Renée looked up again, her face white. "All of the men are wearing Nazi uniforms. And they have lots of decorations on them. As if they might be high-ranking officers." She set the photos on the counter and pushed them away. "I don't think they were just . . . you know . . . privates who were only following orders. This man's wearing an SS uniform. They all look so completely Aryan."

• • •

Kyra arrived not long after Renée and John Franklin left. Her video camera hung on a strap over one shoulder; her long dark hair had been pulled up into a high ponytail. "Sorry I'm late," she said to Maddie. "But has Dad always been this helpless?"

"Well," Maddie replied, trying to assess how much truth Kyra was looking for. "He can take direction if it's offered properly, but he's not big on self-starting or completing tasks that don't appeal to him."

"No kidding," Kyra said. "He asked me to show him how the washing machine worked, and I ended up doing an entire load and starting the second for him. Then I packed them PB and Js and juice boxes to take on their beach picnic for which I got Dustin completely ready."

"It's easy to get sucked in," Maddie said, thinking how often it had been easier to do the work herself than beg and cajole.

"I was almost here when he called to tell me he couldn't find the sunscreen. So I turned around and went back and found it right on the kitchen counter about two feet away from where he was sitting."

Maddie just smiled. She had learned during the death spiral of her marriage and the resulting divorce that no matter how much the children might complain about Steve's actions, they did not want her to chime in.

"He couldn't even figure out how to open the childproof cap on the amoxicillin he was supposed to give Dustin. Why . . ." She stopped, seemingly noticing their lack of action for the first time. "Why are you guys just sitting around with those weird looks on your faces?" she asked. "What's going on?"

Avery filled her in.

"Wow," Kyra said. "So Renée didn't know anything about her stepmother's family?"

"No," Nikki said. "Though I guess it shouldn't be surprising. They were German and they were at war. I don't think membership in the Nazi party was optional."

"Do you think Annelise knew?" Kyra asked.

Maddie had been wondering that very thing. "I'd guess yes except she was only five when her father died and her mother disappeared. So it seems highly unlikely."

"Do you think Renée's going to show everything to her?" Kyra asked.

"I don't see how she couldn't," Avery said. "But I'm glad we won't be there when it happens. And it definitely isn't our business."

"Do you think Joe might want to see the papers and photos?" Kyra asked Nikki.

Nikki went very still at the mention of Joe's name. "W-W-Why?"

Maddie had never before heard Nicole Grant come anywhere near a stutter.

"I don't know." Kyra shrugged. "I mean, Annelise said she saw a man in their cottage that night. Joe seemed to think she might have. Maybe there was someone else there— and maybe it wasn't random. Maybe it had something to do with someone in her family."

"You're making it sound like some Baldacci thriller or something," Avery said. "This is—and was—a very small hotel on Pass-a-Grille."

"With at least one mysterious death. We don't really know what might have happened here," Kyra said reasonably. "But Ilse disappeared. Maybe she went back to Germany for some reason."

Their eyes turned to Nikki.

"What?" she asked warily.

"Can you call Joe and fill him in and see what he thinks?" Avery asked.

"I'm not sure. I know he's out of town. Um, somewhere." Nikki gestured vaguely. "He may not be reachable."

Avery fixed Nikki with a look. "Then maybe you could text him," she said slowly as if explaining something to a child. "So that he can call you back when he's able to."

Maddie gave Avery a look of her own. The cease-and-desist look that every mother learned and used to varying effect. A look, Maddie realized, Avery had rarely experienced.

"If Nikki's not comfortable with it, I can call Joe and ask if he thinks trying to trace Ilse to Germany might be worthwhile." Maddie raised an eyebrow at Avery for emphasis. "And it might help to have someone who knows German read whatever was written on the backs of some of those photos."

"I'll do it," Nikki said. But she said it with all the enthusiasm of someone who had agreed to a double root canal. "I'll do it tonight."

"Okay," Avery said. "Then I think it's time we all stop speculating and get to work."

As if on cue Ray Flamingo made his entrance, moving toward them with an elegance that bordered on regal. He wore a perfectly coordinated ensemble of pale blue polo, creased cream trousers, and calfskin loafers.

"Darlings," he said, hugging them each in turn before removing his sunglasses. "I'm so glad you all are here." The smile he flashed was blinding. "I have had a scathingly brilliant idea that I am dying to share with you."

Kyra's video camera rested on her shoulder. Behind it only her lower face was visible. Her lips were twisted into a smile.

"Ideas are good," Avery said. "Especially scathingly brilliant ones." None of them were immune to Ray's enthusiasm or his dramatic flair. "Lead the way."

"Yes. Come with me." He turned, not checking to see whether they followed.

Maddie was glad he hadn't said, "Walk this way," for Ray was far more graceful than any of them except possibly Nikki, and she wasn't sure she could even come close to duplicating his catwalk strut.

He stopped in front of the closest cottage. "I've been thinking. Adding the new roof decks will require repouring the patios so that support posts can be added. So, why don't we go ahead and extend the patios around the side of each unit? We could wall the area, add lots of foliage, and maybe an outdoor shower so that each courtyard garden would be completely private." He raised an eyebrow mysteriously. "Then we could turn the bathroom window into a glass door." He smiled. "Voila. Many difficult birds done in with one stone."

"I like it," Avery said. "It opens up the bathroom, gives us added visual and usable space. And even if we weren't doing the decks, we'd be replacing the old patios anyway."

"Absolutely." Ray waved a hand airily. "John told me the last time they were touched was back in the early fifties due to some sort of plumbing issue." He shrugged. "This way we end up with something chic and functional."

"The man's good," Nikki said.

"Gifted," Maddie agreed.

"It could work," Avery said. "But like everything else it's going to depend on cost and how much we raise." She smiled. "Still, I think I'm going to have to upgrade from 'like' to 'love' on this."

"But of course you will," Ray said happily. "I told you it would be scathingly brilliant. I don't join those words together lightly."

• • •

Nikki's heart actually skittered at the sight of Joe's name on her caller ID that evening as she walked alone on the beach. "Hello? Joe?"

"Yes." His voice was stripped of all warmth and concern; it gave no hint that the person he was talking to meant anything at all. "You asked me to call."

"Yes. Um, hi." She closed her eyes in humiliation and stumbled over a shell. After spending the day alternately dreading and anticipating his return call, was that the best she could do? *Good God, don't let me stutter again. Just let me get through this call with my pride still intact.* "Thanks for calling."

"No problem. Did you need something?" he asked politely. Her heart skittered faster. She felt slightly light-headed.

"It's not for me," she hastened to explain. "I . . . didn't want to bother you." She winced remembering when she'd asked him to submit to Annelise's interview.

He made no comment. The silence stretched uncomfortably as she walked. Despite her best intentions, and her very real fear of stuttering, she started to babble in an attempt to fill it. "The safe in the women's locker room was opened today."

Nothing.

"And there were documents and especially photos that the others thought you might want to look at."

Still he said nothing. She couldn't seem to slow the skittering. Or regulate her breathing, which had gone kind of shallow.

"It just seemed so odd that they were locked away like that in such a strange place. Renée had no knowledge of their existence. They're from Germany. During the war." Nikki swallowed. "Kyra had the idea that they might somehow provide some kind of clue to what happened to Ilse."

The distance between them echoed heavily in the silence. His loss was a weight pressing down on her chest. She stopped and stood with her feet in the water trying to catch her breath.

"All right," he said finally. "If someone will scan and send them, I'll take a look."

"Thank you," she said, her oxygen-deprived brain grasping

for something, anything to say. But before she could so much as stutter good-bye she realized that the silence had changed. Joe had already disconnected. Fighting back tears, she stood in the water, her eyes pinned on the sunlight that glimmered so brightly on the surface, and did the same.

Chapter Nineteen

Nikki and Maddie sat on Maddie's bedroom balcony sipping coffee and staring out over the pass where seagulls soared in the pale morning sky and pelicans dive-bombed for breakfast.

"How did you not kill him before you divorced him?" Nikki asked, scanning Bella Flora's pool area where Steve Singer's dropped towels and abandoned flip-flops littered the deck. His bathing trunks had been slung over chair backs and left "drying" for days.

"It never occurred to me," Maddie said. "I was in love with him and we were busy building a family and a life. It was a simple division of labor, though I don't remember really discussing it. Steve made a living and I . . ."

"Did everything else?" Nikki guessed.

"No, of course not. Steve coached Andrew in baseball and he helped chaperone some of his Boy Scout camping trips. And . . ." Maddie's voice trailed off as she apparently tried to come up with other areas that had fallen under her then-husband's purview. "I was lucky to be able stay home with Kyra and Andrew—to be there for them. Steve worked hard to make that possible. And I know it was good for the kids."

"And Steve."

Maddie shrugged. "It was good for all of us. We raised two great children. I think we were . . . happy."

Steve came out of the pool house in pajama bottoms and an ancient T-shirt, something Nikki now recognized as his sleeping attire. Without looking to see who might be around, he yawned and stretched contentedly. Within moments his hand had dropped and he was scratching his balls, something he did with alarming frequency. "He seems quite attached to . . . some of his attachments."

Maddie, who could and did blush at the drop of a hat, just laughed. "And Joe's not?"

"Not in such an obvious way," Nikki said almost primly. "And I'm betting William isn't, either."

"I lived with Steve for a quarter of a century and our son for twenty of that. Personally, I think all men have a 'special relationship' with their anatomy. But I'm guessing they feel freer to demonstrate that attachment over time. Will and I are still in the 'honeymoon phase' where touching each other is way more interesting and compelling." Maddie blushed slightly and Nikki wished she were, in fact, still in a "honeymoon phase" with Joe. Or any sort of phase. At the moment she missed him so much she might even have agreed to go on a honeymoon with him. If only she hadn't forced him to give up on her. Regret and guilt sliced through her.

"You aren't going to feed him again, are you?" Nikki asked as they watched Steve amble toward the house. Once you fed a stray they never left.

"I'm not going to cook especially for him, no," Maddie said as Steve disappeared through Bella Flora's back door. "But if I'm putting breakfast on the table, which I am, I'm not going to tell him he can't have any." She smiled and stood. "Speaking of which, I think it's time to get things under way."

"Geema!" Nikki watched Dustin's face light up when his grandmother entered the kitchen and felt the oddest tug.

Steve Singer looked pretty happy to see her, too, or maybe he was just hungry. "Can Dustbin have Mench boast?"

"Absolutely!" Maddie beamed at her grandson. "Do you want to help?"

Within moments Maddie had whisked eggs and milk in a big bowl, heated up fry pans and a griddle, and was helping Dustin, who stood on a chair beside her, to dip the pieces of bread into the egg mixture. Syrup was put in the microwave to warm. Kyra set the table while Nikki set out cartons of milk and orange juice, her stomach turning over at the smells that filled the kitchen.

A boat horn beeped outside and she spied Chase, Avery, and the boys in Chase's boat, *Hard Case*, just off the seawall. "Ahoy there, mateys!" Avery's voice boomed through a foghorn. "Be right there!" The boat putted toward the dock next door at the Cottage Inn.

The stack of French toast grew. More places were set. Steve watched all the activity with a smile on his face but didn't seem at all compelled to move. Or help.

A cell phone rang. Maddie looked up. "Oh. That's mine." Her hands were covered in egg mixture and Dustin leaned against her as he "cookited." "Can somebody grab that?" Maddie called over her shoulder.

Although Maddie's cell phone sat near Steve, Nikki half expected him to ignore it and Maddie's request. He surprised her by picking it up and raising it to his ear. "Singer Bait and Tackle," he answered gaily.

He sat smiling and, apparently, listening before he replied. "Right. And I've got a limo standing by outside to run me over to the gym." He put down the phone. "Some joker who said she was with Aquarian Records, Mad. Wanted to talk to you about being picked up in a private plane." He snorted in amusement. "Back in my day prank calls were simpler. 'Is your refrigerator running? Better go catch it!'" He shook his head, oblivious to the fact that no one was laughing.

"Dad!" Kyra said. "Aquarian is Will Hightower's label. And what's so funny about a private plane?"

"Don't be silly," Steve said. "Why would anyone . . ."

"Want to send a plane for *me*?" Maddie wiped her hands on a dishtowel, ceded her spot at the stove to Kyra, and moved toward the table to snatch up the phone. If he'd been smart, Nikki thought, Steve would already be ducking and apologizing. But then if he'd really been smart, he would still be married to Maddie. Nikki's stomach churned at the thought of how easily bad choices could be made. And how hard they could be to rectify. An urge to call Joe and tell him how much she missed him surged through her. She fought it back. Because it no longer mattered how much she loved him or wanted him in her life. Not until she could turn that love into commitment. Her appetite fled as she watched Maddie turn and leave the kitchen, a mix of hurt and anger suffusing her face.

. . .

Maddie stomped up the stairs, strode through her bedroom, and stepped back onto the balcony. She was still trying to shed her irritation as she hit redial and raised her cell phone to her ear.

"Ms. Singer?" The young woman's voice was polite and respectful. Unlike some people she knew.

"Yes," Maddie said. "I'm so sorry that . . ." What? Her ex-husband couldn't imagine that William Hightower found her attractive? That he might actually want a plane sent for her? "I couldn't get to the phone."

"No problem," the perky young woman replied. "Mr. Hightower asked me to organize transportation for you to the concert. The plane will pick up Mrs. Baynard in Palm Beach and then stop at Albert Whitted Airport for you and any guests you'd like to bring."

"That sounds . . ." Once again Steve's dismissive view of her rose. She pushed it back. ". . . great. Thank you."

"My pleasure," she said quite formally. "I'll email you the details as soon as everything's set up along with my contact information. If there's anything at all that you need or would like to know, please don't hesitate to contact me."

From her vantage point on the balcony, Maddie could see Chase and his sons tying up the boat. Avery jumped out, then retrieved Jeff's walker while his grandsons helped him up out of the boat and onto the dock.

Hitting speed dial, she waited for only one ring before Will picked up.

"Good morning, Maddie."

The upbeat greeting, his obvious pleasure at hearing her voice were balms to the soul. And her ego. When she was with him, the glow in his eyes and the ease she felt in his company convinced her that she was not imagining their connection. But when they were apart the doubts began to nibble away at that certainty. Could she really blame Steve for his disbelief when she herself couldn't quite believe she was in a relationship with William Hightower?

"Mad?"

"Sorry," she said. "It's kind of intense here at the moment. Steve showed up unexpectedly a few days ago to visit Kyra and Dustin. The Hardins just arrived for breakfast and to take everyone out on the boat. And, the renovation project is on but there are a lot of moving parts that still need to be pinned down." She realized she was running on about herself and stopped.

"Sounds like you need to take a deep breath and try to relax," he said. "But I know what you're saying. We're rehearsing almost nonstop down here. I can't believe how fast everything's ramping up. The concert in Raleigh-Durham is part of a trial run in smaller venues. A soft opening. And they'll be recording a few of the new songs live."

"Yes," she said, remembering why she'd ostensibly called. "I heard from Aquarian. Thanks for asking them to make arrangements to get me and Bitsy up there."

"They keep asking what I want. The list is small. You're at the top."

"Right above making somebody pick out all the orange M&M's?" she teased, but his words went a long way toward banishing what lingered of Steve's dismissal.

"I don't really care about the riders and perks," Will said. "I'm writing again, Maddie. Really writing. I feel kind of like some old wine bottle that somebody finally managed to get a cork out of. The stuff's practically pouring out of me." He paused. "I'm sure there's something completely wrong about an alcoholic using wine analogies, but that's what it feels like."

"So how are you staying so calm?" she asked as she heard the sounds of conversation and the scraping of chairs down on the loggia. Someone had apparently figured out that the group was too large for the kitchen table and the day too beautiful to eat in the dining room.

"You would be appalled at how many laps I'm swimming," Will said. "Plus I'm out on the flats as much as possible. And I'm almost embarrassed to admit it, but I sat in on one of the yoga classes the residents take and, well, I look awkward as hell but it is kind of peaceful. Did you know there's a fish pose?"

Maddie smiled at the image of the former rock icon who'd once stared down from a poster on her bedroom wall all folded up on a yoga mat. "Well, that's right up your alley, isn't it?"

"Yeah, turns out half the movements in fly casting belong in a yoga class."

Maddie laughed. "So you mean if I take up yoga I'll be a better fly fisherman?"

"Possibly," he said.

"You don't have to spare my feelings," she said. "We both know I catch way more bushes and bottom than fish."

"True." She could hear the amusement in his voice. Could practically feel the warmth emanating from him.

From beneath the balcony someone called her name.

Dustin raced out to a spot on the pool deck and waved his arms. "Beckfest, Geema!"

"I'm going to have to go," she said.

"Enjoy yourself, Maddie-fan. I'll see you in North Carolina soon. I can't wait to get you in my arms. And show you in person how grateful I am to you for loosening that cork."

"See you then." Maddie ended the call and shoved her phone in her shorts pocket. As she took the stairs down to join the others her step was light, her spirits lighter. She, Madeline Singer, was at the top of William Hightower's "list." A very real part of his life. Steve Singer could take his opinions about her and everything else and lump it. Better yet, he could stick them where the sun didn't shine.

Chapter Twenty

Nikki stood on the seawall smiling and waving as *Hard Case* passed on its way into the Gulf. Chase stood behind the wheel of the boat, which bulged with bodies, life, and good humor. She'd claimed a headache and errands she couldn't put off, but in truth she hadn't had the energy or the stomach for the trip up the coast toward Clearwater.

Making her way inside, she breathed in the quiet, enjoying the novelty of being alone. It was the first weekend in June and the windows were open to catch the morning breeze. By afternoon air conditioning would be necessary.

Too lazy to climb the stairs to her bedroom, she stretched out on the salon sofa, her head propped on a pillow, her hands folded on her stomach. She'd planned to email Bitsy Baynard about the concert plans and confirm her sponsorship details, but it seemed far too much effort. Ignoring the laptop she'd left on the coffee table, she yawned and settled into the sofa with her cell phone clutched in one hand. Joe had been in Tampa for a meeting yesterday and would be at the hotel on Monday morning to talk to Renée and Annelise after the cold case unit had gone back through the family apartment.

She'd been clutching her cell phone in a death grip all weekend. Just in case, which was the most specific thought she'd allowed herself. But it hadn't rung once and didn't seem inclined to ring now. And she definitely hadn't passed up the boat ride in case he came into town early. When dreamland beckoned she accepted the invitation.

She leapt awake sometime later to the ding of an incoming text, then pawed frantically in the loose cushions for her phone. When she finally located it, her heart was pounding. But the text wasn't from Joe. She blinked, trying to understand what she was seeing. The phone number wasn't one she recognized, but as she looked at the message she realized it could only have been sent by her felonious brother. Who currently resided at Butner Federal Correctional Complex in North Carolina. Where he no doubt worshiped at the feet of the even better known Ponzi perpetrator incarcerated there, Bernie Madoff.

She sat up and peered down at the screen. Malcolm had tried to communicate in the past through the prison-regulated email system—she'd agreed to be on his "approved list" for visits and communication partly because she'd felt it might be helpful to Joe and partly because, while she had no desire to speak to or see him, they were each other's only living relatives. But this was not an email. It was a text. Which meant it hadn't come through the monitored TRU-LINCS system, but from a cell phone. Which prisoners were not allowed to possess but which Joe had told her were routinely smuggled in.

She knew it was from Malcolm because it read, *Need to cu, bs* (which had once stood for "big sister" but might now just be "bullshit"). *Ready to share. Only u.*

Her stomach twisted into a knot of anger and fear. Bile rose in her throat. She shivered with revulsion, but could not deny the flicker of curiosity. She felt like Little Red Riding Hood standing at the edge of the forest watching the Big Bad Wolf smile and crook his finger.

• • •

"Are you okay?" Renée Franklin asked her younger sister as they arrived at the family apartment just before noon on Monday.

Annelise nodded, though she didn't look any more certain than Renée felt. John had come earlier that morning to open up the apartment for the cold case unit. Joe Giraldi and Officer James Jackson stood outside waiting for them.

Officer Jackson appeared to be somewhere in his midthirties. He was tall and broad shouldered with friendly hazel-colored eyes and a ready smile. He moved with the grace of a former athlete and had a comfortable air of command about him.

"It's nice to see you both," Officer Jackson said. "My father sent his regards. And he told me to be sure and apologize for all the times your paper ended up in the bushes." He smiled and offered his hand. "I was glad that Agent Giraldi contacted me. After I heard from him I tracked down the case files and took a look."

"The files still exist?" Annelise clung to the young man's hand. She'd begun practically vibrating at her first sight of Officer Jackson and hadn't yet stopped.

"Yes, ma'am."

"And have you found new clues? Fingerprints? Blood spatter that couldn't be detected back then? Trace evidence that will finally tell us what happened to my mother?" The forensic jargon absorbed in marathon viewings of *Forensic Files*, *Cold Case*, and the variously located CSI programs rolled off Annelise's tongue with practiced ease. Renée could hardly bear to see the desperate hope on her face.

"As I'm sure Special Agent Giraldi told you, heat and humidity are the enemy of most trace evidence," the officer said. "And it has been more than fifty years."

"But . . ." Annelise's face began to deflate.

Joe remained silent, allowing the young law enforcement officer to take the lead.

"But that doesn't mean we don't have anything to go on," Officer Jackson said. "My team went through the apartment thoroughly this morning. Plus there are articles of clothing and household items in evidence that we can test in ways we couldn't then. We can also take another, better look at the fingerprints that were lifted at the time, then run them through computer databases that didn't exist in the early fifties. And I've got all of the original detective's notes and records of all the interviews that were conducted."

"Detective Anderson?" Annelise sniffed. "He never even looked for another suspect besides my mother." Her voice had taken on the childish tone that came on when she was agitated.

"In fairness, there were no other leads," Officer Jackson said. "And the man was thorough. He canvassed and did a large number of interviews. There are reams of handwritten notes I'm still working through and lots of follow-up. But the reality is that then, the same as now, a random killer is far less likely than a close family member."

"No!" Annelise stomped her foot, once again retreating into childish anger.

"The fact that she was never found . . ." Jackson said.

". . . only proves that something happened to her," Annelise insisted, her voice growing shriller. "She never would have left me. And she didn't even take anything with her."

Renée put an arm around her sister's shoulders.

Joe Giraldi, who had stood silent until now, stepped forward. "I have complete confidence that Officer Jackson will do everything possible to try to put this to rest. He's going to keep me in the loop and I will keep my promise to contribute whatever I can. But most cold cases are solved through new witnesses who step forward or old witnesses remembering something new."

"That's right," the young officer said. "Agent Giraldi told me that you saw someone that night. And I did see a mention of that in the notes. I thought we might go in together and have you share what you remember."

Annelise's face shone with eagerness. Renée felt only dread. Neither of them had set foot inside since their grandmother had taken them in to pack their things. At that time the door to the bedroom where her father had died had been closed.

She tightened her arm around her sister's shoulders but was not sure for whose benefit, Annelise's or hers. Renée's legs wobbled as they walked into the cottage together.

The windows had been opened but the closed-up smell had not yet dissipated. A slight chemical tang from whatever tests might have been done that morning mingled unpleasantly with the predominant smells of age and mildew. Underneath it all, long-forgotten scents teased at her memory. Her eyes went to the small dinette where the four of them had eaten, and her nostrils quivered with the remembered smells of Ilse's Himmel und Erde, which her father had said translated into "heaven and earth," and was a concoction of potatoes and apples with onion and bacon. On special Sunday mornings her stepmother had served apple pancakes, called Apfelpfannkuchen. After the scarcity of food in Germany during the war, Ilse had sometimes been reduced to tears by the plenty that existed in her new home.

Ilse had been shy and skittish, prone to jumping at sudden movements and loud noises. Her English had been broken and sometimes hard to follow, but cooking even in the cottage's tiny kitchenette had set her to humming and smiling.

Annelise reached for Renée's hand and she grasped it. Renée had been only three when her mother died, even younger than Annelise had been when she'd lost hers. Her memories of her own mother were sparse but Ilse had been young, more like a much older sister than a mother. She'd been standoffish in the beginning, very timid and almost childlike. Her father had treated Ilse as gently as he'd treated Renée and Annelise. He said it was her sweetness that had first drawn him, but he'd also said that Ilse was far braver and stronger than she appeared. Or else she and her mother would not have survived the war.

There had been some who had muttered at David Handleman bringing home a German gentile when so many Jewish girls had suffered so much greater privation and the extermination of their entire families. Nana had been the first to warm to her new daughter-in-law and to say that the heart wants what it wants not what it's supposed to want.

Jackson and Giraldi talked quietly in the corner, leaving them to walk about on their own. The living area was dusty and grimy. Cushions were shredded. Curtains were limp and tattered. Cobwebs hung from the corners and not much air made it through the window screens, which were plugged with sand and grit.

Hands clasped, Renée and Annelise walked into the bedroom they'd shared. The twin beds had been stripped, and the mattresses sagged yellow with age. The nightstand between them was covered in dust; the lamp by which they'd read looked stark without its shade. They'd each had a dresser and a desk on the opposite wall. The closet they'd shared was empty but for a few ancient wire hangers. The Frank Sinatra poster Renée had tacked to the wall above her desk hung in shreds.

Today, children eight years apart would never have shared a bedroom. But spaces had been different then, and so were expectations. The day Annelise was born, Ilse had placed the little pink bundle in Renée's arms and told her that Annelise belonged to her, too. She had taken the words to heart.

She drew a finger over a dusty bookshelf. Annelise opened the nightstand drawer between their beds and pulled out an impossibly small pink *Alice in Wonderland* watch. "I always wondered what happened to this." Her voice caught as she slipped it into her pocket.

"Are you okay?" Renée asked Annelise.

"Are you?" her sister asked, and despite the sheen of tears there was a rare clarity in her eyes.

She'd gone to such lengths to blot out her memories of the Sunshine Hotel and everything that had happened there. She had never wanted to set foot in this cottage again. But now that she was here . . . murmurs of the past reached her. She cocked her head, listening.

"They're not here," Annelise whispered. "I thought they might be, but they're not."

Renée shivered. Because she felt her father and stepmother everywhere. Felt as if they were both calling out to her. Trying to tell her something.

Back in the living area, Officer Jackson and Joe stood waiting for them.

"Right there," Annelise said, pointing to the bookcase behind them. "That's where the man was standing." Her brow furrowed. "But his clothes . . . they were all wrong. Nobody at the beach in the summer would have worn what he was wearing."

Officer Jackson scribbled something on a folder. "Did you hear him speak? Did he say anything to you?"

Annelise closed her eyes in concentration. When she opened them she shook her head. "No."

"Officer Jackson agrees that a session with a sketch artist might produce something," Joe said to Annelise. "Would you be willing to try?"

"Oh, yes," Annelise breathed.

Joe raised an eyebrow at Renée. "Would you?"

"Oh, but I don't . . . I didn't . . ." She stopped mid-protest. What reason could there be now not to try to find out whatever they could?

Slowly, she and Annelise moved toward the other bedroom. It was Annelise who led her through the doorway. Renée's eyes went immediately to the place where she'd found their father lying in a pool of blood that had seeped out of the back of his head. His eyes open and lifeless. The bedroom a mess. She closed her eyes against the image and heard muffled voices. Her father and Ilse.

"What is it?" Joe asked her quietly when they'd rejoined them in the living area.

"Nothing," Renée said, suppressing another shiver. But even she could hear how uncertain she sounded. "I . . ." She shook her head. "It's not easy coming back."

John was waiting for her outside, his eyes worried. Dropping Annelise's hand, Renée waited for her husband to reach her and take her in his arms. But even as his warm solidness wrapped around her, she was thinking about the night her father died. She'd always said she hadn't heard anything. That she'd slept soundly and only known something was wrong when she'd found her father's body. She looked up to see Annelise watching her and another shiver of apprehension crept up her spine. What if that wasn't really the way it had happened? What if she and not Annelise was the one who'd been hiding from the truth all these years?

Chapter Twenty-one

Until that day at the Sunshine Hotel, Nikki hadn't fully realized just how polite Joe Giraldi could be. Or how hurtful she might find it. In the time she'd known him, he'd tracked her, angered her, and even used her to capture her brother, but he had never before ignored her.

She watched from the patio of a nearby cottage where she was supposed to be assessing whether anything that had been pulled out of the unit might be worth saving, as he left the young officer talking with Renée and John Franklin and Annelise outside the family apartment and turned onto the concrete path that led off the property. Sunlight glinted off his dark hair and spotlit his rugged features. She resisted the urge to fall back or duck behind the nearest rattan chair as he approached. When he came to a stop a few feet from her, she was careful not to fidget.

His nod was friendly. His smile was perfectly correct. Or would have been if he'd never held her in his arms, told her he loved her and wanted to marry her. Or, and for some reason most importantly, never seen her naked. "How is everything?"

"Great," she replied through tight lips, which she arranged into a painful smile. "It's nice to see you." Even as she spoke her mind was flooded with contradictory impulses. Stay or flee? Laugh or cry? Truth or consequences?

"It's a beautiful day," he said, beating her to the only safe topic.

"It is, isn't it?" she agreed, drawing in a deep breath of air as if a demonstration were somehow required. She looked up. "There's barely a cloud in the sky."

With the weather covered, they contemplated each other. The silence stretched between them as she once again searched for an impersonal topic. Just as he seemed to be gathering himself to depart, she managed, "Did you find anything of interest in the apartment?"

"I'm not sure," he replied. "But the cold case unit has taken it on, and I think both Renée and Annelise remember more than they realize."

"What do you mean?"

"There's nothing concrete. But I was watching Renée's face in the apartment and something surprised her. Sometimes you can feel that sort of thing. In the gut, you know?" For a brief moment Joe was back, caught up in the explanation. "I've learned the hard way to pay attention when your gut is talking to you. In fact, one time . . ."

She was watching his face when he caught himself and stopped. She waited, hoping for more, but that was it. She searched for some sign, some small "tell" that would indicate he was feeling the same surge of confused emotions that she was. That standing this close and being this far apart was as difficult for him as it was for her. But all he gave her was the polite, slightly friendly face of a stranger. And a smile that didn't reach his eyes.

For a perilous moment she considered telling him that Malcolm had contacted her, that something was up, that she was considering going to Butner to talk to him. It would be such a relief to discuss it with him, to get his far saner reaction to her brother, and at the moment, to life in general. But Joe's normally warm brown eyes were cool; any sign of love or concern for her had been banked if not completely extinguished. While she felt as if her heart was on fire.

No. She swallowed the heat and the emotion along with the words that simmered inside her like a geyser. Joe might be the professional but she'd spent a lifetime hiding her true thoughts and feelings.

She'd made her decision. Joe had obviously made his. There was no reason to prolong the agony. Not that he looked particularly agonized.

She smiled again. "That's great that the case has been reopened. I'm sure it will be a relief to both Renée and Annelise to get some answers. So that they can move on." Which was apparently what Joe had already found a way to do.

Once again they stared at each other. Frozen smile to frozen smile. Mask to mask. Until he finally said, "Well, I guess I should be going." He gave her another nod. Another impersonal smile. "You take care."

And then he was walking away from her, his arms loose at his sides, his stride unhurried. As if he didn't have a care in the world. Or the least bit of difficulty in leaving her behind.

· · ·

Kyra was alone at Bella Flora the next day when she heard a vehicle pull into the drive. Her mother had taken Dustin out in the jogging stroller with her father tagging after her. Nikki and Avery were in Tampa meeting with a potential sponsor that Ray had lined up. Setting her laptop aside, she walked through the center hallway to the formal living room and peered out a floor-to-ceiling window where she saw Nigel Bracken, their lone remaining paparazzo, approaching the pool company truck.

She bit back a smile as the photographer glanced furtively over his shoulder before addressing the pool guy who wore flip-flops, a ratty pair of board shorts, and a pool company T-shirt. A baseball cap had been pulled low over his forehead. A pair of dark glasses completed Daniel's disguise. Unable to resist, she snapped a photo of Daniel and the photographer talking, their heads bent close in conversation.

Her smile turned into a grin as she imagined one day informing Nigel that he had in fact had a conversation with the celebrity he'd been so disappointed to never see. She snorted slightly when Daniel pulled the skimmer out of the back of the truck and handed it to Nigel. Who then followed Daniel around the house to the pool on a circuitous route that came nowhere near the back windows. For a good fifteen minutes after Nigel departed, Daniel did a convincing job of cleaning and testing the pool. Then he came to the back door and knocked lightly.

She opened it a crack. "Yes?" she asked. "Is there a problem?"

"Your pH seems a little off," he replied quite seriously. "And you do have an incredibly unobservant paparazzo hanging around, though he did pay me twenty bucks to let him walk onto the property with me." He grinned, then looked her up and down taking in her bare feet, the cutoff shorts, and her crop top. "Other than that I'd say everything's looking pretty great."

He removed the sunglasses and shot her a wink. "I think the coast is clear. Can I come in?"

"Dustin's out with my mom. I'm not expecting them back for a while."

"Understood. Do you happen to have a cold drink to spare?"

Against her better judgment, she opened the door and stepped back to allow him to enter.

"Thanks." He removed his cap and ran a hand through his dark hair. "That's thirsty work out there."

"Right." She led him into the kitchen. "I'm surprised Nigel hasn't noticed how often we're having pool service."

"He probably thinks you're having an affair with the pool boy." He accepted the Coke and set his hat and sunglasses on the counter. "Which is, I believe, a time-honored tradition."

She rolled her eyes at him and told herself to be strong. She could not fall in bed with him every time the opportunity presented itself. She had promised herself she wouldn't. If only it were as easily done as said.

"He's about to give up and go away," Daniel said. "The British one."

"Good." To give herself something to do with her hands, she turned to the refrigerator and retrieved a Coke for herself, then took her time opening it.

"Not good," Daniel countered. "I explained this to you last time." He took a long pull on the Coke and she watched his Adam's apple, the graceful neck, the fine stubble that covered his face.

"Right. Symbiosis. Got it." She took a sip of her Coke, then held it in both hands as he leaned back against the counter. "Just not interested."

"No?" Somehow without moving he seemed so . . . close. His eyes found and held hers.

"No," she managed. "I'm not interested. Not at all." But her racing pulse and the way her body seemed to be leaning toward his said otherwise. She wished fervently for a vaccine that would boost her immunity to this man. Or that he'd do something atrocious enough to finally set her free.

"Kyra?"

"Hmmmm?" She blinked, realizing she'd missed something.

"I said I'm leaving for location in Montana next week. I'll be there for a good part of the summer. I'd really love for you and Dustin to come out. You could even assist the director of photography or work with the documentary people. Or, I don't know, anything you wanted."

She blinked again trying not to imagine how incredible it would feel to be on a big-budget film set again. It was what she'd studied, what she'd trained for, what she'd dreamed of. Until she'd fallen for Daniel on her first job, and his movie star wife had insisted she be fired.

"Is there a position kept open for naïve production assistants who screw the star because they're stupid enough to believe the star is in love with them?"

"Kyra. You know that's not . . ."

"I'm not that girl anymore, Daniel. I'm twenty-six. I'm a mother. And I'm already committed to *Do Over.*" It wasn't easy, but she managed to keep her voice even. "And where exactly would Tonja be while we were frolicking on set?"

He had the grace to blush. "Europe," he said. "She's shooting a film in the south of France. She's taking the kids for the summer."

He reached for her hand. "I really want you both with me in Montana. But even if you can't come, I'd like to have the time with Dustin."

"He's so little, Daniel. And Montana's not exactly around the corner."

He pulled her gently toward him. "I'll come pick him up," he murmured. "And I'll hire a full-time nanny. There's a great woman named Tabitha Marlowe we once used in London. I'll fly her in. She's worked for the royal family. She's a sort of a combination of the Supernanny and Mary Poppins. I'll send you her résumé."

He was standing too close. She could feel her resistance melting. He was Dustin's father. She wanted them to spend time together. But that wasn't all she wanted.

"You know I care about you," he said quietly. "I have from the first time I saw you."

"Do you keep everyone you've slept with on a string like this?"

"No." He pulled her closer, then turned so that she was

between him and the counter. "There's just something about you that I can't seem to let go of."

He bent his head. His lips hovered over hers.

"It's because I resist, isn't it? Because you have to work at it." Their lips were barely a hairsbreadth apart; their bodies were closer. "I *should* just sleep with you right now. And anytime you feel like it. Just so you lose interest."

"You're wrong," he murmured, his warm breath mingling with hers. "But I'm willing to test that theory."

His lips settled on hers. His hands ran up her sides. Heat coursed through her.

"Kyra?" Her father's shocked voice broke them apart. "What are you doing?"

Daniel let go of her.

"Isn't it bad enough you had such a public affair with that overrated, overpaid prick of a movie star?" Her father shook his head. "Now you're fooling around with the pool boy?"

Kyra winced. Daniel muttered an expletive under his breath.

"What?" her father asked, oblivious.

"This is not the pool boy, Dad. This is . . ."

Daniel turned and stepped forward. He extended his hand. "I'm not the pool boy, Mr. Singer. I'm the overrated, overpaid prick of a movie star."

Chapter Twenty-two

"You've got to do something about Dad."

They sat on the pool deck, drinks and snacks at hand, watching the sunset play out in the sky above them.

"Would you like to rephrase that as a 'good thing'?" Despite having invented their "one good thing" ritual, Maddie was having a hard time getting everyone to participate.

"Fine," Kyra said. "It would be a really good thing if you did something about Dad."

"What did you have in mind?" Nikki asked without much enthusiasm or energy, both of which had been notably absent. "I was thinking we could maybe hit him over the head, put him in a sack, and release him in a different city."

"Good grief," Avery said. "Has it been that bad?"

Kyra and Nikki eyed her. "Not to offend the woman who was married to him or the daughter he helped produce, but you wouldn't have to ask that question if you were living here full-time," Nikki said.

"I've pretty much given up any influence I might have had with your father," Maddie pointed out. "You're the 'host' here and his blood relation, Kyra. If you're hoping for different behavior, you're going to have to ask for it."

"I couldn't believe it when Dad called Daniel an 'overrated, overpaid prick of a movie star.' I mean, I get that Dad doesn't like everything that's happened, but at least Daniel has a relationship with Dustin. And he certainly put a pretty nice roof over all of our heads, including Dad's."

There was no arguing with this. "So you need to spell all that out for him, sweetie," Maddie said. "Your father's life has been turned upside down, and he doesn't seem to be able to right himself."

"So was yours," Kyra said. "And you didn't crumble and take it out on everybody else."

Maddie shrugged. "We learn the most about ourselves when things fall apart. What we do with what we learn is what counts."

Kyra nodded. "I just don't think I can ask him to leave. He is my father. I love him. And so does Dustin." She reached for a Bagel Bite. "I really wish I'd had my video camera to record Dad's reaction when Daniel introduced himself." Her lips twisted into a smile. "But he just keeps taking exception to everything that happens here. If he doesn't like how we do things, maybe he does need to go home."

Assuming he had one, Maddie thought as they sipped their drinks and watched the sky turn a golden red that hovered over the Gulf like a halo. "Anyone else have a good thing?"

Nikki roused slightly. "I'm going with the funds we've raised so far. Bitsy has committed two hundred and fifty thousand. Annelise and Renée have put in another two hundred between them. And Ray and I have a list of potential sponsors to approach. Once we've talked to all of them and see what sort of shortfall we have, I'll try to get the crowdfunding thing figured out."

"Well, that *is* a good thing. Because right now we have just about enough money to take care of reroofing, and either plumbing *or* electrical," Avery said. "Which is really just the beginning of what the property needs. Has there been any response from Lifetime?"

"No." Kyra shook her head. "And given that the first episode of the Mermaid Point season airs in less than ten days, that's not a good sign. If they thought the audience was going to be significant, they wouldn't be ignoring my calls." She sighed. "But if we're looking for another good thing, I think Nigel's pretty close to giving up," Kyra added.

"I still don't think that's a good thing," Nikki said. "And I have to say for a professional Peeping Tom, he isn't particularly observant."

"My good thing is I'm going to a live rock concert. On a private plane. With a backstage pass," Maddie said, trying to steer the conversation back into the positive.

"Not to mention getting to sleep with the star," Nikki said. "Don't forget to put that on the list."

"I do seem to have an overabundance of good things in my life," Maddie said, feeling the warmth of this truth deep inside. "And that includes all of you."

"Well, not to be too half empty," Avery said, "but it never hurts to stockpile the good stuff. Things are moving in a good direction, but we're not home free yet on any front." She put down the Cheez Doodle she'd been contemplating. "I think we all discovered last summer just how unexpectedly disaster can show up and kick the crap right out of you."

. . .

As far as Kyra was concerned, Avery's warning was born out when she returned from a morning run the next day and found a strange car parked in front of Bella Flora's garden wall. A car that turned out to belong to Troy Matthews, Lifetime cameraman and royal pain in the ass. Whom she found seated at the head of the kitchen table, surrounded by the rest of their merry band, devouring a stack of syrup-soaked pancakes. Her mother was at the stove. Kyra's son sat to Troy's right.

"Broy's here!" Dustin exclaimed, holding his fork aloft, his syrup-smeared face alight.

"I see that," Kyra replied, smiling at her son, but not at the cameraman. "What are you doing here? And don't tell me you just happened to be passing through."

"Kyra," her mother said. "I know we want to set a better example than that." She motioned toward Dustin, who was swinging his legs happily as he ate.

"Okay." Kyra arranged a large and patently insincere smile on her face. "Hi, Troy. To what do we owe this unexpected pleasure?"

He smiled the impudent smile that set his blue eyes twinkling. But the man had been shooting them from every possible unflattering angle and light since they'd arrived in South Beach to do over the Millicent and discovered that *Do Over* had been turned into a reality TV show with them as its stars. Most importantly, Troy Matthews was nowhere near as straightforward as he pretended to be and had often turned out to have some unpleasant trick up his sleeve.

"I heard you were shooting a series and thought you might need some help," he said after consuming a large bite of pancake dripping with syrup.

"Oh, where did you hear that?" she asked.

"Around." He lifted a napkin and wiped his mouth.

She looked at him. "We don't need 'help.'"

"You don't think a second camera would come in handy?"

"Not if it belongs to you."

He grinned. "You are direct. Which is one of the things I've always admired about you."

"You're not," Kyra replied. "Which is why I'm wondering who sent you."

"Sent me?" Troy asked innocently.

"Last time I checked, you were employed by the network with whom we have parted ways." Kyra folded her arms across her chest.

Her father watched with interest, but seemed too busy consuming pancakes to speak. Her mother, poised to mediate as always, refilled coffee mugs, then poured the last of the pancake batter onto the griddle. Avery and Nikki followed the conversation as if watching a Ping-Pong match.

Troy took a sip of coffee. "Yeah, well, I got caught doing a 'friend' a favor and I don't work there anymore."

She looked at Troy. He had sent her the Mermaid Point episodes as promised. Maddie, Avery, and Nikki had opted to wait until the series aired to face how the network had dealt with them. Kyra had watched the entire season before making a copy and sending it on to Bitsy. Personally, she'd loathed the camera angles that had revealed their discomfort and ineptitude, burned with righteous anger at each and every extreme close-up of Dustin, and recoiled at the private moments that had been intentionally invaded. But professionally, she could not deny that Troy was a talented shooter and editor and that the episodes, though humiliating, were compelling. Had Lifetime really fired Troy? Or was this some stealth attempt to put someone in their "camp"? "Can you prove it?"

"Kyra!" her mother said.

Kyra looked around the table. "He's been working for the enemy from the beginning. Am I really the only one here who finds this suspicious?"

"What kind of proof are you looking for?" Troy asked. "A termination letter? The lack of a pay stub?"

"Maybe the network sent you to spy on us," Kyra said.

"Why would they do that?" Nikki asked.

This was a good question. But the fact that she couldn't think of an answer didn't make it untrue. "I don't know. But the timing seems awfully coincidental. The episodes are good." The *good* was grudging. "The new season is about to air, I can't get anyone at Lifetime to return my calls, and suddenly out of the blue Troy appears, offering to work for nothing."

"I didn't actually offer to work for nothing," Troy replied.

"Then this conversation is definitely over. Because even assuming we could trust you, there is no money for unnecessary crew or equipment." Kyra had no intention of telling him how close to nonexistent the production budget was.

"I am, however, willing to work for room and board," Troy said, swirling whatever coffee remained in his cup. "And a share of the profits if you manage to sell the programs we shoot."

Kyra looked around the table again searching for allies. "You don't believe him, do you?"

"What harm could he do?" Avery asked. "It's apparently no longer a secret that we're shooting a project. And it's not as if they could take the Sunshine Hotel renovation away from us even if they wanted to."

Kyra knew she was missing something, but she couldn't figure out what. She narrowed her gaze on him. "Much as I hate to admit this, you're good enough to get hired somewhere else. Or work freelance. You don't need to work for us for free."

"I told you, not free," Troy replied. "Room and board and a share of the profits."

This time the word "profits" penetrated all the noise that had accompanied Troy Matthews's arrival. Troy had reason to think there were going to be profits. She looked around the room again taking in Avery and Nikki as well as Dustin and her father and mother, who was still flipping pancakes. At the moment all of them were dependent on what they made of *Do Over*. They couldn't afford to make a wrong move.

"Dad," she said quietly. "Would you mind taking Dustin outside?"

"But I . . ." Although his plate was clean he began to protest. Her mother walked over and cleared his plate and Dustin's. Kyra wiped Dustin's syrup-covered face and lifted him out of his booster seat. Although Steve looked much less happy about it than Dustin, he took his grandson's hand and left.

"Now, then," she said, taking her father's empty seat and motioning to her mother to sit down. The four of them looked unblinkingly at Troy. As if he were a specimen under a microscope. Or a terrorist in need of interrogating.

"I feel like I should be radioing for backup," Troy quipped. "Are you planning to commit violence?"

"Only if you're lying," Kyra said. "Now would be a good time to tell us what's really going on."

"There's nothing going on. I just . . ." Troy began to protest.

"You mentioned a share of the profits. Which means you have reason to think the series has value," Kyra interrupted.

Troy squirmed in his seat.

"What makes you think that?" she asked.

"Yeah," Avery added. "Spill it."

Nikki and Maddie nodded.

"There has been some audience testing," he admitted.

"And?" Nikki asked.

Troy's smile was slow. They watched it grow. "And the audience loved you. They identified strongly with you. They think you're 'plucky.'"

He grinned at Maddie. "And then there's the whole housewife with a rock star thing. It's golden. Not to mention Deirdre dying in the last episode. Half of the audience was sobbing." He dialed his glee back a couple of notches as he noticed their expressions. "Sorry. Plus the Keys are really hot right now. Netflix shot an original series down there called *Bloodline*."

"So why isn't the network returning my calls?" Kyra asked.

"Because they're trying to make you sweat."

"If the show does as well as they think, we could take the new season we shoot to a competitor," Nikki said. "This is great news."

Troy shook his head. "It would be if they hadn't started leaking all kinds of stories about how impossible you are to deal with. They're trying to make sure that even if you manage to shoot a full season, the other networks will be nervous about airing it."

"But that's cheating," Maddie protested. "That's defamation. That's . . ."

". . . a really sneaky way of trying to make whatever we do less valuable," Kyra said, her heart sinking. "Crap."

"It's true," Troy said. "They figure if they can get the other networks to back off, they can swoop in, play the good guys, and get you and the season you've shot for next to nothing."

"Jesus," Nikki whispered. "And I thought Lisa Hogan was ruthless."

Avery just nodded numbly. Which was exactly how Kyra felt. So much effort had already been poured into getting the Sunshine Hotel, raising money, reopening the tragedy that had impacted Annelise's and Renée's lives.

"Don't look so glum," Troy said. "We're not beaten yet."

Kyra stood, squared her shoulders, and looked at this messenger of doom. "You are not a part of 'we.' It's not like you offered us this information. We had to drag it out of you. Thanks for stopping by and all that, but there's no place in this for you."

"Well, not to put too fine a point on it, but you can't really refuse," Troy said, coming to his feet.

Kyra didn't have energy or breath to waste. This was her house, their show. Their disaster. An air of desperation hung as thick as the syrup with which they'd smothered their pancakes.

"When I agreed to send you the Keys episodes without

permission, which as I mentioned got me fired, you agreed that you owed me a favor. Moving in and working on *Do Over* is it."

Once again they looked at him numbly.

"I think I'll go out and get my gear," he said cheerfully. "Then you can show me where you'd like me to bunk."

Chapter Twenty-three

"Good God," Troy complained as he dragged an old and very moldy mattress out of the cottage, then dropped it at Ray's well-shod feet. "What did you do before you went into design? Run a chain gang?"

Ray simply pointed the tip of his imaginary whip at Troy and mimed the snap of said whip as he had all morning. Occasionally he'd hummed what he'd said was the old *Rawhide* theme song that ended with, "Head em up, move em out"—whip crack—"Rawhide!"

"You can quit the gang at any time," Kyra told Troy. "No one's keeping you here."

"I came to shoot, not haul furniture," Troy muttered.

"There's no room at Bella Flora for people who only do one thing," Avery said, to Kyra's obvious delight.

"My dad's even helping," Kyra pointed out.

Avery was not the only one biting her lip so as not to mention just how often Steve had to be found and directed through the tasks he was assigned. "There are no specialists on this shoot," she said instead. "At the moment your muscles are the most valuable thing you brought with you."

She had to admit that Ray was efficient and well equipped. He was also succinct. He'd set them to work with a simple, "Steve and Troy will haul out the mattresses and box springs. The ladies will be pulling out the curtains, blinds, and hardware. Things with a black dot are to be disposed of, things with a red dot will be donated, and things with a smiley face"—he whipped bright yellow smiley face stickers from his pocket—"will be repainted, refurbished, refinished, or repurposed." He had color-coded stickers for each of those options, too.

Troy set his jaw and followed Steve into the next cottage. Avery turned to Maddie, Nikki, and Kyra. "Why don't we divide up, start on opposite ends, and work toward each other?" She pulled an extra screwdriver from her tool belt and handed it to Maddie. She handed Dustin a pail. "Will you put all the screws and hardware in this for me?"

Unlike the other males in the group, Dustin grinned happily.

"Last one to the middle makes dinner," Maddie called over her shoulder as she hurried into the nearest cottage with Dustin right behind her.

• • •

Renée sat in her car next to the hotel property that afternoon working up the courage to get out. When she'd finally dragged herself out of the vehicle, she walked slowly through the opening in the hedge, then took her time on the concrete path, following it past the guest cottages, which hummed with activity. She smiled and nodded to everyone who greeted her, but couldn't quite find the voice to speak or the will to make small talk, as the apartment drew her with the force of a tractor beam.

She paused briefly beside the overgrown hibiscus that had been planted by her grandmother to commemorate the hotel's opening. It was wild, unkempt, and thick with deep red blooms. If their apartment were going to become part of the "new" Sunshine Hotel, the hibiscus would have to be trimmed. Or perhaps she could take cuttings from it and plant them strategically around the other cottages. Or in the private courtyards that Avery was planning. She might even . . .

Stop stalling. It's just an empty apartment.

The front door was propped open. The window screens had been removed and the casement and jalousie windows left gaping. There was nothing there that could hurt her. Nothing to be afraid of.

She inched forward. She hadn't told John she was coming. Hadn't actually known whether she would or not. She didn't want to go inside but couldn't turn away from it, either.

She took another step. Then another. Drawing a last deep breath of air, she stepped inside. Once again the memories washed over her.

She'd stood here just inside the doorway the day that her father had finally come home from the war. It was June 1946; he'd stayed on more than a year working at the American headquarters in Frankfurt and waiting to get permission to marry Ilse so that he could bring her home with him. A choice that her seven-year-old self had bitterly resented. Renée had been wearing her best dress, a bright pink one with polka dots and matching white patent Mary Janes that pinched her toes.

"Look how grown-up you are!" Her father had knelt down and enveloped her in his arms, rocking her back and forth and kissing the top of her head. She'd been okay living with her Nana and Pop Pop, but she'd been so afraid that her daddy wouldn't come back. Like her mother, who had never come home from the hospital. She'd worried about it even after he wrote her her own letter saying that he was fine and asking what she wanted him to bring her when he came home.

She'd only wanted him. But she'd asked for a doll just to be polite. She had not asked for a new mother who looked like a doll herself with porcelain white skin and china blue eyes and a halo of soft blond hair. So unlike Renée's own mother who had been tall and dark-haired like Renée. She'd vowed in that moment that she'd do everything right, be the perfect daughter. So that her father would never leave her again.

When Ilse was introduced, she reached a small white hand down to cup Renée's cheek. "I am so . . . pleased . . . to finally, to meet you," she said in broken English. "Your father . . . he has talked about you so . . . a lot." Her blue eyes were gentle and bright. And even though she was only seven, Renée could feel that it was Ilse who was the most frightened. "I thought that I would luff you."

Renée closed her eyes remembering. People had not liked that her father had brought home someone so patently not like them. To her grandparents' Jewish friends and hotel guests she was too German, too much a part of all that they'd gone to war to stop. Some of them had thought Ilse stuck up and standoffish. They'd gossiped about the fact that Ilse was already pregnant, but Renée had seen how confusing Ilse found her new life. How hard she'd clung to Renée's father. The way she'd tremble or cry out when someone or something took her by surprise.

Once again Renée found herself in her parents' bedroom. Saw her father lying there, his arms and legs akimbo. Saw the blood pooled around his head. The dresser lamp overturned. The sheets strewn across the floor. Had she heard something that night? Had she been up? Had she blocked the memory? Or was she only now wishing that there was one?

She thought about Ilse so quiet and meek, so eager to please. Only fierce if someone she cared about was threatened. She'd been protective of Annelise and of Renée. Determined to find the bridge between the Yiddish words Nana and Pop Pop knew and the German they had been derived from. She'd vowed to speak only English in honor of her new family and country.

Renée closed her eyes and tried to go back. Tried to remember if Ilse had been upset about anything, if her father had seemed worried. If the two had argued. But even now from an adult's perspective, she could recall nothing that would have caused her stepmother to do her father harm and then run away leaving her five-year-old daughter behind. She would have never left Annelise.

Out on the path she heard Dustin's squeal of laughter. The sound of metal objects clattering on the concrete.

Something teased at the back of her mind. Something that hung in the air of the apartment, stirred in the dust. Something that she had seen or heard. Something that if she could only remember might allow all of them to finally put the past to rest.

. . .

Unsurprisingly, Nikki and Maddie were the last to reach the middle. Due no doubt to Nikki's lack of energy and skill with tools and the fact that Maddie had Dustin helping her.

"God, that Ray is a fiend," Kyra said as they exited the van late that afternoon and dragged themselves into Bella Flora. She made an attempt at the designer's whip snap but her movements were nowhere near as crisp as their slave driver's.

"Yeah. He's just lucky we didn't have the energy for mutiny." In fact, Nikki felt short of breath and had no energy at all. She used the last bit of it climbing the stairs, pulling off her sweat-soaked clothes and stepping into the shower. Where she stayed until her skin shriveled and the water began to run cold.

Wrapped in her towel she yawned and groaned simultaneously, a sound that was becoming far too familiar and which she might have to trademark. In her bedroom she eyed the bed with real longing before forcing herself to dress and go downstairs.

"I ordered pizza," Maddie said as Nikki entered the kitchen. "Because the only place I have an ounce of strength left is here." She held up her index finger.

"Works for me." Nikki yawn-groaned as she joined Maddie, Kyra, and Avery, who were sitting at the kitchen table in a stupor. Outside, Steve appeared to be asleep on a pool chaise. Troy was tossing Dustin around in the pool.

"I know we should have something green to go with the pizza," Maddie said. "But I . . . can you guys live with green olives?"

There were nods, but the kind that didn't require much movement. Nikki looked at the pitcher of iced tea on the table but didn't have the strength to reach for it.

"I've been thinking about *Do Over* airing. And whether it's going to help us or hurt us with potential sponsors." Avery picked up the tea, poured herself a glass, and set the pitcher in front of Kyra. "It's not too bad, right? I mean, we decided there was no point in torturing ourselves watching it before it aired since there was nothing we could do about it, but . . ."

"I'm not going to lie. You aren't gonna like it," Kyra said. "But watching it's not that much worse than living it."

Maddie groaned. "Oh, God. I'm not looking forward to seeing myself stutter over Will."

"Yeah. Well, while you're watching you can focus on the fact that your days of stuttering around William are over and that his record company is sending a private jet to take you to his first comeback concert," Avery said.

"That's right," Nikki said, rousing herself to intercept the iced tea as it made its way to Maddie. "He who laughs last and all that."

An incoming text dinged on Nikki's phone. Hoping it was Joe she glanced down, her nerves skittering. But the message was from Malcolm. It read, *I have something important to tell you. Come soon.* The "or else" was omitted, but Nikki knew it was there. Her mind raced. The skittering became a prickle of fear.

The pizza arrived and Kyra placed the box in the center of the table. "I got an extra-extra large so we'd have leftovers. Half veggie, half meat lover."

The others helped themselves. Nikki couldn't seem to tear her eyes from the screen.

"Are you okay?" Maddie asked.

"Hmmm?" Nikki looked up.

"Are you all right?" Maddie repeated.

"I was just thinking," Nikki replied, sliding her phone into her pocket.

"It did look kind of painful," Avery said.

"Very funny." Nikki reached for a slice of pizza more for something to do with her hands than hunger. "No, I . . . I was just thinking I might take Maddie up on her invitation to fly up for Will's concert. It's the day after the first episode, isn't it?" The Butner federal prison was located just outside of Durham, North Carolina, where Will's group was playing.

"Really?" She felt a stab of guilt at Maddie's immediate excitement.

"Yes. I have some business I need to take care of near there. And it might be good to have some face time with Bitsy." This was not exactly a lie.

Maddie shot her a questioning look but said simply, "Sounds great. I'm looking forward to the concert and seeing Will perform and all, but I wouldn't mind having one of my peeps with me."

"I wish I could come," Avery said. "But Enrico's going to open up the ceiling in the main building to see what's what and I need to be here."

Steve came in, a towel tied around his waist, pool water

dripping, his movements careful. He helped himself to a piece of pizza, then looked around. "Is this it?" he asked, as if someone might have hidden the rest of the meal.

Nikki kept her mouth firmly shut. Avery reached for her drink. Maddie contemplated her plate.

"It is unless you want to make something to go with it," Kyra said. "Will you take a piece out for Dustin?"

"Um, sure. Should I take one out for Troy, too?" He said this as if it were a completely novel idea that he was trying on for size.

"That's a great idea," Kyra said. "In fact, why don't you take the rest out with you? Dustin will love the idea of a guys-only picnic." Not waiting for an answer, she removed the remaining veggie slices onto a plate and placed the pizza box in his hands, piled paper plates and napkins on top of it. "I think there are a few juice boxes in the pool house refrigerator if Dustin gets thirsty." She escorted her father to the back door and held it open for him.

"Well done," Nikki said when Kyra returned to the table.

"Masterful," Avery added.

"You're definitely getting the hang of it," Maddie agreed.

"But that's how I handle Dustin," Kyra protested.

"Yes, exactly." Maddie smiled.

"I wish someone had told me that when I was married to Trent," Avery said. "He didn't act much older than Dustin, either."

Nikki tried to imagine managing Joe Giraldi like one might a toddler and failed. Then she wished she hadn't thought of him at all. Because it hurt like hell—way more than her body did after the day they'd spent at the Sunshine Hotel.

A silence fell as they finished their dinner, lost in their own thoughts.

Nikki yawned and didn't care in the least if it sounded more like a groan. "I don't think I'm going to have the strength to come up with a good thing tonight."

"Me, neither," Avery said on a yawn of her own.

"Doesn't matter," Maddie said, yawning in turn. "Sunset's after eight P.M. tonight. Nobody at this table looks like they're still going to be awake then."

"You've got that right," Nikki said, trying but not succeeding to hold back a gigantic and noisy yawn. "I just hope I can find the strength to make it back up the stairs."

Chapter Twenty-four

As if yet another long, hot day of manual labor wasn't enough, the time had come to watch the first episode of *Do Over: Keys Edition*. Avery had tried to lose herself in the work, but had not been able to dispel the dread that had dogged her. The butterflies that had fluttered madly in her stomach all day were still at it when Bella Flora's doorbell pealed. She made it to the foyer before it stopped ringing, threw her arms around Chase and Jeff, and led them back to the salon. With Dustin in bed, Kyra and Maddie were setting out snacks that Avery could not imagine eating. Steve was ensconced in the recliner, and Nikki had carved out a section of the sofa. Troy was there looking far too eager for Avery's liking.

The men helped themselves to food and waited expectantly. Maddie, Nikki, and even Kyra wore the same wary expression she could feel stretching across her own face, the sort a passenger in a speeding car might wear while trying to come up with the position that might allow them to survive the crash.

"How much alcohol are we going to need for this?" Avery asked, wondering if alcohol would slow the butterflies or maybe even put them to sleep.

"I'm not sure," Kyra said. "Are we talking hard liquor or wine and beer?"

"Great." Avery closed her eyes and took what she hoped would be a calming breath. "I was thinking wine. How many glasses do we need?"

Hands shot up, some more desperately than others. Maddie stood. "Let me help you."

"Thanks." Avery took three bottles of wine from the bar fridge, clutched them to her chest, then managed to tuck a liter of tequila beneath one arm while Maddie loaded a tray with wineglasses and a stack of shot glasses.

Chase relieved Avery of her load. "I didn't realize we were going to need quite so much fortification."

"The tequila is just in case of emergency," she said in as flip a tone as she could manage. "I'm thinking it's better to be safe than sorry."

Troy snorted, then attempted to camouflage it with a cough. He raised his video camera to his shoulder but Kyra moved in quickly. "Here." She swapped her camera for his. "You can shoot with mine tonight. So you don't accidentally forget whose side you're on."

"As if you'd let me," Troy said.

"This way there's no question who the video belongs to." She held his gaze. "Because I'll be deciding what we use and what needs to be deleted."

The set of his jaw telegraphed his displeasure. It took him several long moments to rein in his irritation.

Good, Avery thought. Now it was his turn to think before he acted. Just as they'd been forced to do ever since the network had turned the cameras on them.

The wine was poured. The tequila and shot glasses were placed within easy reach, kind of like a fire extinguisher behind glass hung next to the axe required to access it. Chase retrieved the beers he'd brought and offered them to Steve and Troy.

Too soon a brief teaser for *Do Over* played on-screen.

"I just want to go on record as saying that I was only following orders. And there wasn't much in the way of wiggle room," Troy said during the opening commercials.

"It's a little late for excuses now," Kyra said. "And I think the word 'slither' sounds way more appropriate than wiggle."

"I'm just saying I shot what I was told to shoot. And I edited what I was told to edit. This was not my baby."

Oh, God. Even as she told herself not to panic, Avery picked up the tequila, poured herself a healthy shot, and downed it.

Then the *Do Over* theme music was playing. There was an establishing shot of Bella Flora, which dissolved into a shot of them sitting in this very room on Christmas Day. A lit tree stood in front of one of the floor-to-ceiling windows. Crumpled wrapping paper and opened presents were strewn all around it as a narrator's voice set up the scene and the situation.

A shot of Kyra with Dustin in her lap filled the frame. Her hands were clasped around his stomach as he twirled the propeller of a wooden toy helicopter. The camera panned over to Avery. Her face looked huge as she licked her lips and then tore open the flap of an envelope. As they all looked on expectantly her eyes skimmed the card she'd extracted from the envelope. She could still remember how her hand had trembled as her screen image read, "Your next Do Over will start in May. When you turn the home of an extremely high-profile individual into a bed-and-breakfast." There was a cutaway to the rest of them trying to figure out just how high profile that person might be. And then Avery was full frame again as she continued. "That home . . ." Her screen self flipped the card over and hesitated as if waiting for a drumroll. ". . . is located somewhere in the Florida Keys."

The tequila she'd downed did nothing to prevent Avery's gasp as the shot of Deirdre filled the screen. Her mother's voice was wry, her expression challenging as she said, "Has anyone else noticed that we're going to be on another barrier island in the middle of hurricane season?"

Before Avery could blink, let alone pour and drink another shot, the video cut to their arrival at Bud N' Mary's Marina in Islamorada. Shots of fishing boats coming in and disgorging their anglers were followed by shots of deckhands skinning and fileting the catch while other anglers posed in front of really big fish that had clearly not gotten away.

All of them were standing on the docks when Hudson Power, a longtime fishing guide and friend of the homeowner they'd be working for, arrived by boat to pick them up. Which was when they discovered that their renovation was going to take place on an island, as in only reachable by water.

Shots of their stunned faces were followed by shots of Mermaid Point framed by turquoise water. As they drew closer there were glimpses of the island's dense tropical foliage and mangrove-shrouded edges, a tidal pool, a half-moon of beach, and a pavilion overlooking a swimming pool. The soundtrack was one of water slapping the camera boat hull, the buzz of insects, the rustle of palm fronds. There was a loud cock-a-doodle-doo. Avery could practically smell the salt breeze with the faint undertones of fowl and fish.

"Are those chickens?" Steve asked in surprise.

"In the flesh," Nikki said. "And that's Romeo the time-challenged rooster out front. He had a very enthusiastic harem."

Kyra's lips clenched at each close-up of Dustin, of which there were many.

No amount of bracing prevented Avery's eyes from tearing up at the shots of Deirdre, who had been so clearly intent on winning her back. Chase's arm went around her shoulders as she watched her screen self tell her now-dead mother just what she could do with her pile of designer luggage.

Chase pulled her closer.

Nikki poured her another shot as the camera lingered on their faces, revealing their doubts and fears, exposing their least attractive selves for all to see.

Then Thomas Hightower came to greet them and lead them in a scraggly line past the sagging and peeling house to the pavilion where they came face-to-face with Mermaid Point's famous owner.

William Hightower's black eyes were not welcoming as he bowed mockingly, but it was Steve Singer's eyes that narrowed as the introductions were made. He went very still when the camera settled on Maddie's face, which had gone all crimson. Just as it did now as they all watched her screen image whimper and stammer a greeting when she recognized the rock star.

Avery poured a shot for Maddie, put it in her hand, watched her down it.

Steve snorted briefly. A derisive sound that died in his throat when the angle changed and they could all see William Hightower checking Maddie out.

"I told you you got his attention from the beginning," Nikki said, clearly glad that Steve was finally being forced to see just how other men saw the woman he'd taken for granted. His shock at all that followed made it obvious that he'd never really bothered to watch season one.

Kyra reached for the tequila as they watched their initial tour of Mermaid Point, led by the surly William Hightower. They saw the interplay between him and his son and watched him stomp off after informing them that they would not be renovating his studio and that it would, in fact, be off-limits.

Once again the camera lens lingered on their faces as their screen selves watched Wild Will storm away. As much as Avery hated seeing herself as one of the bugs pinned under the microscope, there was no denying that Troy's camerawork and editing were skillful. No one in the room could look away as the horror at their situation mounted. The room fell completely silent as their on-screen selves discovered they'd be living on the houseboat tied at the dock below.

At the commercial break Avery reached for the bottle of

tequila and poured shots all around. "I am not looking forward to watching us schlep our things onto that ridiculously small and ill-equipped houseboat." She was especially not looking forward to hearing the nasty tone with which she'd informed Deirdre that she had to carry her own luggage up to the cramped upper cabin Deirdre had insisted on calling the "penthouse."

Nikki, who'd been uncharacteristically silent, burrowed further into her seat but made no move toward the shot glasses.

Chase shook his head. "How in the hell did you put up with those accommodations?"

"Those network people should be tarred and feathered," Jeff agreed.

Steve Singer kept his thoughts to himself, for which they were all grateful.

Troy attempted to make himself small and unobtrusive, not an easy task for someone over six feet. Despite the tequila, Avery's fury at the hijacking of their show and the way they'd been made to look burned bright inside her. But it was far too late to rail about what had already happened. Better to use that anger to make sure no one could make them look so foolish ever again.

Nikki watched the remainder of the episode with an odd sort of detachment. She could see just how ridiculous they looked, how frightened, how vulnerable. She just couldn't bring herself to care. She'd felt as if someone had wrapped her in a layer of cotton wool ever since she'd decided to go see Malcolm.

A text dinged in on her phone and she started. Afraid that her thoughts of her brother had somehow summoned him. But this time when she forced herself to look down, the text was not from Malcolm but from Joe.

I hate what they've done to you on this show.

A tiny surge of hope pierced the cotton wool slightly. Joe was somewhere watching *Do Over* and thinking about her.

200 · WENDY WAX

Definitely not pretty, she texted back. *Should have turned and fled while we still could*. Not that any of them had had a viable alternative. Or any clear understanding of all of the dirty tricks up the network's sleeve. She held her breath, waiting for his response, and wishing she could turn back their relationship to what it had been then. When Joe didn't respond, she texted, *Wish we were headed to the Cheeca Lodge right now*, then held the phone waiting for a response. She was just about to give up, when his answer appeared.

Yeah. It was only one word but for that moment she could almost feel his solid presence.

Her thumbs hovered over her phone. She wanted to text him back, wanted to share all her hurts and fears. Tell him she was going to see Malcolm after all and why. Ask him for his guidance. His approval. His . . . love. But there was no sign of typing from his iPhone on the other end. No indication that he had anything else he wanted to say to her. Still she held on to her phone as the rest of the episode played out before their eyes, a train wreck she couldn't look away from.

If her taste buds hadn't been completely repelled by the idea, she would have been reaching for the tequila bottle and pounding down the shots along with Avery, Kyra, and Maddie. But the only thing she could imagine being worse than the numbness was being numb and hungover.

She slid her phone into her pocket and tugged the cotton wool firmly back into place.

Chapter Twenty-five

It was impossible to be blasé about boarding a private plane. Especially one sent by a record company specifically for you. Maddie had no idea what model the plane was, how much it cost, or which Aquarian Records megastars might have sat in its oversized leather seats or stretched out on its sofas as she stepped into the main cabin with Nikki behind her that mid-June afternoon. They found Bitsy Baynard, for whom this was not a first and possibly only experience, already sipping champagne and shimmering with excitement.

The steward was male and looked as if he'd stepped off the cover of a romance novel. The pilot and copilot were a comforting blend of military precision and casual courtesy. Their eyes were sharp and their crew cuts were shot through with silver, which Maddie assumed represented many decades of experience.

"May I pour you ladies a glass of champagne?" The steward held an open bottle and two champagne flutes.

"Thank you." Maddie accepted the glass while Nikki opted for sparkling water.

"I'll have hers." Bitsy held her glass up for a refill.

The three of them clinked glasses.

"Are you all right, Nikki?" Maddie asked after she'd taken her first heady sip. "You look a little . . . green."

"I'm fine. My stomach's just a bit . . . off."

"Well, mine feels like there are a million butterflies doing aerobics in it." Maddie took another bubbly sip. "In fact I feel like a little girl going to Disney World for the first time."

"This is the big-girl version of Disney," Bitsy said. "We are going to have a complete and utter blast."

The plane gathered speed, barreled down the runway, then lifted gently into the air. They rose above the sparkling turquoise bay and flew over the northern tip of St. Petersburg, climbing high into the bright blue sky.

Soft music played in the background as hors d'oeuvres were served and glasses refilled.

"I'd almost forgotten how lovely this can be," Nikki said as they banked to the left and watched puffy white clouds fall away beneath them. There'd been a time when she'd jetted around the world on clients' planes, sailed on their yachts, stayed in their villas.

"It is heavenly, isn't it?" Bitsy agreed.

"I don't know, it all feels so surreal. I told you before, I have to pinch myself every time I even think about Will. And this . . ." Maddie looked around the cabin filled with gleaming wood and luxurious leather. The Aquarian Records logo woven into the carpet. "Well, I'm black and blue so I guess it must be real."

"It's real, darlin'," Bitsy said. "And tonight is your night."

"Yes, what did you bring to wear?" Nikki asked, nibbling on a mini quiche.

"Oh, you know. A nice pair of black pants and a top."

Bitsy and Nikki stopped drinking and nibbling.

"And some, um, nice earrings."

"Oh, hell no," Bitsy said. "You are dating a rock star. You're not wearing any 'nice' black pants and top. Nice just isn't going to cut it."

"I totally agree," Nikki said, gesturing with the mini quiche.

"Well, it's a little late to do anything about it now," Maddie said, not liking the determined look in either of their eyes. "We're not going to have more than an hour and a half tops to get ready." Lord knew she'd been quivering with an odd combination of fear and excitement since the whole concert thing had come up. She didn't own "rock 'n' roll" clothes and would feel ridiculous in them if she did. She hadn't come here to make a splash or get attention; she'd come to support Will. "Besides, Will knows what I look like. It's not as if dressing up is going to change how old I am or the way I'm built."

"I know you did not just say that," Nikki said.

"Me, neither," Bitsy added.

"I am what I am. And I'm okay with it." Maddie said it with as much conviction as she could muster.

"'Okay' isn't going to cut it tonight, either," Nikki said. "Not on my watch."

"Or mine," Bitsy said. "You're not going to embarrass Will or us by looking as if this doesn't matter to you."

"That's not what I meant," Maddie said. "And . . ."

"I have to agree with Bitsy on this," Nikki said. "You don't have to be age inappropriate. But you do have to look great."

"Exactly." Bitsy whipped out her phone." It's a good thing we have cell service. I'm going to make some calls and have a few things sent over to the hotel."

· · ·

"I really don't see any reason to go through all this," Maddie said. They'd been whisked from the small airport on the outskirts of Raleigh-Durham and delivered to their hotel in a shiny black town car. A rack of clothing had been waiting in the master bedroom of the presidential suite. The door had barely closed behind the bellman before Nikki and Bitsy were demanding she undress so that the personal styling could commence.

"It's a very good thing I had them send over lingerie," Bitsy said as Maddie reluctantly disrobed. "You are not going to be wearing BMWs when you undress for William Hightower."

"BMWs," she said tentatively.

"That's Big Mama Whites," Nikki explained, opening a glossy black shopping bag with bright pink lettering that formed a pair of lips and pulling out handfuls of lingerie.

"Will has seen my . . ."

"It doesn't matter what he has and hasn't seen," Bitsy interrupted. "You'll move better and feel sexier if you're wearing something 'spicier.'" She plucked a nude-colored pair of panties from Nikki and handed them to Maddie.

Maddie held up the V-shaped satin, flashing back to the lace thong some woman had stuffed in Will's pocket. "I'm more likely to be hobbling with this . . . whatever it is . . . cutting into me." She dangled the undergarment from one finger.

"It's more comfortable than it looks. And it's really flattering. Trust me." Bitsy's horsey face flushed as she winked. "And while you're at it, try this on." Bitsy handed her a low-cut bra in the same silky nude color.

"This is not going to . . ." Maddie's voice trailed off as she slid her arms through the openings. Ignoring Maddie's reticence, Nikki hooked the back and then tightened the straps. "Oh." She looked down at her breasts, which now swelled above the satin cups. A glance in the mirror revealed that rather than binding, the high-cut underwear made her legs look longer and hit her just below the waist. She turned to consider herself from the back. "Not bad."

"Not bad? It's a shame you have to put anything on over

it," Bitsy said. She retrieved the bottle of champagne that
had been awaiting them along with a massive basket of fruit
and chocolates. "Try on the black jumpsuit with the polka-
dot pumps first."

"I thought you had a thing against black pants," Maddie
said, but she was already stepping into the jumpsuit and
pulling it up over her body.

"I only object to 'nice' black pants," Bitsy said, motioning
Maddie to turn so she could zip her up.

Maddie contemplated her reflection in the mirror. The
jumpsuit was smooth and slinky with a low V neckline and
a blouson waist. The pant legs tapered at the ankle. The
black and cream heels shouted "look at me."

"Ooh, that's perfect," Nikki said with an approving smile.
"And it would look great with this triple strand of gold and
silver." She held up a sparkly necklace and fastened it around
Maddie's neck.

"Where on earth did all this come from?" Maddie protested. "How did you . . . ?"

"The concierge had them sent over for our consideration,"
Bitsy said with a shrug.

"I didn't know things like this actually happened," Maddie
said as Bitsy poured her a glass of champagne and Nikki
perused the other outfits. "This would look great on you, too."
She held up a fuchsia pencil skirt and a gauzy white blouse.

"Here, let's take a look." They turned Maddie as if she
were a mannequin, helping her out of the black and into the
fuchsia. Which was startlingly spectacular.

Maddie tilted her head, moved her body. Even without
makeup and her hair all awry, the color lit her face and the
fabric skimmed perfectly over her body, clinging lightly to
her curves. Unable to speak she looked to Nikki and Bitsy,
who were beaming.

"Definitely the pink," Nikki said. "You look outrageously
gorgeous."

"Absolutely gorgeous." Bitsy nodded happily. "Now, hand them to me and pop into the shower. The hair and makeup people will be here at six thirty."

"Hair and makeup?" Maddie asked, not even wanting to think how much all of this must cost. "Now I really am dreaming."

Bitsy laughed as she hung up the garments, clearly enjoying Maddie's delight. "If it helps you can think of me as your fairy godmother. My way of thanking you for inviting me to the concert." She refilled Maddie's glass and sent her off to the bathroom.

"Right," Maddie said, beaming back at Bitsy and Nikki. "Clearly I need to give up and enjoy this. I just want you to promise that I won't be wearing glass slippers and the car isn't going to turn back into a pumpkin at midnight."

"You do look beautiful," Bitsy said later as they were handed out of the car, all of them buffed, polished, made up, and dressed within an inch of their lives.

"Thank you." Maddie did in fact feel like Cinderella trotting off to the ball to try to catch the eye of her rock 'n' roll prince. The last time she'd looked half this glamorous was the day she had to cook on camera with William during the renovation of Mermaid Point. "Will won't even recognize me."

"He will definitely recognize you," Nikki said. "And he'll love what he's seeing."

Maddie smoothed the sides of the skirt and commanded herself not to wobble in the heels. She peeked down to make sure nothing was peeking out from the V of the white blouse and was shocked at the cleavage that looked back at her.

"Don't slouch," Nikki directed, barely moving her lips, which were locked into a smile.

"I'm not slouching. I'm just . . ." Maddie straightened her shoulders as directed. And caught a glimpse of the nude satin bra that was nothing short of miraculous.

She smiled at Aaron Mann, who greeted them on behalf

of Aquarian and then ushered them through the stage entrance of the Durham Performing Arts Center to the greenroom where Will and his bandmates were milling about. There were women in the room. All of them were very young and beautiful with miles of exposed skin that was both smoother and firmer than Maddie's had ever been. A few of them looked up briefly before sniffing dismissively and turning their attention back to Will and the others, clearly seeing no threat to their plans for male domination.

Will's shiny dark hair with its threads of gray stood a head above the rest. His white button-down shirt showed off his golden skin and had been tucked into a pair of black jeans that hung low on his slim hips.

Maddie halted in the doorway, dragged back to reality by the women's dismissal, the way they hung on Will. She was nothing but a middle-aged housewife imposter.

"Oh no, you don't," Nikki whispered in her ear as she stepped up next to Maddie and linked an arm through hers.

"No way in hell." Bitsy took her other arm. With a decisive nod she propelled their threesome in William's direction.

Fear and uncertainty clogged Maddie's throat. If she could have halted their progress without causing a scene she would have. What if she reached Will's side and he realized once and for all just how ordinary she was. What if . . .

Will looked up and spotted her. His face creased into a smile. His brown eyes glittered with warmth. He moved toward them, shedding the young women who'd been hanging on to him. She could feel an answering smile light her face. Her panic fled and her heart, which had been thudding with dread just moments ago, did a distinct about-face and began to do its own little happy dance.

"I was starting to think you weren't going to make it." He took her into his arms and pressed her tight against him. So that she could feel the movement of his muscled body and inhale his warm spicy scent.

"It took us a little longer than expected to get to the hotel and freshen up," she replied.

"It was worth every minute," he said, looking her up and down approvingly. "You look gorgeous." He turned to hug Nikki. "And you must be Bitsy."

"Yes, I m-m-must," Bitsy stammered. "I'm a huge f-fan."

Maddie laughed as Bitsy's polish evaporated. Kyle, Dean, and Robert came over and hugged Maddie, too, much to the young women's shock.

"Thanks," Will said to the blushing Bitsy. "I'm glad you were able to make it. I know it will be more fun for Maddie with both of you here."

"Five minutes!" A young man wearing a headset leaned into the doorway.

"Give me one more kiss for luck, Maddie-fan." Will pulled her into his arms again and she buried her face in his neck, no longer caring about the young girls or their skin. "Aaron will take you down to your seats then bring you backstage. We'll all go out and get a bite afterward if that's okay?"

Bitsy nodded cheerfully. Nikki smiled her agreement. Maddie hummed with happiness.

"I have it on good authority that we're staying at the same hotel." Will's lips brushed against Maddie's ear; a tickle and a promise.

Chapter Twenty-six

Did leaving one hotel room for another on the same floor qualify as a walk of shame? Maddie asked herself this question the next morning when she opened the door of Will's suite to peek into the hallway. After determining the coast was clear, she stepped into the corridor. With her head down she walked as quickly and as quietly as possible, her eyes on her bare feet, the wrinkled white blouse untucked over the rumpled fuchsia skirt. The high heels dangled from her fingers.

She was almost halfway down the hall and to the bed she hadn't slept in when she heard the muffled sound of footsteps on thick carpeting. This was followed by a cheery "Mornin', Maddie." Trying not to wince, she looked up to meet Will's drummer Dean Adams's eyes. "Is he up?"

"Um, yeah." She swallowed and smiled as casually as she could.

"Have a good one."

"Thanks." Head down, she picked up her pace and practically ran into Aaron Mann coming out of his room. Her head jerked up.

"Morning, Maddie." Aaron grinned. "Great night, wasn't it?"

"Yes. I thought the, um, concert was incredible."

Aaron took in her clothing and her bare feet, but he made no comment. "Is he up? We're going to be leaving for Asheville a little earlier than planned."

"Yes." Praying that her cheeks were only hot and not telltale red, Maddie remembered just how "up" Will had been throughout the night and most of the morning.

"The plane will be ready to go anytime after one P.M. They'll drop you in St. Pete and then take Ms. Baynard on to Palm Beach."

"Thank you," Maddie said, forcing herself to meet his eye. She and Will were consenting adults. There was nothing to be embarrassed about.

"Thank you. I'd heard he could be difficult back in the day. Having you here sure has put him in a good mood." He gave her a jaunty salute and headed for the suite she'd just left.

Right. Clutching the heels to her chest, she continued down the hallway careful not to make eye contact with the maid pushing her cart in her direction. Or the room service waiter who tipped his head in acknowledgment. Apparently eight A.M. was hotel rush hour. Thank God she hadn't left in the hotel robe Will had suggested.

As quietly as possible she opened the suite door, tiptoed inside, and closed it behind her. Seeing the second bedroom's door closed, she began to relax.

"The outfit still looks great. Wrinkled but great."

Maddie whirled at the sound of Nikki's voice. The blush was automatic.

"And I'm guessing from the look on your face and the fact that you didn't sleep in your bed that the lingerie was a success, too."

"There may have been a compliment or two," Maddie conceded. Not to mention a great eagerness to remove it. She focused on Nikki's face, which looked slightly pasty. Dark circles rimmed her eyes. "What are you doing up so early?"

"I think in order to 'get up' you have to have gone to sleep. I just couldn't seem to settle down last night." Nikki yawned and pushed her hair back off her forehead, which was creased with worry.

"Yeah. It was quite a day." Maddie glanced toward the closed bedroom door. "I gather Bitsy's still asleep?"

"Yes, she put on her sleep mask and she was gone five minutes later. But before she passed out she told me that she had such a great time she wanted to pledge another fifty thousand dollars to *Do Over*."

"That's incredible."

"I know. I'm afraid to count on it until she wakes up and actually remembers what she said. She was under the influence." Nikki's face brightened briefly. "She also informed me that if she weren't happily married and didn't like you so much she would have been all over Will."

"I think she was all over Will," Maddie said. Though she'd done it with such good humor it was impossible to take offense.

"True," Nikki said. "Thank God Will was such a good sport."

"I think he likes Bitsy as much as we do. She has a good heart. And she does know how to have fun." Maddie looked down at her crumpled clothing. "I'm so glad you two talked me into dressing up for the concert." She smiled and headed for the coffeemaker. "Do you want some coffee?"

"No. It doesn't seem to be agreeing with me." She made a face. "My stomach's been a little temperamental."

Maddie creamed and sugared her coffee, then sat next to Nikki. "So I can't help noticing you're already dressed. I've been wondering ever since you decided to come along what kind of 'business' you could need to take care of here. This morning it occurred to me that business could be your brother. Did I get that part right?"

Nikki grimaced.

Maddie noticed that there was more than weariness in her friend's eyes. "What's going on?"

Nikki looked down at the hands that she'd clasped in her lap then up at Maddie. Her normal certainty seemed to have deserted her. "Joe told me a while ago that Malcolm wanted to see me." She swallowed. "He asked if I'd visit him and see what I could find out. So much of the money Malcolm stole is still missing. I wanted to help. But, then I wussed out."

"So why are you going now? What's changed?" Maddie asked.

"Malcolm's gotten ahold of a cell phone and he's been texting me directly. He wants me to come. He wants something from me."

"But you don't have to go. And surely there's nothing he could do to you if you don't?"

"I don't know. Every time I've tried to convince myself he's a better person than he's demonstrated, he proves me wrong. Honestly, even thinking about him makes me feel sick to my stomach, but I think it's safer to find out what he wants face-to-face. And I guess I'm hoping that he'll let something slip, that he'll give me some idea of where to look for the rest of the money."

"What did Joe say when you told him you'd decided to go after all?"

Nikki looked away. "I didn't tell Joe. I . . . I mean we're not really together so . . . if I find out anything that would be helpful I'll share it. But . . ." Her shrug was painful and un-Nikki-like. "I've got a rental car lined up. It's only about ten miles to the prison. I'll just meet you all at the airport."

"No, you won't," Maddie said.

Nikki met her eyes and Maddie saw the sheen of tears. "It's not like you can tell me what I can and can't do."

"Why not?" Maddie countered. "You seem to feel free to tell me what I can and can't wear."

"That's different," Nikki said. "You were in serious need of an intervention. And I saw the effect that outfit had on Will."

"You're right. I'm glad you and Bitsy made me listen. Glad and grateful." Maddie looked at her friend, who seemed to have lost a big chunk of her usual confidence.

"Damn straight." Nikki swiped at her eyes with the back of one hand.

"I'm not telling you you shouldn't go. I'm just telling you I'm coming with you." She hauled herself to her feet. "Why don't you write a note for Bitsy while I shower and change?"

. . .

Nikki's hands shook on the steering wheel as they approached the Butner Federal Correctional Complex twenty minutes north of Durham. The complex consisted of four squat concrete buildings that sprawled across acres of grassy land. If you didn't look at the razor-wire fences and the way the sidewalks ended in locked gates, you might have been at a modern high school.

The similarities ended when they entered the building labeled *LSC1* and the journey into the prison itself began.

"Don't let him get to you," Maddie said as Nikki left her in the lobby.

"Right," Nikki replied, wishing she knew how to prevent it. Then she turned over her driver's license, had her picture taken, and followed a corrections officer through a series of steel doors. At a security station her shoes were checked for weapons, her left hand was stained with invisible ink that would show up on cell block scanners, and a drug-sniffing dog gave her the once-over. As she progressed farther into the prison, the concrete block walls seemed to get tighter and the hallways darker. The free world felt very far away.

The visitation room was an oblong about the size of a high

school lunchroom. One long side was made of glass and overlooked a courtyard where young children played on equipment. Groups of people sat at tables and chairs and in small seating areas. Attempts had been made to soften the space with greenery and bright paint and even several children's murals; a bookcase with games and books ran along one wall, but sound bounced off the hard surfaces and voices were raised in an attempt to be heard.

She felt Malcolm before she saw him. The first time her eyes skimmed right over him, moved on, then skittered back. He stood alone in a far corner midway between two chairs, which he'd clearly claimed, looking far fitter than he had the last time she'd seen him more than three years ago. His eyes were clear and focused; she could feel them fixed on her as she walked toward him. His blond hair had darkened. His shoulders in the khaki uniform appeared broader, his abdomen tighter. It seemed that prison had agreed with him.

"We're allowed to hug when you get here and when you leave," he said when she reached him.

She made no move to touch him.

With a wry smile he motioned to the closest chair. She studied his face as he took the chair across from her, and she reminded herself how easily he'd stolen from her and then tried to use her. The number of lives he'd ruined. "What is it you want from me?"

"I'd forgotten how direct you can be." He smiled as if this were an amusing trait.

"There's no use pretending, is there?" she asked. "Nothing you've done has indicated that you see me as anything more than another 'mark.' Now tell me what you want so I can say no and be on my way."

"I never meant for all this to happen, Nik," he said.

"So you've said. But you don't really seem to give a damn about all the people whose lives you stole."

"Well, I am serving my time," he said reasonably. "I have a job in the library. And I've been advising some of the inmates about their finances." His lips quirked up into the very smile that he'd always used to such good effect.

"Jesus."

"Oh, don't worry. They don't have enough to bother with. Though there are a couple guys here I knew back in the day. I even met Bernie Madoff in the medical facility. Of course I'm small potatoes compared to him."

"The man is a monster. He lost both his sons and his wife," she said, appalled at the hero worship in his voice. "One of them committed suicide."

Malcolm shrugged. Bile rose in her throat.

"How did you get a cell phone?" she asked.

He glanced over his shoulder but he was smiling when he replied, "I don't know what you're talking about. There are no cell phones allowed in prison." He leaned forward in his chair, though he was careful not to touch her. "Do you remember when we lived in that apartment in Jacksonville and didn't even have a phone?"

She'd spent a lot of years trying to blot out the poverty they'd grown up in, the constant moves to worse and worse places. Her mother's struggle to clothe and feed them after their father's death.

"We were so close," he said. "It used to be us against the world." He plumbed her eyes with his. "Do you remember how hard we worked? How badly we wanted to build new lives?"

What she remembered was loving and cherishing him above all others and then discovering that she'd meant no more to him than any of his victims. "Of course I do. You were the most important person on earth to me," she admitted. "I was so proud of your success." His smile grew but as she looked back into his green eyes, the same shape and color as her own, she saw the calculation in them. "Right up until the moment I discovered you weren't actually a financial advisor but a thief."

"I told you that wasn't intentional. Things just got away from me. And then when things went soft and everyone wanted their money . . ."

"I'm not interested in excuses," she said. "Are you still planning to write your autobiography?"

"Nah. It turns out I'd never be able to sell or profit from it." He seemed to remember himself. "Not even to give the money to the victims."

As if he ever would have. "You need to return the remaining money, Malcolm. Tell the feds where the rest of the accounts are." She'd turned this over and over in her mind, how she might finally get him to do the right thing. "By the time you get out of here you're going to be way too old to enjoy any of that money. Give it up, Malcolm. Do it for our mother, who did everything to give you a better chance in life." Her voice dropped. "And if not for her, for me."

He gave her the same smile and shrug he'd offered when questioned about the cell phone. "I don't actually have access to any of the money. In fact that's why I asked you to come, Nik. I need to ask you a favor."

She was careful not to flinch at his too-easy use of her old nickname. "A favor?" she asked, careful to keep her tone neutral. If her chair hadn't been bolted to the floor, she would have been tempted to scoot away from him.

"Yes."

She didn't trust herself to speak, so she simply raised an expectant eyebrow and waited.

"I'm in a bit of a jam. I need you to access some money for me."

Nikki tried to school her features. This was exactly what Joe had hoped, that Malcolm would confide in her or send her after at least some of the missing money. She knew her coming without telling him wouldn't go down well, but if she could help get back more of what Malcolm had stolen, surely Joe would forgive her?

"I don't see how I could possibly do that," she said, thinking maybe she could outsmart Malcolm. "I'm sure everything in your name has been found and frozen."

She watched his face and was shocked at the twinkle that stole into his eyes. There was pride in them, too. A shiver of apprehension ran up her back as his smile turned smug. "That's true. They've found and seized almost everything that was in my name." He paused dramatically. "But there are safe-deposit boxes in yours." He watched her carefully as his meaning sank in.

"In my name?" she asked in shock. "You opened safe-deposit boxes in my name?"

"Um-hmmm." He'd once had accounts in their mother's name, too, long after she'd died. He'd hidden stolen funds in them and had tried to get Nikki to retrieve the money while he was on the run. "Quite a few of them. The FBI didn't have enough to warrant a search of your accounts." He watched her process this. "Speaking of the FBI, is your boyfriend out front waiting for you? The one you sold me out to?"

She didn't answer.

"Because I don't think he'd react at all well to discovering just how much of the missing cash you're hiding."

"I'm not hiding anything." *Except this visit. Which she absolutely should have told Joe about.* "And no one's going to fall for this." She hoped. "Joe will know you did this when he was closing in on you." She had to remind herself to breathe. Had to swallow back the bile that once again rose to press against her throat.

"I don't think so." She heard the satisfaction in his tone, read it in his eyes. "Those boxes were filled with cash a long time ago. A lot of cash. Everybody needs an emergency stash." He watched her carefully just as a patient cat might watch a startled mouse. "Even your boyfriend might find it hard to believe you knew nothing about the boxes or the money that was stuffed in them. Not when they've existed for so long." There was the merest twitch of his lips as he saw her absorb and understand the threat.

Horror flooded through her as the last vestiges of the boy she'd once known and loved were stripped away. She felt like Dr. Frankenstein, finally forced to face the monster he'd created. "I had no knowledge of any of your wrongdoing. I didn't participate in your scam in any way. I was a victim. And you know it."

Once again, the shrug. The smile. The hint of amusement at having so effectively set and sprung his trap. "And who would really believe that if I decided to have an anonymous tip called in? Perception, Nik. It can be far more convincing than reality. But I don't want to do that. I just need you to pick up cash and bring it to me."

"I won't do it." She stood. "I should have known better than to come here. You're crazy if you think I'm going to get involved in this."

"You're already involved whether you want to be or not. And I'm not crazy." He sighed and ran a hand over his face. "I'm desperate."

"Desperate? For money? Here? What are you going to do with it?"

"Shhh. Keep your voice down. Or I'll really be in trouble."

"What are they going to do to you? Take away your television time? Make you work an extra hour in the library?" Anger bubbled inside her. "You've ruined hundreds of lives and bankrupted countless charities. And now you're threatening to incriminate me when I've done nothing wrong except love and believe in you." She stood and prepared to leave. "I don't really give a shit what you want or what you think you need money for."

Malcolm stood, too, though he was careful not to make any sudden movements. "There's a hit out on me," he whispered. When she didn't respond, he continued. "It turns out more than one of my investors was representing a drug cartel. I have to give them back what they lost. Or I'm dead." He looked genuinely shocked.

"I can put them off for a while, but not indefinitely."

"How ironic. Did you know that one of your clients tried to kill me down in Miami? Does the name Parker Amherst IV ring a bell?"

"No, afraid not. The world is full of nut jobs, isn't it? I'm sorry." His voice turned pleading. "I know you hate me. You have reason to." He paused. "I get that you're glad to see me rotting in jail. But I guess I'm hoping you don't want me dead."

She simply stared at him. She no longer trusted her ability to determine whether he was telling the truth. If, in fact, he ever did. For all she knew this was just another scam. She settled her purse on her shoulder.

He reached a hand out and she shrank away. "I know you, Nik. You're trying to tell yourself I'm making this whole thing up so you can just walk away. But I'm not." He looked her straight in the eye. "I apologize for threatening you. But desperate times call for desperate measures." The smile he gave her was half sad, half cocky. As if he couldn't decide what would work best on her. "I'll give you some time to think it over. But if I don't get a yes from you soon enough to call off the bad guys, I'll have to leak the location of the safe-deposit boxes to the authorities." The smile turned more menacing. "And I wouldn't say anything to your boyfriend about this. Government employees have to be squeaky clean these days. Even a hint of impropriety can torpedo a career."

She wanted to rip the smile from his face. Wanted to shout and scream her anger at him at the top of her lungs. Instead she turned on shaky legs, then fled—at least as much as one could "flee" in a prison. Back through the obstacle course of clanging steel doors and to the front desk, where she managed to retrieve her driver's license. Desperate to get outside and into the fresh air, she motioned for Maddie to follow her.

"What is it? What's wrong?" Maddie asked when they hit the sidewalk.

"I was afraid I was going to throw up or pass out," Nikki panted. Right before she bent and did exactly what she'd been afraid of: heaving the contents of her roiling stomach onto a small patch of grass and then crumpling none too elegantly beside it.

Chapter Twenty-seven

Renée knew that stress did different things to different people. Some drank to excess or turned to drugs, while others cleaned or redecorated. Many people tried to stick their heads in the sand. Renée found solace when her hands were covered in dirt.

As the appointment with the sketch artist grew closer, she replanted and rearranged her flowerbeds, caught each dead frond as it fell from its palm, and pounced on every weed that had the temerity to break ground. As she pruned and pinched and fertilized, she began to imagine the plants and flowers trembling at the sound of her footsteps on her garden's cut-stone paths.

She watched her garden disappear behind her that morning as she left to pick up Annelise for the drive to the county sheriff's office, where they were to meet the forensic sketch artist who was going to try to create a composite of Annelise's alleged long-ago intruder.

"I sat up all night making sure I remembered every detail of what that man looked like," Annelise said, her hands fluttering, her excitement building so that the closer they got, the more animated her sister became and the slower Renée drove.

The sketch artist that Officer Jackson brought out to meet them was a sunny young woman with wavy brown hair, almond-colored eyes framed in thick brown lashes and a dimple creasing one cheek.

"Annie." She'd smiled, reaching out to shake hands. "J. J. tells me he grew up right near you all." She chatted amiably for a good while clearly bent on getting them to relax. Annelise, normally so prickly with strangers, was doing exactly that, while Renée felt herself withdrawing, her answers to the woman's pleasantries growing shorter and shorter, like a morning glory closing up for the night. She'd assumed that Annelise would work with the artist and that Renée would be shown whatever they came up with, but when the pleasantries were over, Annie had given them a friendly smile and invited both of them to come with her.

"Aren't you worried we might corrupt each other's memories?" Renée asked as they took their seats across from where Annie had set up. Not that she had any to corrupt.

"No. We're looking for as much detail as possible." She dimpled. The girl really was adorable. "Sometimes sharing the process can be even more productive."

"Isn't sixty-four years a little long for a face to stay in someone's memory?" she'd asked dubiously while Annie sat down, positioned the sketch pad, and picked up a pencil.

"It depends. Sometimes the more traumatic the event the more it's embedded. It's not an exact science, but people are often surprised about how much they actually saw and remembered. Prompting helps. And I have a catalogue of facial features for comparison if we need it." She gave them one last reassuring smile. "Ready?"

Renée wasn't. But Annelise leaned forward in her chair and nodded.

"General physical description?" Annie prompted.

"Tall," Annelise said immediately. "Big." She hesitated, thinking. "But his clothes kind of hung on him. Like he might have been bigger originally."

Renée looked at her sister, amazed at her certainty and the crispness of her answers.

"Hair?" Annie prompted.

After another hesitation Annelise said, "Light colored and—short." She looked at Annie as if waiting for an argument, but Annie nodded and smiled. "It was close cropped. Like in a crew cut," Annelise continued. "His forehead was kind of shiny in the moonlight. I . . . his hairline was high."

The artist's hand moved constantly; they could hear the brush and scratch of the pencil on the paper as she drew. "Jaw?"

"Square." This time Annelise's reply came more quickly. "Powerful."

"Set of his eyes?"

"Wide. Deep set." Annelise looked down at her hands briefly before her head jerked up in surprise. "I don't know why exactly, but I feel like they were blue!"

Annie's pencil kept moving. "Slant or no slant to the eyes?"

Annelise paused to think. "No slant."

"The nose?"

"Straight. Narrow."

The pencil moved more quickly. "Cheekbones?"

"High and . . . angled." Her voice grew more certain even as Renée mentally leafed through celebrities and public figures that might have infiltrated Annelise's fertile imagination and provided flesh and bone for the "intruder."

"Lips?"

"Thin but . . ." Annelise's eyes closed. Her forehead furrowed in concentration. "Wide."

Renée's heart constricted as she watched her sister. Annelise's eyes remained closed, her chin tilted slightly upward. A small eager smile flitted over her lips as she pulled the strange man everyone had told her had never existed out of her memory so that Annie could put it on the page and thus into reality. Renée felt trapped. Pinned in a web of expectation she knew she couldn't fill or escape. The search for answers that seemed to be freeing Annelise wrapped hands around Renée's throat and squeezed the breath out of her lungs. Each feature Annelise added built the image forming in Renée's mind.

"Can you think of anything else?" Annie asked, her pencil flying over the page. "Any identifying marks? Scars? Tattoos?"

A shimmer of something surfaced then disappeared. Renée drew a deep and ragged breath. Annie was watching. "Renée?" she asked expectantly.

Renée shook her head.

"Don't censor yourself," the artist said, her pencil still moving. "Everything you need is already there. It's just retrieving it that takes some effort."

"I don't have anything to retrieve," she said as that thing, whatever it was, danced out of reach.

"Just say whatever comes to your mind."

Renée closed her eyes as Annelise had and tried to see. But whatever it was continued to elude her. When she opened her eyes and shook her head in frustration, Annelise was watching her, her eyes clearer than Renée could remember.

"All right," Annie said. "I'm going to show you the sketch so far. I'd like you to tell me what looks right and what doesn't so that I can make adjustments."

She turned the sketch pad around. They both held their breaths as they studied it.

"Okay, what feels right?"

"The hairline," Annelise said, her voice going breathy and childish as if she were actually five again. "And his jaw." She studied the sketch. "But his face was narrower in there." She gestured toward the cheek area with fluttering fingers.

Renée looked at her sister as Annie made the adjustments. She didn't know how Annelise could possibly remember this kind of detail, in a room lit only by the moon, from a glimpse at the age of five. But Annelise was intent, earnest, her answers spontaneous. Clearly she was not making things up.

"And I think . . ." Annelise hesitated, closed her eyes again.

Annie turned the pad into sketching position.

"I think he did have a tattoo. A jagged one down the side of . . ."

". . . his neck," Renée finished, surprising everyone including herself. Her fingers traced the lightning bolt that began just below the jawline.

Annie's pencil moved rapidly over the page, sketching, shading. A few moments later she turned the composite back so that Renée and Annelise could see it.

"That's him," Annelise said quietly, the childish hesitation gone. "That's the man I saw."

Renée stared at the face. She had seen this man or someone who looked a lot like him. This knowledge was a kick to the stomach, hard and unexpected. Her sister had told the truth and Renée had refused to believe it. She had driven a wedge between them that had lasted a lifetime because she could not, would not, consider the reality of a deadly stranger in their home. Preferred to believe that her stepmother had caused their father's death and then fled. Why had that seemed easier to believe? She had seen that face before. But it hadn't been the night that her father died. It was in one of the pictures in her stepmother's hidden photo album.

. . .

Maddie was in the grocery store checkout late the next afternoon, a place with which she was intimately acquainted, when she saw the picture of her and Will on the cover of *Fame*, a tabloid that often featured photos of freakishly impossible half-animal, half-human oddities and first-person accounts of alien abductions. She stared at the grainy picture, which had been taken at dinner after Will's concert, and read the headline, *Middle-Aged Magic with Aging Boomer Groupie?*

She moved closer in an attempt to read the first paragraph, which was filled with disdain for the pitiful nature of "star stalkers" who were old enough to belong to AARP. There had been fans down in Islamorada who'd thought Will could do better and the occasional snarky caption or headline, but as far as she knew, this was her first tabloid cover. She sincerely hoped it would be her last.

The picture was especially appalling given how attractive she'd felt that night despite the young girls in the greenroom.

That's because Will made you feel that way. Not because you are, the voice—was it her subconscious?—said.

It's just the angle, she countered.

Right. The voice was as disdainful as the article.

She shuddered to think of how much worse it might have been if her fashion intervention hadn't happened. Unable to stop herself, she reached for the tabloid.

I wouldn't do it if I were you, the voice warned.

Ignoring it, Maddie pulled the publication from the rack and opened it to where the article continued. Photos of Will at the next two concerts showed him with much younger women, all of whom stood far too close and gazed much too adoringly. Her heart stuttered at the shot of him and the guys in the band eating dinner in a restaurant afterward with those same young women draped all over them.

Told you not to look.

It doesn't mean anything, she retorted. *He's not interested in those young girls.*

Her subconscious raised a skeptical eyebrow.

He chose me over them in Durham.

What choice did he have? She imagined her subconscious rolling its eyes as it taunted, *Besides, you're not there now, are you?*

Her subconscious had copped quite an attitude.

I have no reason to doubt him, Maddie protested, even as she remembered the hungry looks the women at the Lorelei had sent him. The thong in his pocket. His explanation that female attention was just "part of the gig." Even Bitsy Baynard had not been immune.

Bitsy's not a cute young thing, the voice countered. Which meant she was now not just talking to but arguing with herself.

Will is not looking for a cute young thing.

All men are looking for a cute young thing. You can't expect a man to keep choosing a PB&J when there's a smorgasbord of delicacies available. The voice had turned downright snarky.

Will loves peanut butter and jelly. She smiled at her memory of his delight in the first "handwitch" he'd shared with Dustin. *Will says he's been there and done that. That he's had enough.*

Do men ever really have enough?

"Are you going to buy that?" the grocery clerk asked, nodding to the tabloid now wadded up in her hand.

"Um . . ."

Go ahead. You can put it up in your room as a reminder.

"Um, no, thank you." She laid the paper down, then used both hands to try to straighten out the wrinkles before placing it back on the rack.

Take that, she said to the voice as she pushed the grocery cart out of the store. Her subconscious was a royal pain in the ass.

Chapter Twenty-eight

Renée stood in her garden, a hose in her hand. She'd been operating on automatic pilot since yesterday's session with the sketch artist and what had turned out to be a brutal drive home. They'd barely left the sheriff's office parking lot when Annelise, who'd slid as far from Renée as her seat belt would allow, turned to her and bit out, "I told you so! All these years I told you so. But you always knew better!" There was no dampening of the eyes, no slow gathering of moisture. It was as if someone had slammed open a tap and sent a flood of tears streaking down Annelise's contorted face to carve out gullies of powder and rouge. "Do you have any idea what it feels like to never be taken seriously?" She'd emitted a harsh yelp of laughter. "No, of course you don't. Not reasonable Renée. Always so calm. Always so in the right! If I hadn't stopped you, the hotel would already be gone and no one would have ever looked into what happened!"

"I'm starting to fear for that plant's life." John's voice yanked her back to the present. "Do they make life preservers that narrow?"

Renée looked down at the bird-of-paradise that she'd been

watering and which was now practically swimming. "Hmmm?" She released the nozzle to stop the flow and took a step back. Her gardening clogs squelched in the mud patch she'd created.

"Are you trying to drown it or just sort of beat it into submission?" John's tone was teasing as he came down the back steps, then walked toward her leaning heavily on the cane.

"Don't come any closer. You'll sink and I don't know how we'll get you back out." The poor bird-of-paradise seemed to shrink away from her, just as Annelise had. Its beautiful orange flower hung heavy and limp. And no wonder. Plants were like animals in that way, sensitive to their owner's moods. If talking to plants soothed them and encouraged them to grow, surely the excess of emotion that had been coursing through her veins had to have an effect as well. Renée took another step back, dislodging her feet from the muck, but unable to dislodge Annelise's words from her head.

"I know you have a lot on your mind," John said gently, reaching his free hand out to her. "But I know you don't want to take it out on your garden."

She held on to his hand as she stepped clear of the mud and toed off the clogs. She wiggled her toes in the grass. "I'll have to resign as president of the garden club if I keep this up."

"Your secret's safe with me. And I don't think the plants are talking."

She smiled at her husband. The man who had been her rock, her constant, smiled back.

"Come. Let's sit." Using the cane to support them both, he led her to the table with the best view of the flower beds. "Tell me what you're worrying about."

She studied her garden, which seemed to be surviving at the moment despite her rather than because of her. Like John, it had helped keep her sane through the rough patches. "We had a huge fight in the car on the way back from the sheriff's office. She shrieked at me. And I shrieked right back. I told her that she wouldn't have been treated like a child if she hadn't acted like one. I said all kinds of pompous, condescending things. But the truth is she's right. We all ignored what she said. We all refused to believe her. But I'm her sister. I should have done better. I should have listened. I should have done something." The tears were hot on her cheeks, her throat clogged with regret.

John placed his hand on hers. It was curled and arthritic but still warm and strong. "You've always been there for her, Renée. You've done everything you could. None of us ever believed she saw someone that night. It just, well, it was all so far-fetched."

"I know." She still couldn't believe how clearly her sister had described the man's face. How shocked Renée had been when she'd realized where she'd seen it. "I feel so confused. So many things I've always thought are . . . wrong. I want to help figure this out and at the same time I still wish we could just tear the place down."

"I know." John's voice was tender. It was the sweetness in him that had first drawn her, the calm core that helped to center her. "You might have been older, but you lost your father that night, too. Along with your life as you knew it."

Slowly Renée reached in her pocket and pulled out the black-and-white photo that she'd removed from the album. "This is the man Annelise saw. This isn't the only picture of him in Ilse's album. He seems to have been a friend of Ilse's brother. And there are a couple of photos of him with Ilse. They looked as if they might have been more than friends."

She studied the face that Annelise had remembered all these years. The "light" eyes that were most likely blue. The short straight hair cut with military precision that was so light it was most certainly blond. His lips were thin and humorless. If he'd been warm or affectionate in real life, there was no sign of it in his features or his bearing. "This note fell out when I removed the photo." It had been folded up into a tiny square, the creases worn into it over the decades. "It's addressed to Ilse, but that's all I could make out. It's in German.

"I know that emblem on his collar indicates he was in the SS," Renée said. She wasn't sure what the single *S* tattoo in the shape of a lightning bolt stood for, but she could see the faint jagged shadow of it on his skin. "I'm not sure what to do next."

John's face wavered in the sheen of tears that remained now that the flood that had scalded her cheeks had finally slowed. "Why don't you just talk with her?" he said. "We've both spent all these years trying to protect her from what we assumed her mother did. I think we need to stop trying to protect her and include her. Ask her what she thinks should happen next." He reached out to wipe a tear from her face. "I think she'll agree that you should show these pictures and the note to Officer Jackson and Joe Giraldi. One of them might be able to find out who he was and whether the note has anything to do with what happened."

"You make it sound so simple."

"Maybe it will be." His smile crinkled the corners of his basset hound eyes. His face had never looked more beautiful to her than it did now.

"You're a good man, John Franklin," she said.

"And you're the best thing that ever happened to me." He leaned over and kissed her.

"Thank you." She smiled up at him as love and warmth and gratitude flooded through her. "I'm pretty sure my garden thanks you, too."

• • •

Nikki collapsed into the chair that night for sunset, already yawning while Maddie set out cheese and crackers. Avery arrived a few minutes later clutching her ever-present bag of Cheez Doodles and a pitcher of margaritas, which she offered to Nikki.

"No thanks." Nikki tried to smile but she had the feeling that even a whiff of alcohol could put her to sleep. She felt bloated and uncomfortable. All she wanted was to climb into bed and sleep for a week or so. Was that too much to ask?

"You don't look so good," Avery said as she poured a drink for Maddie and then herself.

"Gee, thanks," Nikki replied drily.

"I think what Avery meant to say was you look under the weather," Maddie corrected.

"Yeah." Avery took a long sip of her margarita. "Are you sick?"

"I'm fine," Nikki said, wishing it were true. She hadn't felt like herself since she'd fainted four days ago at Butner. Her head throbbed, seeming to bulge and contract with each remembered moment of the visit with her brother and his pleasure at having so neatly set her up.

"I think you should see a doctor." Maddie speared her with a motherly look of concern.

"No. Visiting Malcolm just, I don't know, it threw me," Nikki said. This, of course, was an understatement of gigantic proportions. "All I need is a good night's sleep and maybe a tranquilizer. Do either of you have one?"

"Just this." Avery raised the pitcher.

"You really aren't yourself," Maddie said. "Don't you think we should make sure it's not something more threatening than Malcolmitis?"

"Definitely not." Today she'd Googled exhaustion, bloating, nausea, and dizziness, and ovarian cancer had sprung up. The disease that had killed her mother when she was even younger than Nikki was now. "I appreciate your concern, Maddie. Really I do. But I am not going to a doctor." She was careful not to look Maddie in the eye as she changed the subject. "Where's Kyra?"

"She was getting the guys organized," Maddie said. "I believe they're headed to Chuck E. Cheese."

They were lost in their own thoughts when Kyra came out and plopped into the chair beside Avery. "I just want to warn you that coming up with a 'good' thing today is going to be a real stretch," she said, reaching for the pitcher. "Unless not having to go to Chuck E. Cheese again counts."

"I'm with you on that one," Avery agreed.

"Works for me," Nikki added.

Maddie looked at the three of them. "I've always promised not to be the 'good enough' police but I can't believe no one here can find *anything* positive to say."

"Believe it," Kyra said, downing half of her drink. "Hey, these margaritas are good."

"Damn straight," Avery said.

"How many have you had?" Maddie asked as Avery poured herself another.

"I'm not sure. I did a lot of tasting while I was making them," Avery replied. "But I think the answer is 'not enough.'"

Nikki eyed the pitcher wishing that the idea of feeling fuzzier than she did now didn't make her want to retch. "Not enough for what?"

"Not enough to tell you what I have to tell you." Avery raised her glass to her lips.

The silence that fell now was absolute. All of their eyes turned to Avery. All of them braced. Nikki knew she didn't want to hear whatever Avery had to tell them, but at least it had momentarily shoved the worry over whether she had inherited something deadly from her mother out of her head.

"Which is?" Kyra prompted.

"Our roofing situation is not good," Avery said in an alcohol-primed rush. "Enrico was practically in tears today. And I'm pretty close to bawling myself."

Avery's mantra had always been "there's no crying in construction." But apparently even a lifetime of repeating something didn't make it true.

"What happened?" Maddie asked in the too-careful voice people used at deathbeds and funerals.

"Enrico opened up the ceiling in the main building and one of the cottages to see how much additional support we'd need to add to shore up the new roofs and decks." She paused, and the expression that flitted across her face made Nikki's stomach clench. "The existing beams are so damaged from age and leaks that it's basically a miracle that none of the roofs have caved in yet."

They sat stunned and silent as Avery explained the finer points of roofs and the beams that reinforced them. Nikki blanked out at the specifics, but the desolation on Avery's face sent tremors of apprehension vibrating up Nikki's spine.

"Even if we didn't add the decks or raise the ceilings—and I really think we need to do both—we'd have to install all new support beams. And given the new codes and the threat of hurricanes, they're going to have to be steel."

"So, we're just talking finding more money?" Maddie asked in that same careful voice. As if the word "just" belonged in that sentence.

"I wish it was that simple, not that money is exactly flowing in." Avery scrubbed at her face, then ran the hand through her hair, leaving it wild and Einstein-ish. "It also puts us way behind schedule before we even really start. There's no point in doing interior work until the interiors have protection from the elements." She drew a deep breath and swiped at her hair again. "Plus we don't have enough money to pay for the rest of the work anyway."

Once again there was silence. Nikki wrapped her arms around herself. Despite the warm breeze coming off the water, she shivered.

"Wow," Kyra said. "I hate to jump all over the negative here, but I don't see how we can afford to produce and air the series when we can't even afford the renovation. And it's not like Renée and Annelise are going to let us just sort of piddle around with their property for the next year while we try to figure it out."

"No one's talking about piddling around," Maddie said, though Nikki thought this was exactly what they were talking about.

"No, but we are looking at having to stop work in order to look for money and then starting again when, and if, we find some. That doesn't sound very workable," Kyra said.

"It's not. And you can't schedule good crews that way," Avery said. "They have other jobs and projects. We don't want to be in the position of finally having the money to do the floors for example and then having to wait for weeks for the floor guys to finish somewhere else."

"We have just about five hundred thousand dollars right now. What can we afford to do with that?" Nikki asked, pretty certain she didn't really want to hear the answer.

"Well," Avery said. "Enrico has offered to be a sponsor, but his workmen will have to be paid, and even at cost the materials are expensive. But basically I think we can replace all the support beams, raise the ceilings, and finish the roofs on all the structures and complete the rooftop deck on the main building."

"That's it?" Kyra asked.

"Well, if we can get Hardin Morgan's pool people on board, we can probably afford to resurface the pool. And I'm pretty sure we can redo the pool deck and all the walkways, which could include the new patios for the cottages if Chase will loan us his crew."

"But that's such a small part of what has to be done," Maddie said. "I mean, there's still windows and doors and plumbing and electrical and . . ." Her voice trailed off.

Avery nodded glumly as she turned to Nikki. "Do you think Bitsy would put up some more money?"

The "no" stuck in Nikki's throat. She cleared it. "I can ask. She really enjoyed the concert and meeting Will, but I don't see it. Pathetic as we feel, I don't think *Do Over* qualifies as a charitable contribution. Which is much more Bitsy's thing."

"What have you found out about the crowdfunding options?" Avery asked.

Nikki sat up carefully. Her head throbbed and her throat was as dry as the Sahara. "I've done some cursory searches on the Internet. Kickstarter looks like the best match for us, but we still need two million dollars. Since you have to wait until all the money is raised before you receive the funds, that leaves us in a really precarious position."

Once again they stared at each other. No one ate or drank. Even Maddie, their resident "glass is half full" representative, had nothing positive or pithy to offer. The Sunshine Hotel and *Do Over* seemed to be trickling through their fingers like the sand in an hourglass.

"Let me take another look and follow up with the companies Ray and I have already reached out to."

"Are you sure you're up to it?" Maddie asked quietly.

"Of course I'm up to it," Nikki lied, even though all she really wanted was to climb into bed, curl up like a baby, and sleep for the next decade or so. Which would be just about how long it would take to forget about her brother's threats, the unlikelihood of raising enough money to save *Do Over*, and the fact that she'd pushed away the one person in the world she wanted to curl up next to.

Chapter Twenty-nine

Bella Flora was big but not, as far as Maddie could see, big enough to absorb the number of egos and emotions currently living inside her. With even the roofing, which was almost all they could afford, on hold until Enrico and his crew completed another job, there was nothing for them to do until they could raise more money. Which meant there were way too many people with far too much time—and stress—on their hands for comfort. Tempers had grown short and squabbles were more frequent.

Avery had taken to alternately pacing and scribbling with occasional indecipherable muttering. Nikki spent her days dialing for dollars and flinching whenever Joe Giraldi's name came up. It was clear she was operating on far fewer cylinders than usual. Like a high-performance vehicle running on regular gas rather than premium, she appeared in desperate need of a tune-up. Kyra and Troy recorded their collective misery, the largely abandoned hotel, and each other. As their sparring and jabbing grew nastier, even Maddie began to question just how full their collective glass really was.

The only occupants of Bella Flora who seemed oblivious

to the seriousness of the problems they faced were Dustin and Steve. Who'd eaten every morsel of food on his plate, drunk half the bottle of wine she'd opened, and devoured his dessert even more eagerly than his grandson.

"Is there more ice cream?" He looked at her expectantly.

"Yes." She turned to the sink and actually stuck her hands in the soapy dishwater so that she would not be tempted to get it for him, serve it to him, or dump it in his lap. *He is not my responsibility. He's a grown man able to take care of himself.*

"It's in the freezer, Dad," Kyra said through what Maddie could tell were gritted teeth. "And maybe you could bring the carton to the table in case anyone else wants more."

"Oh. Right." She heard a chair scrape back and busied herself loading the dishwasher, but heat rose to her cheeks as she thought of how completely she'd catered to him in the long years of their marriage. How even now her first reflex was to jump before he had a chance to say how high.

Small arms wrapped around her thighs and Dustin's small head rested against her hip. She shut off the water and turned to lift him up. "Go night night, Geema?"

"Absolutely." She buried her face in his curls and breathed him in, the most soothing scent in the world.

"I can take him up, Mom," Kyra offered.

"I'll do it. Tonight we're going to read *Penguin on Vacation*."

"Ackasun," Dustin echoed, but his eyes were already getting sleepy.

She took her time reading and then tucking Dustin in. Rituals were important and not just for Dustin. She could use all the soothing she could get before she had to join the others to watch the third episode of *Do Over: Keys Edition*. Another half hour of public humiliation packed with unflattering shots, her stammering fascination with William Hightower, and Deirdre once again in the flesh, so alive and determined to win back Avery. When all of them knew just how the season, and Deirdre's life, would end.

"Is he asleep?" Kyra asked, tapping the open seat on the sofa beside her.

"Before I even got him into bed."

Kyra smiled. "Thank God he's such a great sleeper."

"He's a great everything. You're doing a fabulous job with him."

"I don't feel like I'm doing anything. I think it's living in the middle of all these people who care about him. I guess this is our village." She made a face at Troy's back. "Although there are a few residents I wouldn't mind asking to move. I'd even pack his bag for him."

Maddie was careful not to add "me, too" or look pointedly at Steve. "So."

"So. I made you this." Kyra handed her a piña colada. "I think we could all use some form of fortification for tonight's episode. It's mostly that first night at the Lorelei."

Maddie did her best to hold back a groan. Last week's episode had spotlighted the tension between Avery and Deirdre, the discomfort—at least on Avery's part—with which they collaborated. It had also shown Maddie at her stammering worst intercut with far too many close-ups that revealed the adoration in her eyes as Will had so memorably shared a PB&J "handwitch" with Dustin, a moment that had begun to let her see Will in a more human, less rock god, light.

"This may only be a one- or two-drink episode," Kyra said. "But there's a lot of Deirdre. And the, um, altercation at the Lorelei with those nasty fans."

Maddie drew in a deep breath, settled on the sofa next to Kyra, and raised the glass to her lips. After a brief and still-embarrassing recap of the previous week's episode that included her openmouthed gaping/stammering/beached-fish impression, the opening credits rolled. The episode began with shots of them climbing into the Nautilimo, which resembled a floating pink Cadillac, leaving Troy and his audio guy in a spray of water. Somehow the Lifetime crew had gotten to the

Lorelei ahead of them and captured everything from their arrival in the Nautilimo to the nasty fan couple who'd tried to force a drink on Will. The last shot was a freeze-frame of Maddie as the couple yanked their camera out of her hands. Steve's bark of laughter was loud and automatic.

Good God, Maddie thought.

"Great job, Troy," Avery bit out.

"Yeah, stellar," Nikki added, hoisting herself out of her chair.

"I don't understand how you can live with yourself," Kyra said. "Especially here." Kyra was no longer the only one glaring at Troy. If there'd been a rope and ladder handy, he'd already be swinging from the reclinata palm in the backyard. Maddie wouldn't have lifted a finger to cut him down.

Steve was chuckling and shaking his head. "That moment when the flash went off by accident in your hand, Mad? Priceless!"

"Dad!"

"What?"

"It appears the time has come to say good night." Troy stood and offered a slight bow.

"Good-bye would be even better." Kyra glowered.

With a wince, but no comment, Troy headed to the door. Still chuckling, Steve followed him.

"God, that sucked," Nikki said. "Big-time."

Maddie nodded. "It did." Whatever serotonin had seeped into Maddie's system while she'd put Dustin to bed had evaporated shortly after the opening credits.

"Yeah." Tears shimmered in Avery's eyes. "I can't stand watching Deirdre so alive when I know what's coming. And I can't stand seeing how I treated her."

"I know." Maddie put an arm around Avery's shoulders and pulled her close. "But you had good reason and she knew it. It doesn't matter how long it took you to reconcile, only that you did."

"So much time got wasted." Avery's words were a miserable whisper.

"Yeah." For a long moment they leaned against each other.

"I'm done," Nikki said. "See you guys in the morning."

Avery straightened. "I'm right behind you."

"I'm way too agitated to even try to go to sleep." Kyra looked at her phone. "It's not even nine thirty. I think I'm going to get some air."

"I'll come with you." Maddie couldn't imagine trying to fall asleep, either. Stray bits and pieces of the episode zoomed through her brain like asteroids hurtling toward earth. "Will you guys keep an ear out for Dustin?"

They slipped on flip-flops and walked outside into the warm summer twilight. The breeze was gentle and salt tinged. The palm fronds stirred lazily. The Gulf breathed in and out, exhaling small waves onto the sand and inhaling them back again. Without discussion they took the sandy path toward the jetty and walked out onto the fishing pier.

"We need control over the show and our lives," Kyra said tightly. "I can't stand what Troy and the network have done to our show and us."

"I agree, honey. We all do. But we're completely on hold until we have enough money. And even if we can raise it, we have no guarantee we could reach a real audience with whatever we shot."

"There's got to be a way."

"I know." If only she had some idea of how they could achieve this.

They watched the moon rise and the stars begin to come out, their images reflected on the water. Dark shapes glided beneath the surface and she heard the soft exhalation of air that signaled a dolphin nearby. A sound that Will had once pointed out to her as they'd floated quietly out off one of his favorite flats.

Her phone vibrated in her pocket and she pulled it out. As if summoned by her thoughts, Will's face filled her screen.

"Go ahead," Kyra said. "I'm going to walk a little way down the sidewalk." She nodded up past the dunes and swaying sea oats to the first spill of streetlight.

"Hello?"

"Hi, Maddie-fan." She felt a slight shiver of pleasure at the rich timbre of his voice. "You okay?"

"I'm feeling better now," she said. "I'm pretty sure public humiliation isn't fatal."

"No, it's not," he agreed. "Or I would have been dead long ago."

There was music in the background. The tinkle of glassware. Voices. "Hey, Will, hurry up!" The voice was female and impatient.

"Where are you?" She was careful not to ask about the woman who wanted him to hurry up. *Hurry up and what?*

"The Lorelei. We came out to play a set but we took a break to watch the show. Imagine everyone's surprise when we realized how much of it took place right here. Everyone cheered when you stepped up to block the camera and tried to help protect me from that couple."

"I think it was Hudson and the guys who sent them on their way," she replied.

"But you were fierce, Maddie. Like a lioness protecting a cub."

She blushed with pleasure. "Well, they had no right to demand things like that."

Voices rose in the background. More than one of them was female. She clamped her mouth shut so she wouldn't ask whom he was with. But that was all it took for the doubts to surface and for her nasty subconscious to demand to know just what Maddie had expected.

"When do you think you can get down to visit?" Will asked.

"I don't know. We're on an enforced hiatus. We've got to raise more money before we can do anything else on the property. But I'm not sure I should leave. It's a kind of 'all hands on deck' time." She missed him. Missed how she felt when she was with him. "What's going on with you?"

There was more laughter. She heard him cover the mouthpiece with one hand and immediately imagined some woman brushing up against him, trying to convince him to get off the phone and pay attention to her. *Stop it. For all you know he's just ordering another Coke or a hamburger or something.*

"Things are good. Just busier than I expected. The label wants us to do a mini tour of small venues. Apparently nostalgia is big right now. And I guess I'm old enough to be nostalgic as hell. I think there was a theater in Tampa on the list."

"That would be great. Maybe you could stay on a few days or something." Why was she afraid to come out and invite him?

"I'd like that, Maddie-fan. Let me check the schedule."

"Come on, Will!" It was the same voice. Up close and personal.

She pushed herself off the dock and began to make her way to Kyra. *No. Have a little faith. Will wouldn't have called you if he was with some other woman.*

Ha! her subconscious countered. *You know how that works. He doesn't have to be with them for them to want to be with him.*

Don't start assuming things.

All right, her subconscious shot back when Will told her he had to go. *I won't if you won't.* This was followed by a derisive snort of laughter. Apparently her subconscious not only had an attitude; it had a nasty sense of humor.

Chapter Thirty

"Breathe."

"I am breathing," Avery said.

"No, you're hyperventilating. That's not the same thing."

Avery couldn't quite stop the eye roll or manage to do what Chase suggested. The deep breath she took remained harsh and ragged.

They stood between the pockmarked pool and the entrance to the Sunshine Hotel's main building. The patchwork of tarps that covered the roof snapped in the brisk afternoon breeze. Surf pounded against the sand. "We've been at this for almost six weeks and the property looks even worse than when we began. And Nikki and Ray aren't getting anywhere near the kind of response we were counting on from the list of potential sponsors." She paced several steps, then paced back to Chase's side, not quite able to stay still.

"We have to look at this from a different angle," Chase said. "And that's hard to do without enough oxygen to the brain."

She drew another breath, let it out. Still ragged. "What other angle is there?" she asked, crossing her arms over her chest. "I mean, I thought we were in budget hell with the network, but at least there *was* a budget."

"I think we need to rethink the scope of the project," Chase said. "Let go of the elements that aren't critical and then pick a few key places to wow the shit out of everybody."

She paced toward the building, came back again. But this time the thought made it past the layer of panic. Deirdre had had a similar approach to design when money was tight, something she'd dealt with on her father's projects before she went to Hollywood, and on their *Do Over* budgets, which had been intentionally miniscule. A few small, really expensive accents or an eye-popping fabric on a couple of throw pillows were like a magician's sleight of hand. A means of making the audience focus where the magician wanted their attention. "That's not entirely stupid," she conceded.

"Gee, thanks."

She thought about the property. What mattered most. "So we pour in as much as we can here." She nodded to the building in front of them. "Spalike locker rooms, fabulous beachy-chic dining room, comfortable yet luxurious lobby/reception area. All high ceilings, glass walls, acres of terrazzo. And the killer roof deck. Where we'll have the most exciting sunset viewing experience on the west coast of Florida."

"Exactly." Chase nodded enthusiastically.

"And the cottages?" she asked after a less ragged breath.

"I say we focus on getting them weather tight and deal with them once we have more money in place. My crew will be available soon."

"If they can cut up the old concrete then repour the decking, the walkways, and maybe the new patios, we can help with the grunt work," Avery said.

"Have I mentioned that hearing you talk construction turns me on almost as much as when you're covered in sawdust?"

"Blueprint." She arched an eyebrow. "Header. Foundation."

She drew out the last word in mock-suggestive breathiness. She laughed but didn't push him away when he nuzzled her neck. The kiss was sweet and meant, she knew, to soothe more than excite. But nothing could completely distract her from their number one problem: their budget or lack of one. "Even scaling down and relying on sleight of hand, we're still going to need more money than we're likely to get." A lack of funds might be the mother of invention, but a renovation of any size could not be done with creativity alone.

"Well, Hardin Morgan Construction wants in."

"That's sweet, Chase, but . . ."

"Seriously, Avery. Dad asked me to remind you that the firm's behind you. We'll even work for peanuts." He smiled. "Some of us might even be willing to settle for kisses. Or other demonstrations of affection."

Her eyes blurred with tears.

"Plus Enrico's not the only Dante who wants in. And God knows that family has enough skilled artisans to build a city. Roberto even offered to bring his houseboat up and dock nearby to handle the carpentry."

Her heart actually leapt at the thought of Roberto Dante, the head-bobbing, tie-dye-wearing former hippie carpenter, who had done so much for Mermaid Point.

"You know I have a huge crush on that man."

"Yeah. Apparently the feeling's mutual," Chase replied. "I'm twisting arms over at our pool company. And Dad put in a call to our window and door people. We'll find a way to make it happen."

"It means a lot to me having you so on board. And I want to believe we can pull it off. I really do. But even if we rebuilt this place with our own two hands, we have to have enough money for materials and furnishings. I'm trying, but it feels kind of like trying to believe in the Easter Bunny and Santa Claus despite all evidence to the contrary."

"It's not a matter of trying, Avery. You believe or you don't." Chase slung an arm around her shoulders and pulled her close. "You need to get all the way on board, or I'm going to have to give you some serious noogies." He knuckled his fist in her hair.

She snorted. "What are you, like ten?"

He grinned, unrepentant, but he dropped his hand. "And I wouldn't let Maddie hear you doubting. That's a very half-empty attitude you've got going."

"Are you kidding? I'd be happy if the glass were only half empty. I'm afraid there might be a huge hole in the bottom."

"It's going to be okay, Avery," he said with a certainty she wished she could feel. "And I wouldn't count Nikki out, either. Even under the weather like she's been lately, she's a hard woman to say no to."

• • •

"No, I'm sorry. But the answer is no." Bitsy Baynard's voice on the phone was clear and firm. Allowing for absolutely no wiggle room. "Things are a little tight at the moment. In fact, I'm going to have to withdraw some of what I originally promised."

Nikki slumped in the passenger seat of Ray's Cadillac. It was the first day of July. The thermometer showed ninety-one humidity-filled degrees. She'd aimed all of the vents at herself and turned the fan to high when he'd run into the 7-Eleven. Despite the ferocity with which the air-conditioning was blowing on her, she could feel sweat dampening her hair and dripping between her breasts. She felt distinctly light-headed as she wondered just how tight things could be for someone with Bitsy's resources.

A text dinged in. She swiped the screen to take a look. *Malcolm.* Perspiration dotted her upper lip. Her pulse thrummed in her veins. He'd begun texting her at all hours of the day and night. Small bursts of words carefully crafted to look innocuous but meant to bully and intimidate. *How's Joe? Have you been traveling lately?*

She blotted at her face with a crumpled tissue trying to keep her thoughts on the phone call. Bitsy had stood by her when others had not; she'd been unfailingly generous. "No problem, I completely understand. Please let me know if anything changes." They said their good-byes and hung up. Nikki deleted Malcolm's text as she had all the others and stuck her face right up against the nearest AC vent as the car door opened.

"Are you all right?" Ray slid into the driver's seat, dropped a plastic bag on the floor of the backseat, and gave her an appraising look. "You don't look so good."

"Good God. Why does everyone think they have the right to weigh in on my appearance?" Even Dustin had put a small hand out to cup her cheek and said, "Nik-key have owie?" "What happened to manners and common courtesy?"

"Sorry," Ray said. "It's just that your face is so white that . . . hold on." He pulled a bottled water out of the plastic bag, unscrewed the cap, and put it to her lips.

"What are you doing?"

"Shh. Drink." He tilted the bottle up so that she had no other option. "I think you might be dehydrated."

"No. Wait." The water dribbled down her chin, then sloshed down her throat when she stopped talking. She gagged slightly. Swallowed. Drank some more. The water was cold in her dry, parched throat. When she'd drunk all she could, she pushed his hand away. Swallowed one last time. "Don't ever do that again."

He raised both hands palm out. "Sorry. Just trying to help."

"I am not dehydrated." She looked down at the cream blouse now dotted with water stains. "I'm soaked now. But not dehydrated." She glanced down at her watch, drew a steadying breath. "We need to get going. I don't want to be late for our appointment."

"Yes, ma'am. Rearden Lighting coming right up." He put the car in gear and backed out of the parking space. She closed her eyes against the sun's glare but she could feel his eyes on her. "You know, we could postpone this meeting. Or you could wait in the car while I go in."

"No."

"We could postpone and I could take you to a walk-in clinic. Just to make sure there's nothing wrong."

"No." This time she opened her eyes. But was careful not to let them show fear. She'd never felt this awful for this long. Not since she'd had mono in high school.

Another text dinged in. She didn't look at it. She tried to turn her thoughts to the upcoming meeting and pitch, but her mind once again filled with memories of her mother's horrible decline, the way she'd wasted away until her body finally shut down.

"I'm worried about you, Nikki."

"Hmmm?" She tried to focus on what Ray was saying. But her thoughts and worries were spinning in a rush of color and noise, like a merry-go-round whirling out of control.

"Nothing," he said. He turned into the lighting company's parking lot and put the car in park. "Seriously, Nikki. Why don't you just wait here and let me . . ."

"No." Another text. Another worried look from Ray. She graspsed the door handle and pushed the door open. One foot hit the pavement.

"Wait, let me help you!" Ray was out of his door and racing around the car even as she levered herself out of hers. "Lord, you are stubborn."

"You're not the first person to say that," she said, holding on to the door as the world and Ray went in and out of focus. She blinked rapidly, attempted to catch her breath. "And you probably won't be the last." A blast of hot humid air hit her. The merry-go-round sped up. The music became a screech. She took a step. Forced herself to take another. "You see. I'm perfectly all . . ." She did not finish her thought, her sentence, or her step. Her knees buckled and she fell face-first. The last thing she saw was the concrete rising up to meet her.

Chapter Thirty-one

"Hello?" Joe Giraldi's image on the iPhone screen was large enough to reveal a polite smile. His voice came through loud and clear.

"Hello!" Annelise shouted.

"You don't have to yell," Renée said to Annelise, who sat next to her. Both of them were staring at the iPhone propped upright against a small stack of books on Renée's kitchen table. Joe Giraldi's face filled the screen. Their heads, which might have been gray-and-white Q-tips over faces too small to decipher, filled a small box in the corner.

"Thank you for talking to us!" Annelise shouted again as she strained toward the phone, her hands tightly clenched on the table.

"My pleasure," the special agent said. "I got your message and I wanted to let you know that we have a name for the officer in the photos."

Renée felt her sister's start of surprise.

"Who is he?" Renée asked.

"His name is Heinrich Stottermeir."

They waited for Agent Giraldi to continue. "He was pretty

high up in the SS. Not a particularly nice fellow from what I've heard so far. But he was born and raised in Frankfurt."

The photos had made it clear that he'd had some sort of connection to Annelise and her family. "He and Ilse's brother Erik were childhood friends, started their careers together in the Hitler Youth movement. Erik joined a panzer unit. Heinrich moved up the ranks of the secret police."

Renée thought of the photo of him with his arm around Ilse, Ilse's brother on her other side. "I have someone doing a record search in Germany, but a lot of civil records didn't survive the bombing. The Nazis, on the other hand, were quite compulsive about record keeping. Heinrich Stottermeir was reported missing and presumed dead on the Russian front in December of 1944."

"Oh." Annelise drooped in disappointment. There was a tinge of the breathiness that had been absent in her voice thus far. "If he was already dead, then he couldn't have been here."

Renée leaned forward, her eyes on Joe's face. "But we saw him," Renée said. "We have the sketch, and I know I saw him somewhere near the hotel." After all the years of refusing to consider Annelise's insistence on an intruder, all she wanted now was for someone to prove it to be true.

"We're going to follow this lead as far as it will take us," Joe said.

"But what is there to follow if he was dead eight years before our father was killed?" Annelise wrung her hands in distress.

Renée slipped an arm around Annelise's shoulders, but she wasn't sure whether she was trying to give or receive comfort.

"It wasn't unusual for MIAs and other reports from a battlefield to be wrong. And I am curious what someone that high up the chain of command would have been doing on the Russian front," Joe said. "That late in the war there were certainly Germans who had reason to 'disappear.'"

Annelise's eyes were wide. "But how will we ever know for sure?"

"We may not," he said gently. "It's still an avenue we have to look into."

"But how?" Annelise asked again.

"I've been checking in with friends in different areas of intelligence. One of them referred me to a guy who was originally with the OSS, the predecessor of the CIA. He's retired in Sarasota. I have an appointment to see him. I'm taking the photo and note you sent me, in case he's fluent in German. I thought I'd come up to share what I find out and check in with Officer Jackson."

"We'd appreciate it," Renée said truthfully. Annelise nodded but remained silent.

"I'll be there Wednesday afternoon. Why don't we meet at the realty office at three?"

"That would be great. Thanks." Renée prepared to hang up, but Joe didn't move.

"So, um, how's the renovation going?" he asked.

"There's a bit of a holdup," Renée said. "Some problem with the roofs and support beams I think."

Joe nodded. "And, how's everyone at Bella Flora?" he asked tentatively.

Renée bit back a smile. "As far as I know, everyone's fine."

"Good. That's, um, good," Joe said. "I'll see you both on Wednesday, then. At three o'clock." There was one last hesitation before he disappeared from Renée's iPhone screen.

"What was that about?" Annelise asked as Renée levered herself out of her seat and then stood, waiting for the kinks in her body to straighten out.

Slowly Renée moved to the refrigerator to retrieve the pitcher of iced tea. "Let's just say I don't think it's *everyone* at Bella Flora that Agent Giraldi is concerned about."

...

"Nikki?"

Nikki's eyes blinked open only to close as they encountered

the glare of some kind of overhead light. Footsteps quick and sure moved closer. She tried to concentrate on the voice, tried to figure out why it felt familiar, but reaching a conclusion required too much effort. She didn't have the energy to slog through the cotton wool that seemed to have been stuffed inside her head. The footsteps drew nearer—multiple sets.

"Nik?" The voice was warm and comforting. The hand that clasped one of hers was callused but gentle. This time when she opened her eyes a face had replaced the glare. *Maddie.*

Avery stood behind her. Nikki blinked again. Ray Flamingo sat in a leatherette recliner.

"Wow. You look like you landed on your face," Avery observed. "It's a bloody mess."

Nikki's hand moved of its own volition to her cheek. She winced as her fingers made contact.

"You're gonna have a real shiner," Avery said. "Maybe two."

Maddie shot Avery a look.

"Sorry. Just sayin' . . ."

Nikki closed her eyes and groaned. Even that hurt.

"What happened?" Maddie poured a glass of water from a plastic pitcher and brought it to Nikki's lips.

Nikki's eyes narrowed. "You!" she said to Ray.

"What?" He stood and moved behind Avery and Maddie.

"You poured water down my throat. I thought I was going to drown."

"I was trying to hydrate you," he sniffed.

"I don't think 'hydrate' is supposed to be a verb," Nikki said as memory slammed into her. "And hydrating against someone's will?"

Avery and Maddie turned to look up at Ray.

"She did not pass out because I gave her a drink of water."

No, she'd passed out because she had a brain tumor. Or cancer. An incurable kind. Like her mother.

"The paramedics thought you were dehydrated, too," Ray

said. "And that you might have had a concussion from hitting your forehead on the pavement."

"There were paramedics?"

"Yes," Ray said. "They brought you to the hospital in an ambulance. "

"I was in an ambulance?" Oh, God. How could she not remember this?

"Oh, yeah. I raced right behind it all the way down to the hospital. You were starting to rouse when they were wheeling you into the emergency room."

"Wheeling me?"

"Yeah. You know, on the gurney." He leaned in to get a closer look at her. "You really don't remember?"

She shook her head. Which was when she discovered that her face hurt.

"So what happened?" Avery asked.

Nikki couldn't remember anything after the forced hydration. *Definitely a brain tumor.* She looked up at the clock on the wall but had no idea how many hours might have been lost.

"We were in the Rearden Lighting parking lot. We had an appointment to pitch them on sponsorship," Ray said.

"Right." Nikki nodded carefully, trying not to use any of her facial features, all of which were throbbing.

"One minute Nikki was getting out of the car. The next she was planting her face in the concrete."

"That would explain the gravel marks on your chin and cheekbones," Maddie said.

Nikki ran her tongue over her cracked lips and came away with dirt and grit. It encountered something jagged in her mouth and she groaned. "I must have bitten my tongue. And"— she stuck two fingers in her mouth—"I think I thipped a tooth."

"That's a nasty bump on your forehead, too," Avery observed. "It kind of looks like a baseball."

Nikki's fingers moved to her forehead. She winced. "Oh, God. Does somebody have a mirror?"

"No," Maddie said before anyone else could answer. "There are no mirrors here." She moved as she spoke so that Nikki couldn't see whatever was behind her. "The nurse said the doctor will be in shortly." She gave Avery and Ray a look. "I'm sure the swelling will go down. In a few days no one will be able to tell anything happened."

"I don't know," Avery said. "That's one of the biggest honking . . ."

Maddie cut her off with her "I'm the mother here, don't mess with me" look. Ray grabbed Avery's elbow. "Come on, girlfriend," he said. "Let's go make sure there's enough money in the meters." He yanked Avery out the door.

After they left Maddie puttered, refilling Avery's water, repositioning the straw, straightening the paper pillow behind Nikki's head. In the quiet Nikki attempted to assess the damage. Her head, which had felt oddly light and puffy, now pounded. Her face felt like one big scrape. The tooth was definitely chipped. Her nose seemed to still be in one piece; was she imagining that it tilted to one side?

"Ms. Grant?" The doctor stood inside the doorway. She was an attractive woman with chin-length dark hair, a firm jaw, and clear gray eyes framed in dark rectangular glasses. Her white coat covered what looked like a runner's body. "I'm Dr. Gracen. You took quite a fall." She came to the examining table. "Can you follow my finger?" She held up one no-nonsense finger and moved it back and forth, up and down.

"Good." She jotted something on her clipboard. "So, we ran blood work when you first came in." The doctor hesitated. Looked at Maddie. "I have something to share with you that is of a . . . personal nature."

"Oh. Excuse me." Maddie turned to go. "I'll just step out."

"No." Nikki reached for Maddie. She did not want to find out that she was dying without someone else present. Some-one who would care that Nikki's life would be over. Her thoughts turned to Joe, whom she'd shoved out of her life. Her hand clenched tighter to Maddie's wrist. "Maddie's like family to me." Better than family because she didn't judge her or want her to go do something illegal on her behalf. "She can hear whatever you have to say."

"Okay." The doctor moved closer. She had a strangely expectant look on her face. "So in addition to dehydration, we found hCG levels that indicate you're . . ."

Maddie started in surprise. Nikki had no idea what the doctor was talking about. "HCG?" Had she heard those letters together during her mother's illness?

Nikki swallowed. "Is—is that hereditary?" she asked, trying to brace for the bad news.

"I'm sorry?" the doctor said.

Maddie's brown eyes plumbed Nikki's. Her mouth had gone slack with shock.

"What do I have?" Nikki whispered even as she tried to swallow back her fear. "How long do I have to live?"

Dr. Gracen's brow furrowed. "Under most circumstances, motherhood is not considered a life-threatening condition."

"Unless you have a teenage girl." Maddie's lips twitched. "Then there are times you long for death."

"What are you talking about?" Nikki couldn't seem to process what was being said. Between her galloping heart and the pounding in her head, her hearing had gone muzzy.

"You're pregnant," the doctor said. "HCG is called the pregnancy hormone. Based on your levels, I'm guessing you're about six weeks along."

"How could this have happened?"

Maddie and Dr. Gracen simply stared at her, brows raised.

"I'm too old. My eggs are . . . I thought my eggs had expired!" Blood whooshed in her veins, pounded in her ears.

Dr. Gracen laughed. "We're talking the miracle of birth here, not the dairy aisle at the grocery store."

"Joe will be so thrilled," Maddie said, her face glowing with excitement. "Now you can stop worrying that you can't give him the family you think he deserves."

"No." Nikki shook her head in a vain attempt to clear it. This could not be happening. It should not be happening. She was too old. She'd been told she couldn't have children. She wasn't meant to be a mother. "You can't tell him. I don't . . . I can't . . . I have to think about this before I . . ."

"Of course you'll be the one to give him the news." Maddie was still positively glowing with happiness. "Renée said he's coming in on Wednesday. Something about the intruder they think was in the family apartment that night. He'll be over the moon when you tell him."

"No. I'm not. I can't." Nikki shook her head, trying to clear it, hardly able to hear her own words over the roaring in her head. She heard Malcolm's voice, though. His snide comments and threats about Joe. *Joe.* "I'll tell him later. When I'm ready. When I'm sure that . . ." She didn't finish the thought or the sentence. For the second time that day her world went black. But at least this time she was already in a hospital with a doctor at her side. And no concrete was involved.

Chapter Thirty-two

Bella Flora's doorbell chimed with increasing frequency late Monday afternoon as guests began to arrive for what had been billed as a casual cookout but which Avery envisioned as a rallying of the troops and an opportunity to try to explain to Annelise and Renée what was, and was not, happening.

Maddie had been in preparation mode since early that morning making bowls of homemade potato salad and cole-slaw, forming hamburgers stuffed with a cheese, bacon, and mushroom mixture that would have had Avery salivating if she hadn't been so nervous.

Careful not to get in Maddie's way, she'd filled a cooler with beers and soft drinks for Chase to take outside to the loggia and had helped Jeff settle at the wrought-iron table near the grill so that he could help supervise. Her heart had almost stopped with gladness when Roberto Dante's house-boat, which she'd christened the *House of the Rising Sun* down in Islamorada due to the cabin roof's streaks of pink and red paint, had appeared just off the seawall. Her heart had started beating again when the carpenter had beeped and waved before turning to head toward the St. Petersburg

Yacht Club at Pass-a-Grille, where John and Renée Franklin had organized a boat slip.

"I think his engine is smoking," Chase said as the houseboat putted east through the pass into the bay for its short trip north.

"I'm pretty sure it's not his engine that's smoking," Avery replied. Although she'd never seen him handle a hammer while stoned, the carpenter's tie-dyed clothing, long gray ponytail, and soul patch weren't the only part of the seventies he'd clung to. "I hope the yacht club is a tolerant sort of place and that no one ends up with a contact high."

"It is kind of hard to believe he and Enrico are related."

Avery smiled at the comparison. Even Mario, a South Florida master plasterer and tile man who'd helped with the Art Deco Streamline home they'd renovated on South Beach, had been far more conservative. "Their life choices are pretty different, but the Dantes are all incredibly talented. None of our renovations would have turned out half as fabulous without them."

"It's all in finding the right people for the right job," Jeff pronounced just as her father always had.

She nodded and smiled but she felt akin to a passenger on the *Titanic* who'd just realized there was no room left in the lifeboats. Nothing about this project had gone as hoped or planned; how exactly were they supposed to put a good spin on that?

"It'll be all right. We can pull off this renovation." Chase squeezed her hand.

"Not without money we can't," she said quietly.

"Don't look at the whole thing. Just focus on the next hurdle. Then the one after that."

Avery resisted pointing out that her legs were far too short for track and field. "Enrico's waiting for Roberto at the yacht club and will bring him over as soon as he's tied up. I guess we'll hash this out when we've got everyone under one roof."

Dustin played nearby in the playhouse replica of Bella Flora that his father had given him their first Christmas on Pass-a-Grille. The tool belt she and Chase had given him was strapped around his small hips. As she watched, he retrieved a child-sized screwdriver and pretended to tighten a screw.

The doorbell chimed again. With Maddie handling kitchen duties and Nikki still MIA, Avery went to answer it. She opened the door to John and Renée Franklin, who flanked Annelise.

There were hugs all around. Annelise carried a bakery box. Renée held a bunch of fresh-picked flowers and a bottle of wine. Avery escorted them back to the kitchen, where Maddie took the cake box from Annelise and accepted the fruits of Renée's garden with exclamations of delight while Kyra filled bowls with snacks. Avery pinched a Cheez Doodle and examined its puffy cheesiness as Maddie made Renée, John, and Annelise welcome. Within moments each had a cold drink and were basking in Maddie's attention as she pulled a vase from a cupboard and began arranging the flowers into an impromptu centerpiece. Avery popped the Cheez Doodle into her mouth, determined to enjoy its puffy perfection as the Franklins followed Kyra outside. She was licking the cheese coating from her fingers when the doorbell rang again.

"I'll get it," Avery said. "But where's Nikki?"

"In her room," Maddie said, giving the centerpiece a final tweak.

"I don't know why I asked. She's been in there all weekend." Avery pinched another Cheez Doodle, which she wasted no time examining.

"She's still pretty beat up. Said she was worried about scaring people."

The doorbell rang again.

"I'm coming, hold your horses." Avery devoured the Cheez Doodle and then began to lick the cheese from her fingers. It was a calming and satisfying ritual. "I'd really like Nikki to be a part of the discussion tonight." With a last lick she left the kitchen and headed for the foyer.

She opened the door to a stooped and wrinkled older gentleman with a shock of white hair hanging over one eye. A Colonel Sanders mustache drooped on either side of his mouth. "Ma'am." He removed his planter's hat and bowed slightly. "I do believe I've been invited to a cookout here." The drawl was pronounced. The hand that swept the white hair off his wrinkled forehead was dotted with age spots.

"Oh. Come in." She stopped just short of calling him "colonel." "You must be a friend of the Franklins." And, she hoped, a potential sponsor. "Let me take you to them." She led him down the central hallway, walking slowly, mindful of his age and his measured steps behind her.

Steve Singer looked up from the beer he was drinking when they stepped out onto the loggia. Troy began to reach for his camera. Kyra froze for an instant, then gave him a shake of her head.

When Avery and the elderly gentleman reached the table, John Franklin looked up curiously, but it was Dustin whose face lit up.

"Dundell!" He ran at the old man as if he was planning to jump into his arms. Avery reached out to intercept him.

"It's all right, young lady." The man's voice was still old and slow, but there was something new in it. Avery turned to see the man's face begin to change. A dimple appeared from nowhere. His smile as he opened his arms to the little boy was quick and dazzling.

"Dundell!" Dustin launched himself into the man's arms. "You comed to git me!"

"I sure did, Dustbin! I never could fool you."

Kyra looked up, and for a brief moment her face looked as happy as her son's. Troy glowered at the movie star. Steve Singer got up, offered a curt nod, and walked inside.

"I take it this is not, in fact, Colonel Sanders come to

deliver a bucket of extra crispy." Chase smiled and reached out a hand. "Chase Hardin." He shook the liver-spotted hand quite vigorously. "This is my dad, Jeff. Dad, I'm pretty sure this is Daniel Deranian."

Daniel winked and smiled his movie star smile, complete with gleaming white teeth. As he straightened and allowed his true self to emerge, it became difficult to understand how she could have been fooled so completely. With a shrug Avery headed back to the kitchen. Hearing raised voices, she hesitated in the hallway.

"Just who does he think he is?" Steve demanded in an almost childlike whine.

"I think he knows exactly who he is," Maddie replied tartly. "He's Dustin's father. He's also the person who gave your daughter, and by extension the rest of us, this beautiful roof over our heads." Drawers were yanked opened and slammed shut. Silverware rattled. "And I think you need to try a little harder to remember that."

Impressed with Maddie's assertiveness, Avery poked her head in to the kitchen. "Anything I can do to help?" She looked meaningfully at Steve, hoping that Maddie would ask her to show him to the door. Or allow her to encourage him to take a long walk off a short pier.

"Steve's going to go help Chase light the grill," Maddie said in a tone that brooked no argument. "Can you let Nikki know that dinner will be on the table in twenty-five minutes or so?"

"What, you're not planning to send a tray up to Her Majesty?" Avery asked.

Maddie turned the cease-and-desist mother stare she'd been aiming at Steve on Avery. "I don't think she's feeling any better than she looks. It'll do her good to come down. But be gentle."

Avery snorted, marched up the stairs. She knocked briskly on Nikki's bedroom door.

There was no answer or movement. Avery knocked louder.

"Go away." The voice warbled noticeably. "I don't feel good."

"Yeah, I get that," Avery said. "But you need to come downstairs."

"I can't come down. I'm . . ." The voice trailed off as if its owner simply didn't have the strength to finish the sentence.

"You have to come down," Avery replied through the door. "We're going to be explaining the issues with the renovation and the budget and we need a show of solidarity."

"I'm sorry. I can't."

"You mean you won't." Avery felt her temper rise.

Nikki didn't respond. Nor did she open the door.

Avery jiggled the doorknob. She had the oddest urge to put her shoulder to the door and force it open.

"Go away!" The voice had gathered power. "I told you. I'm not coming down."

And people called *her* stubborn. Without debating the advisability of what she was doing, Avery reached into her back pocket, pulled out the screwdriver she'd used earlier, and stuck it into the center of the knob. One twist and the lock popped open.

"Hey!" Nikki's voice was indignant. But there wasn't a whole lot of energy behind it.

"Sorry." Avery pushed the door open and walked into the bedroom. Nikki wore ragged cutoff shorts and a hacked-off T-shirt. She sat on top of the rumpled covers with her legs drawn up to her chest. Avery had never seen her so poorly dressed, not even on Mermaid Point in the sauna of a Keys summer. The sight of Nicole's raggedy clothing was almost more frightening than the black eyes, the swollen cut lip, and the huge lump on her forehead.

"Wow." Avery came closer, unable to take her eyes off Nikki's battered face. "I think this is when you're supposed to say, 'you should see the other guy.'" Avery winced. It actually hurt to look at her. "Only there is no other guy."

"I can't come down like this." Nikki wrapped her arms around her legs, rested her chin on her knees.

The doorbell chimed downstairs. The sound of the door opening and Maddie's greeting reached them. It sounded as if the Dantes had arrived. "You do look like shit," she conceded.

"Yeah, well, that's not exactly a news flash." Nikki sighed, which made her look even more pathetic.

"Listen, I'm sorry you don't feel good. But Maddie said to bring you down. We need someone who can put a good spin on things. My face gets all red and blotchy. I totally suck at it."

"While I'm highly skilled." Nikki's voice had turned droll. Which was slightly better than pathetic.

"I didn't mean that exactly," Avery backpedaled. "But you were a matchmaker. And that requires playing up assets and downplaying liabilities, right? It would help if you could, you know, highlight all the potential sponsors you think might still be interested."

"There are no potential sponsors we can count on. Some of our sponsors have actually taken back part of what they pledged."

"It's not like you to be so defeatist," Avery said. "The Nikki I know doesn't give up as soon as things get a little tough."

"Yeah, well, maybe you don't know me as well as you think you do. Hell, I barely recognize myself." The pathetic tone was back. "And FYI, I think we're way beyond 'a little tough.'"

Avery stood not caring whether she jiggled the bed or not. "You know what? You go ahead and sit up here feeling sorry for yourself all you want. But just remember, it's not only yourself you're letting down."

· · ·

It was a tight fit around the loggia table, but Maddie thought everyone enjoyed the meal. By the time they'd finished it off with Annelise's Bavarian fruit tart and Kyra's brownies, the sun was close to setting. Dustin drowsed in his father's lap presenting the oddest picture: Colonel Sanders and child. Maddie could practically see Avery building up the nerve to discuss the renovation, but it was John Franklin who exchanged a look with his wife and sister-in-law and said, "We noticed that things are not progressing on the property. Is there a problem?"

Avery squirmed in her seat. Large red blotches appeared on her cheeks. "We've encountered a few budget issues," Avery said carefully. "A bit of a shortfall."

"Meaning?" he asked.

Avery cleared her throat. "Meaning we haven't been able to raise quite as much money as we need to complete the project."

"How much more do you need?" Renée asked.

Maddie would have given a lot for Nikki's calm confidence at the table even if it was a façade. Another blotch appeared on Avery's neck.

"To do everything we want to do and have it turnkey for a buyer/operator we'd need another two million dollars." She swallowed. "At the moment we have enough to complete all the roofs and the pool and the decking and walkways, as well as the new patios."

"But that's not even half of what needs to be done," Annelise said.

"We have a lot of companies committed to the project," Chase said. "A number of our suppliers have agreed to donate materials in exchange for television exposure. Most other materials will be provided at cost. So in many cases we're just looking at labor. I have a crew ready to start pulling up the old concrete and then we'll focus on the main building while Enrico and his crew begin on the roofs."

John and Renée bent their heads together. Annelise stared out over the water where the final sunbeams glittered. Dustin was slumped against his father completely asleep. Daniel was listening and watching the conversation with interest.

Enrico stood and removed his baseball cap, held it between gnarled fingers. His bald head reflected the last glimmers of sunshine. "We can begin on the roofs and support beams as soon as we finish our current job in just a few days," he said. "We, too, will need only enough money to pay for the cost of the materials and labor. I have put out a call to the *famiglia*." He aimed a slight bow in Maddie's direction. "Even Mario has offered to come up from Miami to handle the plaster and any tile work if we need him. And I think to see the lovely Signora Singer."

Maddie blushed at the reminder of Mario's gentle interest. Steve scowled. Troy and Kyra shot the proceedings from every conceivable angle.

Roberto stood next. His ponytail hung down between his knobby shoulders; his weathered skin resembled leather. "I'm here for the duration." He bobbed his head gently. "I'm sure that between me and Chase and Jeff and their crew, we can handle all the carpentry. My good friend Fred Strahlendorf has asked if he can come up and take care of the electrical at cost."

"And we still have potential sponsors to follow up with," Ray said. "That effort is far from over."

"Devotion is admirable, but what happens if you run out of money before you can finish?" John asked.

Daniel shifted Dustin into the crook of his arm. He looked as if he wanted to speak but remained silent.

"We're not going to let that happen," Ray said.

"Avery, Nikki, and I have all agreed to put in what we have left from the sale of Bella Flora," Maddie said, ignoring Steve's start of surprise.

"It's not ideal, but it's not unheard of to do a project in phases," Jeff added. "Once the roofs are sound and the structures are weather tight, there's no longer a rush in dealing with the interiors."

"But we can't let this drag on forever," Annelise said.

"We've waited more than thirty years," Renée said. "I think we can give them time to finish the project."

"But what if they get halfway through and can't finish?" John asked. "That would present a lot of problems in finding a buyer."

"We're not going to let that happen," Avery said.

"I'd like to help," Daniel said. "I could contribute to the renovation budget."

Kyra lowered her camera. "Thanks," she said. "I know we all appreciate the offer. But you've already done more than enough."

"What if I just cover the amount the Franklins and Miss Handleman have invested?" he asked, looking at Renée and Annelise. "Plus whatever it would cost to tear down the structures in the extremely unlikely event the project couldn't be completed?"

"That's not going to be necessary," Avery said again.

Maddie watched Daniel's face. He was offering hundreds of thousands of dollars with the same ease she might offer fifty.

"Then the money I'm offering isn't at risk," Daniel said reasonably. "But it might make everyone more comfortable."

Renée, Annelise, and John exchanged glances. It was John who gave the final nod.

It wasn't the kind of victory that seemed to demand a celebration. No one lingered long after the table was cleared. Daniel carried Dustin upstairs. Kyra trailed behind them, ostensibly to finish packing up Dustin's things; she'd agreed to let him go on location with his father, a decision Maddie knew would not sit well with Tonja Kay. Not that Kyra had asked Maddie's opinion or permission.

She gave the countertops a final swipe and brushed her hair off her face. She was tired, but also relieved. Nothing was going as well as any of them had hoped, but at least they could move forward.

The doorbell rang. For once Steve sprang into action without being prodded. She heard the front door open.

"Is Maddie here?" The voice was male. The sound of it had her removing her apron, swiping at her hair again, and hurrying toward the front door.

"Is she expecting you?" Steve's voice was belligerent; his body seemed to be barring the way.

Maddie stepped up behind him.

"There you are. I know it's late. We have rehearsal tomorrow in Tampa and . . . well, I apologize for taking you by surprise."

"It's the best surprise ever." She stepped around Steve in a hurry to get to Will. "This is Steve Singer. My . . . my ex-husband." She drew a deep breath. Telling herself she was not responsible for Steve or his feelings, she completed the introduction. "Steve, I don't think you've been formally introduced before, but this is William Hightower." She did not call him her boyfriend or even her main squeeze. She simply threw her arms around William's neck and kissed him.

Chapter Thirty-three

Kyra reached over to grasp one droopy end of Daniel's Colonel Sanders mustache. Slowly she pulled it away from his skin. The white wig had been crammed into the planter's hat, which sat next to the discarded white jacket. His dark hair stood on end, sweaty from its confinement. White powder still coated his face and hands, obscuring his normally golden skin. Dustin slept in the center of her bed, one thumb tucked into his mouth, his index finger curled around the bridge of his nose. An open suitcase sat near him.

"If I'd known the paparazzi had completely abandoned you, I wouldn't have bothered with the disguise." He rubbed at the glue that had anchored the mustache.

"They didn't abandon us. We bored them into going away." It had been such a relief not to be constantly under surveillance.

"I wasn't joking when I told you that you need them, Kyra." He pulled off the bushy white eyebrows as he spoke. "If you really want to create and air your own version of *Do Over*, you need more than money. You need an audience."

"I wish you hadn't pledged that money. I don't want to keep asking you for things."

"You didn't ask. In fact, you're one of the few people I know who never does. I was glad to do it."

Seeing how ready he was for the subject to change, she went to the dresser to retrieve a pair of pajamas and a stack of shorts and T-shirts, then tucked them into Dustin's suitcase alongside a Pass-a-Grille sweatshirt and his favorite sneakers. "I've packed a week's worth of Pull-Ups. He does okay with big-boy underwear during the day—as long as someone's paying attention. But nighttime's a different story. He needs his . . ."

"I know, Kyra. I've done this before. And Dustin's not exactly shy about saying what he needs and wants."

This was true. But that was surrounded by family. A movie set would be filled with strangers. "But what about . . ."

"Tabitha Marlowe is already in Montana. You saw her résumé and spoke to her references," Daniel said. "She's the best there is, Kyra. Here's her cell phone number." He pressed a piece of paper with the nanny's number into her palm. "She's got yours on speed dial. Plus there's a hundred-member crew. I promise there'll be no shortage of people keeping an eye out and showering Dustin with attention."

This was also true. The production assistants and gofers would kill for the chance to get close to Daniel by showing an interest in his son. She shot him a look. She knew first-hand just how charismatic he was in person, how incredibly hard he was to resist, and what a talented actor he was. A talent he wielded freely and not just in front of the camera.

Carefully she retrieved Dustin's favorite books from the nightstand and began to rearrange the contents of his suitcase so that she could fit them in between his clothes. She applied herself to the task as if the location of each item somehow mattered.

"You could still be a part of that crew if you wanted to be." Daniel moved up behind her. "I have a plane waiting." He said this softly as he slipped his arms around her so that his body cocooned hers. "You could just come with us."

For a moment she feared she was going to turn in his arms and surrender. She allowed herself to imagine abandoning all resistance, to feeling his hands and mouth on her naked skin.

She drew a deep, shuddering breath. It was only Dustin rolling over with a small mewling sound that saved her. Kyra turned her head and detached herself. Through the window she saw movement out near the pool. Her father. Who had smashed his quarter-of-a-century marriage and their family by giving in and focusing only on himself.

"No." She turned to face Daniel but kept her distance. "There's no reason to risk pissing Tonja off more than usual. She may be able to live with you spending a few weeks with your son, and I'm glad you and Dustin will have the time together. But I guarantee you she'd never forgive my being a part of the visit. Besides, I don't belong on that movie set." She looked out the window once more and saw her father sitting alone staring out over the pass. "If things were less complicated . . ." She shrugged. Things with Daniel would never be simple. "I appreciate the invitation, but even if I were a better actress than I am, I wouldn't be up for playing the role you're offering."

A short time later she followed Daniel downstairs and out the front door to the waiting town car. The driver took Dustin's suitcase and the bag of Pull-Ups and stowed them in the trunk as Daniel buckled Dustin into the car seat and settled into the backseat beside him.

Dustin's eyes opened sleepily as Kyra leaned across Daniel to tighten the straps and kiss his forehead. "I love you, little man. Have fun with your dad."

"Luff you." His head lolled to the side. His thumb found its way back into his mouth as his eyes closed.

"You'll text when you land to let me know you both got there okay?"

Daniel nodded.

"And we'll FaceTime at least every other day so Dustin can talk to me."

"You can talk to each other as many times a day as you want." Daniel smiled. "We'll have a blast together and he'll be back before you know it."

She nodded slowly. Watched Dustin's long dark lashes, so like his father's, flutter up briefly then down.

"But if you want to check on him yourself, or you need a break, the invitation stands," he said quietly. "There's a lot more between us than just our child, Kyra. You know that, don't you?" His dark eyes held hers. It took everything she had not to answer or agree.

"Have a good flight," she said finally. "Don't forget to text when you get there."

It was his turn to nod. She stepped back as he reached to pull the door closed, then stood in the spill of the streetlight watching the black car disappear into the night.

She went back inside locking the front door and turning off lights. She'd been pregnant with Dustin the first time she'd seen Bella Flora. She'd also been hopelessly naïve and convinced that the movie star she'd fallen in love with would magically appear to sweep her and their child off to happily ever after. That wasn't exactly how it had gone, but she'd been far luckier than she'd deserved. Lucky to have her mother as an integral part of their lives, lucky to be a part of *Do Over* or whatever they could make of it, lucky to have this fabulous home that was big enough to hold all of them. Lucky that Daniel wanted to be a part of Dustin's life.

In the salon she snapped off the light and looked out at the pool deck. A light shone in the pool house, and she thought her father might have gone inside until she saw movement on the chaise where she'd seen him earlier. Unable to leave him sitting in the dark by himself, she left the house and walked outside. The rising moon cast shadows on Bella Flora's pink walls and darkened her white trim. In the sunshine she often looked like a wedding cake fresh out of the bakery box. At night she felt castle-like, a fortress wrapped protectively around them.

Her feet crunched on bits of sand and gravel. There was movement on the chaise. "Maddie?" Her father's voice was painfully hopeful.

"No, Dad. It's me." Kyra reached his chaise and perched on the edge of the one beside it. The moonlight did not flatter her father. His lips turned downward and his eyes were dark holes in his shadowed face. His arms were folded across his chest. Though he lay on a chaise beside a pool that overlooked the water, he was not the least bit relaxed.

"Of course it's not your mother. She's with that damned Hightower." He turned and looked at her. "She's in her fifties for God's sake, and she's nothing but some rock star's booty call."

Kyra stifled the laugh that bubbled up. Her father was completely serious. "Will's here?"

"Oh, he's here, all right. She took him up to her bedroom five minutes after he arrived." He sat forward and turned his gaze toward the back bedroom where her mother slept. The blinds were closed. The light from a single lamp glowed softly.

"Dad," she said gently. "They're in a relationship. You know that."

"Hmmph!" He expelled a breath of air. "Don't you wonder why? That man could probably have anyone he wanted. What do you think he's doing with her?"

Any thought of laughter evaporated. "You're right, Dad. Will probably could have anyone he wanted but he was smart enough to choose Mom. And he knows just how lucky he is to have her. Something you seem to have forgotten a long time ago." She shifted on the chaise. "And he would never have had a chance if you'd treated her the way you should have. Or valued her the way she deserves."

His jaw jutted out. "You don't know what you're talking about."

"Don't I?" She leaned toward him. "I know who fell apart when you lost everything and who didn't." Her own jaw jutted in anger. "And I know who thought about and took care of everyone else including you. And who only thought about himself."

"You have no right to talk to me this way."

"Maybe not," she said, knowing her mother would agree with that statement. "But you have no right to say nasty things about my mother when all she ever did was try to take care of us."

He looked away and she saw him blink rapidly. Something wet slid down his cheek and she realized with horror that he was crying.

"I never thought she'd leave me." His tone was that of a little boy who'd been betrayed.

"You didn't even try to help her," Kyra said, even further incensed by the whiny tone. "You just gave up and dumped our whole life on her. And then you were angry when she found the strength to carry the whole load."

"I never thought she'd have the guts to leave me." He swiped at his cheek. She heard him sniff but she couldn't leave it there.

"That's because you underestimated her. We all did. But she's one of the strongest people I've ever met." She continued to stare at her father's shadowed face. "I hope I turn out to be half as good a mother and human being as she is." She realized just how true the words were only as she said them. As a child she'd taken her mother for granted. But her mother had always stepped up to whatever challenge had been thrown at her. She'd survived the loss of everything they'd owned to Malcolm Dyer's Ponzi scheme. Then she'd been the glue that held everyone together during that sweat-soaked summer spent bringing Bella Flora, their lone remaining asset, back to life. She'd found a way to turn every place they'd wound up together—even that god-awful houseboat on Mermaid Point—into a home. "And you're the one who started dating first."

He grimaced. "I don't understand how she can be with that . . . that wild man." Her father's voice remained a plaintive whine.

"William's spent a lot of time working on himself. And he appreciates her for who she is," Kyra said. "You wanted her to stay the person you thought she was."

He sighed, ran a shaking hand through his hair. "I came here hoping we could patch things up and I don't know, maybe give it another try."

Kyra looked at him in surprise. "Really, Dad? Because I think you just want your old life back. You haven't done anything that would make her regret her decision since you've been here. All you've done is complain and find fault and expect everybody to wait on you."

He closed his eyes. Shook his head sadly. "I can't believe it's really over. I don't know how I'll . . . Do you think if I . . ."

Kyra remained silent. But even as she watched the pain etched in his shadowed face, she sensed that the pain was about him and the loss of what he wanted.

"Well, I guess I better get to bed." He sat up and swiveled. Slowly he began to lever himself off the chaise. "I'll be out of everyone's hair in the morning."

"But where will you go?" Kyra stood, too. The breeze off the water was warm and heavy.

He shrugged again as he straightened. "I don't know. I'm not sure who I even am anymore. Not without your mother. I hope I'm not too old to figure it out."

Kyra watched the play of moonlight on his face. Once she

had worshipped this man, had thought he could do no wrong. "Well, I know you're still my father. You can stay here as long as you want to."

"And do what?" he asked quietly, his voice thick with sadness.

"You can stay here and help."

. . .

Bella Flora was quiet the next morning when Nikki awoke. Except for the doorbell. Which someone seemed to be leaning on. She groaned, buried her face in the pillow waiting for someone to answer it. The doorbell kept ringing.

"Jesus!" Her brain fuzzy and her limbs heavy, she fought her way out of the sheets that were wound around her, and struggled to an upright position on the side of the bed. Which was when she noticed she was still dressed in the clothes that she'd been wearing for, well, she wasn't sure exactly how long she'd been wearing them. Without looking in the mirror or using the bathroom she so badly needed, she walked down the front stairs, moved to the door, and yanked it open. "What the hell do you . . . ?"

She broke off midsentence when she saw Joe Giraldi's eyes. Which were pinned to her face with a look of abject horror. "What happened?"

Her eyes blurred with tears. She'd been steeling herself against the first time she'd see him, had told herself to remain slightly aloof, not to get close enough for him to guess what was going on. But the horror in his voice and the concern in his eyes almost undid her. "I heard you were under the weather. That you'd ended up in the emergency room. But . . . who did this to you?" His tone of voice made it clear that whoever it was would be extremely sorry. And possibly not breathing.

"No one. No one did this to me. It was an accident." She'd thought she'd keep her distance, but he came in without asking. When he grasped her by her arms so that he could look more closely, the warmth of his hands, not the strength of his grip, made her whimper.

"Sorry." He let go, but he didn't step back. She could see him cataloging her injuries, assessing the damage. "What the hell happened?"

"I was out on a sales call with Ray. And I, um, was apparently dehydrated. I just kind of passed out. I fell down in a parking lot."

"You *kind of* passed out? Isn't that like being a little bit pregnant?"

She blinked at the comparison but was careful not to react. It was just an expression. Maddie was the only one who knew and she'd been sworn to secrecy.

"I take it you went down face-first?"

She nodded carefully, reminding herself not to offer too much information that might trip her up later. The man sweated confessions out of people for a living. He could read faces like some people read street signs. Luckily, hers was so messed up he'd have a hard time reading anything. Still, it would be best to stick as close to the truth as possible without revealing the one thing she didn't want him to know. This would be far easier if her brain wasn't moving so slowly and her heart weren't beating so frantically. His eyes dropped from her face to her body. She saw him taking in the wrinkled halter and the skimpy cutoffs. She'd had no appetite and was pretty sure she hadn't put on any weight. Surely it was too soon for anyone, even Joe, who knew her intimately, to be able to tell. Still, she couldn't keep standing here allowing him to examine her. "What are you doing here? Did you need something?"

His eyes moved over her face. "I'm headed down to Sarasota to talk with a retired agent. I'll be meeting with Renée and Annelise tomorrow to share what I find out. I thought maybe we could . . ." He looked into her eyes. She was careful to keep her expression polite but neutral and her mouth shut so that she wouldn't have to lie to him. She loved him; she'd never been more aware of that fact than at this moment when all she wanted to do was throw herself in his arms and stay there forever.

But she was not a child. She did not need Joe or anyone else to take care of her. She would find a way to protect him from Malcolm and even from herself. Given her age and her past history, the chances that she'd carry and deliver a healthy baby were miniscule. Nothing had really changed. There was no reason to give him false hope or the promise of a family that she'd probably not be able to deliver.

"Never mind. I thought that you might . . . but clearly I was mistaken." Now he stepped back. His brown eyes were shuttered.

She smiled politely and spoke as if to a stranger. "Thanks for stopping by. I know we all appreciate what you're trying to do for Renée and Annelise." Nikki held on to the smile until he'd gotten back in his car and backed out of the drive. Only when she'd closed the door behind her did she allow herself to cry. The sound of her misery echoed through the empty house as she climbed the stairs and threw herself on the rumpled bed, pitiful and alone.

Chapter Thirty-four

The boxes that sat piled on and around the conference room table at Franklin Realty reeked of the past. The young handyman who helped out on the rental properties they managed had hauled them down from the office attic, where they'd been stored since the Sunshine Hotel had closed. For the last few hours Renée and Annelise had been working their way through them in anticipation of Agent Giraldi's visit. Each time Renée opened one she was greeted with a none-too-subtle whiff of eau de mildew and a peek into memories she'd spent a good part of her life trying to forget.

"Oh, look at this." Annelise held up a dinner menu from a long-ago New Year's Eve. "It's from the costume party Nana planned that year. I remember because Mama let me stay up late enough to watch everyone arrive so that I could see the costumes. Isn't that Mrs. Zinberg dressed like the Unsinkable Molly Brown?"

Renée reached out for the photo. "Yes, I think Mr. Zinberg came as her millionaire miner husband."

"And here's Nana as Fanny Brice. Remember how she made Pop Pop dress like Ziegfeld?"

Their Nana had been a force. A "people person" who never knew a stranger, she'd been the beating heart and welcoming hostess who made sure everyone felt included. She had known every winter guest by name as well as their children's and their grandchildren's. Renée had mistakenly believed that it was their grandmother who had run things until their grandfather, a kind, quiet, and gentle man, died. Overnight, Nana had seemed to shrink in size; her brilliance dimmed like a star that had lost its solar system.

"The fashion shows are in here." Annelise pulled out two shoeboxes filled with small black-and-white photos. "This is from the first time she let me model." The photo was of the two of them—Renée with her shoulders back and looking far too self-important in a sundress covered in large poppies. Annelise, who wore saddle shoes and a bright pink poodle skirt, held her hand tightly. "I remember Daddy promised me a Hershey bar if I didn't get the outfit dirty."

Convinced that although the guests should be treated like family, they could not be allowed to grow bored, Nana had planned each day with meticulous care. There had been ice cream socials, beach volleyball, and water skiing for teenagers. The fashion shows had been a part of card luncheons for the mothers—with guests modeling fashions from a local boutique. Overnight slumber parties once a month had allowed the parents who brought their children with them to have a "date night." Renée and her girlfriends had made money babysitting and running arts and crafts classes for the younger children.

For the families there were sand-castle-building competitions, weekly sing-alongs and shell hunts as well as relay races and flag football. The goal had been to provide a fun-filled experience fit for all ages, and it worked. Families had standing reservations each winter, favorite cottages that they thought of as "theirs." In the summer a slightly different version of family fun was planned for the local members.

"Here's a stack of boxes labeled 'Guest Registers.'" Renée reached for the top box, which was labeled with a number one. "I'll go through these. Are you doing okay with the photos?"

Annelise nodded. She'd been quiet but present in a way that Renée was afraid to count or comment on. "Do you think we're just wasting our time on all of this?"

"I don't know," Renée said truthfully. "None of this pertains to Ilse's past and it doesn't look like we're going to find anything Joe would consider helpful, but it can't hurt to organize and consolidate." The center of the table had been divided into piles: one for photographs they wanted to keep, one for hotel history and paperwork, others for family and guests, and even one for those things that defied classification. Precious little had gone into the trashcans she'd placed within reach.

Renée opened the box and extracted the first leatherbound register. It smelled its age and was far from pristine, the binding broken in from use, the wine-colored leather scratched and stained. The writing had faded but was still legible. The first entry was January 1, 1942. "God, it begins with the very first guests."

Annelise smiled. "Before I was even born."

An ache of loss flooded through her at the sight of her grandmother's handwriting. Nana had been mother and grandmother all rolled into one. When Renée's father had been in Germany during the war, Nana and Pop Pop had done their best to fill the void. Renée read through the first months, amused at the notes and comments her grandmother had recorded along, it seemed, with her observations about life in general. It was a good thing their guests had not been privy to some of Nana's drier, less charitable entries. "Well, now we know how Nana had such a good memory."

"What do you mean?"

Renée turned the register toward her. "Look at this. She not only registered each family with the dates of their stay and so on. She made notes about them."

Pop Pop had kept the accounting and bankbooks. Nana had apparently used the guest registers to record what she thought mattered most. For forty-plus years until Nana, who had struggled on alone for five years after Pop Pop died, finally closed the hotel in 1984, she had written notes and comments about each and every one of their guests.

Annelise's laugh was rusty. "She was right about Mrs. Weiner's pug nose. And Myrna Lipschitz's cow eyes. But it's a good thing no one saw her notes about them." She gave the register back to Renée and then held up a photo. It was a picture of the two of them standing in front of the big glass display window of the Corey Avenue Five and Dime. "Look at this. Do you remember all the time we spent there?"

"Of course," Renée said. "We used to get to go there after the movies at the Beach Theatre." She sat forward as something hit her. "We went there the day Dad died, didn't we?" She held her breath as images that she'd been careful not to think about for so many years rose in her mind, taking her by surprise.

Annelise nodded slowly, her eyes clouded with memory. "We saw Abbott and Costello. Do you remember? It was their version of *Jack and the Beanstalk*." Her smile was sad. "And then you took me to look at the barrettes."

For the first time in sixty-four years, Renée allowed herself to remember. She'd been in a hurry at the store and short with Annelise, wanting to get back to the hotel before John's lifeguard shift ended.

"I went swimming that morning," Annelise continued. "Mother made me take a nap because I tried to scare the guests again. But after that we got to go to the movies. And I got two barrettes at the dime store. They were pink and shaped like bows." Her eyes shimmered with tears. Her lips trembled and Renée remembered how annoyed she'd been at her little sister's chattering, all the barrettes she'd insisted on trying on, when all Renée had wanted was to go home. But something had happened at the store. Something odd. She stilled as she tried to remember what it was.

A brisk knock sounded on the door yanking her back to the present. Joe Giraldi walked into the conference room.

"I hope you don't mind," he said. "No one answered the front door, so I let myself in."

"Oh. Of course not. Come in. We've been sitting here buried in the past," she said, even as the long-ago images began to recede. "We were just going through our grandparents' papers and photos. Let me get us all some iced tea." She went to the kitchen and returned with a tray of iced teas and spoons, then placed a sugar bowl and a small plate of cookies on the table where everyone could reach them.

"Thank you." The FBI agent stirred sugar into his tea and eyed the photos and papers with interest. But Renée's mind was flooded with random images of the dime store. She stumbled over the pleasantries as it tried to retrieve and hold on to . . . something.

"So, what did you find out?" Annelise asked Joe softly. "Is there any further information about Heinrich Stottermeir and whether he could have come here?"

"I don't have anything concrete," Joe said, settling back in his chair. "Fortunately, a lot of the files from that time have been declassified, so if we get to the right people we have a shot at getting real answers. The retired OSS agent I spoke to recognized his name. Stottermeir seems to have been working for more than one side during the war. When it became clear that Germany was losing, he began funneling information to the allies." He took a sip of tea.

"Our father was in intelligence," Renée said. "He was assigned to the American headquarters in Frankfurt."

"That's how he met my mother," Annelise added softly. Her eyes were fixed on the FBI agent.

Joe nodded. "The contact down in Sarasota knew Stottermeir's handler and is trying to track him down. He thinks he's somewhere out west. He might be able to tell us whether Stottermeir was in the United States in the years after the war."

The flood of images had slowed and were now moving in an odd herky-jerky motion like an old film running through an even older projector. Without warning, Renée was hit hard with a freeze-frame of the odd man, the same man Annelise had recalled for the sketch artist. The man she'd recognized. "He was here. I saw him at the dime store."

"Are you sure?" Joe asked as Annelise looked at her wide-eyed.

Renée nodded. "I don't know how I could have forgotten him. He was so . . . He looked so out of place."

"In what way?" Joe's gaze was fixed on her face.

She closed her eyes, straining to see. The images sped up and unfurled. "He was dressed as if he was a tourist. But something was off. His clothes were too dark for the beach and . . . I don't know. He had a hat pulled down over his face but he just kept staring at Annelise."

"At me?" Annelise asked.

"Yes." Renée swallowed. "Like he was trying to figure something out." She could feel Annelise's and Joe's eyes on her, but that was all she had.

"I tried to trace your mother, too, Annelise," Joe said carefully. "I looked through what I could find to see if she might have traveled back to Germany. But there's no indication that happened."

"I told you." Annelise's voice quivered; the childish hurt and anger were back. "She would never have hurt my father. And she never would have just left like that."

"If she was involved in the intelligence community, which isn't out of the question, she could have been moved." Joe said this almost gently. "Or even given another identity. She might not have had a choice." He reached for a cookie, examined it. Renée sensed he was trying to give them a chance to absorb what he was saying. To shift mental gears. "We don't really know how your parents met. Or whether there might have been a reason other than mutual attraction that brought them together."

"Are you saying my mother was a spy?" Annelise asked with that breathless tone that Renée had begun to hope she'd never hear again.

"No," Joe said. "I have no proof of anything of the kind. I'm just pointing out that there may be far more to this story than your parents would have, or could have, ever shared. Or that we'll ever know."

"My mother and father fell in love with each other when he helped her after she got hurt! He stayed in Germany until they let him marry her!" Annelise cried.

Renée slid an arm around her sister's shoulders, but Joe's words had her thinking about Ilse. How standoffish she'd been at first, how uncertain she'd seemed even around the man who was her husband. She thought about all the things her father had explained away as the result of Ilse's losses in the war, the shock of moving to the United States, her difficulty with the English language, how unwelcoming so many people had been. Until Nana had come to her defense.

Could there have been another reason for Ilse's behavior? Could she have been more than a disoriented young woman who'd survived the war and the loss of her family before coming to America newly married and pregnant by her American soldier husband?

"Was the former agent in Sarasota able to translate the note Renée found?" Annelise asked.

"No," Joe said. "But Officer Jackson is planning to show it to someone at the sheriff's office who speaks German."

She didn't hear the rest of what Joe Giraldi said. She was too busy examining the puzzle pieces of her family's past and wondering if there was in fact some other way to fit them together.

Chapter Thirty-five

"God, I looked like an imbecile." William Hightower unfolded himself from the salon sofa as Kyra raised the remote and turned off the television with an angry snap of the wrist. *Do Over: Keys Edition*, episode four was now mercifully over.

Her father snorted, but for the first time, wisely said nothing.

"I looked like a nervous schoolgirl," Avery said. "If Deirdre hadn't been there, I wouldn't have even been able to make the presentation." All of them were uncomfortable with having to watch Deirdre brought back to life each week, but Kyra knew it was hardest for Avery. She tried to imagine having to watch her mother this way while bracing for her death. All of them had held their breath during the close-ups of Deirdre, her obvious pride in her daughter clear in her eyes.

"Did you really have to use so many close-ups of Deirdre?" Kyra snapped at Troy. "It's sick."

"They weren't happy with the first edit," Troy said. "I had to go back in and beef up her screen time."

"Right." Just as he'd beefed up the tense but evolving

relationship between Deirdre and her daughter. Which came in second only to the close-ups of Dustin.

"And I looked like a monumental witch when I called Will out on his behavior," Maddie said, trying to smooth things over, as always.

"He deserved it," Nikki said with less than her usual sarcasm.

"I did," Will acknowledged.

"I chased you out of your own home." Maddie sounded quite pleased with herself though the shots of this happening during the episode had clearly shown her distress.

"You did," Will teased. "But that was when I realized just how feisty you were."

Maddie laughed.

"And you did get us the go-ahead we needed," Nikki pointed out quietly. Her face had turned a chalky white.

"Only after deviously plying me with lasagna and ice cream," Will said. "I think that was the first home-cooked meal I'd had in like twenty years."

"The sauce was from a jar. You still have the taste buds of a teenager," Maddie pointed out.

William shrugged, not at all offended. "I wish I had time for a little ice cream right now." His tone and the look he gave Maddie made it clear he was talking about something that could not in fact be scooped out of a container.

Will laughed as Kyra's mother blushed. Her father looked away.

"But I have to get back to Tampa. We're doing morning radio and TV to promote the concert. To which I've been directed to arrive, and I quote, 'bright eyed and bushy tailed.'"

"I actually feel sick to my stomach from watching what you and the network did to us." Kyra glared at Troy, who looked far too pleased with himself.

"You're not the only one," Nikki said as one hand fluttered to her throat. "I can't seem to shake this bug."

"Well, I think we should just stop watching these episodes," Avery said. "I mean, what's the point?"

"It doesn't matter whether *you* watch or not. What matters is that a ton of other people want to," Troy countered.

"Why? Do you get a bonus per humiliation viewed?" Kyra's patience had begun to evaporate shortly after the opening credits.

"Your Facebook and Twitter are flat. They pop slightly with each episode but that's not enough. Kim Kardashian has twenty-five million Facebook fans and she doesn't even *do* anything. You need to get the paparazzi back here pronto if you want to do your own thing," Troy said." Tell them, Will."

Will's nod was reluctant. "You're looking at someone who prefers hiding out on an island"—he winked at Maddie—"though not necessarily alone. But Troy's right. If you want to do your own thing you have to have plenty of people who want to watch you do it."

"This is serious," Troy said very seriously. "You need those paps back even if you have to do something humiliating to get their attention."

"You are the last person on the planet that I'm about to take advice from," Kyra snapped. "I still don't think you're being honest with us."

"Think what you want," Troy snapped back. "It's your funeral. Or *Do Over*'s anyway." With a curt nod he left the salon. Kyra was still staring after him when the pool house light went on.

Avery and Nikki headed upstairs. Kyra stood with her father as her mother walked William to the door. There was a lengthy silence during which she had no doubt they were kissing good night. This was followed by murmurs and quiet laughter.

Her father's stiff posture and pained expression made it clear he was as aware as she was of the long and intimate good-bye taking place in the foyer. The door finally opened and closed. The bolt was thrown. Kyra could hear her mother humming happily as her footsteps receded up the stairs.

"Dad . . ." she began, alarmed by the sadness etched on his face.

"No. It's . . . it's just that I really want to hate him . . . but . . ." He swallowed. "She seems so happy."

Kyra nodded.

Her father drew a deep breath. "He'll never be good enough for your mother," he finally said. "But then as you've already pointed out, neither was I."

• • •

Nikki stood naked in front of the bedroom mirror trying to come to terms with what was happening to her body. Her breasts had grown larger and heavier. They'd already been far less perky than they'd once been. Now they sagged pendulously, reminding her of those long-ago *National Geographic* pictures of topless African women whose primitive tribes had been discovered in a distant jungle. Blue veins were visible on what had once been relatively smooth white skin. Her waist already seemed thicker, and her stomach had begun to round and swell slightly. Even her thighs, which had remained relatively tight due to decades of running, had begun to "relax" unattractively. She could no longer remember the last time she'd had the energy to run, and was afraid to turn around for the back view given how jiggly her bottom already felt.

A knock sounded on the door. She froze.

"It's Maddie. Don't even think about not answering."

Nikki pulled on a robe, then opened the door.

"May I come in?" Maddie asked politely.

"I didn't think I had a choice," Nikki replied in a voice so sulky she knew it could not be hers. "Sorry." She stepped back and opened her palm in invitation. Once Maddie was inside, Nikki closed the door quickly. As if there was a horde of people waiting to push their way inside. "It's just that I'm always nauseous now. And I never know when I'm going to have to get to a bathroom to either pee or throw up." She paused to swallow back the bile that once again rose in her throat. "How can they get away with calling it morning sickness when it goes on all day?"

"I'm not sure," Maddie said. "But it usually disappears after the first trimester."

"Really?" Was that her voice sounding so desperate?

"Really." Maddie nodded. "Whatever you want to make people believe, your 'bug' needs attention." She pulled a slip of paper from her pocket and handed it to Nikki. "This is the address of the OB-GYN practice Kyra used. You need to make an appointment. I'll be glad to go with you."

Nikki shook her head. That would make things way too real.

"Or you could ask Joe."

Nikki didn't move.

"How did he react when you told him?"

Nikki's tongue felt as thick as her thighs, as heavy as her breasts. "How did you know he was here?"

"Pass-a-Grille is way too small for secrets." Maddie looked at Nikki's frightened white face. "I know he's got to be excited."

Nikki remained silent, but it was a miserable and highly uncomfortable silence.

"I refuse to believe you didn't tell him that he's going to be a father."

Nikki remained silent but the disappointment in her friend's eyes hurt. "I don't see how this pregnancy is going to end well. I have been pregnant before and there were . . . issues. I don't have the least confidence that I'm going to carry this . . . pregnancy . . . full term." She could not bring herself to say the word "baby." Could hardly let herself think it.

"And I . . . I just couldn't do it. Not yet." Possibly not ever.

"Nikki." Maddie's voice softened. "You can't spend your

entire pregnancy waiting to lose your child. There are lots of women who have healthy babies in their forties and even fifties. I saw an article recently about a woman in her seventies that gave birth without difficulty."

"Not me. I'm not cut out for motherhood anyway." God knew Malcolm was proof of that. "And I still can't believe this is happening. I'm just going to wait. And if everything goes all right, I'll figure out some way to tell him."

"Nikki, you're not thinking clearly. You . . ."

"And whose fault is that? This . . ." Once again she choked on the word "baby." ". . . this thing that's taken over my body and my brain and is barely bigger than a blueberry according to that copy of *What to Expect When You're Expecting* that you left on my bed. That's who." She began to cry piteously. "Everything is just so . . . such a mess."

Maddie sat on the edge of the bed and pulled Nikki down beside her. She tilted Nikki's head against her shoulder as Nikki blubbered incoherently. "It's all right, Nik," Maddie said. "It's just the hormones kicking in. You're going to be fine. And so is the baby. And once you tell Joe . . ."

Nikki cried harder. Maddie hadn't seen Joe's face when she'd practically pushed him out the door. He didn't love her anymore. How could he? She wouldn't blame him if he never spoke to her again. She cried even more piteously. Nothing, not Maddie's soothing pats or her comforting words, could stop it. There was so much she had to figure out. There was the money for *Do Over*. Finding it was her responsibility. And then there was Malcolm. She had to end the threat that he posed to her and to Joe. Somehow she had to find a way to put things right. But she could do nothing but sob like a child.

"Shhhh." Maddie smoothed back her hair as tears streamed down her face. She could feel her nose running, the snot mingling with the tears. She was beyond pathetic. She simply couldn't do this. She couldn't be pregnant. She couldn't tell Joe. She couldn't lift her head from Maddie's shoulder.

"It'll be all right," Maddie said again, still stroking her hair. "Really, Nikki, I promise you. Everything will work out fine." Nikki wanted to believe her. Really she did. But Maddie always thought everything was going to get better. She insisted on believing that every glass was half full. Nikki had proof to the contrary.

"You'll see," Maddie said, having to raise her voice to be heard over Nikki's sobs. "I'm going to make you a doctor's appointment. And then you're going to tell Joe. Joe deserves to know. And I have no doubt he'll do the right thing."

Nikki sobbed harder. She cried an ocean of wet, salty tears. She did not want Joe to "do the right thing." She did not want Joe to marry her. All she wanted was for him to love her.

But he does. The voice was soft but insistent. *He does love you. He told you so. Repeatedly.* But that was before she'd been so nasty to him. Before she'd pushed him away. The soft voice was no match for the fear and anxiety that coursed through her. Or the foggy mushy place that used to be her brain. Words were easy. A baby was real and forever.

"Here, let's get you under the covers." Maddie's voice was soft and soothing. "A good night's sleep will make you feel better."

Nikki allowed herself to be tucked in. She fell asleep while Maddie was still clucking comfortingly beside her. Just as a real mother should. Nikki didn't have a clucking bone in her body.

But her dreams were harsh and torturous. Reminding her in their unrelenting intensity that she was not Madeline Singer and never would be. Any more than she could be Joe Giraldi's wife. Or the mother of his child.

Chapter Thirty-six

Roberto Dante arrived at the hotel on foot a few days later. The sleeves of his tie-dyed T-shirt had been hacked off long ago. A tattoo of a crossed handsaw and hammer ran down one bare sinewy arm, and his gray hair and soul patch were braided. With his tool belt slung over one shoulder he might have been an aging bandito. If banditos smiled dreamily and bobbed their heads to the seventies rock playlist reverberating in their heads.

"How are things going at the yacht club?" Avery had been worried that the sailing set would find Roberto a little earthy for their tastes.

"Couldn't be better," he said. "The women sailors are very friendly. One of the Broad Reachers, that's the name of the women's sailing group, brought me a whole tin of homemade chocolate chip cookies." He smiled. "Perfect for munchies. Even had a couple for breakfast."

"Hey, man!" Enrico called down from the rooftop. "What took you so long?"

It was 7:59 A.M., but Enrico and his crew had arrived just after sunrise to erect the scaffolding, which now encased the main building, and were scrambling all over it like ants at a picnic. The new steel support beams were stacked nearby. A Dumpster sat within dropping distance. A crane stood ready to hoist the beams into place.

"Let's see where we are." Roberto led them inside the main building. They stood in the center of the emptied room and stared up into the ceiling, which had been ripped the rest of the way open. Temporary support poles bore the weight of what remained of the old roof.

"Love this beach and this neighborhood," Roberto said as he eyed the center point of the room and buckled the tool belt low on his hips like a holster. Matching hammers hung from each side like pistols.

"Haven't I been telling you that for years?" Enrico came to stand beside his taller, funkier cousin.

"Not abandoning the Keys, man, not ever. But this is nice." He double-checked the measurements, walked back outside, and eyed the beams. He and Enrico directed the crew members into position. "You ready, old man?"

"Ha! We'll see who has to keep up with who!" Enrico waved one of his guys over another foot, then signaled the crane operator into position. "Let's rock and roll!"

Avery spotted Ray Flamingo making his way toward the building in sherbet-hued clothing that billowed in the slight breeze. While all about him were sweating in the mid-July heat and humidity, he looked cool, calm, and collected. He carried a large portfolio and an easel.

"What have you got for me?"

"These are exterior views of the cottages with their new façades, roofs, and walled patios based on your ideas." He set the first board on the easel.

"Oh, they're wonderful. And I love these colors. What are they called?"

"We have Flamingo Pink, Blue Mambo, and Banana Leaf.

I thought we'd do an assortment of each." He gave her a few minutes to study the wide planking that would cover the concrete and the burnished steel trim on what would be new windows and doors. "I've also done a one- and two-bedroom-unit floor plan that incorporates the remodeled baths and kitchens as well as a sample courtyard garden." He placed these in front of the other drawings and waited for her to absorb them. "I figured we could flesh them out and do finishing boards when we're ready to move into that phase of construction." He said this as if there was no doubt in his mind that there would be one.

"Looks good," she said, sincerely wishing she had as few doubts as Ray.

"Here's how I'm seeing the main building roof deck. We're still going for the wow factor but we don't know what we'll be able to afford in the way of finishes and furnishings. I'd still like to see us go high end, but in the meantime I think we focus on maximizing the space and making it as flexible as possible." He pulled out several boards that showed the space divided in a variety of ways. "If we buy modular pieces and go with planters with lock-down wheels, we have almost endless ways of utilizing the space, which would make it ideal for events. We could even handle a wedding ceremony up there." He smiled mysteriously. "And the pièce de résistance—we do a Plexiglas railing so that there's uninterrupted views from every position whether you're sitting or standing."

"It's perfect," she said, meaning it. "And if we manage to raise the money this place deserves, we'll go with the best outdoor furnishings and décor money can buy. And if we don't . . ."

"It'll still be damn fine." Ray gave her a rare grin. "I promise you that. We are not going to let a little thing like lack of funds stop us."

Ray took his confident *GQ* self off to check and remeasure

the locker rooms, then left to call on a potential sponsor. Avery stood in the center of the property and drank in the site. The main building and the scaffolding around it hummed with activity. The sound of shouting and hammering and drilling mingled with the caw of seagulls and the wash of incoming waves. Money was a huge problem, the construction schedule far from ideal, but at the moment the Sunshine Hotel looked, sounded, and smelled like an active construction site. Avery breathed it all in and focused on enjoying it. Because she had no idea how long it would last.

• • •

Nikki had fled upstairs to her room after her first whiff of the meal that Steve had unaccountably prepared. Troy had taken one look at the soggy beige casserole, swallowed uncomfortably, and announced that he had plans to eat out. That left Kyra, Maddie, and Avery staring uncertainly down at their plates in a kitchen that looked as if a world war had been fought within it.

"What is this, Dad?" Kyra asked after her first tentative bite of the main course. "I, uh, can't quite identify the main ingredient."

"It's tuna noodle casserole," he said, seeming surprised she had to ask. "I found the recipe on a rack in the store with a list of all the ingredients. I didn't know they did that. And I remembered that your mother used to make it when you and Andrew were little." He smiled almost shyly. "Would you like some more?"

"Um, no. Thanks. I kind of filled up on the salad." Which had been made of wilted lettuce, an undercooked egg, a half-rotten tomato, and a salad dressing that was made of mayonnaise mixed with other ingredients she couldn't identify. Kyra was unable to make eye contact with her mother, whose shocked gaze roamed the kitchen. Avery's eyes were fixed on the bag of Cheez Doodles that sat on the counter. Which said something for Avery's vision, given the number of things the bag was buried under.

"What made you decide to cook today?" Maddie asked, pulling her gaze from the war zone.

"Well, there wasn't much for me to do at the site today since Dustin's not here. So I wanted to try to be useful."

Kyra stifled her groan and picked up her fork. Her father had apparently listened when she'd read him the riot act. There was no way she could refuse to eat the meal he'd prepared. Slowly, she raised a forkful of casserole to her mouth. This time she swallowed it whole so that she wouldn't have to chew and therefore taste it. When she opened her eyes, her mother was watching her. Avery's eyes were back on the Cheez Doodles; those eyes were filled with longing.

"That's so nice of you, Steve," her mother said. "You know what would really top this meal off?"

"What?" His expression indicated he couldn't imagine anything improving on what he'd already served. But then he'd been so busy serving and watching them eat, he hadn't had so much as a forkful yet.

"I think there's a bottle of Chardonnay in the wine refrigerator in the bar. If you wouldn't mind getting it and opening it—I'm pretty sure there's a corkscrew in one of the drawers—it would really round things off."

"Okay." He stood and turned.

As soon as he left the kitchen, her mother stood and picked up their plates.

"What are you doing?" Avery whispered.

"Shh!" Quickly and expertly Maddie scraped their plates into the trashcan. Several huge spoonfuls of the casserole followed. She hid the evidence under large wads of paper towel. "Not that I think he's likely to ever look in the garbage can." Then she freed the bag of Cheez Doodles and ripped the bag open as she carried it to the table. "Here." She took a large handful before handing the bag to Avery. "Go ahead and put some on your plates. You've got to eat something." She crumbled Cheez Doodles on top of the casserole.

Maddie managed to wash her hands despite the dishes and pans overflowing in the sink. She'd just slid back into her chair when Steve returned with the bottle of wine. "Do you need help getting the goblets?"

"No, be right back."

As soon as he left, Maddie scooped another large spoonful and buried it in the garbage can. Then she scooped most of what remained in the casserole dish onto Steve's plate. "Parenting 101," she instructed. "Good intentions, like good behavior, should be praised and encouraged."

"I don't know," Avery said, munching on a Cheez Doodle. "I don't think we should encourage him to keep cooking."

"It's the effort we want to encourage," Maddie replied. "We'll just have to try to get out in front of those efforts a little better in the future."

"You mean like when Andrew got on that juicing kick and started making us those green smoothies all the time?" Kyra asked.

"Exactly," Maddie said.

"I don't know," Avery said again. "It sounds kind of like faking an orgasm. You could just end up eating a whole lot of crappy food from a chef who has no idea he needs to do better."

Kyra put a hand to her mouth to cover the resulting snort of laughter as her father returned. He poured them each a glass of wine, then noticed the almost empty casserole dish. The little that remained was now covered in a fine layer of crumbled Cheez Doodle.

"I hope you don't mind that I added a topping and that we ate so much while you were gone." Maddie raised her glass in toast. "We couldn't quite help ourselves."

He smiled at the compliment and took a bite from his plate. He chewed carefully, considering. "The Cheez Doodles do add a certain . . . something."

That something was flavor, Kyra thought. And the cheese did sort of mask the smell.

"Everything's better with Cheez Doodles on it." Avery smiled and downed her wine. Her mouth and fingers bore evidence of her statement.

Steve took another bite and then another.

"How was William's concert?" Avery asked.

"It was great," Maddie said. "They're really sounding good and the Tampa Theatre was packed."

Her father took another bite. He winced slightly as he chewed. Kyra wasn't certain if it was the topic that had been introduced or if he had finally tasted the tuna casserole beneath the cheesy topping. He reached for his glass of water and drank most of it down in one long gulp. "Anyone for dessert?" he asked finally. "I made, well, the recipe said they're a cross between banana bread and peanut butter brownies."

"I'm really full," the three of them said in unison.

Maddie set her napkin on her plate. "I'm going to check on Nikki. Why don't I take one up to her?"

"Sure." Without clearing anything out of the way, her father went to the counter and retrieved a brownie pan. After hacking unsuccessfully at it, he plopped a lopsided rectangle onto a small plate.

"What's wrong with her?" Avery asked.

"Hmmm?"

"Nikki's been sick for a while now," Avery said. "What do you think it is?"

"I'm not sure but I'm going to make sure she sees a doctor. In fact, I've scheduled an appointment for her." Maddie stood. "Thank you for . . . dinner," she said to Steve. "I know we all appreciate . . . the effort you went to." She scanned the trashed kitchen, the dirty bowls and containers on the counter, the crumb trail across the floor.

"You're welcome," he said, blushing slightly. "I'm glad everything turned out so well. I'm kind of an old dog trying to learn new tricks, but I intend to keep at it."

"Great. That's really great." Her mother fled and practically ran up the back stairs. As if the ghosts of meals past were pursuing her.

Chapter Thirty-seven

The demolition of the cottage patios and original concrete paths that bisected them had been going on for days. Everywhere Renée looked there were pulverized chunks of concrete. The ground lay in ripped-up clods all around them. Even worse was the constant whine of the concrete saws that pierced the air. The sound plucked at Renée's nerves. Jangled up her spine. Yanked her back to that horrible week in 1952 when an underground pipe had burst and had to be replaced. The grounds looked and felt much like this the week her father died. But then it had been jackhammers not concrete saws, which according to Avery had not yet been invented.

Even when one saw would stop another would be whining. The sound reverberated in the air and ricocheted off the cottage walls. If power tools had existed in the Middle Ages, the concrete saw might have convinced far more heretics to convert than the rack ever had.

How she could have imagined that this would be a logical time to rethink the hotel grounds she did not know. Yet here she stood, staring at the hibiscus and surrounding trees and vines that obscured the family cottage, trying to do just that.

Just do it. She placed the pencil tip to the pad, trying to blot out the noise and all it conjured, and began to draw.

The jungle could be tamed, the grounds brought back just like the buildings. All she needed was a workable plan to present to the garden club, of which she'd been president more times than any other member.

She'd had a view of the hibiscus from the window of the bedroom she'd shared with Annelise. It was a part of every memory, every dream, every nightmare. All these years she and everyone else had believed that she had dealt better with their shared tragedy than Annelise had. While Annelise had freaked out, acted out, and obsessed about uncovering the truth and exacting some sort of revenge on whoever had caused their father's death and abducted her mother, Renée had accepted reality and moved forward. She had been "healthy"; Annelise had not. Renée had married, borne and raised two children, loved and been loved by John. Annelise had done none of those things. When Annelise had refused to allow the hotel to be demolished and the land sold, Renée had once again moved on, treating the hotel as if it no longer existed, blacking it out in her mind. Virtually every single day of her adult life, she had driven past it, relieved when the trees and vines had swallowed it, convinced that it had no hold on her. That it was only a remnant of the past that had nothing to do with her current life. She'd told herself this over and over until she'd believed it. She'd pitied Annelise for getting stuck and for lacking the ability to move on.

She stopped sketching. Squeezed her eyes shut in an attempt to blot out the damned sound of the concrete being destroyed. But the truth refused to be shut out. She might have been the better actor, but she had not moved on or handled the loss like an adult. She had been like a child who closes her eyes, puts her hand over her ears, and spouts noisy gibberish so that she can pretend she doesn't see or hear the things that frighten her.

She forced herself to open her eyes. Adjusted her grip on the pencil. The hibiscus bush swayed gently, its heavy red blooms nodding and winking knowingly at her. *No.* It was too large. It had overstepped its bounds, gobbled up ground. She'd cut it back, remove large clippings. When the walled patios were complete she'd incorporate a piece of the hibiscus in every single one of them.

Skirting the bush, she walked to the family cottage.

The door was propped open, as were the windows. She walked inside. It was empty now; stripped of its contents and its personality, there was nothing there to differentiate it from the other two-bedroom units. Strangers would rent it one day and never know that her father had died there.

The concrete walls buffered the noise outside. Images wavered in her mind's eye. Her father and Ilse behind the closed bedroom door. Had she heard them that night? She moved toward the bedroom. Stopped and closed her eyes trying to hear, trying to remember. And then, there it was floating on the edge of her memory. Voices. Strained and cracked as if they were . . . arguing. Her eyes flew open as she realized the argument had taken place in an odd mixture of English and German, the words harsh and guttural. Was it just Ilse and her father? She stood perfectly still, barely breathing, her heart racing. Or had there been a third voice? Oh, God. Could it have been Heinrich Stottermeir? If she'd knocked on the door, could she have altered what happened? Would the night have ended differently? Could her father's death have been averted?

Renée held her breath desperately trying to remember, trying to shut out everything else so she could decipher the words that she'd tried not to hear that night and then spent the rest of her life blotting out. Guilt rushed through her. If she'd made herself remember sooner, if she'd spoken up, could she have saved Annelise from all these years of turmoil?

· · ·

Nikki sat in the waiting room of Drs. Gabianelli, Gutschen-ritter, and Payne OB-GYN leafing through a *Life & Style* magazine, which in her current condition seemed an intentional insult since she no longer had a life or a style.

Maddie had made the appointment, overseen Nikki's consumption of a ridiculous amount of water, then dragged Nikki out of the land of denial (a.k.a. her bedroom at Bella Flora) and to the doctor's office to keep that appointment.

"I'm so full I'm going to burst." She turned to Maddie. "Please let me go to the bathroom. I'll only pee a little bit."

"Sorry. You have to follow the instructions. The extra water is so they can do an ultrasound."

When her name was called, Nikki sloshed her way to the examination room. Maddie came with her.

Polite and professional in a white lab coat over a beige dress and wearing low heels, Dr. Payne appeared to be in her early fifties. As she washed her hands, Nikki wondered if she'd been born with the last name or married it. Payne seemed an extremely troubling surname for a doctor. Even worse than Tease for a hairstylist or Storm for a meteorologist. A long line of unsuitable names presented themselves as the doctor approached. This was what her brain did lately; it either fixated on unimportant minutiae or checked out completely until someone or something yanked her back to the present. You didn't have to be Freud to know that her brain was working overtime to relieve itself of her unpleasant reality. Which included her brother. Who despite being incarcerated seemed able to do, communicate, and send pretty much anything he felt like. Including the package that had just arrived with the six safe-deposit box keys tucked into their individual numbered envelopes from six different Florida banks.

She thought about the safe-deposit boxes and Malcolm's threats while the doctor introduced herself, made chitchat about the weather, then opened the manila folder that contained the forms Nikki had filled out.

Nikki began to count ceiling tiles as the doctor palpated her abdomen. They were laid out in an even pattern. With rows of small perforations dotting each tile.

"Did you hear that?" Maddie's voice made her lose count.

"I'm sorry?" Nikki roused and forced herself to focus on the doctor's face.

"I said I would estimate you're ten to eleven weeks," Doctor Payne said. "You're almost through your first trimester."

Nikki nodded numbly.

"Doesn't that mean the nausea and morning sickness should go away soon?" Maddie prompted.

"Usually," the doctor replied smiling. "Shall we take a look?"

"We're going to see it?"

"Um-hmmm. And probably pick up its heartbeat."

"A heartbeat?" Nikki's brain kicked all the way in. The pregnancy had seemed unreal. None of this should be happening. "We could hear a heartbeat?"

"Someone hasn't been reading her *What to Expect When You're Expecting*," Maddie said.

It was true. She'd barely gotten through the initial cheery chapters because none of it had seemed remotely applicable to her. The only thing she'd been expecting was heartache.

"This will be a little cold." The doctor spread a thin layer of gel over Nikki's bare stomach. Then she positioned a monitor so that they could all see it, turned on a knob, then began to skim a metal wand over Nikki's stomach. It took Nikki a few moments to understand what she was seeing.

"Is that . . . is that the baby?"

"It is."

"But it looks like E.T."

The doctor smiled. "Yes. There's a lot of head from this view." She pointed to the monitor. "And here's the sac." She circled the monitor with her finger. "Those are the hands and feet."

Nikki watched in fascination. "It's moving. Is that normal?"

"It is. Doesn't it look like it's waving?" Sure enough there was a back-and-forth movement.

Nikki's heart fluttered in her chest as her brain tried to absorb what she was seeing. There was a baby inside her. Joe Giraldi's baby. "Oh, my God. I can't believe it. It's . . . it's real."

"It's real, all right," Dr. Payne said. "And that's its heart." She gestured to something that pulsed in and out. Nikki watched, mesmerized. "Shall we see if we can pick up a heartbeat?" She moved the wand slowly, and suddenly there was a scratchy racing sound. Staticky lines kept pace on the screen.

"It's so fast."

"Just as it should be," the doctor said.

"There's a baby. With a heart and everything." She turned to Maddie, who was also smiling crazily.

"And . . . oh . . ." The doctor hesitated. "Let me see what this is . . ." Fear pinched out Nikki's excitement as the doctor moved the wand. The doctor's hand stopped moving. "Well look at that." She smiled. "There's another sac." She pointed to the screen and Nikki saw it. It reminded her of the screen in the fighter jet that Tom Cruise was flying in *Top Gun*. First there was only one "bogey" then one moved out from behind the other and there were two. "You're carrying twins." Her finger circled first one baby-filled sac then another. They floated next to each other while the tadpole E.T.s did what looked like calisthenics.

"The sacs are separate, which indicates fraternal rather than identical twins."

"Are you sure about all this?"

"Definitely sure," the doctor laughed. "And those are nice strong heartbeats. Just the way we want them."

Her own heart was beating just as frantically as the baby's. *Babies.* She hadn't even believed she was carrying one baby.

How could there be two? She looked down at her stomach. "I don't understand how this could have happened."

Maddie laughed. Dr. Payne said, "If you haven't been undergoing fertility treatments, I assume it happened in the usual way."

Her period had been so infrequent; she'd assumed she was going through menopause. "I was told a long time ago that I'd never conceive again and that if I did, I'd never carry full term. How could this happen now when I'm practically menopausal?"

"I think the operative word is 'practically.'" The doctor smiled once again. "Doctors are occasionally mistaken. And plenty of women in their forties get pregnant and go on to give birth to healthy babies. Older mothers are more liable to have multiples."

Nikki looked back at the screen, still trying to absorb what was happening, what she was seeing. Both babies seemed to be waving. And possibly blowing raspberries. She hadn't believed in this pregnancy enough to be frightened before. But now she couldn't take her eyes off the screen. They were so tiny, so vulnerable. There were two of them! "Oh, God. I can't believe this is really happening."

Maddie reached out and took her hand. "It looks pretty real to me."

"Let's get a picture so you have proof," Dr. Payne said, moving the wand slightly and then holding it still. The monitor did a freeze-frame documenting both sacs floating side by side, their occupants frozen mid-wiggle. "My assistant will give you paperwork and help set up regular visits. You can call with questions anytime. You're welcome to bring your partner with you to any and all visits."

Partner. Her brain shied away and ran in another direction . . . "Oh."

"Oh, what?" Doctor Payne asked. The monitor spit out an image. Dr. Payne handed it to her.

Nikki's eyes blurred with tears. "I can't believe they're real."

Joe would be so excited. So proud. She swallowed as she imagined his reaction. When she finally found the nerve to tell him. Her hands shook as she buttoned her blouse and pulled on her pants. She was going to have to find a way to tell him. But first she was going to have to put a stop to Malcolm's threats and demands. So that they were rid of him and Joe's career and reputation remained intact.

Chapter Thirty-eight

"Who did this?" Nikki walked into the kitchen, where Maddie was filling a pitcher with ice and sliced fruit. Avery was busy ripping open yet another bag of Cheez Doodles. Steve was peering into the oven.

Maddie poured a bottle of red wine into the pitcher. A shot of brandy and triple sec followed. "Did what?"

"This." Nikki held up the business suit, the vintage coral Chanel suit with the Peter Pan collar. "My lucky suit. The one I wear to call on potential sponsors. The one I was wearing when I introduced that Saudi prince to the woman who is now his wife." She held up the jacket and skirt with its silk print trim and button closures. Which had shrunk to a miniature imitation of itself.

Avery stopped what she was doing to look. "Wow, that's small!"

Nikki could see her trying not to laugh, which only infuriated her further.

The suit had been her first real splurge. Her first validation of her success. One of the few vintage pieces she had not sold for cash when Malcolm had bankrupted her. "How could this happen?"

Steve turned from the oven, a bewildered expression on his face. "I don't know. I washed it in cold water. And I put it on a low setting in the dryer."

Maddie winced. Avery bit her lip.

"Are you frickin' kidding me?" Nikki's temple throbbed. "First of all, you should not be touching my clothes. Second of all, haven't you ever heard of dry cleaning?" She tried to calm down. But while the nausea had, in fact, finally begun to recede, her emotions were pretty much calling every shot. "Seriously, Maddie, you were married to this man for twenty-five years. Didn't you require him to do anything?"

"Nikki," Maddie began.

"It's not like I did it on purpose," Steve interrupted. "I was trying to help."

"Shrinking people's expensive and irreplaceable clothing is not helpful. It's, it's . . ." Her mind went blank. She could not think of words that were bad enough. ". . . criminal."

"Well, you should know!" Steve snapped.

Her temple throbbed harder. Did pregnant women stroke out when they got upset? "What do you mean by that?"

"I think that would be obvious," Steve said.

Kyra came in. "What's going on? I thought we were going to do sunset toasts." She noticed Nikki and the shrunken suit. "What happened?"

"Your father washed my suit!" Nikki all but shouted. "In the washing machine!" She took a deep breath but it just made her light-headed. "I can't take any more of his 'helping.' It was easier when he just sat around and whined!"

"Nikki, please." Maddie had stopped mixing the sangria. "I know Steve's sorry. Maybe he could replace the suit."

"This suit is not replaceable. It was designed by Coco Chanel. I paid close to a thousand dollars for it."

Steve snorted. "A thousand dollars for a pink suit? Thank God you were never frivolous like that, Maddie."

Kyra and Avery both looked like they were having a hard time holding back their laughter. Nikki would kill them if they laughed at her and her pitiful, miniature suit.

"I'm sure my dad didn't mean to do that," Kyra said. "I'm sure he's really sorry. Right, Dad?"

Steve nodded even as smoke began to seep out of the oven he'd turned his back on. Maddie rushed over, yanked open the oven door, and pulled out a cookie tray of burnt offerings. The smoke detector went off as she dropped the tray in the sink.

"Are those my Bagel Bites?" Kyra asked in dismay as Avery clambered up on a chair to turn the siren off.

"They were." Steve looked downcast. "And I'm afraid that was the last of them."

"It's okay, Kyra," Nikki snarled. "I'm sure he's really sorry. Right, Steve?"

"Hey!" Steve protested.

"Why don't you air out the kitchen, Steve?" Maddie put a restraining hand on his shoulder. "Kyra, can you carry the pitcher of sangria outside? Avery's got the Cheez Doodles. Nikki, why don't you put the suit down for now and carry out this tray of glasses?" She removed the miniature suit from Nikki's hands and laid it carefully across the back of a kitchen chair. Then she put the tray of glasses in Nikki's hands, presumably so that she couldn't use them to wring Steve's neck. "I'll grab some of the Ted Peters smoked fish spread and crackers."

Outside, Nikki tried to focus on the water and the sun that was just beginning to set, but her insides rose and fell like a boat on a choppy sea; so did her thoughts and emotions.

Avery poured a glass of sangria and handed it to Nikki. "I think you need this. Maybe it will help you calm down."

Nikki stared stupidly down into the glass. Fruit slices floated in the red liquid. It smelled sweet with sugar. Nutmeg floated on the top. She had two babies floating inside her.

"I think this might taste better right now." Maddie arrived just in time to swoop in, remove the glass from Nikki's hand, and replace it with the glass of ice water she'd brought with her.

"I'll drink it," Avery said, reaching for the glass in Maddie's hand.

"Will you pour me one, too?" Kyra plopped down in a chair. She reached for a cracker and slathered fish spread all over it, then added a drop of Tabasco.

"We all need to calm down," Avery said as Maddie poured a glass for Kyra. "What's going on?"

"Well, Troy has taken some time off," Kyra said. "He claims he's gone to work some of his contacts on our behalf. But I think he's just gone to look for a paying gig. Every time I start letting down my guard he does something squirrelly. I don't trust him."

They all heard the emphasis on the word "trust." Maddie knew there was more to Kyra's scowl than just Troy taking off. "And?"

Kyra took a long drink of the sangria. "And I called to talk to Dustin a little while ago and some woman who was not the nanny answered Daniel's phone."

"Maybe he was on set and it was just whoever could get to the phone or something," Maddie said.

Her daughter looked at her. "That would be great except random people don't touch a megastar's personal cell phone, let alone answer it. Plus she told me that Daniel was 'resting' and maybe I should just call back later."

"And you're jealous," she observed, more tartly than she should have.

"I'm actually starting to feel some empathy for Tonja Kay," Kyra said. "Even when Daniel's not intentionally looking, there's a horde of women trying to get noticed and hoping to be 'chosen.'" She drained the last drops from her glass. "You're lucky that William doesn't give you reason to worry."

Ha! Maddie's subconscious had arrived. And it arrived scoffing. *What about those post-concert photos in Orlando? And the two girls photographed tiptoeing out of his suite?*

He said they were trying to tiptoe in, she informed her mocking subconscious. *And that he had them escorted out of the hotel.*

He always has an explanation, doesn't he? And what do you think is going to happen when it's easier to say yes than to fend someone off?

"Anyone have a good thing to toast?" Maddie asked, mentally shoving her subconscious out of the way.

"Let's see," Nikki said through gritted teeth. "I now have a perfect gift for a five-year-old fashionista with an appreciation for vintage designer clothing." The complaint was aimed squarely at Maddie.

In deference to Kyra's presence, Maddie managed not to point out that she and Steve were no longer married and that she had not invited him here, but just barely. "I really don't think it's fair to hold me accountable for Steve's actions," she snapped. She drew a deep breath of air into her lungs in an attempt to calm down. "Now. How about you, Avery?"

"A good thing?" Avery shook her head. "Not me. In fact we've got way bigger problems than overly amorous movie stars and shrunken designer clothing. We're still pretty much out of money. We're going to have to downsize our plans again unless we come up with more." She gave Nikki a pointed look.

"Hey, I'm not a miracle worker," Nikki retorted.

"That's for sure," Avery muttered.

Maddie's subconscious opened its mouth. Maddie shut it for her.

"Does *anyone* have something good they'd like to share?" She looked at Nikki, wishing that Nikki would hurry up and tell Joe about the babies so that they could celebrate her pregnancy. A celebration of any kind might help break the tension that crackled between them.

"'Fraid not." Nikki's jaw jutted.

"Fine," Maddie snapped. "I guess it's up to me, then." She took a drink of the sangria and stared up at the red-streaked sky as she swallowed it. "Renée showed me the hotel guest registers. There were families that stayed there every year for decades. Multiple generations that their Nana kept notes about and treated like family."

"That's nice," Kyra said without much enthusiasm.

"Yeah, great," Avery added with even less.

"Right," Nikki mumbled, staring not at the sky but into her glass of water.

Maddie chafed at their dismissal. But as usual she chafed silently.

The rest of the sunset was a work of art done in reds, purples, and golds that no one commented on or even seemed to notice. The cicadas tuned up and mosquitoes came out to eat as dusk turned to night.

Nikki was the first to flee. "I'm beat. I'm out of here."

"Me, too." Avery got up. "I'm going to Chase's. I'll be on-site in the morning. We should have the last of the old concrete up and in the Dumpsters tomorrow."

"I'm done, too," Kyra said, standing. "And I sincerely hope Dad cleaned up after himself."

She picked up the tray.

Maddie made no comment as she scooped up the empty pitcher.

"He's going to have to get with the program," Kyra said as they made their way inside. "And I can't believe I'm saying this, but I hope to hell he stops 'helping' soon."

• • •

Upstairs, Maddie took her time getting ready for bed but slept fitfully. Near dawn she thought she heard someone in the kitchen but resisted the urge to get up and see who it was.

The house was still quiet when she went down to the kitchen hours later and put on the coffee. From the kitchen table she watched a small sliver of Pass-a-Grille come to life. Saw boats round the pass and head into the Gulf, saw pelicans and gulls dive for breakfast. At eight A.M. she began to worry that Steve might show up determined to cook another meal, so she scrambled eggs and fried sausage patties, then popped bread into the toaster.

She heard movement in Kyra's bedroom but heard nothing from Nikki's. She buttered toast, poured a glass of orange juice, and filled a plate with eggs and sausage, then carried it upstairs. Balancing the breakfast tray, she knocked on Nikki's door. She knew Nikki was stressed out and all these years later she still remembered just how completely pregnancy hormones could jumble a woman's thoughts and hijack her emotions. But Nikki was going to have to get ahold of herself and she most definitely needed to talk to Joe.

"Nikki?" Maddie knocked again. When there was no answer she pushed open the door. "I brought you breakfast." Maddie stopped in the center of the room. Nikki wasn't there. The room was neat. The bed was made. A note sat on one of the pillows. Worried now, Maddie crossed the room, placed the tray on the nightstand, and picked up the folded piece of paper.

Had to go take care of some things. Sorry to bail. I'm no help to anybody right now.

Maddie walked to the window. Nikki's Jag was not in the driveway. She racewalked to the closet. Nikki's suitcase and a chunk of her wardrobe were missing, but she hadn't taken everything. Maddie tried to think what Nikki might have to "take care of." She knew someone had been texting her and that those texts had upset her. And then there was the pregnancy. *The pregnancy.* Nikki wasn't thinking clearly and she was most definitely freaked out, but . . . Her emboldened subconscious immediately began to bring up worst-case scenarios.

No, Maddie scolded back. *You should be ashamed of yourself for even thinking that.*

Is that right? her subconscious sneered.

But Maddie had no answer. And she didn't have the degree of confidence she wished she did. She had only a prayer. That Nicole Grant might be afraid, under pressure, and in command of less than all of her faculties. But she would never do anything that might endanger those babies.

• • •

The midday August sun was a burning orb of yellow, an oven set to broil that Avery would have given anything to be able to turn off. The air was heavy with humidty. The palm fronds hung limp and unmoving. Even the insects seemed to be hiding out waiting for things to cool off.

There was not a man on that site who had not removed his shirt, though the abdomens revealed varied in size and appearance from washboard to beer keg. The water they poured and squeezed over their heads evaporated as it slid down their bodies. But there was no shortage of sweat, which dropped in rivulets and briefly soaked whatever it fell on before it, too, disappeared.

Enrico's crew scampered over the new roof, careful not to touch the scaffolding with bare hands or bodies. Chase's crew was spread out around the property. The whine of their saws as they chopped their way through the concrete walkways, pool decking, and patios was high pitched and unrelenting. A cacophony of sound that never really stopped and had to be shouted over.

Maddie and Kyra had gone back to Bella Flora for lunch and hadn't yet returned. Avery, Roberto, two of Chase's best carpenters, and Ray Flamingo huddled together in a small patch of shade studying the plans for the rooftop deck. Ray and Avery were the only ones still wearing shirts, which clung like soaked second skins. Avery had tied one of Chase's spare T-shirts around her forehead, but it didn't stop the sweat from forming or from dropping wherever the hell it felt like, including on the plans. "Sorry!" She swiped at her sweaty face with an equally sweaty forearm and tried to summon cool thoughts. She might have thrown herself into the nearby Gulf of Mexico, except that at this time of day the sand scorched like the Sahara and the Gulf water belonged in a bathtub. She tried to focus in on the plans. She was excited about finally beginning the rooftop deck. And if they could just find more money, she knew they could . . .

There was a shout. And then another. The saws fell silent—not all at once—but before she realized what was happening there was . . . quiet. A horn beeped on the street. A seagull cawed overhead. A goose bump slithered up Avery's spine as Chase rounded what was left of the path that led back to the cottages.

"What is it?" she called as she moved toward him, trying to read his face. "What's . . . Has there been an accident?"

It took him several seconds after he reached her to catch his breath. A small crowd formed around them. Construction sites could be dangerous places. People lost digits and limbs and sometimes even their lives. She'd seen Chase handle many things but she'd never seen him quite this frazzled.

"What happened?"

"Back in the last patio. One of my guys . . ." He panted, drew another breath. His eyes locked on hers. "One of my guys found a skull. There may be a body, or what's left of one anyway. It was buried in the concrete."

Chapter Thirty-nine

Officer James Jackson and his partner, Officer Jennifer Hart-well, arrived about thirty minutes later. A team from the medical examiner's office wasn't far behind them. While the forensic team conferred with the officers and then quickly taped off the area and went to work, Avery, Chase, Ray, the Dantes, and members of their crews huddled in front of the main building in various states of agitation and distress.

Gerald Pitts, who had unearthed the skeletal remains, stood in the center of a fascinated audience expounding on his experience and gesticulating with large callused hands that shook slightly. "When I found the skull, it wasn't attached to anything and I didn't understand what it was at first. God, I thought I was going to lose my lunch."

Since it was her construction site, Avery had gone to see for herself. One glimpse of what lay in the torn-up earth had immediately made her wish that she hadn't. Now she tried not to listen as Gerald went on to describe the skull in stomach-turning detail. She had watched Deirdre die, had seen Max Golden dead, and her father laid out in his coffin. But there was something primal and frightening about a body devoid of flesh, about what had once been a living, breathing person shorn down to its underpinnings.

Chase put an arm around her shoulders. "You okay?" he asked when Gerald finally ran out of steam and gruesome adjectives.

"Sort of." Despite the heat a cold knot of dread formed inside her. She texted Kyra and asked her to let Maddie know what had happened. Then she paced the area between the main building and the pool trying not to picture the skull or imagine whatever else might be unearthed in the ground beneath that patio. It was uneven going now that the concrete was gone, the sand beneath it shifting and crumbling.

The workmen lingered in whatever shade they could find waiting to be interviewed by Officer Hartwell. Gerald went first. Others who had been cutting concrete in the same area followed. Those who waited drank from thermoses. There was little conversation. The sun still shone, the sky a vibrant blue painted with white puffy clouds. The shouts of beachgoers, the whine of boat engines, and the caw of gulls still reached them, but here the air was somber and funereal.

"I absolutely cannot believe this," Ray said after both of their interviews, which were quite perfunctory as neither of them had been anywhere near the cottages. "It's really quite macabre, isn't it?" His shudder was no less real for its theatricality. "Do you think it's Annelise's mother?"

Avery couldn't think who else it might be, but she had no energy for speculation. It would be a long time before she figured out how to erase her glimpse of the remains and Gerald's lurid description from her memory. And then there was the fact that they'd already lost half a day's work they could ill afford and had no commitment as to how much longer they might be shut down. By the time Maddie and Kyra arrived the interviews had been completed and the crew released. Enrico and Chase stood talking next to the scaffolding. Ray and Roberto were once again going over the roof deck drawings. Avery stood alone unable to focus, let alone participate.

She watched dully as Kyra climbed the scaffolding, her video camera slung over her shoulder. When she reached the top she raised the camera to her shoulder and began to describe the activity below, activity Avery did not want to hear about or envision.

"This is so unbelievable," Maddie said, her voice bleak, her shiver mirroring Avery's.

"John, Renée, and Annelise are here," Kyra called down softly from the scaffold sometime later. "Officer Jackson is talking to them." There was a brief pause. "Now they're headed over to the area that's being excavated."

Kyra paused. She did not continue. Her play-by-play was rendered unnecessary by the scream that rent the air.

• • •

Annelise's scream went on and on. It was a horrible keening thing. The force of it sent her to her knees where she rocked back and forth, her head bent, her eyes locked on the patch of upturned earth and what lay exposed inside it. Renée would have liked to drop beside her, oblivious to everything and everyone but herself, but her knees remained locked, her mind unable to cede control to her emotions no matter how turbulent. Slowly she lowered herself to the ground, her knees creaking in protest. Even more slowly she focused her gaze on what had been unearthed.

The skull was no longer attached to the rest of the skeleton but it lay at a slight angle nearby. Its eyeless sockets stared up at them. Its jaw hung open as if cut off midway through its own long-ago scream.

She wanted to believe that the skeleton belonged to Heinrich Stottermeier. That he had been the intruder. That the third voice, if in fact she'd heard one, had been his. And since she seemed to be making this up as she went along, that maybe he had died and Ilse had somehow survived. Though where her stepmother might have gone if that had been the case, Renée had no idea.

But the skeleton—she stumbled over the word in her mind even as she looked at it—was largely intact, apparently female, and exactly her stepmother's size. Annelise sobbed incoherently as they watched the technicians complete their work, their movements professionally precise, yet oddly gentle. Annelise's sobs began to turn into words. Those words were saturated with pain, but laced with triumph. "I knew she'd never run away! I knew she'd never leave me!"

"It's all right," Renée whispered. "Everything's going to be all right." The words were automatic. As was the arm that reached around her sister's shoulders, the hand that brushed back her hair.

Below, latex-gloved hands moved carefully, exploring, dusting, detaching, saving. Bits of fabric clung to bone. Annelise gasped as they recognized the scraps of pale pink fabric dotted with tiny rosebuds that were brought up in clear Baggies. Ilse had had a peignoir set, a nightgown and robe, made of it.

A band of tarnished metal encircled one bony finger, which was no longer attached to its hand. Renée gagged at the sight of it. Recoiled at the same moment Annelise did when a technician bagged it. The ring had never, until now, left Ilse's finger. It was the one their father had had engraved with the line lifted from the Book of Ruth. *Where you go, I will go, and where you stay, I will stay.* It had been Ilse's most prized possession.

"At least now we know," Renée said. In view of the ring, there was no point in even suggesting that it might be anyone else.

"Oh, God," Annelise cried. "I can't believe she was buried here all along. People have been walking all over her grave."

They clung together long after Ilse's remains had been

recovered and taken away. It was John who finally helped them up off their knees and onto their feet. Officers Jackson and Hartwell escorted them to the car, carefully picking out a path through the ditches and troughs that now bisected the property.

"I'll drive you wherever you'd like to go," Officer Jackson said as he helped them settle into the Cadillac. "Jennifer will follow us in the cruiser."

It didn't occur to any of them to argue. None of them could imagine driving even the short distance to their home. When they got there Renée used the last of her strength to tuck Annelise into the guest room bed before crawling into her own.

• • •

Maddie watched John, Renée, and Annelise depart. Sandwiched between the two police officers, all three of them appeared smaller and more stooped, their steps slower and more tentative than Maddie had ever seen them. Although they were free to leave, she, Kyra, Avery, and Chase remained at the main building unable to summon the collective will required to do so. They were still there when Officer Jackson came back to find them. Although they hadn't seem him arrive, Joe Giraldi was with him.

"Was it Annelise's mother?" Avery asked. Chase's arm was once again around her.

"We'll need to wait on DNA for a positive ID, but based on the fact that the original detective noted that the patio was poured shortly after she disappeared and given the personal items found with the remains, it seems pretty certain," J. J. said.

"How are Renée and Annelise?" Maddie asked.

"Renée's pretty stoic. Her sister isn't doing so well," the officer said. "In my experience with cases like this, assuming something and knowing it are very different things." He turned to Joe. "I was just saying to Agent Giraldi that foren-sic science can reveal a lot of the 'what' and even the 'how.' I'm hoping that we'll hear something from Stottermeir's former handler that might help us understand the 'why.' But it's not unusual in a case this cold to have to settle for less than a complete explanation."

"Any idea how much longer we'll be shut down?" Avery asked.

"I would imagine they'll continue to work the scene for a few more days, but I'll check and let you know," Officer Jackson said. He, Chase, and Avery left.

Joe remained behind. He seemed to be looking for some-thing. Or someone. "Do you have a minute, Maddie?"

"I'm going to get a little more video," Kyra said. "Just let me know when you're ready to go."

"All right." She and Joe watched Kyra disappear around the side of the building. Maddie turned back to face Joe, but she waited for him to speak.

"Is Nikki around?" he asked finally. "Or is she playing hooky back at Bella Flora?"

Maddie stared up into the agent's face. It looked uncreased and unworried. His tone was a little too light for her liking. "Why do you ask?"

"Do I need a reason?" he asked.

"I don't know, you tell me." Maddie waited and watched.

He shrugged. "I haven't heard from her. I just wanted to be sure she was all right." He held her gaze but his gave nothing away. At least nothing important. Even smart men could be so incredibly stupid.

"You haven't heard from her," Maddie repeated. "And has she heard from you? I mean in any way that would make her feel you really cared to know what she thought or felt?"

"Of course I . . ." He stopped, closed his mouth.

"Ah, so she might not be sure you'd want to hear anything that might be troubling her?"

He went still in the way of a lion scenting prey that she'd seen once on *Wild Kingdom*. She needed to be careful what she said and even what she didn't.

"Is something troubling Nikki?" No matter how carefully he shuttered the dark eyes and pretended otherwise, he cared.

"Maybe."

"Then if you're as close a friend as she thinks you are, you would need to tell me."

Maddie thought about the children Nikki was carrying. *Joe's children*. She thought about the ambivalence with which she was carrying them and her fear that Nikki's thinking might be muddled enough to do something Maddie knew Nikki would regret. Something from which she might never recover.

His eyes were like lasers. She could feel them searching her face, and possibly her mind and heart, for the truth. But Nikki's pregnancy was not her secret to share. Malcolm was a different thing altogether. He had some hold over Nikki that Joe could possibly do something about. But this, too, was a dicey matter. No wonder Nikki was keeping her distance—she could feel Joe's eyes probing.

"Would you be surprised if I told you that Nikki went to see her brother in prison?" Maddie asked.

"Not entirely." His gaze still gave nothing away. Neither did his answer.

"And if I told you that he'd been texting her nonstop and harassing her and maybe even threatening her?" Maddie asked.

"Then I'd have to make him stop," Joe said quietly. "I'd have to break him into tiny pieces and scatter those pieces to the corners of the earth."

"Because you love her."

"Because he's the scum of the earth and that's what he deserves."

This was not exactly the answer Maddie was hoping for.

"The thing is, she hasn't completely confided in me. But I'm pretty sure he's trying to get her to do something for him. Something that she doesn't want to do but may feel she has no choice about."

"Is that it?" His eyes plumbed hers as he searched for more.

"That's all I know. Or think I know." And definitely all she should say. "Except that it's possible that she's not thinking as clearly as she usually does." She clamped her lips shut and dropped her eyes.

"Thank you." He said this quietly and then, with none of his earlier feigned nonchalance, turned to leave.

As she watched him go, she prayed that she'd said and done the right thing. She would have loved to tell Joe everything, but she'd made a promise to Nikki. "Please, God," she whispered to herself as he strode out of sight. "Don't let that promise be the thing I regret for the rest of my life."

Chapter Forty

Renée padded quietly down the hall to the guest room where she'd sat with Annelise until the sleeping pill finally kicked in. Now her sister lay on her side, curled into a tight protective ball, whimpering and twitching, but at least she was asleep. She stared down at Annelise's ravaged face, shocked to see what the years and distress had done to it. When had the high, smooth cheeks sunk in on themselves? How had the skin grown so taut and thin, the age spots so prevalent? When had her little sister's mouth turned permanently downward so that her unhappiness was apparent even in repose? She looked far older than her nearly seventy years. If Annelise was "old" what did that make her?

Leaving the bedroom door open so she would know if she were needed, Renée went into the family room and lowered herself onto the couch. Moonlight streamed in through the windows; she could hear the wash of the tide on the sand barely a block away. A pile of boxes sat near her feet, brought down from the office attic. She lifted the lid of the closest box, which had been labeled and dated in her grandmother's hand, and pulled out the first photo album. New Year's Eve

1950. The eight-by-ten was a black-and-white of the hotel lobby. The windows had been hung with long silver fringe, paper lanterns strung above the entire space. In a corner on a raised platform a tuxedo-wearing trio with a sequin-gowned singer performed in the glow of a spotlight. On the improvised dance floor, the terrazzo shining like marble, couples were frozen midstep or midsway, all of them wearing formal attire. Her father had served as official photographer, and this album was filled with what Nana always requested: close-ups of the couples who danced in each other's arms or lingered in the dining room over tables draped in white linen, their faces bathed in candlelight. Photos that would be given to each guest before they checked out of the hotel and that undoubtedly graced family albums all over the Midwest.

As she turned and studied the pages, Renée recognized every face, every couple whether they were hotel regulars or local beach club members.

The Grossmans, who came each year from Detroit and who took a second cottage for their daughter and her children for the entire month of December. The Rosenzweigs and Weintraubs from Cleveland. The Schwartzes and Jacobsons from Chicago. New Yorkers might favor the East Coast and particularly Miami, but in the late fifties and sixties, midwesterners took advantage of the newly inaugurated national interstate highway system to make their way to Florida's west coast and St. Petersburg Beach.

Renée traced the outline of Nana's and Pop Pop's figures at the center of the group photo taken just after midnight each New Year's Eve. On New Year's Day another would be taken of everyone—grandparents, parents, children, longtime employees, plus all the Handlemans, a shot her father would set up and then take with the aid of a self-rigged timer. Always Nana would remind them that "the reason *our guests* come back every year is because they know they are family."

"Renée?" John stood in the doorway, his eyes half closed and his voice thick with sleep. "Is everything okay?"

"I wanted to check on Annelise. And then, I don't know, I couldn't seem to go to sleep. I was just looking at the old New Year's pictures."

"Really?" He yawned and came to sit next to her. The sofa dipped as he pulled her close. She rested her head on his shoulder. It was narrower and frailer than it had once been. But John's strength had always radiated from the inside out.

"It's no wonder," he murmured. "What a day. I never believed Ilse would have ever done your father harm. But I did think she might have had a reason to run. She always seemed oddly frightened. As if she were somehow waiting for the rug to be snatched out from under her."

"You've never said that before." Renée lifted her head.

"Haven't I?"

"I feel like I've started remembering things I didn't even know I knew," she said. She hadn't only been unable to fall asleep, she'd been afraid to. Afraid not of seeing what had been left of Ilse's body, but of hearing words and seeing images that had begun to take shape in her mind. "I think I heard them arguing."

"Who? Your father and Ilse?"

"I don't know. That's what I thought. But I'm starting to wonder. There was a lot of German even though Ilse and my father always spoke English. I heard the word 'Juden!' And Ami refers to American, I think. And mein! Mein tochter! That means 'daughter.'" She closed her eyes. Trying to remember was less frightening with John by her side. "Ilse was the one who sounded hysterical. Which doesn't really make sense, does it? I don't think I ever heard her raise her voice in all the time I knew her. But I'm pretty sure I heard her say, 'Nein! Not yours!'"

For the first time, she could see herself standing in the kitchen with the glass of water she'd gotten up for, feeling that something didn't fit but not understanding what. "I don't know. I thought it was just the two of them. That they were arguing for some reason. And in the morning when my father was dead and Ilse was gone, I thought that proved it. But I think there might have been a third voice." Tears gathered, pricking her lids. Had she heard Ilse pleading? A noise? Some sort of scuffling? Had she really said, "Not your *tochter*!" And why would she say that to her husband? "Oh, God, I should have knocked on the door. I should have done something."

The tears pressed more insistently and it took her a few moments to recognize what they were. "And why am I only remembering now?"

"Shhh," he soothed. "Don't worry. I don't know what you could have done about any of it."

"I'm crying," she said, shocked at the unaccustomed wetness on her cheeks. She never cried. Never.

"It's all right. You're allowed to. You have every right. You're just always so busy being strong and taking care of everybody else that you push your own problems and worries aside. But that doesn't necessarily make them disappear."

He pushed her hair back off her face. "Annelise isn't the only one who lost a parent that night. And you'd already lost your mother when you were even younger than she was when Ilse died."

She looked at her husband, made herself consider what he'd said. What would she do without him? "How'd you get so smart?" She pressed a kiss to his forehead. Another to his weathered cheek.

"I guess after all these years my wife finally started rubbing off on me."

"I love you." She smiled, cupping his cheek in her hand. "I'm so lucky to have you."

He shook his head and cupped the hand that cupped his cheek, the touch warm and comforting. "I'm the lucky one," he said gently. "And I thank whoever is in charge up there every single day for giving you to me."

She sighed when John put his arms around her. She buried her face in his chest and thought again about her father and Ilse. In comparison to the decades she'd shared with John, they'd had so few years of happiness. And Annelise had had almost none at all.

. . .

Nikki would have given a lot to be wearing her "lucky suit." The one that would have given her confidence to not act like what she was: a desperate family member of a convicted felon, acting on his behalf while trying to figure out how to turn the tables on him. For the entire five-hour drive to Tallahassee in the Florida Panhandle, she'd racked her brain to come up with a means of retrieving the cash Malcolm had put in her name without drawing undue attention.

In the end she'd had no choice but to show her ID and sign in. Despite the absence of her lucky suit, no one had tried to stop her. As she emptied the safe-deposit box, she debated what she would do with the money—assuming she got out of the bank without tripping up. Pay it to whoever threatened Malcolm's life (if, in fact, there was a shred of truth to this story)? Turn it in to the authorities (this would include Joe) so that it could be disbursed through proper channels to Malcolm's victims? Or, and she was ashamed of how much she preferred door number three—keeping it to give to the victims she knew personally (that would be herself, Maddie, and Avery) so that they could use it for the damned renovation, which was still stalled in every possible way. Once she figured out whom the money should go to, she'd have to come up with a way to keep Malcolm from carrying through on his threats against Joe and her. Every part of this both alarmed and exhausted her.

"Ma'am?" She'd left the vault and was crossing the bank lobby when the voice sounded behind her. "Wait. Just a minute. Ma'am!"

Nikki's brain weighed the words and the urgency behind them as her feet did a stutter step. She didn't want to stop, though. She couldn't. The front door was just a few steps ahead of her.

"Ma'am! In the green shirt!"

Caught. Mind racing, Nikki prepared to turn around. She must not raise her hands in surrender. *Stay calm.* She hadn't done anything illegal. It would only be illegal if anyone found out that the money she'd retrieved from the safe deposit box was stolen and put there by a convicted felon. She gauged the number of steps to the door, then forced herself to turn slowly. "Yes?"

"You dropped this." The bank employee moved quickly toward her.

Nikki had to force herself to hold her ground, to keep her smile steady.

The young woman stopped directly in front of her. "Ms. Grant?"

Nikki braced for the words *you're under arrest.* Or *please come with me.* "Yes?"

The employee reached out and . . . handed Nikki her driver's license.

Jesus. "Thank you."

"No problem," the young woman said. But she stared at Nikki a beat or two longer than seemed necessary. As if she were memorizing Nikki's features. Or possibly wasn't really a bank employee at all but a . . . *Enough.*

Nikki nodded, smiled once more, and turned clutching her driver's license in her hand while using her elbow to hold the purse, now stuffed with wads of cash, tight to her side. It took everything she had not to sprint out the door.

"Get a grip," she said once she'd gotten into the Jag, locked the doors, and turned on the ignition. She sat slowing her breathing and waiting for the air-conditioning to blow cool. "If you're going to jump every time someone speaks to you, you might as well carry a neon arrow over your head that flashes the words 'guilty person.'" Redirecting the vent to the sweat-soaked blouse that now stretched too tight across her breasts, she pulled out the list of banks, which criss-crossed Florida. She'd come northwest to Tallahassee. The next bank was in Jacksonville on the opposite coast. It was only 164 miles due east on I-10, but it was already three o'clock. Even if she made it before the bank closed, she'd have to race in and out; someone in a bank in too big a hurry would be calling attention to herself. She could go ahead and make the drive now, spend the night in a hotel near the bank, and go in the next morning at a time when the bank would be busy enough that she could go unnoticed. "No worries," she told herself. "Everything's under control. You don't have to decide what to do with the money now. You just have to retrieve it." Decision made, she backed out of the parking space and made her way to the interstate.

In the morning she lay in bed and stared out at the rain slanting down on the hotel window. She'd overslept yet still felt like it would take a few more hours to be truly rested. Feeling as heavy as the iron-colored sky, she got up and moved slowly into the bathroom, where she took her time showering and dressing. She longed for a cup of coffee, but Maddie had insisted that she needed to cut out caffeine. *For the babies.* Now she eyed the two chocolates that she'd dis-covered in the bottom of her purse. *They have caffeine in them,* Maddie's voice said in her head. But at the moment Nikki didn't care. They were small. How much caffeine could they possibly contain? Besides, where were the perks that pregnant women were supposed to be entitled to, she wondered as she unwrapped the first gold foil and popped the candy in her mouth. Wasn't she allowed, even expected, to eat?

She considered herself in the full-length mirror as she savored the final chocolate. The sleeveless white blouse did gape a bit around the buttons, but its peplum hid the fact that she'd been unable to button the waistband of the black pencil skirt she'd paired it with. The black-and-white-patterned pumps smartened the plain pieces up a bit. They were now her go-to dress shoe because of their kitten heel.

Her breakfast done, she checked out of the hotel and headed for the second bank on Malcolm's list. This time she entered the bank lobby with her head high and a pleasant smile on her lips. A greeter showed her to the safe-deposit vault. With far less dithering than in Tallahassee, she signed in, showed her ID, and went inside. It only took her a few minutes to find the numbered box and remove it from its spot. Glancing over her shoulder even though she knew she was alone, she carried it to the vault table, opened it, and began to remove the bound bills. Yesterday's box had held a lot of hundred-dollar packets but had not been full. This box was tightly packed and held more than twice as many stacks of hundred-dollar bills. Her mental calculator put the total so far somewhere around $500,000. If the safe-deposit boxes continued to bear this much fruit, there'd be more than enough to renovate the hotel, cover production of a new season, turn in a huge chunk to the government, and still pay off whoever was threatening Malcolm's life. *This money may be in your name but that doesn't make it yours. If you keep any of this, you're no better than your brother.*

She brushed the thoughts aside as she exited the vault and began to make her way through the lobby. Once she had retrieved all the money she'd figure out what should be done with it. No one seemed to be watching or even noticing her at all. Relieved, she nodded good-bye to the greeter and covered the last few steps to the door glad to see the rain had stopped. Then she was outside into the hot, muggy air, exultant at how smoothly the retrieval had gone and striding across the parking lot to the Jag. Which was when she saw the man standing next to it. A man who looked an awful lot like Joe Giraldi.

"What are you doing here?" she asked as he folded his arms across his chest and leaned back against her car. An overnight bag sat at his feet.

"I could ask you the same thing. In fact I *am* asking you the same thing." Joe's eyes were dark and steely. The tic in his cheek apparent. He was wearing the blue pin-striped suit, crisp white shirt, and red tie in which he liked to make arrests.

"How did you find me?"

"I'm with the FBI," he said drily. She wished he'd put his sunglasses on so she wouldn't have to see the way he was looking at her. "We do have one or two resources at our disposal." His cheek ticked his disapproval again. "And FYI, the next time you decide to do something illegal and want to avoid detection, it's best not to use your credit cards."

She knew this, of course. Anyone who'd ever watched an episode of *Castle* knew better. She'd just been so intent on getting this taken care of and getting Malcolm off her back that she hadn't been thinking clearly. As if on cue a text dinged in. "Who says I'm doing something illegal?" she demanded, careful not to look at her phone. She did not want him to know that she'd been communicating with . . .

"Is that Malcolm?" He held out his palm, making it clear he expected her to hand over her phone.

"What in the world are you talking about?" She tried for shock and righteous indignation; only the shocked part rang true.

"I know he's been texting you," Joe said, lifting the phone out of her fingers. "And threatening you."

Once again, she was at a loss for words. As many times as she'd known she should tell him and worried about him finding out, she hadn't prepared any kind of defense or explanation.

"He's not just threatening me," she said. "He's been threatening to implicate you." She paused. "And also someone's put a hit out on him."

It was clear from his lack of reaction that none of this was news to him. She tried not to fidget under his regard, but it was hard to stand up under his merciless gaze when she knew just how much right he had to be angry.

"There's nothing Malcolm can do to me or my career no matter how much he might want to. And while I'm guessing everyone who's ever known him for more than five seconds would like to see him dead, there is no hit," Joe said grimly. "No one but your brother is demanding money."

"What?" This time the shock was real and automatic. She'd known this was a possibility but still had not been able to take the chance that something would happen to Malcolm that she could have prevented. "How do you know that?"

"Because the person who smuggled that cell phone in to him works for us." He watched her face as the implication of just how much he knew sank in. His nod was as sharp as his voice. "He's played you again, Nikki. Like he's been playing you his whole life. And for some reason you just keep going back for more instead of asking for help from someone who could have given it."

Tears formed, blurring her vision. Her brother, whom she'd practically raised, was a selfish, self-absorbed, and criminally greedy human being who'd bankrupted hundreds of people, charities, and institutions. Once again, he'd proven that he didn't give a single shit about her. Her lip began to tremble. She ordered it to stiffen up.

"It would have been nice—and a whole lot smarter—if you'd confided in me. Because now I'm in an awkward position." Joe looked at her as if he were trying to figure out what he'd ever seen in her. "If we don't clean up this mess right away, I'm going to be forced to arrest the woman who appears to be carrying my child."

Nikki's head jerked up. "How do you . . . ? What makes you think that?" She couldn't believe Maddie had told him.

He looked her over, his angry gaze lingering on her breasts in the too-tight blouse and the bulge of the waistband that she'd been unable to pin closed. "I think that because I know your body better than I know my own," he bit out. "And because you recently used your credit card to pay the firm of

Gabianelli, Gutschenritter, and Payne for an OB-GYN appointment that included an ultrasound." He let that and his anger hang in the air like a dark cloud. "I can't help wondering when you were planning to tell me."

Guilt flooded through her. Tears formed again for what had to be the second time in five minutes. She should have listened to Maddie. She should have told him. She . . . The self-recriminations stopped. "You were checking up on me. You knew about the appointment but you never called." Anger coursed through her, shoving the guilt aside. "That ultrasound could have been for a tumor or something!"

Joe stepped closer. Leaned over her. "But it wasn't, was it? What was your plan, Nikki? I'd like to believe you were going to tell me at some point. And I have to think that you know me enough to know how happy I would have been to find out that we were going to have a child together." His hurt and anger rained down on her, showering her in its white-hot ash. He had every right to that anger; she knew he did. But he did not have the right to make her feel so small and miserable. She yanked her eyes back up from the asphalt. "Not a child!" she shouted, surprising them both.

"What?"

"It's not a child, damn it! It's children. I'm pregnant with twins!"

For an instant, surprise softened his eyes. He tamped it down. Within seconds they were once again hard and unforgiving.

His hand shot out again. "Give me the list."

"What list?" Any control she'd started with was completely gone. Her mind might be moving at a turtle's pace, but her mouth and her emotions were flying at warp speed.

"And the keys."

"I don't think so," she said, staring him in the eye.

"Then think again."

"I'm not handing over anything or going anywhere until you tell me where we would be going and why."

"Get in the car," he said tersely. "I'll drive."

"Where are we going?" she asked again, her anger flaring.

His sigh was one of disgust but also of capitulation. "We're going to retrieve the cash. Then you're going to turn it in. And you're going to do it in front of witnesses so that there can be no question that you were colluding or doing anything other than retrieving the money on behalf of your brother's victims."

"But . . ." she began.

"The list and the keys. Now."

She handed them over and then stomped around the car, yanked open the passenger door, and sank into the seat. He threw his bag in the trunk, adjusted the driver's seat, and buckled his seat belt.

"How long until . . ."

"No. Don't speak. I don't want to even hear your voice." He looked at her as if she were a stranger. "And for God's sake don't cry."

She'd lost him. She hadn't trusted him and now she'd lost him. Nikki struggled to control her thoughts and her emotions as Joe peeled out of the parking lot with an angry squeal of tires. As it turned out, not speaking was a lot easier than not crying. She kept her head turned and her eyes trained out the passenger window as billboards, scrub, and exit signs blurred by.

Chapter Forty-one

Officer Jackson looked slightly uncomfortable that afternoon when he arrived at the house to share what had—and had not—been determined about what happened that July night in 1952. Renée showed him to a chair in the family room, then took her place on the sofa between Annelise and John. The box of photo albums still sat nearby.

Annelise's attempts to regroup and regain her bearings had met with mixed results. She'd lost weight since the remains had been discovered, and appeared almost skeletal herself. Today she seemed wan but calmer and Renée hoped that whatever the young policeman had to say would offer enough closure so that all of them, and especially Annelise, could begin to move on.

"So." Renée took hold of Annelise's hand. Her too-thin body trembled against Renée's like a twig caught in a stiff breeze. "What can you tell us?"

The policeman glanced down at his notes, then leaned forward in his chair. "We have confirmed the original finding that your father died of blunt-force trauma. His head wound was the result of contact with the corner of the bedroom dresser. Photographs of the scene confirm that there was an altercation. At the time it was assumed the altercation took place between David and Ilse and that she fled."

"And now?" Renée asked.

"Now a new analysis of bloodstains on the deceased's pajamas and the carpet sample indicates that someone else was there at the time of death and also lost blood. That person had the same blood type as Heinrich Stottermeir, according to his military records."

"But that only proves someone with the same blood type was there." Annelise squeezed Renée's hand. "It doesn't prove it was Stottermeir."

"No," Officer Jackson said. "But his fingerprints do. We know he was in the apartment because when we ran the prints lifted from the bedroom through the IAFIS database—something that didn't exist in 1952—we got a match. Stottermeir was definitely there. Based on blood spatter and the location of his fingerprints, he was definitely a part of the altercation."

Annelise clenched Renée's hand more tightly. "And the . . . my mother?"

Renée closed her eyes trying yet again to hear and to remember. Every night she dreamt that she was standing in front of the refrigerator with the glass of water in her hands. But while the moments in which she stood there straining to hear became increasingly clear, the memory never changed and it never went further. Had she already been back in bed when that struggle had taken place and her father's head split open?

"We have DNA confirmation that the skeletal remains that were unearthed are Ilse's. It's clear she was involved in the struggle that took place. The bones in her hands display dents and splintering. Her right wrist was fractured."

Beside her, Annelise seemed to have stopped breathing. She had not stopped trembling.

"Her neck was broken perimortem," J. J. said.

"What . . . what does that mean?" Renée asked as Annelise's hold on her hand tightened.

"It means that her neck was broken at or around the time of death," he replied gently. "Official cause of death is listed as spinal shock. Which means that . . ."

". . . death would have been instantaneous," Annelise whispered, her relief evident.

Renée drew a deep breath and felt Annelise do the same.

"We heard back from Stottermeir's handler, Jim Newsome, in Round Rock, Arizona. Apparently Stottermeir used a number of aliases after the war. The cold war was heating up and although it's unclear how many sides of the fence he may have been playing by 1952, he did travel in and out of the United States. It wouldn't have been difficult for him to locate your mother."

"And the note I found in the photo album?" Renée asked.

Jackson pulled a piece of paper from the file in his lap. "It's an apology of sorts," he said quietly. "He expresses regret for 'losing control of himself.' But he then absolves himself for 'exercising a husband's rights' since they had been promised to each other and would one day be married."

"Oh, God," Annelise said, her eyes pinned to J. J.'s face. "She was pregnant with me when she got here." Annelise's voice was once again breathy and childish; the hand that still clung to Renée's trembled. "Was . . . could Heinrich Stottermeir be my father?"

"No." Officer Jackson shook his head. "That's one of the few things I can say with complete certainty. Based on your, your mother's, and his blood types, he couldn't have been your biological father. But, of course, he wouldn't necessarily have known that."

Annelise breathed a sigh of what could only be relief. Renée did the same.

"A good number of OSS files were declassified by the CIA

in the 1980s. Others were declassified more recently. Some relating to intelligence operations during WWII are still being withheld. Former agent Newsome is willing and able to answer questions that pertain to your parents and Heinrich Stottermeir. He's actually standing by now if you'd like me to call."

At Annelise's nod, Officer Jackson punched in the number. She drew several deep breaths while the introductions were made via speakerphone. Clinging to Renée's hand as if it were a life raft, she said, "Can you tell me . . ." Another breath. A swallow. "Was my mother a spy?"

"No," Newsome replied without hesitation. "She did provide a cover of sorts for your father's extended stay in Frankfurt. But it appears that however their relationship began, the marriage and their feelings for each other were real." He paused then and his voice gentled. "I met your father on several occasions. He was a fine man."

John's arm went around Renée's shoulders. Annelise leaned in closer. "But why would Stottermeir show up all those years later?" he asked. "What did he want?"

"I don't know," Newsome said. "But he was obsessed with Ilse. When he learned that she'd married and moved to America, he was furious. When he discovered that she'd had a child, he became convinced that the child was his."

No one interrupted as the former OSS agent continued. Renée didn't think she was the only one barely breathing.

"We had no warning he was headed to Florida. I don't know what he intended. I think he'd convinced himself that Ilse was there because she thought she had no other option. To the end he insisted he didn't mean to kill anyone. That she jumped on his back while he was fighting off Handleman and when he flung her off she slammed into the wall. When he realized she was dead and that Handleman was dying, he disposed of her body and ran."

Beside her, Annelise shuddered. Tears pricked at the back

of Renée's eyelids. All these years the government had known what had taken place that horrible night in July and no one had told them.

"What happened to Stottermeir?" John asked.

"The Russians wanted him," Newsome said matter-of-factly. "And we wanted to be rid of him. I believe he spent his last days in a Russian gulag."

It was John who escorted the officer out while Renée and Annelise continued to sit, their hands clasped.

Annelise was the first to speak. "I wanted so badly to find her, to know that she didn't leave of her own free will." Her voice wobbled. Tears pooled in her eyes as she met Renée's gaze. "And now that I do know, I just feel worse."

"I know," Renée said, watching her sister's face and trying to hold back her own tears. Once she'd allowed herself to cry that day at the hotel, it was as if the floodgates had opened; she had not yet figured out how to close them.

"But at least we finally have some answers. You were right about pretty much everything. I was wrong. We were all wrong to doubt you."

Annelise's smile was sad. She made no move to wipe away the tears as they slid down her ravaged face. "I used to fantasize about hearing that from you. But it doesn't really change anything. My mother has been lying in the ground all these years while everyone thought the worst of her." She let go of Renée's hand. Her eyes narrowed. Her tone stiffened. So did her shoulders. "You were right about one important thing, though. The hotel should be torn down and the land sold. I'd do it with my own two hands if I could." Annelise stood slowly. "I want it gone as soon as possible. I don't ever want to have to see it again."

Renée looked at her sister in surprise. After all these years of begging her to do just that, it was the last thing she'd expected. "But we gave Avery and Maddie and the others permission to renovate. We pledged money. And we gave them our word."

"I don't care," Annelise said. "Everything's changed. And it's not as if we put anything in writing."

Annelise had been deadly serious. Nothing Renée said seemed to make an impression or come close to changing her mind.

Two days later she and John sat uncomfortably on either side of Annelise as she presented "their" decision to Avery, Chase, Maddie, Kyra, and Steve Singer in the salon at Bella Flora.

"But we've already started construction." Avery's shock was apparent in her voice. "I know we're behind schedule, but we can still make it attractive to a buyer."

The others voiced their agreement. They'd assembled expecting to discuss details of design and construction and been blindsided with a complete change of plan.

"We no longer want to sell it," Annelise said. Renée had to clamp her mouth shut as eyes locked on her and John at Annelise's "we." "The circumstances have changed." It was odd to see her sister so adamant, so in charge. The dithering breathiness was gone, smothered by this new resolve. "We're going to tear it down."

For a long moment no one spoke.

"But we agreed," Maddie finally said. "We've raised money and sponsorships."

"Renée. Please," Avery said. "You and John know how much has already been poured into this project. Let us finish. Let us show you what I know it can be."

"Renée and John have agreed," Annelise said. "There's no point in showing anyone anything." She stood. Renée and John followed suit like puppets whose strings had been pulled. "Thank you for everything you've done. If you'll excuse me, I'll wait out in the car," Annelise said. She turned and headed down the central hall toward the front door.

"I'm sorry. I know you would have done a spectacular job." John handed Avery the envelope he'd brought. "This is a signed and notarized document promising to pay back sponsors and out-of-pocket expenses out of proceeds from the sale of the land. Needless to say, we'll pay for the demolition ourselves."

"I'm sorry, too," Renée said, hugging each of them in turn. "More than I can say. After all these years, I was looking forward to taming that jungle and to seeing the hotel brought back." She found a smile and hoped they understood the apology in it. "But it's a relief to know what actually happened and to see Annelise . . . reconciled. And I think it's finally time to let go and focus as best we can on healing." She took John's hand and the two of them walked slowly toward the front door.

• • •

Despite her mother's attempts to get them to look at their collective glass as half full, as far as Kyra could tell the collective mood at Bella Flora was downright empty.

"I can't believe they yanked the whole project out from underneath us like that without warning or anything," Avery exclaimed repeatedly as she paced the grounds, too anxious and too agitated to sit still. Maddie cleaned house, doing load after load of laundry before Steve could get to it, and cooked comfort food that no one but her father ate.

Kyra sat alone in front of a video monitor watching the footage they'd shot at the Sunshine Hotel. The video of the buildings and grounds was good, but as always it was the shots of the people whose history was tied up in the hotel and those who'd been determined to bring it back that drew her. She replayed a sequence she'd shot in which Renée shared the guest registers her grandmother had kept and talked about "Nana's" personality and philosophy as a hotelier. This—not the nuts and bolts of remodeling or their own much-too-publicized lives—was what *Do Over* should be about. If only she could find a way to make it happen.

She checked the *Do Over* Facebook page and Twitter feed, which the network had taken over without warning and wall-papered with countless close-ups of Dustin. Each new episode brought new fans and followers, but those viewers seemed most interested in her mother's budding romance with William Hightower and Deirdre's attempts to win over the daughter she'd abandoned. They "liked" and reacted to the obstacles the network had thrown in their way. Time and again it was the personal problems each of them wrestled with that elicited the most interest and response. Was that only because that was what the network had focused on? Or could Troy and Daniel be right? Would a straight renovation show elicit the same kind of response and gain any audience at all?

She frowned at the thought of Troy Matthews, who had become as hard to reach as the network heads had always been. She'd left three messages that had gone unanswered and had no idea when, or if, he'd be back. All the more reason to remember that he was undoubtedly just as devious and motivated by self-interest as the network, no matter what he claimed.

Leaving her computer, she moved to the window. Despite the heat, her mother puttered with the planters, trimming and pruning. Her father lounged on the pool steps, a paper-back in his hands. Every once in a while when he thought Maddie wasn't looking he stole a peek. Kyra watched them, seeing her father's hopefulness, her mother's inattention. If she'd still wanted to, Kyra could have pretended they were still married, that their family was still intact. But despite the murkiness of their current situation, she couldn't even bring herself to wish it. Her mother had found the strength to move forward; surely her father would have to do the same.

Her phone rang. Daniel's face filled the screen. When she answered, it wasn't Daniel but Dustin who greeted her.

"It's me, Mommy!"

"Hi, sweetie," she said, smiling at the glee in his voice. "Are you having a good time?"

"Is fun! I been acting today. Jes like Dundell!"

"Really?" she asked, hoping for a no.

"The tyreckther tolded me I was a natchral."

"That's great, sweetheart," she said. Then as casually as she could, "Please put your dad on the phone."

"A lady's rubbing him. He can't right now."

"Dustin?"

There was muffled female laughter in the background. A rustle of movement. Then Daniel was on the phone. "I don't think that was an accurate description of what's going on."

"Oh? And what is going on there?" Kyra asked.

"First of all, the woman rubbing me is a masseuse. I pulled a muscle doing a stunt yesterday and I'm having a massage. Purely medicinal."

There was more female laughter. Kyra felt a quick stab of jealousy, which she pushed aside. "Well, as long as everyone's clothed and behaving themselves, I hope your muscle recovers. But I'm not okay with Dustin performing on camera. And I know you know that."

"It was just a small cameo," he rushed to reassure her. "They added a flashback sequence of my character as a small child and you have to admit he's a dead ringer."

"Still not okay. I'm serious, Daniel. We agreed that would never happen without a discussion."

The doorbell rang downstairs.

"Won't happen again," he said way too smoothly as she turned to head for the stairs. "We're having a great time together. I'll deliver him back to you all in one piece before you know it."

The doorbell sounded again; she hung up as she reached it and tucked the phone in her pocket. A UPS truck idled in the drive. The deliveryman held out an envelope addressed to her. He handed her a pen and asked for her signature.

Her mind still on the conversation with Daniel, she opened the envelope and stared down at the letter. Which was from the network legal department. It had been sent, it said, to inform them that they were in breach of contract. That they were not allowed to "quit" the series. And that if they did not come back to work, they would face legal action.

Kyra couldn't seem to catch her breath. The words blurred and then came back into focus. Her head pounded in fury as she continued reading the document. Which claimed that the title *Do Over* did not belong to them. That they had all signed enforceable noncompetes. And that if they attempted to produce a renovation television show and sell it to another network, Kyra Singer, Madeline Singer, Avery Lawford, and Nicole Grant would be prosecuted to the full extent of the law.

Chapter Forty-two

Joe practically marched Nikki into Tampa FBI headquarters, signed them both in without comment, then deposited her in a chair in the first hallway they came to.

"What?" she snapped. "You're not going to handcuff me?"

"Don't tempt me," he growled. "And stay where you are. Do not move." He turned his back, knocked on a closed office door, and disappeared inside.

As soon as he was out of sight, Nikki got up and went in search of a ladies' room, glad Joe wasn't there to comment. When he'd complained about the frequent stops during their interminable "road trip," she'd informed him that she wouldn't have to go to the bathroom so frequently if it weren't for him. She'd then swept into the truck stop bathroom as regally as one could when one urgently needed to pee. Putting his angry face behind her had become almost as important as emptying her bladder.

The FBI bathroom would never be called lavish but it beat out most of the fast-food and truck stop bathrooms she'd visited over the last three days and afforded her a few minutes of much-needed privacy. Not to mention a brief respite from Joe Giraldi and his anger, which she'd countered with her own again and again until they'd built a wall of it between them as hard and unforgiving as stone. Whatever happened next, it was clear there would be no going back to what had been. Trust had been broken on both sides. She couldn't imagine how they could possibly get beyond that.

She washed her hands and splashed water on her face. After a brief internal debate she pulled out her makeup bag and went to work on her face. Not because Joe would notice or even look at her, but because she suspected that when turning in $3.2 million in stolen cash to a government agency, a woman might want to don armor.

"There." Her face still looked pale despite the foundation and blush, and the cover stick hadn't completely eradicated the dark circles under her eyes, but the Visine had helped and so had the liner and mascara. A quick French braid hid her hair's lack of sheen. She felt nothing like herself, but at least she resembled her.

"Nicole Grant?"

Nikki looked up and met the woman's gaze in the bathroom mirror. She had short dark hair and a pixieish face. The black pantsuit and crisp white blouse identified her as a special agent.

"Guilty," Nikki said. "On second thought, maybe I should clarify that."

The woman smiled slightly. "No need. I'm Maura Hastings. I was sent by Agent Giraldi to make sure you hadn't escaped."

"Still here," Nikki said. The knot of dread remained, but she was almost eager for this whole thing to be over. These past three days had been an agony. She'd understood Joe's hurt and anger and knew that she deserved it. She even got the strategy—she'd been crazy to think she could just go retrieve the money and then either keep it, hand it over to Malcolm, or waltz into FBI headquarters to turn it in without coming under suspicion. Especially now that she knew the FBI and Joe had been aware of her visit with Malcolm and of what he'd asked her to do almost from the beginning. And yet he'd betrayed her equally in sneaking around, knowing things about her that he shouldn't, that she wasn't ready to share.

She'd clung to her anger and tried to give as good as she got. Still, she'd been unprepared for how much his distance would hurt. How awful it would feel not to share the same bed or even the same hotel room. How lonely it would be to sit so close to him in the confines of the Jag and be worlds apart.

"Without honesty and trust we have nothing," was the only thing he'd said on the subject, and only after he'd finished berating her. "But I think those things go together." He'd said this as if she were the only one who'd behaved badly. As if he weren't the very definition of the pot calling the kettle black.

She came out of the ladies' room to find him glowering at her. She glowered back.

"I've handed over the money to the special agent in charge," he said, motioning to the office he'd disappeared into earlier. "You're going to have to make a statement. I suggest you try to stick with the truth since all of your conversations and texts with Malcolm were recorded." His words were razor sharp. His jaw and eyes hard. Nonetheless he'd managed to warn her.

The formal statement was nothing compared to the road trip she'd survived. When she'd finished she'd asked, "You're sure that Malcolm's life was not being threatened?"

Joe's eyes glittered with anger, but he'd remained silent.

"We're certain," the agent in charge said. "He concocted the threat to get you to act. We have made certain that he won't be accessing a cell phone again for a very long time. And he's been moved to a somewhat less cushy location."

Joe smiled with what she recognized as grim satisfaction. When the interview was over he walked her to her car, retrieved his bag, and handed her the keys. "Are you all right to drive?" he asked curtly. "If not, I can get someone to drive you to Bella Flora."

"I'm fine. Thanks." She looked up into his face, searching it for some sign of warmth, for a remnant of the love that had always seemed to shine out of his eyes and that she'd stupidly taken for granted.

Her eyes filled with tears. Again. She wanted to tell him how sorry she was and knew she should at least attempt to explain. But he'd rejected every one of her ill-formed apologies and she had no idea how to explain her fears let alone her actions. She barely understood them herself. She felt incredibly pathetic and tired as she got into the driver's seat and lowered the window. God, she was tired. "So," she said. "Take care of yourself."

She put the car in gear. He didn't step back and he hadn't stopped glaring at her. "What?" she snapped. "Whatever you're thinking just say it for heaven's sake. I feel bad enough without all this silent condemnation." Tears threatened again. She'd really had it with the tears.

"You feel bad?" he asked in a deadly calm voice. "I've been trying to figure out how you could be pregnant and not tell me." It was not a question. "Which led me to wonder if the reason you didn't tell me is because I'm not the father."

She blinked in surprise.

"I mean why else would a woman I love and have asked to marry me not share that information?" He put his hands on the edge of the car and leaned in. "Are the babies mine? Or did you sleep with someone else?"

The tears evaporated. Incinerated by the anger that flashed through her. "How can you ask that?"

His eyes blazed hot. He'd always been so calm and

controlled, his emotions strong but held in check. "How can I not?" he snapped back. "I mean, I keep trying to understand how you could have not told me. And the only thing that comes anywhere close to explaining it is if I'm not the father."

She clenched the wheel. She'd never wanted to slap someone as much as she wanted to slap his face now. "You can't actually think I slept with someone else!"

"I don't know," he said. "The idea never occurred to me until I found out about your pregnancy on my own. Because you see, I never thought you were the kind of woman who would carry a man's child and not tell him. So, you'll have to forgive me if I find it a little challenging to know what you would and wouldn't do."

She turned the key in the ignition, gave it gas. The engine sprang to life. "They're yours, all right, you sanctimonious asshole!" she shouted. "Courtesy of you and your gold-medal sperm!" She revved the engine, threw the car into gear. "I may be a lot of things, but I'm not a cheater. But if you want a paternity test, be my guest!"

A crowd of dark-suited, white-shirted agents had stopped to watch the altercation but Nikki didn't care. They could all go to hell. Nikki mashed her foot down on the accelerator and felt the Jag surge away from the curb. It was her fondest hope that she'd managed to run over at least a few of Joe Giraldi's toes in the process.

· · ·

Avery paced Bella Flora. Then she paced the grounds that surrounded it. When more space was required, she paced the beach, covering it in long sweeping arcs and loops that she did not choose but which seemed to choose her. They had lost the Sunshine Hotel. They'd not only failed to complete it, they'd failed to save it. Soon it would be torn down. Bulldozed. Obliterated from the face of the earth. She felt its loss deep in the pit of her stomach and, oddly, in her heart.

Because she had seen what it could be and she had believed that she could bring that vision to life. And she had failed.

As she paced and fretted, she imagined her parents turning over in their graves. She saw them shaking their heads in dismay, wondering where they'd gone wrong. Chase had stopped arguing with her, had given up trying to talk "sense" into her. Even Jeff, who had sat her down and tried to explain that not every building or structure was meant to be saved or even rehabilitated and that no one and nothing lasted forever, had thrown up his hands in frustration.

Intellectually, she understood that what they both said was true. Knew that she was being childish. And still she railed at the unfairness of it. The Sunshine Hotel had been their only opportunity, a perfect one at that, and she had let it slip through her fingers. Now they'd lost *Do Over*. The list of losses and mistakes tormented her. Kept her awake at night. A dozen times a day she decided to go to the Franklins and ask to present their case once more. Half a dozen times she picked up the phone. But she never made the call.

Because Annelise and Renée were entitled to change their mind. Entitled to tear it all down if they wanted to. And she needed to come to grips with the fact that there wasn't a damned thing she could, or even should, do about it.

Maddie intercepted her as she paced past the jetty. "We're going to do sunset out here on the beach. Can you help me get things set up?"

Avery looked up at the sky in surprise. "I didn't realize how late it was."

"No, you seem to be missing a lot of things. Chase called. He tried to reach you but he said your cell phone kept going to voice mail."

Avery patted her pockets.

"It's on the kitchen counter. I actually found it in the hamper. You might want to call and tell him you're okay."

Her eyes met Maddie's.

"Lie if you have to. The man is worried about you."

"Right."

"Bring the pitcher of margaritas and the Cheez Doodles with you when you come." Maddie gave her a gentle push. "Kyra and I will set up the chairs and a couple of small tables. And you might as well start trying to come up with a good thing or two."

• • •

Nikki got stuck in rush-hour traffic on the Howard Frankland Bridge. She tried not to look at the faces of the other drivers who seemed so intent on getting back to homes and families and people who loved them.

Her eyes got damp. Again. *Jesus.*

Shortly after she'd sped away from FBI headquarters, her anger, which she had clung so tightly to, had begun to dissipate. She tried to reinflate it but she was too tired to do it justice. By the time she neared the Pinellas County side of the bridge, she felt needy and pathetic and as flat and rubbery as a spent balloon.

She took the Fourth Street exit off the interstate and went into a McDonald's to use the bathroom. No longer eager to get back to Bella Flora, where there would undoubtedly be questions she did not want to answer, she ordered fries and an ice cream sundae for dinner, then took her time eating them. When traffic had died down she got back on the road but stayed on Fourth Street rather than getting back on I-75. Which meant she drove at a snail's pace and stopped at every light.

By the time she got to Pass-a-Grille the sun was in full flight and beach traffic had dwindled. Those bent on watching the sunset were either already on the beach or headed there on foot.

Maddie's and Avery's cars were in the drive but when she dragged herself inside, the house felt empty. Dropping her bag at the foot of the stairs, she headed toward the kitchen.

There she found Steve Singer with his hands in a wooden bowl and a book open on the counter in front of him.

"What are you doing?" she asked.

"Kneading bread."

"Why?" she asked without heat or real interest. "Tired of shrinking irreplaceable expensive clothing?"

He glared at her but it was child's play after Joe's steely looks.

"Where is everybody?"

"They're out on the beach," he said.

Too restless to go upstairs, she wandered outside and followed the sandy path toward the jetty. Maddie, Kyra, and Avery sat near a stand of dunes staring out over the Gulf.

"Well, look who finally decided to come back," Avery said. "Where the hell have you been?"

"Hello to you, too!" Nikki replied.

"Now, now," Maddie said, offering Nikki a smile and getting up to give Nikki her seat. "Is everybody doing okay?" she asked quietly with a pointed look at Nikki's stomach.

"Fit as a fiddle," Nikki said as Maddie sat down on the cooler.

"I'm glad." Maddie's smile was tinged with relief, which made Nikki wonder just what Maddie thought she'd been up to. "Are you sure?"

"I think I'll survive," she said wearily before turning back to Avery. "What gives? Something crawl up your ass and die?"

"Maybe I'm wondering what makes you think you can just take off and disappear without telling anyone where you were going or when you'd be back."

"And maybe I don't remember signing articles of indenture. Or being put under house arrest." Though God knew if Joe Giraldi had his way she'd probably be sharing a cell with her brother right now.

"You agreed to help," Avery persisted.

"And I have. But I had something I had to take care of. Now I'm back. I don't really need to take your shit," Nikki said, her store of anger having apparently replenished itself. "Why don't you just tell me what I missed?"

Maddie grimaced but didn't intervene. Kyra sipped on a frothy red drink, but looked miles away. Which was beginning to look like an enviable location.

"Let me give you the short version," Avery said. "We dug up a skeleton underneath one of the patios. It was Annelise's mother. Annelise and Renée have decided to bulldoze the hotel. We will not be renovating." She waved her half-empty glass for emphasis as she spoke. "And the network lawyers have informed us that we're in breach of contract and that unless we come back and do the show the way they want it for the pittance we originally agreed to, they're going to sue."

"You're joking," Nikki said.

"Afraid not." Avery drained the remainder of her drink.

"Here." Kyra refilled Avery's glass, then poured one for Nikki. "Strawberry margaritas," she said as she placed the glass in Nikki's hand. "I suggest you drink it quickly. You're behind. But there's another pitcher where that came from."

Nikki looked down at the icy red mixture. Her mouth actually watered. "Thanks," she said, reluctantly handing it back. "I can't."

"Now who's joking?" Avery asked.

Nikki shifted in the chair trying to get comfortable. Her waistband was too tight and her bra no longer fit. She was in desperate need of a shower and possibly a new life. "Not me. Is there a bottled water in that cooler?"

"Since when?" Avery demanded, apparently seeing this as a personal affront.

"Nikki can't drink alcohol right now," Maddie said.

"Why not?" Avery's tone was indignant; Kyra's curious.

"Because I'm pregnant."

Nikki's admission was met with silence. Avery was the

first to recover. For some reason she looked to Maddie for confirmation. "Is she serious?"

Maddie nodded. Her face broke into a smile. When Nikki didn't object she said, "Nikki and Joe are having twins!"

"Correction. *I'm* having twins. *Joe* wants to take a paternity test."

"I don't believe that," Maddie said.

"Believe it. He found out by accident." She did not have the strength to explain the whole Malcolm fiasco and was still too angry to admit that Joe had had her under surveillance. "And he can't seem to forgive me for not telling him." She felt tears forming and swiped at them with the back of her hand. "He thinks the only reason I'd have is that they're not his."

"Good grief," Maddie said.

"How far along are you?" Kyra asked.

"About thirteen weeks."

"Wow. You were already through your first trimester and didn't tell him?" She took a sip of the margarita. Nikki would have liked to rip it out of her hands and down it herself. "I can kind of see why he might be upset," Kyra continued. "I tried to tell Daniel right away and we weren't, well, you know. In the same kind of relationship as you and Joe."

"Why didn't you tell him?" Avery asked, clearly curious. "If they're his and everything?"

"I don't know!" Once again it seemed easier to argue than attempt to dissect or explain her muddled emotions. "I just . . . I can hardly believe it myself."

"Well, at least you have something to look forward to." Avery finished the margarita. "But I get the disbelief thing. That's how I feel about the hotel reno. I can't quite absorb how wrong everything went. I keep fantasizing about sneaking onto the property and disabling the bulldozers. Or staging some sort of protest. It's driving me crazy. I can't quit right in the middle." She blew a bang out of her eye. "And then there's the network."

"Yeah," Kyra said, explaining the document she'd received. "We can't go back to them. But what do we do about the lawsuit? It takes money to hire attorneys."

"What does Troy say?" Nikki asked, glad not to be the topic of conversation. The knot of worry tightened. If she was going to be a mother, especially a single one, she needed financial security. She needed this show to work.

"I haven't heard from him and he's not answering my calls or texts," Kyra said.

"Yeah, you're not the only one who disappeared on us," Avery observed.

"At least Nikki came back," Kyra said. "I think he's gone for good. And I have a bad feeling he's sold us out. Maybe he was just here to spy on us and report back so that they'd know what we were doing."

"This is depressing as shit," Nikki said. Yet in spite of the devastating news, she felt slightly better for having her secret out.

"Yeah. Don't even think about asking us to come up with one good thing, Maddie Singer," Avery said with a slight slurring of her words. "Because all this shit really sucks."

"There's a ton of suckage going on," Kyra agreed.

The first smile in recent memory tugged at Nikki's lips. "It is downright suckalicious."

"Yeah," Maddie said, surprising them. "You know it's bad when you have to invent new words to describe it." She raised her glass in toast. "But the good thing is we now have a whole new collection of adjectives at our disposal."

There was laughter. It began with a few tentative giggles that turned into shotgun bursts as they tried out their new vocabulary and culminated in hearty snorts that had nothing to do with alcohol, the sunset they'd forgotten to watch, or anything but their relief in being together. Nikki gave in to it, too, and as her hands rested on her jiggling stomach, she wondered if the babies growing inside her could feel the merriment that had at least briefly replaced the anger and panic that had been churning inside her.

They laughed for some time, not at all concerned with the odd looks from passersby or the curtain of darkness that finally fell around them. They were still chortling and trying out their new vocabulary words as they carried the chairs and cooler back up the path to Bella Flora. Nikki knew they all feared that if they didn't find a way to save *Do Over* and subdue the suckage, this might be their last laugh together. A thought too horrible to be borne.

Chapter Forty-three

The clatter of pots and pans carried up the back stairs from the kitchen. Kyra turned on her side and reached blindly for a pillow, intent on burying her head beneath it. The hearty curse that accompanied a loud bang eliminated any chance of slipping back into sleep. Her eyes opened to the early morning light, then slid to Dustin's empty bed. She missed him, missed waking to find his sturdy little body snuggled up against hers, missed his stress-busting sunny smile and his arms looped around her neck. FaceTime chats, even on an almost daily basis, were poor substitutes for the real thing. In just a few days Daniel would bring her baby home. *Daniel.* Who had given them Bella Flora. And who was catnip to women.

She flipped onto her back and stared up into the ceiling not wanting to hear the noise coming from below; to acknowledge it was to be forced to deal with it. Her thoughts flitted randomly through her head. Her childish naïveté about Daniel's feelings for her, her certainty that he'd want to marry her when she'd found herself pregnant. Her mother's "glass half full" philosophy coupled with just how hard she would work to fill that glass.

The whir of a blender turned jagged as if metal were being pulverized. The sound was replaced with a heartfelt "Damn!"

They had lost the hotel, and their former network didn't consider itself "former" and had threatened to sue them. Her thoughts turned to a life without *Do Over*. She had a toddler. Freelance video work required travel. Feature film work was even more demanding. Unless you were a major movie star with a traveling nanny and a boatload of money, movie making and motherhood did not go well together. If she wanted to do what she was trained for, she had to find a way to control the work. *Do Over* without a bully of a network would have been perfect. But without the funds to renovate and produce, there could be no *Do Over*. Nor could they hire attorneys to free them from the network.

"Crap!" Her father's voice rose again. "Shit!"

With an expletive of her own, she got out of bed, washed her face, brushed her teeth, and pulled on shorts and a T-shirt. Downstairs she found her father standing in the middle of a totally trashed kitchen.

"Jeez, Dad. What happened?"

He held up a casserole dish with oven-mitted hands. His face was smeared with food and sweat. Coffee stains and something oily ran down his shirt. "Your mother always called these breakfast soufflés 'never fail,' but that's not entirely true."

She looked at the lumpy mixture that hadn't solidified or risen. Then she looked at the egg-splattered floor and the reclaimed wood countertops covered in stringy clumps of melted cheese. She was surprised Deirdre hadn't come back to haunt her father given the mess he'd made of pretty much every space she'd designed.

"Please," she said, reaching for the casserole dish. "Please stop. You have zero aptitude for cooking. And even less for cleaning and laundry. You have to stop trying."

"You think a man can't do this?" her father asked. "All the best chefs are male."

"I didn't say it was chromosomal." Kyra walked to the coffeemaker. The pot was half filled with wet grounds soaking in tepid brown liquid. "You're not a chef. You can't be a chef when you can't even make a pot of coffee."

She dumped the remains in the sink and rinsed out the carafe. Then she set about making a fresh pot.

"Well, I'm sorry I'm not up to everyone's standards," he huffed. "You complained that I wasn't helping. Now I'm trying to help and nothing I do is good enough." His voice had turned whiny.

"This is not the kind of help we need!" She looked at her father, really looked at him. "Are you paying attention at all? Have you noticed what's going on? We are in deep shit. We have no project because we lost the Sunshine Hotel. We need money to renovate something so that we can produce a television series. And hire attorneys to defend us."

She expected him to lash out but his shoulders slumped in defeat. He set the casserole dish on the stove, removed the mitts, and ran a hand through his hair. That hand must have been coated in oil or butter because his hair now stood up in uneven clumps. "I do know. I guess I've just been trying not to."

"That does seem to be your modus operandi, doesn't it?" she snapped. "I don't think it's working particularly well for you. Or us!"

"Ah, Kyra," he said. "I wish I had money to give you. Here I am living on your good graces and trying to show your mother that I've got it back together but . . ." He looked down at himself, the floor, the kitchen. "It's not going anywhere near as well as I'd hoped."

"Dad. It's not *going* anywhere. You and Mom are over. And no amount of attempting to cook and shrinking people's clothes is going to get her back." So this, she thought, was tough love. How in the world did her mother bear it? "She and Will are a couple. I don't know how it'll end up, but she's happy. You need to find a way to be happy, too."

"That's a lot easier said than done."

"That's for sure," she agreed. "But the father I grew up with didn't just give up when things didn't work out. You dumped everything on Mom when you lost all our money. And now you say you want to help. But what is it you're doing?"

He hung his head. Like Dustin sometimes did when he'd done something he knew was wrong or didn't get his way. She expelled the breath she'd been holding. She drew another breath in an attempt to calm down. "Do you really want to help us?"

"Of course I do, kitten. I just don't seem to know how."

"Then stop making excuses. And stop pretending to be something you're not. You know finance. That was always your specialty. Money is exactly what we need. And we need it fast."

"I'm sure Daniel would help you if you asked. He *should* help you."

"Daniel already gave us this house. And he insisted on guaranteeing demolition and payback of sponsors if we failed to complete the renovation. He's been more than generous. And this isn't just for me or for Dustin. Maybe we could, I don't know, take out a mortgage on Bella Flora? And then we could all pay it off together?"

It was her father's turn to sigh. But for once he seemed to have been listening. And thinking. "You won't qualify for a mortgage, sweetheart. You'd need a serious credit history and a steady income for that. There are ways to borrow money against an asset. You could borrow from a hard money lender. But the interest rate would be steep, and if you weren't able to pay the loan and the interest off at the end of the allotted time, they would take the asset."

Her mother walked into the kitchen. Given the wind-blown hair and the sunburnt cheeks, it appeared she'd been out for a morning walk. Frowning at the mess, she side-stepped the egg spatter on the floor, eyed the misshapen undercooked contents of the casserole, then poured herself a cup of coffee.

"I was just asking Dad if he'd take a look at whether we might be able to borrow money or take out a loan of some kind."

She made no comment about the mess, but instead looked at Kyra's father. "That's a good idea. Could you take a look at the financial possibilities for us, Steve?"

Her father looked surprised; that surprise turned to pleasure. "I was just telling Kyra how much I want to help." His chest puffed out slightly. "I think I'll take a walk on the beach to clear my head a bit. Then I'll see what I can come up with."

Kyra watched him go. "Wow. That worked way better than my attempt at tough love."

Her mother smiled. "'Good cop, bad cop' was created for a reason." She considered the abandoned soufflé, then began to pull things out of the refrigerator. "I think your father's forgotten who he is and what he accomplished before Malcolm Dyer stomped all over us." She added milk and cheese to the mixture, then tossed in another stick of margarine. After a few moments staring into the refrigerator she withdrew a jar of salsa and poured it in, too. "I think even a soufflé can be saved or reimagined under the right circumstances." She turned the oven back on. "Everyone needs a purpose, or at least a goal."

"What's yours?" Kyra asked on her way to the utility closet to retrieve the mop.

"Hmm." Maddie picked up the casserole dish and slipped it back into the oven. "It used to be being a good mother."

"Check." Kyra affixed a new wet cloth onto the mop head and went to work on the egg spatter. "You definitely got the mother thing right."

Maddie smiled and bowed her thanks. "Then it was surviving. Keeping our heads above water."

"Check—mostly anyway." Kyra put some muscle into the mopping.

Avery arrived sniffing happily like a mouse on the scent of cheese. "Is that soufflé I smell?"

"Sort of." Maddie smiled and poured a cup of coffee for Avery.

"And now?" Kyra asked. "What's your goal now?"

"I'm still thinking about that," Maddie replied. "But I have to admit I wish there were a way to talk Annelise out of bulldozing the hotel."

"Amen, sister." Avery looked up from her coffee, distracted by the scent of warm, melted cheese.

"Why?" Kyra asked her mother. "I mean, I agree, but why do you say that?"

"Because I think we all need *Do Over*, or something like *Do Over*, to pour ourselves into. And because I'm totally pissed off at the network for the way they've treated us and how they've hijacked your idea and our program. I don't think it suits any of us."

"Amen!" Kyra and Avery said together.

Nikki wandered in, her hair in disarray, her eyes still cloudy with sleep. Already Kyra thought she saw a softening of her features, a thickening around the middle. The idea of her as a mother was almost as hard to fathom as her mother having a sex life had once been. Life certainly was full of surprises, some more pleasant than others. As she watched, Nikki walked over to the coffeepot and put her nose as close to it as possible.

"What are you doing?" Avery asked.

"I may not be allowed to drink it but nobody said I couldn't inhale it. Maybe I'll be like Bill Clinton and inhale but not ingest." She took one more whiff. "Sorry," she said, noticing their eyes on her. "I think I interrupted something that sounded an awful lot like a prayer meeting. What were you talking about?"

Maddie laughed. "I was just saying that the biggest thing I learned when our world fell apart was to be proactive. There is no reward without risk and certainly not without hard work. If we're going to go down, I say we go down fighting." She looked at all three of them. "What do you say?"

Kyra knew she wasn't the only one wondering how big a fight they might be talking or how great a risk they'd have to take, but in the end she'd much rather go down swinging. "I'm in," she said.

"I'm up for a fight," Avery said. "A little bloodletting, as long as it's not ours, might make me feel better."

"Me, too," Nikki added. "And may I add a final amen!"

Chapter Forty-four

The front door of Franklin Realty swung open. Renée looked up and spotted Joe Giraldi.

"Welcome," Annelise said.

If Joe was surprised to see her sister rather than Renée at the front desk, he didn't show it.

"Thank you," he said, offering them a smile. "You're both looking well."

Annelise preened a bit at the compliment, and Renée was thrilled to see such a normal reaction. The agent, however, didn't look his normal calm and collected self. In fact, she thought his eyes resembled those of a bear caught in a trap and unable to decide whether to stay put or gnaw off a foot to escape.

"I've been helping out," Annelise said. "Answering phones and all."

"It's been great having her here," Renée said honestly. If slightly nerve-racking. Each day she waited with some trepidation for the new stronger Annelise to weaken or have some sort of meltdown, but so far she'd come in each morning as scheduled and handled the tasks she was assigned without difficulty. She suspected that Annelise's surprise at this equaled her own.

"I heard from Officer Jackson that they were able to track down the retired agent in Arizona and that he clarified a lot of what happened the night your father died."

"Yes." Renée smiled. "I can't tell you how much we appreciate your help."

Annelise nodded her agreement. "It feels as if history has been rewritten."

"How's the renovation coming?" Joe asked in an obvious attempt to change the subject.

"Oh, that's done with," Annelise replied before Renée could even think of an answer.

"They've already completed the project?" Surprise shone on his face.

"No," Annelise said tightly. "We decided not to renovate."

"Why not?" he asked.

Renée moved cautiously toward her sister, but Annelise said only, "Because now that I know my mother was buried there all those years, even the sight of the place hurts."

No doubt hearing conversation, John came out of his office to investigate. He and Joe exchanged greetings.

"Your sister-in-law was just telling me you've halted the renovation," Joe said.

"Yes," John said. "We're going to bulldoze the buildings and list the land."

"That's a shame." Joe hesitated as if trying to decide whether to continue. "Not to overstep, but I have some familiarity with family members of victims looking for closure. In my experience it's not the buildings or the location where the crime took place that are the problem. It's the memories. And, of course, you carry those wherever you go."

Annelise stiffened. Once again Renée braced for an

explosion, but her sister said simply, "And how does one handle those memories?"

Joe's smile was even, his eyes a bit less bear-in-trap as he focused on Annelise's question. "Everyone does it differently, of course. Sometimes it's by finding a way to honor the victim. Other times it's a matter of toughing it out. At some point, from what I've seen, the good memories begin to outweigh the bad. You start to remember the people you lost as they were in life and not as they became in death." The observation was no less comforting because of its straightforwardness. Annelise's shoulders relaxed a bit, which made Renée's relax, too.

"Well said." John motioned Joe to a wing chair and took the one opposite. Renée leaned against the edge of Annelise's desk.

"You know what I remember?" John asked quietly. "How much David Handleman loved the hotel. How glad he was to be home from Germany and a part of running it." His smile was soft with memory. "And how much he wanted Ilse to love it, too."

Renée nodded, caught her sister's eye. "Do you remember the sunset walks?" Once again she waited for Annelise to freeze up, shed tears, or storm out, but once again she smiled.

"You would skip ahead of us. Daddy would carry me on his shoulders and point out the dolphins when a pod would swim or feed nearby. Sometimes he'd tease us with a horseshoe crab or a clump of seaweed." Annelise laughed softly. There was a hint of her old childish breathiness, but this child had once been happy. "Sometimes we'd just sit under the shade of an Australian pine and have a picnic."

"Australian pines?" Joe asked.

"Yep. They used to be all over the island until the freeze of 1961. Took me decades to get used to how naked the beach looked without them," John said.

Renée looked at her sister and the faint smile that still lingered on her lips. "The beach is just as beautiful either way."

Annelise got up but not in order to change the subject or escape. "I'm going to fill in for a friend at the Pass-a-Grille Historical Society this afternoon." She gave Renée a fleeting kiss on the cheek, said good-bye to Joe and John, and left. No tears, no drama.

Renée and John shared a smile.

"That's the first time she hasn't spit nails at the mention of the hotel," John observed. "I have wondered if she'd be any happier once the place was pulled down or if she might regret it. I feel bad about leaving the ladies in the lurch."

"Me, too." Renée checked her watch. "It's a little early, but I think we're entitled to a drink."

"I'm in," John said.

"Joe?"

"The man looks like he could use something with a bit of a kick. I'm guessing the Chivas Regal will do the trick."

Joe nodded his agreement.

"Coming right up." Renée went to put a tray together. "Neat or on the rocks?"

"Neat," Joe said.

"Ah," John replied. "I knew you were a man after my own heart."

When Renée returned with the tray, the desk chair had been pulled over to join the wing chairs. She set the drinks tray on the low table between them.

"*Salud.*" They clinked glasses and raised them to their lips.

The warm liquid slid easily down her throat. John shot her a wink. Joe looked from one to the other.

"I wish I understood women half as well as you seem to, John," Joe Giraldi observed.

"Ah . . . I thought you looked a little harassed. Is something wrong?"

"Shall I leave you two alone?" Renée asked, careful not to laugh at the idea of her husband as an expert on women. Despite the agent's attempt at a light tone, it was clear he had something to discuss.

"No," Joe said. "I think I may need a woman's opinion."

"Renée's got no shortage of those," John observed wryly.

"Now look who's talking," she retorted. Both of them were smiling.

Joe took a long sip of his drink.

John sipped along companionably. "I'm flattered, but I have to say I'm a little surprised you've come to me. It's been a while since I courted a woman."

Renée sipped her scotch and smiled.

"I considered talking to Maddie," Joe admitted. "But I don't think I'd be all that welcome at Bella Flora at the moment. Not if Nikki had anything to say about it." He took another sip but didn't seem to be finding it particularly soothing. "You and Renée have been married even longer than my parents. And, well, my parents would hardly be objective considering this concerns their son and their potential grandchildren."

"You've got my attention," John said. "And I think Renée's eyes are about to pop out of her head. Don't stop now."

The agent shifted uncomfortably in his chair. "There's a bit of a problem between Nikki and me."

"Oh?" John asked. "Why's that?"

"I may have accused her of sleeping with someone else."

Renée was careful not to gasp.

"Do you have reason to believe that? That's a pretty serious allegation," John said quietly.

"No. I just . . . well, I found out completely by accident that she's pregnant and I was so angry that she hadn't told me that I started spewing whatever came out." He looked down into the amber liquid. "And I may have thrown my weight around a little. Well, more than a little."

Renée closed her mouth, but only after she'd taken a couple of large swallows. Nicole Grant was pregnant. And neither she nor Joe seemed to be celebrating.

"Thing is, I thought I understood women. I have dated a few in my time."

"No doubt," John said.

"So, I'm a little curious how you and Renée work things out when they get screwed up. More specifically how you apologize when you've been an idiot and then how you get Renée to do what you want her to."

John snorted. Renée thought he was going to spray scotch all over the place. "Well, at least you've got things in the right order."

"Damn straight," Renée said. "And the apology has to be sincere. And abject. Abject is good. And you might want to consider getting down on one knee and begging. With a ring in your hand."

"Been there, done that," Joe said. "I can't believe I'm admitting this. But I couldn't get her to say yes."

"Hmph." John took a drink, swirled the amber liquid around in his glass. "Women can be stubborn. Their reasons for things can be, well, let's say men and women look at the world from different angles. You know, that Mars and Venus thing. But you don't strike me as the kind of man who gives up just because somebody says no."

"That's true. But things are a little complicated. She's not just pregnant. She's having twins. You'd think she'd want to be married, wouldn't you? Especially to someone who hasn't been shy about telling her how much he loves her. And wants children." He shook his head in disbelief.

"That's life, son. It's complicated and messy. But that's what keeps it interesting."

"This is way more interesting than I bargained on."

They sat and sipped in silence for a few minutes.

"Sounds like you need to try again," John said. "Do what Renée suggested. You tell her how you feel. Include the love and adoration. Then you add the abject apology. And maybe jewelry."

"And what do you think the chances are that those things will work?" He looked to Renée.

"I don't know," she said truthfully. "There's something missing here. I'm not sure you can convince her unless you know what it is." The glass was wet in Renée's hands, the alcohol warm in her stomach. "But you need to give it your all. You don't want to be fathering those children from a distance."

"No," Joe said quietly. "That's not something I could do or allow." He took another drink but didn't seem to be enjoying it. "And if that doesn't work?"

John considered this for a minute, then he looked at her. "Renée? Can you step out for just a minute? I don't want you to hear all my secrets."

"As if you have any left after all these years," she retorted even as she got up and walked away. She stepped into the next room and pulled the door closed behind her, leaving it open a tiny crack as she had no doubt John knew she would. She had to hide her laughter when John told Joe Giraldi his never-fail strategy for "managing" her and convincing her to do what he wanted.

As if the old softy had ever tricked her into anything that she hadn't already decided to let him think he'd tricked her into.

• • •

"I'm not comfortable about this, kitten," her father said to Kyra. "Your mother won't like it." They sat at a table on the back deck of the Wharf restaurant, overlooking the bay and munching on grouper po'boys and fries. Given the veritable boat parade and view of Tierra Verde, it would have been a relaxing lunch if her father hadn't seemed so intent on talking her out of the very decision he'd helped her make.

"But you said yourself that if I got a hard money loan, I'd probably need someone to guarantee it. You even suggested John Franklin, which I think is a complete stroke of genius." They had an appointment thirty minutes from now to discuss the details of the loan with John.

"It would be safer to ask Daniel for the money when he brings Dustin back this afternoon. I'm afraid you don't fully understand what can happen if you do this and become unable to pay off the loan." Beads of sweat dotted his forehead. Kyra was pretty sure it wasn't because of the heat. "You could lose Bella Flora."

"I can't ask Daniel, Dad. I don't want to treat him like some sort of money train. And I wouldn't even consider risking Bella Flora except we need to do a renovation and have enough left over to hire a good attorney to deal with the network for us. I just can't see any other way."

"But, sweetie. If things don't work out and you can't pay off the loan . . ."

John Franklin said the same thing an hour later after Annelise—*Annelise*—had shown them to the conference room and Renée had delivered cupcakes and soft drinks.

"I do understand the risk," Kyra said again. "You and Dad have explained it about a dozen times. But we can't wait around for someone to save us or the show. And I'm the only one with an asset large enough to borrow real money against."

The Realtor steepled his hands on the table. His brown eyes were filled with concern. "I'm going to say this one last time. I don't think you should do this."

She nodded and smiled so that he'd understand that she'd thought this through. If she let herself think about the risks too much, she'd lose her nerve entirely. "I'm going to do this. Because I believe in *Do Over* and us. But if the worst happened and you had to pay off the shortfall, at least I'd be losing Bella Flora to you." She looked at him. "And you're the only person I know who loves her as much as we do. You've always said she was the best house on Pass-a-Grille."

"Oh, she is," he said, but there was no mistaking his reluctance.

For a moment she allowed herself to imagine the loss in vivid detail. Walking away with nothing into an uncertain future. But her mother's words came back to her. Like her mother, she would be proactive and if she got taken down, she was going to go down fighting. She looked the Realtor directly in the eye, then did the same with her father. "I promise I understand what I'm doing."

"All right." John opened a folder and withdrew a typewritten sheet of paper, which he placed in front of her. "This is the current estimated value of the house and grounds. This is the amount of the loan plus interest that I've agreed to guarantee." He pointed to each number in the column and waited to make sure she'd absorbed it. There were an awful lot of zeros.

She swallowed, gave one last nod, then signed and dated the document. Her knees were slightly wobbly as she stood and followed John out to the front room. There Renée stopped them. "Hold on just a second. I'll send the rest of the cupcakes back with you for Dustin."

"You must be looking forward to having him home," Annelise said as Renée went to box up the cupcakes.

"That's for sure. Bella Flora has been really quiet without him," Kyra said.

"It certainly has," her father agreed.

Annelise smiled. Kyra realized there was something new in the smile, something that hadn't been there when she'd yanked the hotel renovation away from them with no thought of anyone or anything but her own feelings.

Kyra pushed away the resentment that still lingered. She

was speaking before she'd even thought what she might say. "We have the money to finish the renovation now. It would mean so much to all of us if you would reconsider letting us bring back the hotel. Or at least show you and explain why you should reconsider."

Annelise began to shake her head. Was Kyra imagining that there was regret, even apology in the movement? "Couldn't you just agree to listen?"

The "no" was not immediate, but Kyra could feel it coming.

"Listen to what?" Renée asked, returning with the bakery box.

"We have the money for renovation, and we'd really, really appreciate a chance to discuss all the reasons why renovation makes sense."

John and her father remained silent. Renée's reaction was everything Kyra had been hoping for, everything Annelise's was not.

"Oh, please, Annelise," Renée said eagerly. "Couldn't we just agree to listen?" She placed the box in Kyra's hands.

Annelise said nothing for what felt like an eternity. Kyra held the box so tightly she feared for the safety of the cupcakes. She held her breath when Annelise turned and met her sister's eyes. "All right," Annelise said finally. "But I'm only agreeing to listen." It was clear she didn't believe there was anything they could say that would sway her. "But you better make it soon. The bulldozers are already on-site. Demolition is set to start on Monday."

"Oh, thank you!" Kyra said. "Thank you so much." She left immediately, pretty much dragging her father out, afraid to give Annelise a chance to change her mind.

She practically floated to the car, her feet barely touching the sidewalk. Dustin would be home soon, Daniel was bringing him, and she was about to deliver not only the money they needed but also the chance to win back the renovation.

"Well done," her father said as they climbed into the

minivan and headed back to Bella Flora. "You're not afraid to go after what you want. I'd like to say you're a chip off the old block. But in truth you remind me of your mother." Kyra knew from the way he said this that it was very high praise. "But I don't think I'd mention where the money's coming from just now. It would only upset her."

Kyra nodded. The last thing on her mind was giving anyone anything else to worry about.

Chapter Forty-five

Kyra basked in her father's compliments all the way back to Bella Flora. A good deal of her rosy glow faded when she discovered Troy Matthews lounging by the pool. As if he had every right to be here.

"What are you doing here?"

"Sunbathing," he replied. "Do I look like I'm getting burnt to you?" He sat up and handed her the sunscreen. "Will you put a little on my back? I should probably flip over."

She stared at him in disbelief. "I'm thinking sugar water would be better."

"Sugar water?"

"Yes, we could slather it all over you."

"Really? We?"

"Yes. It would probably take a few of us to get you staked to the nearest ant pile."

Her father laughed and excused himself.

Troy sighed in feigned disappointment. "I think you're going to feel bad about this latent hostility you have toward me when I tell you what I have for you."

"My hostility is not latent," she said. "If it feels that way, I'm doing something wrong."

"Seriously, Kyra." He looked up at her. "I've got some really good news."

"For who?" she asked. "Because in my experience, the person you care about most is you. And your good news is not necessarily our good news."

Her mother came out bearing glasses of iced tea.

"Please don't feed and water him," Kyra said. "Once you do they never really go away."

"Troy says he has an offer of some kind for us and I think we need to hear what it is," Maddie said.

"An offer?"

"Yes, I was just getting to that when you threatened to stake me out to an ant pile."

"Well I have news, too," Kyra said.

"You can both fill us in," Maddie said. "Avery and Nikki should be out any minute." She pulled two straws out of her pocket and set them next to the iced teas. "Have you heard anything from Daniel, Kyra?"

Troy's cocky smile slipped slightly at the mention of Daniel Deranian.

"He texted before takeoff that he thought they'd be landing at Albert Whitted around four P.M."

"Perfect," Maddie said. "I thought we could have a welcome home picnic for Dustin. It's too hot to even fire up the grill, so I'm making 'handwitches.'" Her smile turned slightly dreamy. Kyra imagined she was remembering William and Dustin eating smooshed PB&Js together on Mermaid Point.

"He'll love it," Kyra said. "And I agree, it's way too hot to fuss."

Avery and Nikki came outside blinking against the harsh sunlight. The five of them settled at the table on the loggia.

"All right, let's have it," Avery said. "But I only want to hear good news. If anything else goes wrong, I plan to throw myself into the Gulf and start swimming to Mexico."

Nikki grimaced. "What does it say that I envy the fact that you *have* a plan?"

"Good grief," Maddie said. "I think we need to dig down deep to try to tap into our inner optimists. Surely things can't get any worse."

No one argued. But no one seemed inclined to do any internal digging, either.

"Want to flip a coin to see who shares their news first?" Troy asked. "Or should I go ahead since I'm the guest?"

"You left off 'unwelcome' and 'uninvited,'" Kyra pointed out. "You showed up under questionable circumstances and disappeared the same way."

"No, I came here and worked for you for free," Troy said. "Then I left to try to find you a new gig. I came back when I found one."

"A new gig?" Avery said. "Okay, Troy goes first."

Kyra swallowed her objections and sat back, arms crossed.

"Bottom line, HGTV wants you," Troy said. "They don't care what the show is called and they don't need it to be reality TV. Their whole channel is design and construction and they'd be a much better fit. They've been watching your numbers and they seem to think you can resolve the threat of a lawsuit."

"People know about the lawsuit?" Nikki asked.

Troy nodded. "I think that's still part of the plan. They're doing everything they can to make you as unattractive as possible to other networks. But I think HGTV will be willing to wait until things are settled and you're free."

"I don't know," Avery said. "I've already done a show for HGTV and it didn't end well. I was treated every bit as badly by the program head there as we have been at Lifetime. I'd still rather do our own thing."

"But you need a whole lot of money for that. And a

project," Troy countered. "Last I heard you didn't have either."
He spoke directly to Kyra, his voice challenging while his
eyes seemed to be sending all kinds of contradictory signals
that she was too irritated to want to try to decipher.

"Yeah, well things have changed a bit since you left on your
'mission to save us.'" Kyra air quoted. "We now have access to
one and a half million dollars." She paused to let this sink in.
"If we can bring the reno in at a million, we'll have enough
left to fight the network's lawsuit if we need to."

"What did you do? Run to your 'boyfriend'?" Troy aimed
air quotes back at her. "Or should we just call him your sugar
daddy?" Troy's face was tight with anger. "He doesn't even
need those movie star looks to hold on to you, does he? Not
as long as he's got all that money."

"Troy," her mother admonished. "That's not fair."

"You can believe whatever you want to," Kyra shot back.
"You are the biggest . . . oh never mind." She turned her back
on him. "Does it really matter where the money came from?"

"Yes, of course it does," Avery said. "We wouldn't want
anyone put at risk. But I don't see anything wrong with Daniel
wanting to help. He is the father of your child, and it's not like
he'll be out on the street if something goes wrong."

Kyra was careful not to flinch at the thought of being out
on the street, since it would be them and not Daniel who
would be there. Nor did she correct Avery's assumption.

Nikki did flinch at the "father of your child" comment,
but said only, "As long as you're not taking on anything you
don't think you can handle?"

"No," Kyra said, relieved it was only a half-truth and not
a full-fledged lie.

"You're not committing yourself to something you might
come to . . . regret?" her mother asked softly.

Kyra forced herself to meet her mother's eyes and realized
that Maddie was worried that she had somehow obligated
herself to Daniel in ways she otherwise might not have. It

was with relief that she was able to say, "No, absolutely not." Because that, at least, was true. She was committed to trying to save *Do Over* and no matter what happened, she would not regret that decision.

"I'm feeling some actual hope here, but I'd feel even better if we had a project," Avery said. "Or knew where to find one."

"That's the best part," Kyra said. "I saw Annelise and Renée. And Annelise is, I don't know, something's different. The bulldozers are already on the property and they're set to begin demo on Monday."

"That's the best part?" Avery frowned.

"No. The best part is that they agreed to hear us out. I think if we come up with something they can get excited about, we might have a shot at finishing the Sunshine Hotel."

"Oh, my God." Avery jumped up and threw her arms around Kyra. "I feel like one of those death row inmates who's being led to the gas chamber when the last-minute call from the governor comes in." There was another bone-crushing hug. Then she hugged Maddie. "For giving birth to Kyra!"

There were celebratory hugs all round. Only Troy kept his arms to himself.

"I'm going to call Chase and Ray right now," Avery said. "What do you say we have that picnic at the hotel? We'll need as much time as possible there before sunset so we can figure this out without having to do it by flashlight."

. . .

Daniel and Dustin pulled up in front of Bella Flora just before five P.M. They arrived in the longest, most pimped-out white limousine Kyra had ever seen. All it lacked was a flashing neon sign that read, *Here I am! Look at me!*

Kyra gritted her teeth. "What in the world is he doing?"

"He's obviously not planning to sneak in under the radar," Troy said tartly.

She ignored the cameraman, not quite able to believe what

she was seeing. Just when she was getting ready to go out and remove Dustin from the car, the driver, dressed in a fancy uniform with brass buttons and a matching cap, got out and hurried around to open the door.

Neither Daniel nor Dustin wore a disguise of any kind. For a man who had been so gleefully inventive and had wardrobe and makeup people at his command, it was decidedly odd to see the two of them so . . . them. They strolled up to the front door chatting animatedly, Dustin moving and looking like a mini version of his famous father. Each step was a money shot if ever she'd seen one, assuming there'd been a photographer there to capture it. The only thing that might have been more adorable would have been if Dustin were riding on his father's shoulders. They were at the front garden gate when Daniel swept Dustin up into that very position. They sort of chortled at each other before ambling up to the front door. Just your everyday A-list movie star and his illegitimate child.

"What's going on?" Kyra asked as she met them out on the front loggia.

"Just enjoying the day." Daniel slid an arm around her shoulders and gave her a long, lingering kiss. It was the sort of public display of affection that they'd been careful not to give in to even when they were actually seeing each other.

"Have you lost your mind?" she asked, pushing him away, eager to get back inside before someone saw the three of them together.

"Not that I'm aware of," he replied amiably, still standing too close and showing no inclination to go inside. He leaned down so that she could take Dustin from his shoulders. Dustin looped his arms around her neck and started kissing her.

"Bliss!" she exclaimed as he gave her a butterfly kiss with the thick dark eyelashes that were so like his father's. Lifting his shirt she blew a very loud raspberry on his belly. Daniel reached out and tickled him. For at least those few moments they might have been a real family, the kind that had the right to be seen together in public, to tease and to tickle. All three of them were laughing by the time they went inside and closed the door behind them.

"Quite a show you put on out there." Troy stood in the foyer, a one-man unwelcoming committee. "Too bad there were no paparazzi there to see it."

"It is, isn't it?" Daniel said, not at all perturbed.

Her mother came out of the kitchen smiling, her arms open wide. Her father wasn't far behind. Dustin clambered down and raced to them. When the kissing and hugging died down, Maddie walked over to greet Daniel. "It looks like Dustin had a great time. Would you like to stay for dinner? We're having a picnic on the beach behind the Sunshine Hotel."

"I'm sure Daniel needs to get going," Kyra said.

"Actually, I'm not going anywhere," Daniel said. "I'd be glad to stay for dinner. I've been wanting to see the hotel. After that I'm checking into the Don CeSar. The Don's a big enough hotel that word should get out. I plan to stay there until someone notices."

"Running low on adoration?" Troy asked.

Daniel shrugged. "I have it on good authority that the *Do Over* cast can't afford to be forgotten right now. So I thought I'd hang around. At least until word gets out that I'm here."

. . .

Nikki told herself it wasn't running away since she was headed in the general direction of the Sunshine Hotel. But the truth was, she'd had to leave Bella Flora because she couldn't bear watching Daniel Deranian and his obvious affection and attachment for his son. Every time she looked at him, all she could see was Joe Giraldi, he of the angry tic in his cheek and the righteous indignation.

He'd had the nerve to ask if he was the father and basically called her a liar and a cheat. After he'd known that Malcolm was trying to use her and was not in danger, had known that she was being watched.

Her bare feet pounded the sand, splashed through the too-warm shallow water. Zinc oxide ran down her nose. The oversized straw hat flopped as she walked. All around her, people seemed to be enjoying themselves. She took every smile, every laugh as a personal affront. How could they be so happy when she was so miserable? How could they go on about their lives when her body and her entire life had been hijacked? With each step the litany of losses rang louder. Her company, Heart Inc., was ancient history, *Do Over* was in the toilet, and the one time she'd let herself fall all the way in love, what had happened? She'd driven Joe away. She had babies growing inside her for Christ's sake. And their father was off somewhere trying to convince himself they weren't his.

She stomped along, not exactly walking but definitely not running. The doctor had said she could jog if she wanted to. Ha! She'd probably never have the time or energy to ever run again. If she managed to carry these babies to term, which still seemed grossly unlikely, she'd have two babies and no job or money. She'd undoubtedly get fat and ugly. And by the time the babies went to school she'd be . . . oh, God, she'd be ancient! People would think she was their grandmother! She walked on, her thoughts churning. Here she was worrying about herself when the people she should be feeling sorry for were her babies, *her* children, who wouldn't exactly be hitting the mother jackpot. She was selfish and self-absorbed, and her mothering of Malcolm had produced a conscienceless monster. What if she screwed up her children? What if she was such an awful mother that . . .

"Hold on!"

It took her a minute to realize someone was talking to her. Her sunglasses had fogged up due to the warm tears that seemed to form at the least provocation. She swiped at them with her forearm before turning. She blinked and removed the foggy glasses certain she was seeing or—in her mental state—imagining things. But no. There he was. Dark glasses. Determined chin. Bare chest. Unfairly attractive. Joe Giraldi.

She turned back around and walked faster. She had nothing to say to this man.

"Nikki! Stop!"

"Or what?" She threw the words over her shoulder. If he hadn't arrested her by now, chances were it wasn't going to happen. Anger coursed through her, hot and powerful. She'd like to see him try to arrest her. She'd chew him up and spit him out. She'd . . .

"Nikki." His voice sounded next to her ear. His hand grasped her shoulder. "Nikki," he said again. "Please stop. Or at least slow down. I'm afraid you're going to collapse or hyperventilate." His eyes went to her stomach and came back to her face.

She kept her chin up and she didn't exactly acknowledge him. But since she was feeling slightly light-headed, she did slow down. She would not give him the satisfaction of fainting in front of him.

"Nikki, seriously. You've got to . . ."

She stopped abruptly and turned. If he'd had lesser reflexes he would have plowed into her. "I don't have to do anything. Especially not for someone who called me a cheater. If you don't want to have anything to do with me or my children, go right ahead and believe whatever you want. And then, then you can just get the hell out of my life."

She blinked back tears. Thank God for the foggy sunglasses.

"Nikki," he said. "Stop it. Please. I came to apologize."

"Well, go ahead then and be done with it," she said and hoped to hell her lip hadn't just quivered.

"I'm sorry. I know I overreacted. I just . . . I've never been quite that angry. Or hurt."

She managed to remain silent. And she was pretty sure her lip had stopped quivering.

"First I kept waiting for you to tell me that Malcolm had contacted you. Then I waited for you to tell me that you were going to see him. Then I waited for you to tell me that he threatened you. But you never did."

When she didn't respond, he continued. "And then I accidentally found out that you'd been to the doctor and could be pregnant."

"You were tracing me and my credit card. I don't think that qualifies as an 'accident,'" she bit out. "And none of this would have happened if you'd told me about the investigation."

"Nikki, I couldn't do that."

"Because deep down you didn't trust me not to tell Malcolm." Her glasses fogged again. She ripped them off.

He sighed. "Because I'm not allowed to share the details of an ongoing investigation. Period."

She did not want to accept this. Didn't care if it was the truth.

"I am sorry, though," he said.

"You accused me of cheating on you." The tears fell then, which really pissed her off. Her lips weren't the only thing quivering.

"I know. That was completely out of line. I just lost control. Part of me wanted to make sure you felt as bad as I did." He wiped the tears from her cheek with the pad of his thumb. "But can you please tell me why you didn't let me know you were pregnant? Don't you want to have children? Or is it just me you don't want?"

Oh, God. She tried to hold on to her anger, but it was seeping out of her like a lifeboat that had sprung a leak in the middle of shark-infested waters. She did want him. She wanted him more than she'd ever wanted anything in her life. The realization struck her with the force of a blow to the gut. She loved this man. She was incredibly lucky that he loved her. Lucky to be carrying his children. He'd been honest with her; she owed him the same in return. *Please God*, she prayed silently. *Please don't let me screw this up.*

She reached out and removed his sunglasses so that she could see his eyes.

"I got pregnant twice before," she said finally. "When I was married. And I had miscarriages both times." She drew a deep breath, surprised that the long-ago pain was still there. "It was . . . well, it was awful."

His eyes were dark and stormy with emotion. His hands fisted at his sides. But he didn't interrupt.

"Then the doctor told me that I'd never carry full term. I don't think I even listened to the reasons why." She swallowed around the lump that rose in her throat, forced herself to continue. "But I was told it would be better if I didn't get pregnant. And I never did."

Joe's eyes held hers. "Yeah, I noticed you were a little fanatical about taking your birth control pills."

"Well, I had a reason. And then when my period got so erratic . . ." She shook her head. "Well, I guess I'm not going through menopause after all."

He gave a bark of laughter. It loosened the knot of anxiety that she'd carried inside her. It was crowded in there with the babies.

"And honestly, you know I practically raised Malcolm. And look how he turned out. He doesn't care about anyone or anything but himself. Even though I keep forgetting that. I'm not exactly mother of the year material."

"Ah, Nikki." He slung an arm around her shoulders and without discussion they turned back toward Bella Flora. "Malcolm's lack of moral fiber and conscience aren't on you," he said. "I've been in law enforcement long enough to know there are simply some people who have neither. The really dangerous ones are able to cover it up with an overabundance of charm."

"He's got that, all right. I've known him his whole life and I still keep falling for it."

"You want to believe. That makes it easier for him. He doesn't even have to win you over."

She took a deep breath and scrubbed at her eyes. She felt limp with relief, barely resisting the urge to lean her head against his shoulder.

"Are we okay?" he asked.

She nodded, not trusting herself to speak.

"Can I kiss you?" he asked, bringing them to a stop and turning her to face him.

She nodded again.

"Good. Because as mad as I was at you on our little road trip I could barely keep my hands off you."

"You could have fooled me. You were a complete and utter maniac."

He tilted her chin up and brought his lips down on hers. The kiss was long and thorough, but achingly gentle.

"Well, I'm going to be a father. I may be feeling a little overprotective." His lips hovered over hers as he spoke. Then he kissed her again.

It occurred to her that this could be the moment that he'd ask her to marry him again. She was shocked at how much she wouldn't mind if he did.

But though he kept his arm around her the whole way back and then left her at Bella Flora with one last extremely enthusiastic kiss, the word "marriage" never crossed his lips.

Chapter Forty-six

Avery left to meet the Hardins for an initial walk-through while Maddie packed a cooler of drinks and assorted sandwiches. Kyra and Dustin rode in the limo with Daniel, who seemed disappointed that he couldn't affix a sign that read *Follow me!*

Nikki had come back from her walk looking decidedly more relaxed and said a very long good-bye to Joe. An odd smile flitted on and off her face. Despite her general aversion to minivans she'd decided to ride with Maddie and Steve.

"I'm not going to have to own one of these, am I?" Nikki asked as she slid into one of the captain's chairs in the back. "I mean, it's not a requirement or anything?"

"No." Maddie laughed. "But you'll probably want one. Two car seats will fit a lot better in one of these."

"Yeah, the Jag's probably not going to cut it," Steve added, ignoring Nikki's strangled groan. "I got rid of my Corvette when Kyra was born. I hardly missed it at all after the first year or two."

They arrived at the Sunshine Hotel and found Avery, Chase, his father, and Ray Flamingo in deep discussion. Troy had gotten there ahead of them and was already shooting.

Daniel stood next to Kyra. "It's like a time capsule from the fifties, isn't it?"

Maddie nodded.

"Bohzer!" Dustin raced toward the bright yellow earth-mover parked near the main building.

Maddie's heart sank at the sight of it. The idea that a shiny new high-rise or multimillion-dollar home might soon stand in this spot made it sink even lower.

"Up!" Dustin said, raising both hands above his head. "Want to ride the bohzer!" The cab was locked, but Daniel sat Dustin on a flat space above its track where he made driving and zooming sounds for a few minutes. As soon as his feet were back on the ground he raced out onto the beach with Daniel behind him.

Avery, the Hardins, and Ray Flamingo stood in a knot between the main building and the pool, their expressions intent. Not wanting to interrupt, Maddie wandered over to the low concrete wall and stared out over the beach. The late afternoon sun still glowed bright, sending shards of sunlight glinting off the aquamarine water. Seagulls soared and dipped in the sky, unperturbed by the parasailer that floated by. At the water's edge a family of four left the decidedly lopsided sand castle they'd been building to peer out into the Gulf. Daniel and Dustin, who'd been tossing a football around, went to see what they were pointing at.

"Geema!" Dustin raced toward her a short while later, his legs pumping as he attempted to outrun his father. "We sawed dolpins! A whole family of dolpins! They were eating!" He arrived out of breath, his dark curls bouncing. His face was smeared with sand and flushed with excitement. "Can I give the dolpins a handwitch?"

Daniel laughed aloud. Maddie saw Kyra's eyes seek him out, watched them share a smile. "I think they like fish better," Steve said. "But I'm sure if you ask her nicely, your Geema will break out the peanut butter and jelly."

...

Avery and her crew came over to join them on the blankets that had been spread out on the sand. She and Chase got Jeff settled in a beach chair braced against the low concrete wall while drinks came out of the cooler and sandwiches were passed around. Avery sat between Chase and Ray, an unwrapped sandwich in her lap. She leaned back on her hands, her face turned up to the sun. The pose appeared reflective, but Maddie could feel the energy coming off her and imagined she could see the wheels turning in her head.

"I have a catalogue in the car with a reproduction lifeguard stand in it," Ray said, his sherbet-colored shirt fluttering slightly in the hot breeze. "When I first came across it, I could practically see John Franklin sitting up there in his nineteen-fifties bathing trunks and muscle T-shirt trying to get Renée's attention."

"He told us that he kissed her for the first time right over next to that cabbage palm," Maddie said, pointing to the nearby stand of trees. She remembered the expression on his face when he'd shared the memory. "Their whole history is tied to this place."

"Have you reached any decisions?" Kyra asked.

Avery looked at Chase and Jeff, older and younger models of each other, before answering. "We've agreed that even with the new infusion of capital we can't do everything. That we have to do what matters most and focus on the most valuable part of this property."

"Which is?" Kyra asked.

"What we're all staring at." Jeff nodded toward the Gulf and its white sand frame.

"Which means we were right when we decided to deal with the main building and the pool area," Chase added. "A million dollars sounds like a lot but it'll only go so far."

Dustin finished his sandwich and crawled into his mother's lap with his juice box. Daniel smiled down at him.

"This beach has a really nice casual vibe. It's less showy than South Beach or even Fort Lauderdale," Daniel observed, his shoulder brushing Kyra's. "But it's really comfortable."

For a moment Maddie wondered if he was referring only to the beach. The movie star looked far more relaxed than she'd ever seen him. Not, she reminded herself, that she'd ever seen him at home with Tonja and their children.

"It's true." Avery leaned against Chase as she spoke. "We've been discussing letting go of the high-end finishes we originally envisioned and can't really afford for a while. The plan now is still to go retro but make sure that it's casual and family friendly. We'd include the soda fountain, a great new casual dining room, and break the lobby up into conversation areas, card and game tables, all of it overlooking the new pool and beach."

"Plus the men's and women's locker rooms," Chase added. "And the rooftop deck. Which would leave us with . . ."

". . . a fully functioning beach club," Maddie finished. She looked back at the hotel trying to envision it as it once was and might be again.

"But what about the cottages?" Nikki asked. "What would we do with them?"

Ray sat up, his rolled sleeves revealing lightly muscled forearms. He was the only one of them not sweating. "I think we should finish the roof and exteriors including new doors, windows, and patios. Then paint them the way we'd planned in those great midcentury colors—Flamingo Pink, Blue Mambo, Banana Leaf—and leave the interiors unfinished for now."

"It could work," Avery said. "We'd create a viable local beach club. People could buy yearly memberships. And there could be activities and parties like the Handlemans had for their guests."

Despite the heat, Maddie's arms goosebumped. "I love it. Especially the idea of re-creating the Sunshine Beach Club."

"We could finish the cottages later," Chase said. "Or whoever bought it might want to."

It was Nikki's turn to sit up. "Why not sell them as timeshares? People could pay for two weeks a year. Or a month. Or, I don't know. There could be a sliding scale." Her voice grew more animated.

"And once enough people bought time in a one- or two-bedroom, it could be built out," Jeff said.

"For $150,000 bucks we could finish out a one-bedroom unit to their specifications," Chase added. "Maybe charge $200,000 for the two-bedrooms depending on finishes. John Franklin will know what they might go for."

Troy moved among them, stepping carefully, shooting each person as they spoke. For the moment, at least, Kyra seemed content to be in the moment rather than try to capture it.

"They could be fabulous," Ray said. "The shells would stay the same, but the interiors could be customized."

The sun dialed it back a notch. As it began its end-of-day swan dive, the beach began to empty. The family who'd spotted the "dolpins" earlier began to gather up their sand toys and beach towels. The father hefted a cooler onto one shoulder while the mother packed up an oversized straw bag.

"But who would they be marketed to?" Nikki asked. "There are lots of hotels on the beach already. And there are only ten units here."

"But they're not beach clubs that you can belong to," Maddie said, her eyes drawn again to the young family now heading back up the beach. As she watched, the children raced ahead of their parents. Midway, for no apparent reason, the little girl did a cartwheel, then turned to run back to retrieve a purple pail. On her way back she raced past her brother squealing with what sounded a lot like happiness.

Just like John had told them the children used to back when he was lifeguarding.

"I know exactly who would want to join the beach club and buy time-shares on this property." Maddie felt the smile crease her face as certainty flooded through her. "Is it too late to ask the Franklins to come over and hear our idea?"

. . .

"Oh!" Annelise came to a stop at their first sight of the bright yellow bulldozer. Renée stopped with her. "It's so . . . big."

Renée couldn't get her feet to move. The two of them stared at it dumbly. It was big. Big and yellow.

"What is it?" John asked coming up behind them.

"I wasn't expecting . . . I didn't realize . . ." Annelise's voice trailed off, but Renée knew exactly what she meant. Agreeing to bulldoze the hotel and actually seeing the bulldozer that would flatten it were two very different things.

Despite all the years of wishing for the hotel to come down and the property to be sold, she had never allowed herself to imagine it. Or think what it would be like to step onto this lot once it was reduced to sand and rubble.

"I just wanted it gone but . . ." Annelise began.

"I know." Renée resisted the urge to lean against John, who'd moved up to stand between them. If it felt this awful now, how would it feel when the land sold and someone else's home or condo building went up on it?

"Ladies?" John crooked his arms and they each slipped an arm through one. Renée's heart thudded dully in her chest as they walked carefully through the overgrown grass and rubble, supporting each other as they traversed the uneven ground.

"Neh Nay!" Dustin left his mother's side and came running to her as she and John and Annelise reached the others. She was surprised to see Dustin's father follow him. He shook John's hand firmly and offered what seemed to be a sincere greeting while Dustin threw his arms around Renée's thighs, which was as high as he could currently reach. She hugged him back, noticing as she straightened that Annelise stood alone near what had been the deep end of the swimming pool where the diving board had once been. Her eyes were fixed straight ahead. No doubt staring into the past.

"You used to love to scare the guests with your underwater disappearing act."

Annelise smiled sadly. "I never did it again after that day."

"I know." Renée put her arm around her sister's shoulders. It had been a day of "lasts." The dividing line between their "before" and their "after." The night their father had died and Ilse had . . . The day both their parents died, she corrected herself.

She turned her gaze to the low wall where much of the group sat. But what she saw was herself, pretending the wall was a tightrope when she was five or six. Sitting with her father and Pop Pop eating ice cream sandwiches. As a teenager it had provided an uninterrupted view of the lifeguard stand. She had spent so much time trying to forget the bad things, that she'd forgotten the good things, too. She had, as the old expression went, thrown the baby out with the bathwater.

Avery came forward to greet them, her eyes bright with anxiety reminding Renée that she and Annelise weren't the only ones who would be affected by the hotel's fate. There were hugs and waves and friendly nods. Somewhere along the way these nice young people who had come to own Bella Flora had become far more than that. They were shown to webbed beach chairs like the one Jeff Hardin sat on.

Sunset was not far off and they sat in the gathering dusk listening to the cicadas tuning up, the occasional caw from a circling gull, the rustle of the palms. The soundtrack that she and Annelise had grown up with. The past washed gently over her like a warm Gulf swell on a summer day, and she realized with regret that if they sold the property she'd never tame these grounds, never divide up the hibiscus bush, never share this place with her children and grandchildren. They'd let it molder all these years. If they tore it down and sold off the land, she'd most likely never set foot here again.

Avery stepped up in front of them. Maddie joined her. "Thank you for coming. We all really appreciate it."

Beside her Annelise drew a deep breath. Her hands were clasped tightly in her lap. "I don't see any display boards or artwork. Will we have anything that will help us reach a decision?"

"No," Avery said. "As it turns out, our idea is a lot less about finishes and construction or even timetables and budgets than we originally thought."

"And a lot more about the Sunshine Hotel and Beach Club and what it's meant to be," Maddie added.

"What does that mean?" Annelise asked.

Shadows lengthened as Avery and Maddie described what they had in mind, with occasional clarifications or additions from the others. While Jeff Hardin and Steve Singer looked on approvingly, Troy Matthews and Kyra Singer shot video. Daniel Deranian sat with his son on his lap and seemed, at least to Renée, in no hurry to get back to the world he normally inhabited.

"So you're saying you want to not just renovate, but re-create the Sunshine Beach Club?" Renée asked when they'd finished. It was the last thing she'd been expecting when they arrived. From the look on Annelise's face she, too, had been taken by surprise.

"Yes," Maddie said eagerly. "With the same kind of activities and personal treatment families used to get in your grandparents' day."

"But who on earth would run it?" Annelise asked.

"You could sell the club," Nikki suggested. "Or hold on to it and hire a management company."

The shadows lengthened. Each answer seemed to beget more questions.

"I don't see it," Annelise finally said. "Those days are over. People have their own pools now. And anyone can go to the beach. Why would they come here to do those things?"

"I think families would enjoy it," Daniel Deranian said.

"You'd bring your family, then?" Troy asked archly. Kyra gave him a death stare.

"Part of my family," Daniel said.

"I can't help feeling that 'retro' is just a new word for old-fashioned." Annelise remained unconvinced. But Renée found herself picturing Nana, remembering the personal connection she'd forged with all their guests. She had had only one child, but in a time when entire Jewish families had been exterminated, she had created an extended family right here on Sunshine Beach.

"No," Ray insisted. "Retro is all the rage. And the structures here are a perfect example of midcentury modern."

"The architecture is fabulous and with Renée's help the grounds will be, too. But it's not just the structures," Maddie said. "Young families are yearning for those old kinds of connections, a way to anchor their children to the family in this fast-paced world."

Annelise sat very still. Renée could feel her resistance. But a sense of rightness, of a calm certainty she hadn't felt in decades, settled over her. Renée turned to her sister. "They're right," she said. "The Sunshine Hotel and Beach Club was never about the buildings." She looked at the hull of a pool and the torn-up concrete, at the low-slung building that sagged and gaped but had been the scene of so many celebrations. "It was always about the people. The families. Including ours."

She reached for her sister's birdlike hand and her husband's stronger one. "We've both been hiding from our memories in different ways. But I don't want to tear it down and forget it anymore. I want to remember and share those memories. And maybe give new memories to the guests who come here." She met her sister's eye. "Think what an honor it would be to Nana and Pop Pop. And to our parents."

"But no one would take the time to do the things Nana did. Or even know how to make it feel like it used to."

Renée saw the tears in her sister's eyes and felt them gather in her own. But this was a chance to turn the pain and uncertainty they'd lived with for so long into something good. She was casting about for an answer when Madeline Singer spoke.

"But we do know how," Maddie said as the sun oozed into the water leaving a red-streaked sky behind. "Because your Nana left very explicit notes and instructions. And a long list of guests whose children and grandchildren already have wonderful memories of the Sunshine Hotel and Beach Club that they might want to build on."

Annelise nodded and smiled. She gently squeezed Renée's hand in agreement.

Chapter Forty-seven

The grand reopening of the Sunshine Beach Club took place on a postcard-perfect October day under blue skies and taffy-pulled clouds. Guests mingled on the new white concrete pool deck enjoying the salt-tinged breeze off the Gulf and temperatures that hovered in the midseventies. Hawaiian-shirted bartenders mixed tropical drinks for the adults and nonalcoholic versions for the children all topped off with brightly colored paper umbrellas. Similarly clad waiters passed family-friendly hors d'oeuvres right out of the fifties: mini burgers, hot dogs, and pizzas, along with deviled eggs and celery stuffed with cream cheese and Cheez Whiz. There was not a pâté or a foie gras in sight.

Adults chattered in ever-moving and morphing groups as children cannonballed into the pool under the watchful eye of a lifeguard who sat atop the retro lifeguard stand Ray had insisted on ordering. Others raced onto the beach and back again whooping with delight.

A sizable crowd enjoyed the proceedings and the sweeping beach and bay views from the rooftop deck with its modular cushioned seating and movable wheeled planters. Small hands and noses pressed up against the deck's Plexiglas sides enjoying the same view of the pool and beach as their parents and taller siblings did. On a makeshift stage set up in front of the cabbage palms, William Hightower and his band broke into their current hit "Free Fall." A largely female audience crowded around them. Bitsy Baynard stood at the very front swaying to the music and singing along, number one fan and cheerleader.

Renée, John, and Annelise stood near the ribbon-wrapped glass doors of the main building in what had turned into an impromptu receiving line.

"I can't believe how many original guests have family members here today," Renée said as she accepted a hug from Sheila Rosenzweig, who'd been a small child when she'd first come with her parents, and who'd arrived with two of her six grandchildren. Fran Lebow chatted with Jan Rothstein's grandson. Myra Shonenbaum had only heard about the Sunshine Hotel; she and her husband had come to see it for themselves.

"Wait until they get to go inside," Annelise said. "I love the photo wall Ray created. And the soda fountain is just the way I remember it." Her sister's face had filled out in the last months and her smile had become more ready. Every once in a while the fanciful child she'd once been shone clearly in her eyes.

"I hope we have enough ice cream sandwiches," Renée said, noting the vintage ice cream coolers that Ray had tracked down and borrowed for the occasion.

"We have enough ice cream sandwiches and Good Humor bars to feed every family in Florida for a year," John teased, but he, too, had thrown himself into the details of this party. All three of them had been a part of the phone tree Maddie and Nikki had organized, and had called many of the invited guests personally.

"The grounds look beautiful," Carol Franks said.

"I know that's your doing," her sister Margie said. "You always did have a green thumb."

Renée flushed with satisfaction. Months of pruning, paring, and transplanting had tamed the chaos into a lush tropical paradise. Guests followed hibiscus-lined paths accented with birds-of-paradise and frangipani, which wound through the brightly painted cottage shells where Franklin Realty associates stood ready to explain the time-share and ownership options. A long line of excited guests stood in line reading brochures and studying renderings while they waited to be escorted to Nikki, who was the "keeper of the contracts" and sat at a shaded table on the covered patio that bracketed the main building. Joe Giraldi stood talking with Officer Jackson nearby.

"Are you ready?" Maddie escorted Annelise and Renée to the double glass door and handed them a large ceremonial scissor. Troy and Kyra shot video and stills as they cut the ceremonial ribbon and led the way inside what was now a high-ceilinged light-filled space.

Avery joined the group, eager to hear their reactions.

"Oh, my gosh, it's so perfect."

"Just like I remember, only better."

"Oh, look at the photos. I think that's my grandmother!"

"I can't believe they still have the old keys. We always stayed in the Happy Crab."

The guests hurried across the newly refurbished sand-colored terrazzo with its blue and black bits that stood out in the sunlight now streaming into the room through south- and west-facing glass walls. They exclaimed over the card and game tables and pulled levers on the vintage pinball machines. Others were drawn to the seating areas that broke up the long space. They dropped down on the clean-lined sofas and love seats and admired the reproduction free-form Noguchi tables, and Arne Jacobsen—style Egg chairs, which had been upholstered in brightly colored fabrics designed to hold up under damp bathing suits and tracked-in sand.

The doors to the locker room halls stood open so that they could check out the newly refurbished wood lockers, benches, and tiled showers. Others made a beeline for the dining room with its floor-to-ceiling glass walls and bright white Saarinen–style Tulip tables and chairs.

"If you get any closer you're going to trip someone," Chase said.

"Shhh," Avery said, glowing as one man lifted his young daughter onto his "favorite" stool at the soda fountain and asked if she wanted to try an ice cream sundae with a cherry on top.

"At least I'm not flirting like your father." She nodded toward the photo wall that Ray had covered with black-and-white candids of the Handleman family and their guests. Jeff Hardin leaned on his walker as Annelise pointed to a shot of herself atop her father's shoulders at three or four years of age.

Chase smiled and puffed out his chest. "Hey, we Hardins are known for our charm."

"And your modesty," she said as Ray walked up to join them.

"Great job on the interiors," Chase said, clapping the designer on the back.

"It's great," Avery agreed, her smile slipping just a bit. "I wish Deirdre could have been a part of this."

"In a way she is," Ray said. "I don't think I mentioned this before. I never could figure out exactly how to bring it up. But I learned a lot of what I know from her just like you did."

"You knew Deirdre?" She thought at first she hadn't heard him right.

"Back when I came out and my family couldn't quite deal with it, I ran away to Hollywood. You know, to be a designer to the stars."

Avery watched his face. "At least you didn't leave a husband and child behind." The hurt was still there, not completely dislodged by the reconciliation with her long-absent mother.

"No. I was an eighteen-year-old with a lot of dreams and almost no training. I met her when I was parking cars at a private party." He looked around at the chattering people, the space they'd created. "She taught me, Avery. And she mothered me as best she could, which we both know was not her strength. But she talked about you all the time. She had such regret for leaving you. I know she took me in in part to atone for leaving you. She saved my life, Avery. And you remind me of her. In all the best possible ways."

"Oh, crap," she muttered as her eyes teared up. "Don't you dare make me cry right now."

"I know you'd never do that," he said, swiping at his own eyes. "After all, everyone knows there's no crying in construction."

There might not be crying in construction, but there was definitely sweating. Which was what Nikki was doing at that very moment. Despite the balmy seventy-four degrees, the shaded table at which she was seated, and the glasses of ice water that Joe Giraldi kept pushing on her, Nikki's personal thermometer seemed stuck on high and didn't seem like it had any intention of coming down.

"Are you sure you're okay? You look . . ." Joe began.

"Don't say it. It's not polite to point out that a woman is sweating." She picked up a brochure and fanned her face. She'd pinned up her hair and wore the skimpiest clothing a woman who was five months pregnant could possibly leave the house in, and still she was overheated.

"Believe me, I learned that lesson the hard way." Only last week he had made the mistake of suggesting she might want to stop coloring her hair in case the dye adversely affected the babies. "You've got to keep drinking liquids, Nikki. All the manuals say so."

"Go away," she said. He'd been hovering nearby through the entire party, though he'd tried to pretend otherwise. "I'm working."

"Drink up." He pushed the fresh glass of ice water closer. "Then you can file this paperwork." He set a completed contract in front of her.

"Why would you buy a two-bedroom cottage here? You already have a house."

At his look she took one sip of the water and no more. If she drank another ounce she was going to have to pee again.

"I'm going to be working out of the Tampa office for a while," he said smoothly. "And so I thought it might be a good idea to own something locally."

"What?" Her eyes flashed but even she wasn't sure why. "Why in the . . . ?"

"Look, I know you don't want to get married," he said quickly, his eyes pinned to her face. "So why don't we just go ahead and take that option off the table right now."

"Oh. Okay." She tried to look relieved. "Good."

"I figure we can worry about that down the road if either of us ever want to. The main thing is the babies, right?"

"Right." *Off the table?*

"Nonna Sofia did suggest a shotgun wedding," he said, still watching her. "But I told her I'm not allowed to threaten people with a firearm when I'm not on duty."

"Right," she said again. "Absolutely. No one would want to be forced into a marriage. Just because they were going to be a parent or . . . anything." She dropped her eyes to the paperwork. He was committing $200,000 plus for a two-bedroom unit with all the upgrades. But he'd decided he no longer needed to commit to her.

"Things are going great and I want to be here with you and our children." He gave her a blinding smile. "But you were right. There's no reason we have to be married when we can just enjoy each other and be hands-on parents together."

"Right." She searched for a smile but knew the one she came up with was nowhere near as blinding as his. She nodded her head, though, and tried to look satisfied. He was giving her the space she'd said she wanted while being supportive. She looked up and thought she saw a glint of humor steal into his dark eyes. But no, she had to be imagining that. "Lots of people have babies without getting married," she agreed. The man had finally given her what she'd asked for. It wasn't as if she could complain about it.

. . .

It was late by the time Maddie was able to make her way back to the stage area. She was tired, but happy. The party had far exceeded all of their expectations. Bitsy made room for her near the edge of the stage as Will struck a final chord, brought the last set to an end, and thanked the audience. Handing off his guitar, he stepped away from the microphone and shot Maddie a wink. As he began to move toward her the crowd of women surged forward and surrounded him. Soon the only part of him that was visible was the top of his dark head.

Her response was visceral and immediate. She wanted to walk over there and pull those women off of him. Wanted to stake her claim and assert her "rights." But these women, these fans, were a part of what he did. He'd told her repeatedly that they didn't tempt him and that she was what he wanted. Somehow at some point she was going to have to find a way to believe it. In the periphery a digital flash went off; someone with a profile that reminded her of Nigel Bracken appeared off near the pool bar.

Steve materialized beside her. He was standing too close, but his attention was fixed on Will, who had left the last of his admirers behind and was moving toward her.

"You don't deserve her!" Steve shouted as Will drew near. His tone was belligerent, his manner oddly menacing.

"What in the world are you doing?" she hissed at Steve.

William kept moving toward her, his dark eyes intent, his skin burnished by the sun. His body appeared loose and languid but when he came to a stop in front of her, she could feel that post-performance energy coming off him. There was something else there, too, something she couldn't quite identify. Without acknowledging Steve or even speaking, Will leaned down to kiss her. Despite the crowd and her ex-husband glowering beside her, she ultimately succumbed to the feel of Will's lips moving on hers. Vaguely she became aware of someone tapping on Will's shoulder. People around them murmured.

"It's okay, Maddie," Will breathed quietly. "Not sure if anyone told you but . . ."

Another tap, harder this time. Will straightened and turned. Bitsy gasped.

"What do you think you're doing with my wife?" Steve's voice was loud and harsh. Maddie's eyes flew open. There were screams. Bitsy's was loud and shrill in her ear. Digital flashes went off.

"Oh, no! Will!" Maddie shouted. "Look out!"

Will turned to look at her just as Steve's fist connected with his cheek. William swayed slightly. After a few almost ballet-like steps, he crumpled to the ground at her feet.

"Out of my way, luv!" The voice was Nigel Bracken's. "Step aside. That was bloody brilliant!"

The potato-faced pap named Bill charged forward beside the Englishman. Their cameras fired in a cacophonous burst as they captured the tableau of Steve Singer glaring down at the prone form of William Hightower with Maddie standing in openmouthed shock behind them.

• • •

Maddie was no longer shocked several hours later as she left the hotel with Will's arm around her. But she was irritated.

"That was quite a show you all put on there." John Franklin chuckled as he, Renée, and Annelise walked with them to their cars. "You definitely put the Sunshine Hotel and Beach Club back on the map."

"And hopefully the cast of the program formerly known as *Do Over*, too," Troy said.

"I'm only sorry I missed it," Renée said. "But I think it was best that we had all the children gathered to watch the magician inside."

"It was quite a show, all right," Avery agreed with a yawn. Chase and Jeff had left earlier with Bitsy right behind them. A car waited nearby to take Will to join his bandmates for a flight to Nashville.

"That felt incredible," Steve said, flexing his fingers. "I may have hurt my hand a little, though." Dustin slept soundly on his shoulder.

"You'll forgive me if I don't feel too bad about that," Will said drily, exploring the bruise on the side of his face with tentative fingers. "You may have won the toss but you were supposed to pull your punch. It's a good thing it didn't land a couple inches over. I happen to know from experience it's kind of hard to sing with a broken jaw."

"Sorry." Clearly Steve wasn't. "I guess I got a little carried away."

Joe Giraldi snorted. "J. J. debated arresting both of you. He thought it might get more attention. It took a while to talk him out of it."

"Am I the only person who didn't know what was going to happen?" Maddie asked tightly.

"No," Kyra said. "Because if I'd known the paparazzi had been invited to witness that charade, I would have put a halt to it."

"We were just trying to help, kitten," Steve said, looking extremely pleased with himself.

"I've told you all along that you need them if you're going to have a successful program of any kind," Troy said.

"It was actually Daniel who came up with the idea and reached out to Nigel," Steve said.

"Yeah." Troy sounded less than happy about this.

"I hate the hell out of it," Will agreed. "But it's a sad fact of life."

"Good night, all." Joe walked Nikki to the Jag and leaned in to kiss her good-bye, then left in his own car.

"I'll miss you, Maddie-fan," William whispered in her ear. His kiss was hot and sweet. She wished as she so often did that he didn't have to leave. "I would have liked a little warning," she said, keeping her tone light. "But thanks for taking one for the team."

When the car disappeared into the darkness, she climbed into the minivan and back into her real life, the one that included her grown daughter, her sleeping grandson, and her ex-husband at the wheel.

• • •

It was way beyond sunset. In fact midnight was long past when Maddie pulled a robe on over her nightgown and wandered outside. The moon was full and round and bright. Its light shimmered on the smooth surface of the bay and reflected itself in Bella Flora's back windows as if they were mirrors. The night was still, the air fresh and clean. The silence was broken only by the occasional jump of a fish or the croak of a frog.

She wrapped her robe more tightly around her and took a seat at the wrought-iron table, pulling her bare legs up beneath her. A door creaked and someone stepped outside. "Mom?" Kyra's voice asked tentatively.

"I'm over here," Maddie whispered back. "Trouble sleeping?"

"Yeah." Kyra came to sit beside her. She wore an ancient fuzzy pink robe and slippers that her brother had given her one long-ago Christmas. "You, too, huh?"

"I was thinking about opening a bottle of wine but I was too lazy."

The door creaked open again. "Hey, who's out here?" Avery asked. "Oh, hold on." She came and put an open bottle of wine and a glass on the table. "I'll grab a couple more glasses."

"What's on your mind?" Maddie asked when she and Kyra were alone.

"I was just thinking that we can't really afford to wait around and see what happens before the lawsuit is resolved. I was thinking we might already have enough footage to cut together a one-hour special on the Sunshine Hotel and Beach Club's history and reinvention. It wouldn't be part of *Do Over* and we might be able to sell it to HGTV. I do have to pay back the money that I borrowed. And while tonight went well, we don't know how many people will join the club or purchase time-shares."

"I thought that money came from Daniel," Maddie said, searching Kyra's face.

"Mostly," Kyra said, not meeting Maddie's eye, which was never a good thing. "Besides, I'll go crazy if I'm not shooting or editing something."

"I know the feeling," Avery said, returning with the glasses in time to hear Kyra's last comment. "We've only just finished part of the hotel and I feel like we need to find a new project." She took a long sip of wine. "Did you know that Ray was a protégé of Deirdre's?"

"I may have known something of the kind." It was Maddie's turn to shift uncomfortably in her seat. She had to force herself to meet Avery's eyes. "I just felt that he was the perfect choice and I was afraid you'd reject him if you knew. I'm sorry. Given how much I hated being left out of the loop about Will and Steve's faux fight, I wish I'd told you."

"Nah, you were right," Avery said. "I would have sent him packing. And he did a really great job."

Maddie smiled to herself and took a sip of wine, savoring the warm fruitiness that trickled down her throat. Bella Flora hunkered almost protectively behind them, moonlight flattering her angles and curves.

They were drinking quietly and staring out over the pass when the door creaked open once more. Nikki came out yawning, a shawl pulled tight around her shoulders. "If I ever get through a night again without having to pee ten times, it'll be a miracle."

"Well, you'll have a few other reasons to get up then," Maddie said.

"Yeah," Kyra agreed. "I'd get as much sleep as possible now. It's going to be in short supply for a while once those babies come."

Nikki lowered herself into a chair and rested her arms on the slight bulge of her stomach. "I still can't quite believe this is happening. Or that everything will go all right and I'll actually become a mother."

"You better start believing it," Maddie said. "This is about as real as it gets."

"Have you and Joe set a date?" Avery asked.

"Well. No, not exactly," Nikki said. "In fact, all of the sudden he seems perfectly okay with just being co-parents but not getting married at all."

"Joe said that?" Maddie asked. "Joe Giraldi? The man who's been asking you to marry him for a good year or more?"

"Yep," Nikki said not at all happily. "That's the one." She sighed. "In fact, he took one of the two-bedroom cottages and he's going to be working out of the Tampa headquarters. But, well." She shrugged. "Marriage no longer seems to be an option."

"Men," Avery mused. "Can't live with 'em. Can't . . ."

Maddie sent her a cease and desist look. "On the bright side you'll have all the best parts of a relationship. You know, date nights and weekend getaways, and . . ."

"I don't think Nikki's going to have a lot of free time or energy for any of those things," Kyra said, ignoring Maddie's warning look.

Maddie tried the look again, slightly worried she might

be losing her touch. "You know Joe and his family will be there for you and the babies," she said. "Plus, we have Bella Flora and each other."

"That's right," Avery said, raising her glass. "To Bella Flora!"

"Bella Flora!" All of them toasted and drank except for Nikki, who had begun to brighten. "To us!"

"We'll raise the twins together," Kyra said. "Dustin can be their big brother."

"To Dustin!"

"And we will be your village," Maddie said quietly. A solemn vow and promise.

The breeze was soft and cool, the night gentle. They had Bella Flora and each other to guard their backs.

"To my village!" Nikki raised her hand as if it held a glass.

They talked and toasted through the night and into the dawn. The blanket of their friendship wrapped snugly around them.

SUNSHINE BEACH

by Wendy Wax

Discussion Questions

1. In order to renovate the Sunshine Hotel and Beach Club, Madeline, Avery, Nicole, and Kyra must help solve the mystery of what happened to Renée and Annelise's parents. What else do the characters learn as they renovate the club? Does each woman have to make peace with a certain part of her own past to move forward with changing her life?

2. Renée and Annelise suffered a brutal loss when they were children and have dealt with that loss very differently. Renée feels the Sunshine Hotel and Beach Club, the place where the loss occurred, should be torn down while Annelise doesn't want it touched. How do these different approaches to the hotel reflect how each sister has dealt with her loss? Do you think that's a result of their ages at the time of the incident, their personalities, or both? How does solving the mystery of their parents' deaths help the two sisters? How do they each change as a result of what is discovered? How does that change their view of the hotel?

3. Avery has to come to terms with the unexpected death of her mother, Deirdre Morgan. Do you think that is made more complicated, since she had just reconciled with her mother? Do you think Avery regrets not allowing her mother back into her life sooner?

4. When Steve Singer comes to stay at Bella Flora it changes his relationship with his ex-wife, Madeline, and his daughter, Kyra. How does each relationship change? How do Kyra's feelings toward her father change the longer he lives in the house? What does she learn about him?

5. Maddie chooses to let Kyra reach her own conclusions about Steve. Why do you think Maddie handles it this way? Do you think it was the right strategy? How does Steve change during the course of the novel? Do you think he learns any lessons? How does Maddie and Steve's relationship transition throughout the book? What do they each learn about the other? As Kyra's view of Steve as a father changes, does it influence how Kyra feels about Daniel Deranian's parenting skills?

6. Do you think Kyra is still in love with Daniel? When she lets Dustin stay with his father on the movie set do you think she has any sympathy for Tonja? Why or why not?

7. At the end of the book Kyra takes a loan against Bella Flora to raise the money the women need to renovate the hotel and fight the network lawsuit. Her father and John Franklin are very concerned about the risk involved. Do you think Kyra is making a wise decision? Do you understand why she is willing to risk Bella Flora? Do you think she should have told Maddie, Nikki, and Avery the truth about where she got the money? Do you understand why she didn't, and

why she didn't want to take a loan from Daniel? Have you ever taken a similar risk?

8. Nicole is struggling with how to tell Joe Giraldi that she is pregnant with his baby. Have you ever found yourself scared to reveal a secret that affected another person so closely? Do you agree with how Nicole handled the situation? Why do you think it was so hard for her to tell Joe? Why is Nicole so scared to trust Joe's love? Why is she reluctant to marry him? Do you think her feelings have changed by the end of the book?

9. Why do you think Nicole feels obligated to visit her brother Malcom Dyer in prison, after all he has put her through and after all the lies he's told her? Why do you think she wants to believe in him and trust him? In contrast, why is it so hard for her to trust Joe?

10. Daniel Deranian and William Hightower have both been celebrities for a long time and they both encourage Maddie, Nicole, Avery, and Kyra to keep the paparazzi like Nigel Bracken interested and reporting on the women's activities at Bella Flora. They feel that relationship will help the women to promote and protect their television show, *Do Over*, and that it's a mutually beneficial relationship. Do you think that's true? What do you think about reality television stars who are famous simply because they're willing to have their lives filmed? What role do the paparazzi play in their celebrity status?

11. Madeline feels like she'll never be able to compete with the young, gorgeous rock-star groupies who hang on William Hightower. Do you think her fears are reasonable? Do you think women are under an enormous amount of pressure

to appear young, thin, and beautiful no matter their age? Why do you think William values his relationship with Maddie? Could you relate to Maddie's insecurities?

12. Maddie and Kyra are navigating complicated relationships with high-profile stars. Maddie is romantically involved with the rock star William Hightower, and Kyra's son, Dustin, was fathered by Daniel Deranian, a major movie star. What difficulties are presented for each woman because she's involved with a famous man? How are their challenges similar and different?

13. At the end of each day, Maddie asks everyone to share one good thing to toast at sunset. Why do you think Maddie feels that tradition is so important? Does it help each character? Does it help some of the women more than the others? Do you have a similar daily ritual?

14. Avery, Kyra, Maddie, and Nikki each faced different challenges. Which woman's story resonated the most with you? Why? What do you think each woman learns by the end of the novel? What causes the breakthrough for each of them?